Praise for Award-winning Author
C. Hope Clark

"Page-turning . . . [and] edge-of-your-seat action...crisp writing and com-
pelling storytelling. This is one you don't want to miss!"
—Carolyn Haines, *USA Today* bestselling author

"Her beloved protagonist, Callie, continues to delight readers as a strong,
savvy, and a wee-bit-snarky police chief."
—Julie Cantrell, *NY Times* and *USA Today* bestselling author

Murder on Edisto selected as a Route 1 Read by the South Carolina Center
for the Book!

"Ms. Clark delivers a riveting ride, with her irrepressible characters set
squarely in the driver's seat."
—Dish Magazine on *Echoes of Edisto*

"Award winning writer C. Hope Clark delivers another one-two punch
of intrigue with Edisto Stranger . . . Clark really knows how to hook her
readers with a fantastic story and characters that jump off the page with
abandon. Un-put-downable from the get-go."
—All Booked Up Reviews on *Edisto Stranger*

Hope Clark's books have been honored as winners of the Epic Award,
Silver Falchion Award, and the Daphne du Maurier Award.

The Novels of
C. Hope Clark

The Carolina Slade Mysteries

Lowcountry Bribe

Tidewater Murder

· Palmetto Poison

Newberry Sin

The Edisto Island Mysteries

Murder on Edisto

Edisto Jinx

Echoes of Edisto

Edisto Stranger

Dying on Edisto

Dying on Edisto

An Edisto Island Mystery: Book 5

by

C. Hope Clark

Bell Bridge Books

This is a work of fiction. Names, characters, places and incidents are either the products of the author's imagination or are used fictitiously. Any resemblance to actual persons (living or dead), events or locations is entirely coincidental.

Bell Bridge Books
PO BOX 300921
Memphis, TN 38130
Print ISBN: 978-1-61194-942-1

Bell Bridge Books is an Imprint of BelleBooks, Inc.

Copyright © 2019 by C. Hope Clark

Printed and bound in the United States of America.

We at BelleBooks enjoy hearing from readers.
Visit our websites – www.BelleBooks.com and www.BellBridgeBooks.com.

10 9 8 7 6 5 4 3 2

Cover design: Debra Dixon
Interior design: Hank Smith
Photo credits:
Landscape (manipulated) © C. Hope Clark

:Lgtl:01:

Dedication

To Karen Carter, owner of the Edisto Bookstore. A woman who has believed in the Edisto series from the start. If only I could live on Edisto Island and share books, stories, and wine with her on a regular basis.

Prologue

Slade

BODIES WEREN'T foreign to me, but they weren't commonplace either. Trying to keep my feet out of the water, I stooped over, not too much, to study the corpse floating face down about three feet away. The ears were chewed on by some kind of creature. A denim shirt clung to a pudgy back, and the torso gently rocked though no boat stirred the South Edisto River.

The last body I'd discovered in Newberry, my most recent major case, made me vomit my breakfast burrito, and if I hadn't skipped lunch today, I'd have upchucked here, too.

We were supposed to be on vacation. Or rather, I'd been ordered by my boss to take a vacation.

"Go take basket weaving or something," he'd said, his way of telling me to get out of his hair for a while and quit finding investigations where there were none. Sorry, but when I thought there was a case, there usually was a case. My record proved it. He sort of pissed me off.

So I'd Googled basket weaving and South Carolina Lowcountry, and made reservations for a week at Indigo Plantation. I was from this piece of the state, and revisiting would be nice. Plus, I planned to make the biggest, gaudiest basket in the world, and set the damn thing on his desk when I returned.

Patiently, Wayne had stood guard on dry land, while I searched for the right grass for a basket, along the edge of the river. But as I waded calf deep in the water, a heavy something bumped me from behind. Imagining a gator, I screamed, teetered, and fell, making the lawman come running.

Wayne saw the body before I did. "Don't touch it, Slade!" he'd yelled.

From sitting waist deep in brackish water, slick mud under my butt, I scrambled like a crab at surf's edge, putting distance between me and the dead man. "It touched me first," I yelled back.

Gently but quickly, he rolled the man over and checked for a pulse. I'm sure my eyes rolled. Skin color and missing eyelids told us what we needed. I couldn't stop staring though I was sure I'd regret it in my dreams.

"Stay here and guard the scene," Wayne said, in his federal agent voice, the boyfriend in him gone. "Don't disturb anything. And don't let anyone else disturb anything."

Then off he waded to shore and left me. Just like that. Before I could ask what to do if the body tried to float off.

Chapter 1

Callie

A BEAD OF SWEAT rolled down her back as Edisto Beach Chief Callie Morgan drove her patrol SUV down Pine Landing Road, grip damp on the wheel, eyes straight ahead if not slanted to the right. Away from that patch of dirt she'd have to pass.

A beautiful road to a tourist, or a naïve resident who hadn't kept up with current events. Dripping moss off live oaks. A deerstand here or there attesting to the wealth of wildlife. Sun flittering through the silent canopy. Humidity making the air dense enough to drink, and with a salty flavor. Typical South Carolina Lowcountry. Typical Sea Island August weather.

The allure she was supposed to appreciate.

But a hundred yards ahead stood the haunting section of road that ignited a bass drum beat in her heart. But guilt kept her from racing past. She deserved the pain of penance.

She hadn't been down Pine Island Road since that night Seabrook lay bleeding out, when she'd emptied her Glock into the guy responsible. Too late to save a man she'd just come to love. Foot off the gas, she eased past the place where bodies littered the roadside last October. But her mission today lay at the end of the road, not here, so she told herself to look ahead instead of behind. In more ways than one.

Pulse loud in her ears, she finally reached her destination. She had a lunchtime date long overdue but felt no hunger. She was meeting Raysor, whose patrol car she saw parked two rows from the front.

Fifty-plus cars were strewn across the grassy five acres of lawn, some wedging between trees and flora into the tangle of wetland jungle that skirted the property. No room for her vehicle at first blush, so she drove on past the renovated plantation house turned bed and breakfast.

She'd heard the owners had spared no expense for the inaugural Indigo Festival on Edisto Island held in the run-down plantation home brought back to life, and they apparently hit the ball out of the park. Like her, a dozen vehicles trolled for parking. That freshly established grass wouldn't last long with business like this.

Folks all the way to Charleston were a-twitter over this place. Callie'd heard the owners had drawn heavy traffic last week as well, even before this week's official Indigo Festival, and in spite of the late summer heat. Kudos to them. Edisto could stand to have more quality tourist attractions sans dolphin floats and octopus beach blankets.

Deep-pocket outsiders were learning to love this island, craving to feel at home alongside the natives, and this fresh influx of folks couldn't help but bring affluence with them. A sweet and sour impact. At least Indigo had been careful finding a balance between preserving history and earning a dollar—a fine line the island had danced on since agricultural life fled the island decades ago.

Too bad making things appear old-fashioned and genuine took so much money.

A pair of women walked right in front of her vehicle, and Callie braked hard. They didn't even notice; their attention stuck on the milieu awaiting them two hundred feet ahead. Callie eased forward, allowing them their distraction.

The old house's architectural detail was jaw-dropping both in the old house and the addition. The wide sprawling field of the plantation's namesake indigo grew right up to the processing barn, a plant she'd never seen. Presumably they'd hired some farmer from Tennessee to extract that blue hue from green leaves and attempt to recreate a crop that served Edisto farmers well centuries ago. The venue sold clothing and scarves colored with the results in the gift shop. Yeah, she'd read the brochures.

Impatient, Callie made a slot for herself outside the cordoned area against the house and switched the ignition off. Hiding inside the cool car, her pulse remained amped. *Deep breath.* Local law enforcement shouldn't appear all agitated and off kilter. With fingertips, she softly rubbed her chest as if soothing the back of a child.

Watch people. Interest outward.

An older couple strolled past, dealing with the heat better than she'd expect, smiling, holding hands. She managed a smile of her own. A boy around ten appeared lost, and Callie about went for the door handle to help until he caught up with another kid who'd been temporarily obscured by a hydrangea bush. She settled.

Better. Collect yourself and go inside. You're late.

Indigo Plantation wasn't in her Edisto Beach town jurisdiction, but still, she'd been remiss in dodging the invitation to tour what was considered to be one of Edisto's future defining venues. She'd also missed the owners: a wealthy herd of four men to whom Indigo Plantation was one of many ventures, but she didn't lose sleep over that. She was considered a political figure, one of the "importants," but her constituents lived on the water. This was a token visit in the most complete sense of the word, and she was happy meeting only the manager.

Her mother had scolded her yesterday for being tardy with her call on the new business. Beverly Cantrell lived forty-five miles away in Middleton, as mayor, and she'd leaped at the chance to attend the private meet-and-greet a month ago before the grand opening in July. She'd returned dropping names and shoving those brochures under Callie's nose, requiring they be read, frustrated that she'd had to make excuses for her daughter's absence.

As had her lunch date, Deputy Don Raysor, the barrel-chested, middle-aged deputy loaned to her from the county. Scolded her, that is. At least he'd been loyal enough to wait until today and meet her out here. Except he came in his car, allowing her to come alone in hers. He understood why.

He'd been on Pine Landing that night, too.

Calmer, she exited the vehicle.

"Hey, Chief Morgan!" came a voice from across the parking area.

She automatically turned and waved. People recognized the "diminutive lady cop" way faster than she recognized them.

Following the carved wooden signs, Callie hurried past the main entrance to the addition, comprised of the restaurant and gift shop, and positioned to take in sunshine off the river and reflect the white and yellow paint. Stepping in, she easily found Raysor, who had iced tea at the ready for both of them. Before she could get seated, a fifty-something blonde came over in blue slacks and white blouse, tastefully embroidered with Indigo in script over her heart. "Can I get you something, Chief?"

"Ice cream," Callie replied, the heat making a full meal less alluring.

"Vanilla cheesecake, Amaretto peach, banana caramel pecan, Bordeaux cherry?"

What happened to chocolate or vanilla? "The first one," she said, then as the woman left, she sucked down a huge draw from her tea before facing the deputy. "How long you been here?"

"Not long," he said, ignoring the fact they'd radioed and coordinated to meet an hour ago.

She took a moment to take in the eatery, scents of toasted bread and something fruity in the air. "Great place. Hope they can weather the off season." A few of the twenty tables were empty, but business still brisk. "You toured anything other than the food?"

"Nope. Thought we'd meet the manager, owner, whatever he is, together. You know . . . to represent the beach and the county. Like we get along and all that." His chubby grin drew the same from her.

"Yeah. As if. So the ads say classes, tours, and a historic bed and breakfast with four-poster rice beds. Classy. Mother's impressed."

Raysor waved, flippant. "Well, if the esteemed Beverly gives her affirmation, then we have no choice but to follow her lead, do we? The royal stamp of approval."

A man in his forties, decked out in dress khakis, white shirt, and a blazer in blue that Callie now understood represented the Indigo brand, appeared from a hallway connecting the restaurant to the main house. Their waitress pointed him toward the two uniforms.

"Here we go," Callie said.

"Yeah, he asked about you earlier." Raysor wiped his mouth on a napkin before grinning and rising from his chair.

"What's his name?" she whispered while pushing out a smile.

"Forgot."

"Nice, Don."

She reached out a hand first, and the gentleman swallowed it in his. "I've heard so much about you, Chief Morgan. I'm Swinton Shaw, the manager of Indigo Plantation, but call me Sweet."

She grimaced. "And you say that without joking." She gripped and made him shake, indicating strength behind the gentility. She preferred the former to the latter when meeting fresh people.

He winked. "'Sweet' is my mother's doing. We can't run far from our mothers, can we?"

"No matter how hard we try," Callie said, withdrawing. "I heard you met mine, and no doubt she left an indelible mark." She motioned to the table. "Congratulations on the turnout. Sit, unless you're too busy."

"I can spare five minutes," he said, gaze straying to a waiter then to the hostess podium before allowing his attention to rest at their table.

Callie got a good measure of him before he slid up a chair. A full foot taller than she, not that she wasn't accustomed to being dwarfed, but in her career, size had proven more of a handicap to the criminal element as they continued to underestimate her. She rather enjoyed the ability to catch people off guard with her size-four physique and unspoken history as a detective in a major city. Not that it mattered here. Mr. . . . um . . . Sweet, carried all the traits of a Southern gentleman.

His outdoorsy tan married well with the colors he wore, his dark, peppered hair long, slightly waved and brushing his collar. Dignity layered atop an ability to maybe captain a boat or fish the creeks. "You have a reputation of your own," he said, waving for the waitress to bring him whatever it was he normally wanted when he greeted guests. "The first woman chief of Edisto Beach. You command respect, and I hear nothing but good about how you keep this place safe."

"I'm still employed," she replied, noting what sounded like a Georgia accent.

Raysor crossed a booted foot over the other knee, bumping the table. "Don't let her size fool you. Last year she solved a six-year-old serial killer case we never knew existed."

Sweet's cordiality paled. "Serial killer?"

"Don't listen to him," Callie said, and welcomed the cup of ice cream from the waitress then watched the lady set a water and lime before the boss. "So Sweet . . . How far out are you booked for the B&B?"

Humor in his eyes, he stared down at her. "Meaning how long do we think we can keep this concept afloat? Trust me, we researched the B&B business before breaking ground, and our goal is to surpass anything conceived, much less attempted, on this island. A place to harbor overnight guests without competing with the house rentals on your beloved beach, yet entice your visitors with our other attractions. A small dock for our guests to catch your existing boat charters. A festival for indigo in the summer, and the Hoppin' John Festival for New Year's."

Pausing, he seemed to wait for all that to sink in. Admittedly, they'd chosen prime times to hold their festivals. Little else happening in both cases.

He continued. "Our indigo doesn't just stop at our little shop either, as we attempt to supply dyes to businesses and textile entrepreneurs up the coastline. Natural cotton doesn't mean anything without the natural dye. And we'll have seasonal classes on sweetgrass baskets, thanks to one of your local residents, as well as textile arts that vary from month to month. We're attempting to marry with the natives rather than compete with them."

Callie raised a brow at Sweet's allocution and took another bite of ice cream to hide a smile.

"A little thick?" Sweet asked.

"Maybe a pinch," she said. "But I like it. Call if we can help. While I don't have jurisdiction over this part of the island, I might be closer than calling the mainland. We get along that way." She pointed her spoon at Raysor. "Don here is from Colleton County, by the way, so I'm sure he speaks for them, too."

Sweet's gaze hung on her. "Very nice to hear."

A silence passed between them. Callie juggled her thoughts, a tad unsettled at the obvious attention. The man had six, maybe seven years on her, but not enough to be too old. After all, she'd almost bedded her old boss last year . . . a man with a decade plus on her.

Raysor cleared his throat. "Mind if we walk around?"

Sweet seemed to remember he had another guest present. "Don't mind a bit. Inform me of any safety issues you feel need addressing."

He reached out to shake Raysor's hand, then did the same in a slower, softer manner toward Callie, holding onto the grip. "I'd love to chat again. Learn about more than textbook history of Edisto. When this week's chaos settles, I can reach you at the station? Or maybe meet you someplace for dinner?"

As long as it's work-related. "Sure," she said, then motioned to Raysor. "I really need to get back to my own seasonal chaos. August is crazy at the beach."

"Come on, Doll . . . Chief." The deputy tripped over the casual reference, his nickname going back to when they first met and didn't exactly like each other. Their feelings changed, but the moniker stuck. "I'm curious, and like Mr. Shaw said, we can give the grounds a once-over."

Sweet tipped his chin. A noble, mannerly gesture Callie couldn't help but appreciate. Then she watched him leave from whence he came. When she looked at her partner, he smirked from ear to ear.

"Oh, shut up," she said, and headed to the door.

The wet, briny heat slammed into them, with minimal breeze to cut the effect. Short sleeves did little to cool an officer wearing a vest and leather belt with gun, magazine, cuffs, and assorted other tools weighing it down.

Shades on, they walked around the exterior of the house. "Damn," Raysor said as they faced toward the South Edisto River and frontage that cost a ridiculous penny or two. Paths meandered in several directions with signs blending into the landscape, but Callie led her partner to the edges of the indigo field. They soon strolled through the modernized showplace and barn, grateful for its air-conditioning.

"If he actually asks you out to dinner, would you go?" Raysor asked, leaning against a post, not in the least bit interested in how the worker behind the gate made blue dye.

"Day to day works for me, Don. I'm not into forecasting."

"Maybe it's time you traveled further down the road, Doll."

She scoffed at him. "You're like an old maiden aunt with your matchmaking."

"As one of his oldest friends, I imagine Seabrook would want you to be—"

Her stop-sign palm in his face halted him. "Don't . . . please."

So he stopped and watched the throng around them instead.

She preferred not to discuss her deceased lover. The wound wasn't oozing after ten months, but it wasn't healed yet, either.

Instinctively she turned away from the conversation toward the dye exhibit. The representative spoke as he stirred the dye vat. "Indigo is not as cheap a dye as what already goes on your blue jeans," he said. "But your current dye," and he pointed to the various pairs of denim on the tourists, "comes from overseas, mostly the Orient, because United States laws prohibit the use of cyanide in making the dye you're wearing in most of your jeans."

Gasps rolled through the people.

The comment caused Callie to tip-toe and strain to see, but her lack of height prohibited seeing over the other visitors. So instead she moved to look out the picture window. People casually came and went, not a one of them without humidity dampening the edges of their hair.

Amongst the ambling strollers, a tall, bearded man in his late forties stood out, trotting, scanning the people while bee-lining it toward the house. A controlled urgency in his face, his stride.

Callie pushed through the door and headed toward the guy. "Can I help you, sir?"

"Yes!" He made a pivot, reached her, then continued fast-walking, taking her by the arm to the barn.

She wasn't fond of being handled and shrugged him off. "Want to tell me your problem?"

"Not here," he said, glancing around.

Raysor approached, and the stranger muttered from behind a taut jaw. "You, too. Come with me, please."

A few people paused seeing a stern man and two cops. Unspoken, the three of them eased further into the building with this new stranger trying doors before finding one open.

They entered, and after shutting them inside, he turned. "My girlfriend found a body near the water."

Raysor cocked both brows. "Say what?"

"Wait a minute," Callie said. "Are you sure?"

The tall man in cowboy boots reached in his pocket and drew out a federal badge. "Senior Special Agent Wayne Largo."

Son of a bitch. Just what this island needed, another death. She'd seen no sign of security. Guess it was on her to secure the scene and call in the right jurisdiction. "Let's go then."

Callie quickly maneuvered them out of the room, past the tourists, and to the outside. Largo kept their pace regular but not hurried now that he had uniforms beside him for all the world to see. No need for a panic. "This way."

"Anyone else see?" Raysor asked.

Wayne shook his head. "Not when I left."

Raysor released a few huffs and puffs after forty yards or so. "So your girlfriend was ok with a body?" he asked, careful of civilian ears.

"She knows what to do . . . and what not to. She has experience with investigations."

"Good," the deputy said.

"She's a tough cookie," said Largo.

The crowd thinned the further they walked. A quarter mile now. Perspiration easily returning to trickle down Callie's back. "But she's not an agent?"

"No," Largo said. "However, she's managed a handful of serious cases with Agriculture. A longer story for another time."

"Oh, I think we can walk and talk at the same time," she said. "Take me to the scene. What's your partner's name?"

"Carolina Slade, and I said she's not my partner." He pulled out his phone.

"I'll handle any calls, Agent Largo." The girlfriend wasn't an agent. Not his partner, but the woman ran cases. A detective, maybe? Why didn't the man just spit it out?

"Whoa, hold on," shouted a voice from behind. "What's happening?"

With dark hair—cut tight and neat, a fit and striking young man trotted to catch up. An Indigo Plantation polo, of course, and cargo pants. "I'm security. Something going on?"

Funny, Sweet didn't mention a security staff. "Chief Callie Morgan. Mr. Largo here says a body was found on the water's edge on the outskirts of your place."

He froze. Obviously bodies weren't in Mr. Security's experience portfolio. "Damn," he said. "We sure don't need that."

"None of us does," she said, noting that Largo and Raysor had given her the unofficial lead.

Largo struck out again, the security man matching pace but hugging close to her. "You're from Edisto Beach," he said. "I'm Marion Tupper, ex-Charleston County Sheriff's Deputy."

"Nice to meet you." Well then, Mr. Tupper had to have some experience. Even beat cops ran across death. She wasn't fond of this parade. Any visitors crossing their path would certainly pique an interest.

Not that she didn't trust Marion, but she preferred not to ask questions of Largo in front of the security guard. He was a civilian regardless of his history, and securing the scene didn't include reading a civilian in on all the details.

"You usually call Charleston County SO, right?" she asked.

"Yes, ma'am."

"Let's see what's here before you call them, okay?" she said.

"Yes, ma'am," he replied.

Ma'am. She liked that. He'd recognized the pecking order.

"Thanks, Marion. Excuse me a moment?"

With the only sound being footsteps on grass or the occasional sand and shells, she heard the periodic snort from Raysor. She caught up to Wayne's side and lowered her voice. "How did your partner find this body?"

"Hunting for sweetgrass to make a basket. She took a class out here."

"A class." She curled her finger twice, beckoning to him. "Bring that badge back out. What kind of agent are you again?"

He slipped it out of his pocket. "U.S. Department of Agriculture. Office of Inspector General. You've probably never heard of us, but we are a federal law enforcement agency."

Huh. Her husband had been a US Marshal, killed by a Russian mobster when they lived in Boston. She had a fair knowledge of federal law enforcement, but Agriculture?

And this girlfriend. A partner, but not a partner. A female who understood investigations but wasn't the law. Callie wasn't sure who this other party was, but so far she wasn't impressed, which lessened her impression of the agent. She'd figure the details soon enough, but right now they needed to deal quickly with the poor sap who died possibly too conveniently during the biggest celebration Edisto Island had since the October plantation tour.

The island itself was not her jurisdiction, but people didn't understand jurisdiction. All tourists saw was the uniform. All natives knew, however, was that since she'd appeared on Edisto, she'd solved cases. Cases they never knew they had, each involving a body.

Nope, not only did Edisto tourism not need this sort of scandal, but she also didn't need to be, yet again, the lady chief who attracted bodies to Edisto.

Chapter 2

Slade

WAYNE COULD'VE just called 911. Stewing about that a few moments, I soon simmered down when I realized he was doing damage control for Indigo. Probably hoping to keep this as low key as possible for an attraction only open a month and deluged with camera-toting tourists.

I sat on the closest dry patch of ground, watching the path. Not a well-traveled trail, but then how could one tell when the whole place was spit-polish new while made to *seem* three hundred years old?

Then I coaxed myself to glance at the body again. So this was what a floater looked like.

God, the guy had to belong to somebody. I shivered, even in this hellacious heat, because three years ago I'd once worried about my children being found in one of these creeks. My son still had the occasional nightmare from that kidnapping.

I hoped this guy didn't have a wife nearby. Not sure how I'd handle that. But then, his condition dictated he hadn't just fallen in. I'd have heard if there had been a search party. That sort of thing made the news. So . . . no search party yet. And how did he get here, or more importantly, where did he come from?

I wished he had eyelids left to close, so he wouldn't stare like that. Scooting my wet butt around, I put the sight of the body to my back.

My phone! Tugging it out of my pocket, I checked if it worked, then the time. Twenty minutes had passed, and here I still sat in the sun, sweating down to my bra since my undies were already soaked. Where was Wayne? There had to be cops somewhere on Edisto. The local law surely watched over this cash cow of an event.

I jerked my head up. I heard it before I saw it . . . a small, ten-foot, piece-of-nothing boat puttering toward the Atlantic with what sounded like a fifty-year-old motor, coming around a bend a half mile north. As it approached, a leathery old codger seemed to squint, laser-focused on us, meaning me and my body buddy. The boater tapped his friend who then studied us, too.

We didn't need company. Distance disguised a lot of ills, like my mud-slimed legs. Waving, I stood, gathered my bag, and waded into the water a little bit, pretending to study my grasses again.

With my nonchalance, they ignored the lump in the water, maybe considering it a palmetto log. They puttered on, puffs of white smoke trailing, leaving me a lone cat-call over their shoulders.

Turning, I lost my balance in the muck, went down with one hand catching myself in the water, but not before it mashed a leg of the corpse.

"Yow!" With a yelp, I backtracked, splashing, my dark water phobia as unnerving as the dead dude.

As the body wafted side to side like driftwood, a piece of paper popped out from under him . . . on the river side, and started to float toward deeper water.

Crap. Evidence.

Scampering out of the water and toward the jungle, I grabbed a three-foot stick and returned. The paper drifted six feet from the body now. With my heart thumping, I waded into the water, stretched . . . and missed, pushing it a foot further. Wouldn't take much for the tide to just take it and go. Damn it!

Deep breaths. Lakes, rivers, oceans, all dark water gave me panic attacks. I knew what lived down there . . . what you couldn't see. Man wasn't made to swim in water that contained creatures that couldn't walk on land.

However, with a confident breath I waded waist deep, stabbed the paper, and backtracked as fast as the water would allow me . . . to the water's edge where fishes couldn't eat me. Wet to my ribs, for Pete's sake.

Come on, Wayne.

The stick sort of pierced the paper. Damn. I was screwing the hell out of evidence.

I peered around . . . what would it hurt to take a peek at it? Held delicately by one corner, it appeared to be a small map, maybe twelve-by-twelve inches if completely unwadded. Mass produced on glossy paper as if from a tourist center.

The woods rustled, clumsy footsteps. Not my stealthy Wayne.

Behind waist-high reeds along the water's edge, I fought to hide my muddy sneakers, wet shorts, and the body in the water behind me. I dropped the paper on the ground.

"Something wrong?" asked a fiftyish woman. Bet she had a friend somewhere nearby. Yep, another woman emerged. Both in capris and wide-brimmed straw hats I recognized from the gift shop, with ribbons of that blue I'd long tired of.

"I said," the woman repeated, shading her eyes though she wore sunglasses, "is something wrong?" The ladies whispered to each other.

Oh, go off and dye something.

"Nope," I said, "just slipped into the water trying to see a fish. Waiting for my friend to come back with a towel and more shoes." I stooped down and pretended to analyze a reed. "I took the basket making class and am learning the grasses, like this one."

They started over to see.

Wrong move. "Watch out for snakes, though. I've seen three in the last hour. The last one right over here." I pointed to my left like I loved snakes. "They enjoy this type of brush."

One woman put on the brakes and bumped into the other. "Oh, well, if you're okay." With painted smiles, they left. Thank God.

Walking to a drier part of ground, I sat again, my salt-water-logged britches sticking to places I'd have to unwedge when I stood.

Having grown up in Ridgeville not far from here, Edisto and I knew each other, but we weren't getting along well today. Still, I missed the Lowcountry. Some unspoken attraction had drawn me down here. If you unplugged and took in this place, it took care of you, a healing of sorts. This, however, was not the welcome I expected.

"Slade?"

I jumped up. "Wayne?"

From around a copse of palmettos and myrtles, he appeared with two cops in tow and a younger guy in cargos. The different uniforms threw me. The lady cop wasn't big as a mouse, and suddenly I felt twenty pounds overweight.

"Carolina Slade, I assume?" She reached out a tiny hand. I took it. "I'm Edisto Beach Chief Callie Morgan." She turned to the rotund older deputy. "And this is Deputy Don Raysor of the Colleton Sheriff's Office."

Edisto Beach and Colleton County. Curious since this place was in Charleston County. The lines ran close out here, though, so maybe I was off.

The deputy nodded, no smile, like the lady chief. I glanced at Wayne who gave me no clues.

"What do we have here?" Chief Morgan asked, walking closer, but not treading on what could be clues.

I stepped to where I'd discreetly dropped the map and pointed. "This floated out from under him."

She turned. "You touched it?"

"To keep it from floating into the Atlantic." I held a flat hand up to my belly as a measure. "Waded up to here to save it, which for me, was no easy feat."

"It has a hole in it."

"I used a stick."

She delivered a cool glance at the deputy whose mouth flat-lined. Yeah, I'd made a lasting impression.

"Coroner is on his way," she said, then motioned to the body. "Y'all recognize him?"

Wayne shook his head. "We're sort of on vacation. Not from here."

"We work in Columbia," I added, "but I was raised not far from here."

"On Edisto?" the deputy asked.

I shook my head. "Ridgeville."

Again the two uniforms exchanged glances. Ridgeville was an hour away. Maybe that wasn't close enough for their tastes.

Chief Morgan, though five inches shorter than me, exuded an in-charge attitude, more than making up for the height difference. "Agent Largo, you said *this* was your partner?"

The moment she addressed me as a *this*, I sensed my stock drop a thousand points. So with a deeper voice than I'd planned, I said, "They call me a Special Projects Representative with the US Department of Agriculture." I kept my gaze fixed to her green eyes. "I manage internal and minor investigations until they turn criminal. Then I call in the Inspector General." I pointed at Wayne. "Like him."

"So since I'm not aware of any cases out here, this is, I guess, a pleasure trip?" she asked. "Not that I care. Just trying to wrap my head around who I'm dealing with." She cut a glance at the deputy. "Your names go in the report, regardless."

She thinks we're having an affair? That was quite an investigative leap with no facts. Her stock fell a few points with me, too.

She started taking pictures with her camera. "Have you seen this guy in your stay here?"

"I met him last night at dinner," I said.

Wayne gave a light frown. "When?"

"You didn't see him," I added. "He came by the table when you went out of the restaurant to take a call."

Wait, that didn't sound good. But if it mattered, I couldn't deny meeting him. I stumbled deeper in the explanation. "He introduced himself as . . . as . . . Andy, Arnie, something with an A, asked me what I liked best on the menu, then left. I have no idea where he sat or who he was with or what he ate or which room he stayed in . . ." I took a breath. "He's a stranger."

"See him meet anyone? Argue with anyone?" the chief asked.

I shook my head. Wayne stood stoic. He did stoic well, which often made me more the comedic relief when we worked together.

"First," the chief started, "this map is part of a con." She offered it to the deputy whose expression showed he recognized whatever the con was.

"Care to share?" I asked. She'd already been told I did investigations. For the federal government, no less.

But she ignored me. "Secondly, who comes on a vacation alone, especially to a place like this? There might be another person."

"Not necessarily," I said. "What if he's a reporter, travel agent, or food critic out here for the event?"

They all went silent.

Yeah, take that, Chief. I said I did investigations.

Chapter 3

Callie

"WHAT'S WITH ALL the foot traffic here, Carolina?" Callie said, studying the driver's license, then the tracks, the sliding spots in the muck, the muddy, wet mess of a woman before her.

"Please, the name's Slade," she replied, holding up her hands. "Hey, I didn't see him until I tripped over him. Then I had to fish out the map. After that I sort of fell again. Then two ladies came along, and I tried to block their view of the body."

Slade looked to her boyfriend for guidance who pretty much let her stand on her own. Callie sure wouldn't have paired these two on the street. Largo seemed to have some semblance of calm wit about him. He even pulled off cowboy boots on the coast. Self-assured and observant. She'd noted he continued to scan the scene, imprinting the details.

But the crazy non-agent, non-partner friend of Agent Largo could be right about her suggestion the victim might've been alone. A travel writer was not uncommon on the island. A wife would've reported him missing already.

A white stripe swept down one side of Slade's shoulder-length haircut with the same lack of precision as Callie's, but their commonality seemed to stop there. Especially with the comedy-of-errors she appeared to represent all over the crime scene.

A crime scene that wasn't hers. "Don, can you call the Charleston SO?" Time to pass the reins.

"Sure thing, Chief." Raysor stepped off from the group.

The guttural puttering of an old engine attracted notice as a small johnboat cruised by. A lone, dark-tanned local waved, his other hand on the motor's control. Each of them gave a slight wave in return.

The security officer's walkie went off. A staticky voice came across as if through a tin cup. "Marion? Update please."

Mr. Shaw, or rather, Sweet, sounded way less cool than he had almost an hour ago.

Apologetically, Marion stepped aside, leaving Largo, Slade, and Callie to stare at each other.

Largo took a step toward Slade. "We'd help, Chief, but I suspect you'll have plenty of uniforms out here soon enough."

"Yep, you're probably right," Callie said, with a breathy "Thank God" at the end.

The floater bobbed from a small wave that had ultimately reached them from the boat now taking the bend in the distance. Refocused on the body, Callie tried once again to find something familiar, failing. The last floater Callie'd experienced was a stranger, too, but before the case concluded, she'd cried tears for the man she'd unexpectedly come to know. He'd washed up into Big Bay Creek, on the edge of her world, but this one was miles from Edisto Beach, clearly a Charleston issue. Thank God again.

Largo intently studied the scene, stepping lightly to his right, obviously mentally playing with logic. He whispered a few times to Slade, who shrugged more than gave answers. The basket weaver.

In her old role as a detective in Boston, Callie'd seen more bodies than any ten federal agents could lay claim to. Most feds were prima donnas, leaving the dirty part of murder to the locals, preferring the bigger umbrella, more white-collar sort of crimes. The depth, breadth, and complexities of Bean Town had thrown her into the paths of every sort of law enforcement imaginable, but an agriculture agent was not one of them. Nobody rustled cattle around Beacon Hill or Fenway Park.

"Where are y'all staying in case we need to talk to you?" Callie asked, using the collective pronoun to include all LEOs. Interviewing these two wouldn't take long. They might be a little extra baggage for the investigation but appeared innocent enough.

Slade answered. "A little blue and white cottage at 607 Dolphin Street at the beach."

That surprised Callie. "Not here at Indigo?"

"Nope," Slade replied. "Came here out of curiosity. And to make a basket for my boss."

Yeah, this bird sure wore different colored feathers than most.

Dolphin was only two blocks long, unpaved, with most of the houses occupied by natives. They'd be easy enough to find.

The sun beat down with a vengeance, and in the rush nobody had brought anything to drink. "Why don't we move toward the shade?" Slade motioned to Raysor on the phone to do the same.

Marion returned and waited until they'd all regrouped. "Chief. Mr.

Shaw wants to speak with you."

Callie expected to reach for a walkie, then saw Sweet make his appearance pounding down the trail toward them.

"Chief!" came the familiar voice. He trotted over, apparently having run from the B&B, his white shirt limp and damp from the trek. "This way." Hand on her shoulder, he steered her into the jungle woods, away from listeners. Mosquitoes and gnats swooped in for the surprise blood offering, eager to taste ears, noses, and sweaty necks.

"Listen, Callie." He still worked to catch his breath, a soft sandalwood cologne wafting off hot skin. His touch still rested on her shoulder, warm and firm. "I need *you* on this."

"On this," she said, easing out from under the touch. "Meaning manage the body on your property?"

With a glance over his shoulder at the others ten feet away, he nodded. "Yes. These Charleston cops come from off-island. Marion just checks doors and such. You," and he sucked in a deep breath in a big finale of having collected himself. "You understand how a situation like this can sabotage an entire season for anything tourist-related. You love Edisto. This affects all of us, so what can we do to keep you on this case?"

A gnat stuck in her eyelash, and she yanked off her shades to pick it out. "Charleston will have to run the investigation, Mr. Shaw."

"And if I call the owners?"

Callie had no clue who the owners were, but no matter. Charleston SO would dictate how this investigation ran. "I'm sure the owners mean well, but the sheriff's in charge."

Shaw shifted his interest to the body, studying the polestar which had guided them all to the river.

"You recognize him?" she asked.

"Don't think so." The answer slid out slow. Uncertain. Almost a bit fearful to say he did.

He tried to rest a hand on her shoulder again, and she moved so his attempt fell short, and instead she placed hers on his moist back. "Try not to see the . . . damage," she said, feeling how stiff he was. "Mentally step back and observe the clothing, the height, the shoes."

Giving Sweet a moment, she glanced behind her. Marion gave his boss space. Raysor remained on his phone. Largo and Slade watched, his arm around her. She whispered something to him, and he squeezed once affectionately and shook his head.

Callie pushed aside the slight ping in her chest at the natural easiness between them, and rubbed Sweet's back before she realized what she was doing. "Recognize anything?"

"No." Retreating from the nastiness, he joined Marion, patiently sweating in wait. Bet Indigo Plantation didn't have a contingency plan for this.

Raysor's cheeks flamed red. "You look hot, Don," she said.

"Because it's damn Hades hot, Chief." Leaning over, he wiped his temple on his sleeve. "Charleston's on their way and appreciates us guarding things."

Sweet seemed to return to life. "Marion. Run tell them to send out drinks."

"We don't need anybody else out here," Callie said. "Bottled water suits us fine, and Marion can bring it."

Sweet motioned toward his help. "Head on, Marion. Show us how fit you are and make it fast. And don't tell another soul what's out here. Put a sign on the trail entrance saying closed."

Then he addressed the so-called investigative duo, arms out in apology. "How can I make up for ruining your vacation?"

Agent Largo shook his head. "No apology necessary. We're just glad we found the guy rather than civilians."

"No, no," Sweet continued, patting Wayne's shoulder, ignoring the comment about civilians. "Let me comp a free night to your stay."

Slade gave a chagrined expression. "Um, we're staying on the beach, sorry. I came for the sweetgrass baskets. And to see the indigo."

"No problem," the Indigo manager replied without hesitation. "You have an outstanding invitation to stay *two* nights then. I don't want this to be the lasting impression of Indigo Plantation for you." He pulled out his phone. "Excuse me, if you don't mind. Have some damage control to take care of."

"I can imagine," Largo said. "Good luck with that." He shook his head in condolence when Sweet turned and moved deeper into the woods.

Callie wiped drips off her forehead before they reached her eyes. She sympathized for Sweet. Anyone with a tourism bent held their breath hoping that neither scandal nor liability reared its head during peak season. A dead tourist squarely fell in that realm.

Charleston SO would arrive soon, and they'd have questions. If the body had been hers, she'd have checked it out, patting it down like she had the last floater, adding much to the irritation of the deputy coroner who felt it his sovereign task to touch the body. It's how last time she knew the guy had been robbed of his gun and conked on the head before they got him to the morgue.

But that had been in her jurisdiction. She studied this body, staring at the sky, buoyant and listless . . . without a mark on him. She'd left the map on the ground where Slade had dropped it, but Callie recognized it easy enough. The property of Mr. Teach Drummond, Edisto's own pirate.

Every tourist region had its good names and embarrassments, and Teach fell into the latter. Each commercial season, which normally thrummed loudest from April through September, every venue, restaurant, and store around Edisto maintained vigilant oversight of their brochure racks, to sift out Teach's cheap material he paid kids to slip in. He operated via a website, wandering the area in his blend of worn-out jeans, cracked boots, and a blouson top open to show a chest-full of white hair, a stark contrast to the dyed ebony black that hung long to his ribs, braided in an assortment of ways, always with wilted, greasy ribbons. The purported ancestor of Edward Teach, aka Blackbeard, meaning Callie likely had no idea what Teach's real name was. He saved the hat for when he welcomed tourists to his boat and wore a daily bandana otherwise . . . just as greasy.

The local joke was to gift him new ribbons, the wilder the design the better. His response was always to flamboyantly untie the old and weave in the new, with a deep bow at the end of the impromptu show.

The map wasn't really the issue here since Teach passed them out by the hundreds each week, but Callie also knew that those maps led to "treasure" and "artifacts" up and down the North and South Edisto Rivers, mostly South, in honor of Blackbeard himself. Bottles hidden with miniature coins, shark's teeth in cinched bags, and ever with the promise of a particular bounty owned by the original pirate that had never been found during his days of terrorizing Charleston Harbor in the early 1700s. Most of the finds came with a twenty percent discount off a tour on his ship.

The dead guy in the water had either fallen prey to the con or picked up the map out of curiosity.

She leaned against a tree. They'd been in the heat for just under an hour.

"You still need me here, Doll?" Raysor asked low and gravelly. "The guys at the beach are probably cursing my name about now."

"And it's cooler there with the breezes, and sweltering out here," Callie added with a half-grin.

The Colleton deputy emphasized the point with a swipe where his tight-clipped hair clung to the rolls of his neck. "Wish I was sittin' in an air conditioned patrol car."

"Go on. I got this, Don. If you pass that security guy, make him give you something to drink."

"Damn straight."

Watching him lumber off to the path, she hoped he had a spare shirt at the office. Most of them did this time of year. She was the only one who could scoot a mile away from her office, snag a change at her house, and even squeeze in a mini-shower. What had once been her family's vacation home was now hers, and a string of unexpected catastrophes in her world had led her to appreciate the location.

So much of her soul had taken root in the sand that she doubted she could live anywhere else.

Fluttering her uniform shirt a little, she guiltily noted the patient couple now seated under a stand of pines and volunteer palmettos. The woman Callie'd labeled as odd sat quietly melting beside Largo, playing with her bag of reeds.

"Slade, right?" Callie said, approaching them.

The woman rose. "That's right. Got more questions?"

"No, I—"

"We were thinking . . ."

"Slade," Largo said, tugging on Slade's damp shirt. "Not our case."

"Hey, we're players in this," she said before returning attention to Callie. "Now, somebody has to have seen this guy around here." She waved upstream. "He couldn't have floated all that far. What's that way? And how did he get in the water? If there's no boat, there's no accident, if you ask me. I say this is deliberate."

"Slade, listen to me." Largo stood and leaned down to her ear. Callie watched the muscles bulging in his jaw and the tightening of Slade's in return.

"You two can go, if you like," Callie said, pretending not to notice the minor skirmish. "You're renting on Dolphin. Let me take pics of your licenses, and we should have anything we need to reach you."

"Thanks, Chief," Largo said. "We'll check in with you before we leave in a few days."

"Appreciate that."

Largo walked off with just a hint of a swagger, a man so natural in boots and the outdoors. Slade watched him, too. Then saw Callie watching him, but instead of concern, looked at Callie and asked, "But what if this dead guy—"

"Come on, Slade!" the agent hollered.

With a heavy sigh, she followed him.

Callie wondered what the hell Largo saw in this oddball, off-the-wall woman, because he had the appeal to snare just about whomever he wanted.

Chapter 4

Callie

ONCE LARGO AND Slade disappeared, Callie took another glance at the body, then noticed Sweet. He continued a long-winded explanation into his phone, several times glancing at her with a smile, but his stiffness revealed the strain of the call. If she had to guess, Indigo Plantation's owners were none too happy about a body highlighting their inaugural season, and their new manager was getting an earful about how to minimize smudge on the virgin brand.

Settling in the shade, seated on a log to avoid the ants, Callie fanned herself with her pocket notebook, checked her messages, spoke to her office a second time to make sure no bedlam was happening on her beach while she babysat someone else's problem. Another twenty minutes passed when, finally, voices caught her interest.

About the time Callie recognized Marion's chatter, he appeared around a curve of wax myrtle shrubs, weighted down with an Indigo cooler, biceps taxed. But his head was turned, conversing with two uniforms and a plainclothes gentleman behind him whom Callie would guess to be a detective from Charleston County Sheriff's Office.

The jurisdiction was confusing to outsiders. Rural Edisto Island belonged to Charleston County, all sixty square miles of it. At the end of the island sat the tiny town of Edisto Beach, belonging to Colleton County, acquired in a coup back in the 70s. The beach gave Colleton half its property tax revenue, a fact Charleston regretted to this day. The rivalry popped up on occasions like these.

"Where'd everybody go?" Marion asked, gladly dropping the cooler with a whump in the grassy sand. Callie stood. Sweet nervously gave the scene his back. The security guard quickly passed out iced water bottles.

"Detective Chuck Roberts." Badge on his belt, the detective thrust out his hand. Cargo pants and an SO polo shirt clearly pegged him as the man in charge, having graduated past the uniform stage of his LE career.

An easy ten inches shorter and a hundred plus pounds lighter, Callie gripped the offer as if she matched pound for pound, ever used to making up for size in the opening seconds of an introduction. "Edisto Beach Chief Callie Morgan." She waited to be invited to call him Chuck. He didn't offer.

"Fill me in, if you don't mind," he said, moving toward the water.

"A couple found him floating just as you see him," she said.

He raised hands to his waist and *tsked* once from the corner of his mouth. "What a mess."

"The woman literally stumbled over him, then she remained here, standing guard while the man came hunting some kind of authority. He found me first. I happened to be here to meet the manager and offer whatever services I could in their new business."

The man ordered the two uniforms to discreetly guard the perimeter, then turned to her. "And where are all these people now?"

"That," and she pointed toward Sweet, "is the manager. You've already met Indigo's security." She gave a gentle thumb motion toward Marion. "And I let the couple return to their vacation."

About a decade older than she, Detective Roberts scratched alongside his tight haircut, studying the ground as if her presence suddenly pained him. Callie could've felt the condescension with her eyes closed.

So she stepped in the ring first. "You don't have a problem with that, do you? I spoke with them, snapped pics of their IDs, acquired their names, address and phone numbers, and said we'd be in touch."

Swatting at gnats, he addressed her, his thick brows knotted. "Guess that means an even longer day for me, doesn't it? Think you could've thought twice about that, Chief? How many deaths have you even worked on that lovely beach of yours, Chief?"

If he emphasized Chief one more time . . . and she hadn't gotten to the fact Largo was an IG agent, but he could find out on his own now. "I am not your problem, detective." She pointed to the body. "Take your frustrations out on how that happened and make all of us happier."

He exaggerated bending over to match her height. "Listen, little lady. This is my county, and if you don't mind, I'll take it from here."

"Not fighting you for it," she replied.

Amazing how in this day and time they still let Neanderthals walk the earth. Edisto might be at the farthest end of the county, but she didn't draw the lines, and she damn sure didn't have to bother with this dinosaur any longer. "Then give me your card so I can text you my notes, I'll leave you to it." She leaned to see around the oaf and locate Sweet, to give him her condolences for the mess she was leaving him with and tell him good-bye.

Only he approached them, sliding his phone in his chest pocket. "I assume you're from Charleston County?" he asked the detective, reaching for a greeting.

"Detective Roberts. Call me Chuck."

There it was.

Detective Roberts accepted the greeting with a congenial shake, his facial wrinkles smoother, his position now balanced, unchallenged, and right with the world.

"I'm Swinton Shaw, manager at Indigo," Sweet said. "Excuse the call, but the owners are a bit rattled by all this."

"Completely understandable, and we'll do our best to keep this as low-key as possible. The body wouldn't happen to be a guest, would he?"

"I'll have to ask my staff, or maybe Chief Morgan would be glad to," he added, with a congenial glance at Callie.

"Sweet," she started, then fought to hide her own cringe at the first name slip. Especially with such a name. "As I said, not my jurisdiction."

The detective's phone rang. Then Callie's. A small hint of satisfaction appeared on Sweet's face about the time Callie realized he'd lost some of his tension.

Studying caller ID, Roberts raised his phone. "Gotta take this, sorry." He left earshot.

Callie, however, saw Charleston Sheriff's Office on hers and paused. Guess it wouldn't be hard for the SO to call Marie and get her number, but the bigger question was why? A thank-you maybe?

"Chief Morgan."

"Chief . . . it's Callie, right?"

Still puzzled, she maintained her professionalism. "Yes, sir. Is there something I can help you with?"

"This is Sheriff Mosier. I'd heard good things about you from my Boston connections."

"Always good to hear," she said. "And nice to finally speak to you. Sorry we haven't had the chance to meet yet."

What the hell? And what prompted him to check into her past, considering she hadn't given the sheriff's office any need to fact-check her career? Beverly might've been right this time. Her mother was forever leaning on her to socialize more—which meant play more politics in the tri-county area.

"We have a request we'd like you to entertain, if you don't mind," said the rich, deep voice. The confident bass tone alone could garner that man votes in the next election. "We'd be highly honored and would hope you'd consider it the same."

"Yes, sir." He wasn't in her chain of command, but the sheriff of a county as large and affluent as Charleston merited respect.

"I understand you've covered for us on that body at Indigo, down in your neck of the woods. Much obliged. Well, we believe you might be a major asset to us if you would join forces with us in this case. Maybe even take lead in some instances. Detective Roberts is a good man, but he's not Edisto-familiar, and we fully understand that a local has much more talent to draw from. It's the least we can do for the poor man who died."

Callie hesitated. Appreciation for the floater wasn't driving this sheriff; however, she'd bet a year's pay politics did.

She almost said no thanks, but voices echoed in her head. While her mother's scolding would be the loudest, she could more so imagine what Raysor would say. Possibly the Edisto Beach town council and its anti-Callie Morgan chairman, Brice LeGrand. She even heard a trace of Mike Seabrook's urging in her ear. *Play nice and cooperate.*

"Yes, sir. I am honored. Just how much leash do you want me to run with?" she asked.

"All of it," he replied. "And Roberts understands fully. He shouldn't be a problem."

At the detective's name, Callie's gaze traveled to Roberts . . . and recognized disgruntlement and the pure pissed-off glower in his eyes. Yeah, he would cooperate fully and be thrilled to do so.

He didn't care that this was about Edisto Island's reputation and livelihood. Why have Charleston uniforms all over an area, freaking out tourists and natives alike, when the sheriff's office could use someone who not only blended into the environment, but was also well-trained in homicide investigations.

She hung up a split second before Roberts did, and the unspoken air between them almost hummed with *oh shit*. She didn't ask him if he knew. He stood motionless, too stubborn to concede he'd gotten the same orders. Sweet, however, panned a satisfied gaze over them. In spite of jurisdiction, he'd gotten his way.

But regardless of the sheriff's reasons, and in spite of whoever Indigo Plantation's owners thought they were, she would pursue this case as if it were solely hers, answerable only to justice.

The detective broke the ice first, and Callie kicked herself for letting him beat her to the punch. Alpha dogs vying for leadership. "What would her highness like for us to do first?" he asked.

She held out her hand. "Let's start over, Chuck. Call me Callie."

He took her grip and reeled her in. "Roberts," he whispered. "And I ain't your bitch. Just keep that in your sand-filled head."

She forced a smile. "First, I suggest you call your coroner and have him arrange to come by boat to collect our guy. I'm sure Indigo Plantation would appreciate discretion, and with the right amount of it, the tourists won't have a clue. Work for you, Mr. Shaw?"

"Yes, ma'am," he replied, reciprocating her smile.

Keeping the press in the dark ranked almost as high as solving the death. The owners, Sweet, the sheriff's office, and frankly, all of Edisto Island would appreciate prudence. Employment wasn't plentiful out here, and Indigo offered the economy a boost. That community benefit and deep pockets commanded the town's protection.

Besides, journalists, bloggers, and newscasters made her skin crawl. They'd hounded her last year when she solved a case Edisto didn't even realize they had. The first woman cop on Edisto, then chief. Then when she took out Seabrook's killer . . . Her name alone could attract some of those news hounds . . . news whores.

Nope, no reporters. Not if she could help it.

But she felt as though she'd stepped into a realm she couldn't see. Politics, wealth, and murder offered all the potential ingredients for invisible motive and complicated cases. Just asking her involvement triggered suspicion, but she could be overthinking this. A guy probably just drowned. The players didn't want attention. Giving it to a small town chief kept it out of Charleston eyes.

It felt right, but it didn't. Nothing pure about justice sought with so much effort on sweeping it under the mat.

Regardless, no choice but to move forward. Yes, for the dead man. For Edisto. But for what else she wasn't sure . . . yet, there was something else. A ghost of worry had already taken residence in her bones.

Chapter 5

Callie

"RUN ALL THE license tags in the parking lot," Callie said to the two Charleston cops. "Tuck your cars in amongst the thickest part of the parking lot to remain obscure. Then one of you stand guard over the body until the coroner arrives."

Roberts lifted both hands in a question. "Guess that just leaves me, your highness."

How was she to deal with this iconoclast? "Roberts. You received orders, and I've been offered an investigation I can't refuse. Can we at least agree we didn't ask for the assignment? Let's just do this together without waves."

"Again," he said, puffed up and arms crossed, in spite of the heat and humidity no doubt making his arms sticky. "What's my assignment?"

Whatever. She tried. "Keep out of sight, for one. All of you. The point is to make mine the only face on this case. Nobody, to include any potential killer, will worry about seeing me since I'm commonplace. And Roberts, you address the body and the coroner. When you have cause of death, call me."

His complexion might've been mistaken for sunburn if they'd been outside long enough. She tried not to dwell on his attitude.

With a beckon toward Sweet, she continued to assume control. "Mr. Shaw, I'll need a list of your guests, please. I'd say eliminate couples and focus on those traveling alone since nobody's come forward missing a significant other; but, then again, who's to say there isn't another body?"

Sweet jerked, eyes wide. "Another body?"

"Or the other party is the killer," Roberts said.

"Assuming this is a murder," she added. "But we've got to determine identity ASAP to start putting these pieces together. Sweet, we'll need that list quickly."

She assumed Roberts's silence meant concurrence. Grateful for the sunglasses, she tried craning her neck at these men standing so damn close. No intimidation there at all. No sir.

"Would you like a list of all my employees as well?" Sweet asked, still a tad pale from the mention of a second potential corpse on his plantation.

She smiled to ease his discomfort more. "Yes, those who've worked in the last, say, forty-eight hours. And if this lovely officer here can get cracking on those license tags, we might be able to narrow down potential names."

The smell of Roberts's sigh spoke of fast food burgers. He pointed at Callie then Sweet. "I'm coming with you two." He turned to one of his men. "Steve, call me when the coroner arrives."

Everyone studied Callie. They were going to make this hard, weren't they? "Okay, Mr. Shaw, lead the way."

At the end of the path, Marion peeled off toward the house, instructed to keep his mouth shut. The other officer went for their patrol car.

"How about a cold glass of tea while I fetch those two files for you?" Sweet asked, holding the door open to the restaurant.

Nobody argued.

While Sweet disappeared into the hallway connecting to the B&B part of the place, Callie picked a table and sat, halfway expecting Roberts to sit elsewhere, but he settled across from her. Soft cornflower blue and white murals of Southern history lined the walls between an ample number of windows, allowing the outside to come in, the décor meant to soothe.

She glanced at her watch. "Let's wish for an accident," she said low, the room almost bare at four p.m.

Mute and seated sideways in his chair, Roberts kept his focus on where Sweet exited. The same waitress from earlier scurried over with two glasses and positioned them on puffy soft, Indigo logo coasters. "Can I order you something?" she asked. "Mr. Shaw says no charge."

"A scotch," Roberts growled.

The lithe fifty-something lady acted disconcerted, unsure the message.

Callie released a soft chuckle. "He's teasing. It's just awful hot today. The tea's fine, um," she searched for the name tag, and the waitress pinched it, lifting it a smidge. "Jackie," Callie finished. "That ice cream was quite good earlier."

"Yes." Seemingly grateful for a positive conversation, Jackie smiled.

"Before we opened, we were allowed to taste test them all. We settled on the four. Vanilla cheesecake, Amaretto peach, banana caramel pecan, Bordeaux cherry." The same recitation from before.

"And your favorite is?"

Smacking, Jackie scrunched her nose. "Overwhelmingly banana caramel pecan."

"You almost make me want a dish."

The waitress half turned. "Won't take a second for me to get you one."

Callie shook her head. "We're just parked here a moment waiting for Mr. Shaw. Maybe later."

With a nod, the lady left, moving to the other tables, straightening what already seemed neat to Callie. Another waitress came out, and Jackie gave instructions to her. Probably the senior of the wait staff, Jackie appeared cognizant of Sweet's expected presence.

Roberts took his tea down half a glass, uninterested in conversation. Not the best detective personality. Thing is, Callie knew they'd visit Indigo time and time again before all this was over, and if chit-chat with a waitress now about ice cream opened a door later, what's the harm being civil, if not nice?

And a good detective got along with the devil, if needed.

Sweet came in, papers in hand, his expression serious. He chose not to sit. "Let's take this into my office."

Staff watched, trying to appear they weren't, but Roberts's polo clearly stated Charleston Sheriff's Office, and Callie wore a uniform. With Sweet's smile gone, Callie sensed the whispers. She prayed Marion Tupper remained silent as ordered, not feeding the gossip.

The three left the cheerful restaurant, rounded one hallway, through the lobby, then down another hallway to an office accented with period pieces to match the faux-history flavor. Mostly oak, aged dark, with curved legs and glass atop the desk and side tables. Brocaded lampshades on brass lamps. A deeper blue in the drapes, not curtains, cream-colored paint on the walls, and deep blue and maroon rugs on the cream carpeted floor. Sweet shut the door and motioned them to two chairs in front of his desk.

"We're not that big, so we're talking sixty guests at our best, assuming no singles." He laid the list before him. Neither detective claimed it, instead inching their chairs closer.

"Only one single," he said. "We're not exactly a singles destination."

Callie studied the underlined name, the address, phone number. The credit card only listed the last four numbers. "Nothing jumps out to me," she said. "What about you, Roberts?"

"Nope." He pulled out his phone and started typing.

"Oh, no need searching," Sweet said, and blew out long and hard. "I know him."

Callie tensed. "You said you didn't recognize him." Or maybe Sweet's recognition of the body had to be cleared by corporate headquarters before acknowledging same to a cop?

The leather chair gave a mild creak as he shifted and clenched palms. "That's not what I meant. I recognize the name Addison Callaway. He's a travel writer. Appears unannounced, canvasses resorts, B&Bs, restaurants, anything tastefully tourist. Avoids the neon and highly commercial, and unless he approves of you, he'll brand you as cheap. The monied tourists go elsewhere." He blew out long. "I hadn't gone over the registration in detail, and if someone isn't well-versed in the hospitality world, they might not even know who he is. Apparently, nobody did."

"Well," Callie said, waiting. "Is the body him or not?"

Sweet shrugged. "He doesn't flash his face around for obvious reasons, just like this one. He was checking us out. Fits the description of him, though."

"Got him," Roberts said. "You're right. Few pictures. Good ones anyway. Just a lot of opinion, and apparently a lot of people think he's worth a damn."

Sweet slumped in his chair, frustrated. "Because he's vicious. He loves you or he hates you, and either way, he's revered for colorful wording. His travel blog alone reaches a quarter million people, but where he excels is on Instagram and Pinterest, with photography and short, catchy comments. That takes his audience up to maybe a million." His fingers danced on his own smartphone. "Give me a sec." He scrolled and flipped sites. "Whew, nothing about us yet."

"He matters that much?" Roberts asked.

"Oh my God, yes," Sweet replied, sliding the phone into his pocket. "His pieces appear in *Food & Wine, Conde Nast Traveler, Southern Living, Travel + Leisure* . . . his writing attracts millions when you take into account his reach." He stared from one detective to the other. "What the hell am I going to do about this?"

Roberts laughed. "About what? Unless you killed him."

Sweet's jaw slacked, mouth agape. "Jesus, is someone going to think that?"

"Mr. Shaw, come on," Callie said, soothing. "We haven't confirmed it's him. We haven't proven he was killed. Let's not jump to conclusions." Roberts wasn't being much help. "Detective, think you could check with your officer and see where he is on those tags? We'll need to cross-check driver's licenses of those guests, too. Especially Callaway. Where's he from?"

"Florida," Sweet said. "Though he stays on the road. But I can tell you what car he came in." He opened his laptop and typed a few strokes, scrolling. "A Lexus. A rental." He wrote down the tag and held it out, unsure which detective to pass it to.

Roberts took it. "And what will her highness be doing? In case *my* boss and *my* sheriff need an update?"

She glowered. "I'll keep you apprised and give you any leads to follow I can."

Watching his anger rise in return, she regrouped, trying to appeal to him instead of the oh-so-eager temptation to argue. "I'll be working on a timeline," she said. "But then, you'd know that."

He stood and left the office.

She hated how her heartbeat had quickened, her adrenaline spiking a tad.

Elbows on his desk, Sweet waited with interest. "Wow."

She turned on him now. "You insulted him by requesting me."

"The owners thought—"

"Bullshit," she said, biting the T on the end. "You called them. You made the request."

He dropped his hands to the desk and crossed them. "You do what you have to do in order to protect the business," he said. "My logic is sound, Callie."

It was, but oh, the ripples he'd made. Not necessarily for him and Indigo, but for Callie. If she expeditiously and guardedly controlled this situation, the Charleston Sheriff would be indebted to her, not that she needed his blessing on Edisto Beach, but still, not a bad chit to hold onto. But Roberts would hate her for stealing his glory.

If she mismanaged this case, however, she'd burn bridges. The sheriff, Roberts, Sweet . . . and Edisto Beach Councilman Brice LeGrand would have their way with her career.

Brice. Damn how she hated his breathing over her shoulder. She preferred answering to a captain in Boston rather than this twit and the rest of the council. Not that the others hated her . . . most had voted her into the position, but Brice wielded a heavy hammer on this tiny beach thanks to his lineage, and he had methods of getting his way. Thus far, Callie stayed a step ahead of him, her reputation continuing to outshine his.

"Write down that tag info for me," she said. "And who manages the cameras? You or Marion?"

He pulled up his laptop. "Both. Check this morning?"

"Check everything since Callaway arrived," she replied. "And make a copy to take with me. I saw the cam on the check-in desk, the entrance to the dining room, the barn, and the main entrance. I'm sure you have others. You wouldn't have one on each hallway to the rooms, would you?"

"Sure do." Pulling out his radio, he called for Marion.

"I'm here, boss."

"Ask them at the desk to give you a copy of the driver's license for Addison Callaway, then find him on the cam footage dated to when he checked in. Copy that?" He studied Callie. "We're creating a timeline for the detectives," he added.

"I'm on my patrol. Stop that?"

"Affirmative. Shaw out."

Callie wasn't happy at what she heard. "Why didn't you tell us you had copies of driver's licenses?"

"Nobody asked," he said.

Eyes narrowed, she studied him, wondering what else he knew and hadn't said. "You heard me ask Roberts about driver's licenses."

Sweet sighed. "I just preferred to share information with you than Roberts. I really don't like him."

"We're both working this death, Sweet. Neither of us is any more worthy than the other. You understand? Roberts already thinks I've stolen his thunder thanks to you and your boss."

His slight shrug didn't assure her much.

"How about showing me to Callaway's room?" she asked. No point in any more discussion of Sweet's choice to play the political trump card. He considered the move discerning and necessary. Like with the waitress, she needed his cooperation.

"Are you legal going into his room?" Sweet asked.

"I'm as legal as you are," she said. "It's called knocking on the door, no different than housekeeping. And each room does have a phone, right?"

Sweet shook his head at the stupidity of his oversight and put a call through to the room. No answer.

They rose and left. En route, she texted Roberts. *ANY SIGN OF CALLAWAY'S CAR?*

The reply was simple. *NO.*

YOU MIGHT CHECK THE RENTAL PLACES AT THE AIRPORT, IF YOU DON'T MIND.

He didn't respond. She'd assume he got the message.

The main building was two stories with a minimal number of choice rooms, price upped due to the proximity to the restaurant. The newer building to the south held fourteen additional suites. Callaway went with the furthest and most obscure room, on the second floor of the main building to the rear.

With no response to their knocks, Sweet opened the door, and Callie couldn't help but note the room's river vista first. Next she catalogued the rice bed and early American accompaniments, again with the whole Indigo blue theme going on. Beautiful acreage and landscaping with the indigo and finally the massive span of grass leading to that picturesque river bank.

Callaway had already been working an angle. On a notepad beside a closed laptop were scribbled comments like "slow to serve breakfast" and "indigo . . . yawn." Then "blog?" And another, "not even magazine-worthy?" with two underlines below it. Finally, "local color might help."

"Don't touch anything," she said, as Sweet reached to turn a page of notes.

"He was going to roast me."

"Not anymore if the body is his," she replied. "Let's back out of here until we make a solid ID. And neither you nor your staff needs to come in here. Not until we find him or determine he's the body."

Sweet kept studying the desk.

"Sweet! You hear me? Don't come back in here."

Jostling himself, he quickly replied. "Sure, sure." He stood still, his thoughts not quite caught up. "So what now?"

"We try to define the details from when he checked in. Did he speak to any of your staff, and if so, did he mention where he'd been or what were his plans?"

"Suggest we start with the concierge," he said, his willingness marred with a twinge of uncertainty.

"A concierge?" she asked. "A place this small and you actually have a concierge?"

"Riley. She juggles a few other duties, but she has an ingrained knowledge of the island's activities, eateries, recreation."

Callie read harder. "Riley Stone? I recognize that name. Her family's lived on Edisto for, what, three generations? Thought she was going to College of Charleston?"

"Graduated, then I hired her," he said. "Now you see why I wanted you on this?"

Employment. Part of the reason Edisto needed Indigo, Callie thought. "Let me start with her."

Sweet glanced at the clock on the nightstand. "It's not quite six yet. We ought to find her near registration somewhere."

As they reached the lobby, Callie noted the small, antique French carved oak desk situated to the side of registration, so the concierge would quickly adjust between the two locations. With all the period furniture throughout, Callie'd not noticed this piece. The desk had dolphins carved into the feet. A young lady sat behind it, reading her phone.

Sweet's voice came out deeper, more boss-like. "Miss Stone?"

The phone disappeared, but not before she almost dropped it. "Sir?"

"Not again, please," he scolded.

"Yes, sir."

"This," he motioned to Callie, "is Chief Morgan."

Callie reached out to shake the girl's hand that already shook at being caught slacking. "Congratulations on landing a job on the island," Callie said. "We need to keep more young people like you around here."

"Yes, ma'am," came the less than enthusiastic reply, giving Callie a sense that a momma or a daddy had something to do with Miss Riley landing a job near home.

Callie pulled out her notebook. "Have you had any dealings with a guest named Addison Callaway?"

"Oh, yes, ma'am." The girl seemed eager to compensate for the phone faux-pas.

"Do you keep a log of any kind?"

Her face fell. "Um, no, ma'am." She turned to Sweet. "Was I supposed to?"

Gently he shook his head. "No, but we might start. Just answer the chief's questions."

"When did you see him?"

"I saw him go to dinner day before yesterday right before the kitchen closed at nine. I was working extra hours because of the opening. He'd asked me about some local stuff right before that."

To let her feel useful, Callie scribbled as if the girl gave her good intel. "Did he ask your assistance with, say, reservations or directions?"

Two staff members about her age walked by and kept walking but studied over their shoulders just the same. Riley let them leave the room before answering. "He asked about a lot of places. The Post Office. I told him about Whaley's. Oh, and he asked about the new place, Ella and Ollie's."

Though they had a remarkable menu, Ella and Ollie's would always be Grover's to Callie. Where her old boss Stan flew in from Boston and met her, let her imbibe to excess to make Callie vent and get over herself back when panic attacks ruled her day. God, what a mess she'd been when she first moved here.

"Were reservations ever for two?" Callie asked.

"No, ma'am. But he asked about boats."

Callie flipped a page. "What kind of boats? For what?"

"He said he wanted to see Indigo from the water, see the dolphins he kept hearing about. I sent him to Craven's and the marina but warned him we were a little far up the river for him to kayak himself unless he had experience."

Craven's rented kayaks and canoes, plus wind boards and whatever other trendy contraptions one could enjoy on the water. The marina housed the bigger boat rentals, or you could hire a captain to take you out. Several boat owners earned a living taking folks out to fish, sightsee, or experience nature.

"Did he give you any idea which boat he preferred?"

The girl shook her head. "Oh, Mr. Shaw. That reminds me." She reached in the lone drawer of the antique desk. "I confiscated more of these yesterday in the gift shop. I remember because Mr. Callaway had one. Said he found it here, so I searched until I found them all. Throw them away?"

"I'd appreciate it, Riley."

Callie held out her hand, and Riley placed them in it. A dozen copies of the treasure map like the one found near the body.

"What was your impression of him?" Callie asked, peering up from the map.

"Ma'am?"

Callie lightly shrugged as if her question was simple, informal, and without pressure. "Was he pleasant? Soft-spoken? Or more pushy . . . maybe entitled?"

She took a second to think. "Formally nice is maybe more like it? But still acted like I owed him, too. Like I ought to count myself lucky he flirted with me."

"Flirted?"

"Asked me to go out on the boat with him once I made that suggestion on the charter instead of the kayak. Said I sounded like I could *handle myself*." She used air quotes around the last two words.

"So how'd you get out of it?" Callie asked.

"I told him I had to work."

Face red from the heat, Roberts appeared. "Coroner's here," he said, leaning down low to Callie. "And Callaway's car is missing."

"Any ID on the body?"

"Nope."

"Phone?"

"Sort of falls under the heading of ID, and the answer's the same." His mouth held a straight line. "Cameras?"

"Already have the security guard checking them," she said.

"How far back?"

"Day before check-in to now."

"Keep an eye on your phone," Roberts said.

"Sure," she replied almost to his back as he spun and walked a few feet away, making a call.

Callie just stared.

"Is all law enforcement this competitive?" Sweet whispered close.

"No," she said calm and oh-so-even. "Only when civilians try to tell us how to do our jobs or muck around in assignments they shouldn't."

She glanced at her phone and opened several pictures from Roberts. The driver's license pic versus the frontal view of the dead guy. Some crime scene angles of the body and its placement around the water. Kudos to Roberts for sending these. Though puffy and nibbled on, the facial features appeared similar enough. "Pretty sure it's him all right." She held the phone over for Sweet to see. "Now we find his car and connect the dots as to his disappearance."

Roberts returned. "And when he died," he said, not catching Callie's attempt to avoid the mention of death in front of Riley.

But Riley hadn't heard, her young smile lit up toward a pair asking directions to the beach.

Callie gave Roberts his expected *good-boy* nod. With the *who* reasonably solved, now she had only to determine *why* and *how* Addison Callaway wound up dead on the banks of Indigo Plantation.

Chapter 6

Slade

"I WON'T LET THE boat tip over," Wayne said from the rear corner of Craven's Boat Rentals, where I'd pulled him away from a confused salesperson behind the counter.

Teeth clamped, I almost wanted to swat the lawman. "Do you not remember Beaufort? That case that landed us on a shrimp boat? Honest to God, Wayne, I swear a shark swam by me after we got thrown into the ocean." My hand instinctively went to my ribs where I harbored a scar from our target's knife.

We'd floated in the water for an hour, in the middle of the night, me scared out of my head, at least until I passed out from loss of blood. Not a good ending to the last time we'd gone on the water.

A mother watched me while pretending to assist her first or second grade son pick out a tee shirt. To our right, an older, white-haired pair tried on beach hats, though the lady had taken more than a glance in our direction. Maybe I'd said shark too loud.

"You shouldn't have sneaked on the boat," Wayne whispered lower.

"I had to save your ass," I said.

Shaking his head a few times, he reached for my shoulders. "Forget all that. We'll just be in a creek. Both of us. Relaxing. Never out of sight of land. On vacation. You remember what vacation means, right?"

I shrugged him off, shaking my head. "Dark. Water."

The dark water phobia had existed in me as long as I could remember. To the days when I was six and went to Sea World in Florida. When I almost wet my pants standing there as an eight-foot shark circled the tank, and monster manta rays lazily watched me, wordlessly declaring the water was theirs and not mine. Telepathically communicating with me, my face pressed against the glass, inserting images in my brain of my leg crunching in their mouths.

Forget they were in the tank and I was not. The ocean was clearly their turf, and I wasn't setting foot in it ever again.

"I'll watch you from the land," I said about the time the bell tinkled above the door.

"Hey, Chief," said the counter person.

"Hey, Rick," said the voice I'd heard enough of today. The lady cop who figured I had not one lick of sense. Could read it in her eyes, hear it in her voice while we were out at the plantation. I'd protected her damn dead body, thank you very much. I dragged Wayne behind a stand of boogie boards wide enough to hide us, yet keep us within earshot.

"Slade," he grumbled.

"Shush," I said.

"Need to ask you two things," the chief said to the store person. "Hope you can help me. Looking for a guy."

I heard the gasp. "You think some criminal came in here?"

"No, no, nothing like that," she assured him. "Recognize this man?"

At first I thought she showed a picture of the floater, but fast realized she had some sort of ID by now. Driver's license maybe.

"Yeah," Rick said. "Reserved my biggest boat yesterday morning. I worried he didn't know what he was doing with it and suggested a charter, but he said he could manage, so I told him he better get here at the crack of dawn because it usually got snatched quick by families. It has a small motor. Less manual labor."

I cut a discerning glance at Wayne who held a finger in front of his lips.

"Boat come back okay?" she asked.

"Oh yeah," Rick said. "It's out back on the trailer. Appeared at the marina this morning, but I don't believe he delivered it."

"And how would you know that?" the chief asked.

I heard a drawer scrape open. "Because I hold a person's driver's license when they rent one of my boats." He slapped something on the counter. "Appears your picture matches mine. He didn't return the boat by the time I went home last night, so I just added another day to his charge, figuring he got absorbed in his recreating, you know? When you find him, tell him he's still gotta pay for the extra time. He can't be far."

"Why?" she asked.

"His car's still outside. A rental."

The chief didn't immediately reply. A pause held conversation in check, and I wondered how Callie'd express herself without saying their mutual friend had passed on.

"I'll take his license, if you don't mind."

Rick sounded clueless. "Wait . . . what if he shows up?"

"Then send him to me," the chief replied.

Good answer in a comical, morbid way.

"And I'll have to ask that you carefully, without touching it any more than you have to, secure that boat someplace until I can bring someone to go over it. The shed maybe? Will it fit?"

"Wait," he said, dragging out the word. "What's really going on?"

Time to rescue the conversation. I walked out, just out of Wayne's reach. "How you doing, Chief Morgan. Fancy seeing you here."

After a brief look meant to put me in my place, she smiled. "You renting a kayak?"

"Never in a million years," I said, to which Rick scowled. Guess he thought Wayne and I were just trying to decide which color canoe or something. "Mind if I ask a question of our friend here?" I asked.

Gently she waved toward Rick, seeming more curious than accepting of a partnership.

"You're not renting a boat?" the man asked.

"Never mind that," I said. "This guy," and I pointed to the enlarged copy of the driver's license still on the counter, the real license beside it. "Did he get a pirate map here?"

"Maybe," he said.

I motioned to a stack next to the register. "You leave these maps out in the open. Everywhere else on Edisto, the business owners not only hide but toss out these things. Seen it happen three times since we've been on the island. Why not here?"

Chief Morgan turned toward Rick, waiting. Guess my question piqued her curiosity. Score two points for me.

Rick gazed around the shop, then beckoned us in, urging discretion. The chief, Wayne, and I leaned in.

Our guy tapped the stack of maps on the counter. "I give Drummond consideration because his maps make people want to treasure hunt, which means they usually need a boat. A mutual relationship."

"Why don't the others like him?" I asked.

Rick's already tanned, shoe-leather complexion darkened with a pinch of temper. He tapped his chest. "I'm the only one who gives our pirate the time of day without a threat. Can't account for the others."

"Businesses out here threaten him?" Wayne asked.

"Not quite," Chief Morgan said. "But the pirate hasn't made many friends for all the years he's lived here. Did a stint in the Navy, from what I heard, then spent a few years at the yacht clubs in Charleston. He retired and went full-time out here."

"And he's not a bad guy," Rick added. "And if you wanna talk about threats, you ought to talk to the guy you're hunting for. He's some smart-ass blogger claiming to be somebody special. Or so he says. He could threaten. Gives you a bad headline if you don't give him a freebie. I Googled the guy while he was walking around the store. He's huge. Any press is good for me, so yeah, when he asked me to set him up to meet with Drummond, I did it."

Wayne lifted one of the map brochures and opened it. "What's your competition think about your partnership with Drummond?"

With a deeper frown, Rick shook his head, his voice hard. "Don't give a damn. I'm the only kayak rental on the island, so it don't matter no how. Besides, most tourists don't want to fork out bucks for a charter. And Drummond's boat ain't the most seaworthy vessel, so I'd be a safer, more reasonable price, just without Drummond's drama." He paused, studying Wayne harder. "And I'm asking you to leave him alone. Guy's just earning a living same as me. Damn blogger dude didn't even give Drummond any business, the son of a bitch."

I nudged Wayne to back away, sensing Rick's temper rising at us for wasting his time *and* not renting a boat.

"So that's why the missing man rented your boat," I said. "How long did you speak to this . . ." I turned the driver's license paper around, "Addison Callaway? Did he give any indication where he was going? Or why? Or with whom?"

Rick looked at the chief, his thumb motioning at me. "Who the hell is this woman?"

Wayne chuckled once behind me.

Chief Morgan gave a shadow of a smile, too. "I want to ask you the same questions she is, Rick, so sure, go ahead and answer, if you don't mind. She's all right."

Using me or accepting me? I went with the former considering her tone.

A bit tardy in his response, ol' Rick rubbed the counter then leaned stiff-armed on it, gnawing the inside of his lip as if it represented the words he wanted to say but probably shouldn't. The man was fast losing patience in us. "What were your questions again?"

"Did he say where he was going? Or why? Or with whom?" I repeated.

"The sound, maybe up the river," he said. "I don't get involved with the why. He could be having sex with dolphins for all I care."

That painted a picture I didn't want to see. But at least Rick continued.

"Like I said, I don't know the why. But he came in, took a map, read it while standing about where your man is there, and then asked if I knew our local pirate."

"What about this pirate?" I asked.

"Teach Drummond," the chief filled in. "Thinks he's a descendent of Blackbeard."

The door tinkled again, warning us of a family of six piling in.

Rick shouted, "Be right with you folks," then spun on us. "I'm losing business here."

"Then talk faster." I turned my head and shouted out to the family. "We won't be more than a minute more. Trust me, he's worth waiting for."

Then I returned to Rick. "What were Callaway's plans?"

"To meet with Drummond," he said. "Said he'd put in a good word about this place in his travel blog if I got the guy to give him a free tour, but Teach is tough, man. He ain't giving nothing away. Pissed off that blogger 'cause he returned in a mood and rented my biggest boat."

Callaway was definitely not growing on me. "Say if he was going with someone?"

"Nope, but I told him he ought to hire a local. Otherwise he might go out a few hundred yards alone, decide it's not for him, then change his mind, and I would've lost a day's rental. Kind of a city fella from those fancy tasseled loafers."

The chief spoke. "Did he listen to you and find someone? You recommend anybody in particular?"

"He was alone when he made the reservation, but he had a friend the next morning when they picked up the boat at the marina." He gave a twisted scowl of a smirk. "A young woman less than half his age. Light skinned black girl. Nice lookin' though don't think boatin' with this guy was thrillin' her much. Might've hired her to handle the boat, like I said." He sneered again. "Not sure he hired her to do anything else, but wouldn't be surprised if he did."

Wayne lowered his tone. "You rent the boat to him for free?"

Rick's complexion darkened. "Maybe I did, maybe I didn't."

"Just asking," Wayne said. "Wonder how many other business owners around here he did that way?"

"All sorts," Rick said. "Folks aren't so happy about the blackmail business he was in."

"Like who?" I asked.

He held up his palm. "Ain't rattin' on my peers. You got a cop standing right there beside you. Let her find 'em. I'm done." He turned to the lady and her son waiting patiently behind us. "Come on up, ma'am. My apologies for making you wait."

She slid around us to the counter, in essence scooching us away. The chief led us to a corner, near a counter of *rare* shells and crafted jewelry and stood so she could watch who came toward us, situating Wayne and me where we couldn't be seen.

"Not sure Rick can tell us much more anyway," I said. "But damn, we learned there's another person involved."

"Agreed." She paused as though debating with herself.

Wayne shrugged. "We could help. Your pirate sounds sleazy, and my guess is that he's not a fan of cops."

She glanced to her left, double-checking for ears, and reached over to slide a rack on the counter three inches out of her line of sight to the entrance. "No, Drummond won't talk to me or my officers. Too many times we've had to deal with complaints about him trying to capitalize on other businesses' crowds, brochure racks; hell, he even solicits in private parking lots."

"Sounds like an enterprising bastard," Wayne added. "So why not let us touch base with him? As fresh faces and a pair on holiday."

The chief lightly scratched her neck. "He'd shoot his mouth off if I did it."

"Right," Wayne said.

My lawman was smart. The chief had shown no interest in me, but Wayne? He was a whole other package. For some reason people swallowed his logic a lot quicker than mine. Tall, dark with salt and pepper hair always needing a trim. His beard more of a three-day stubble that he pulled off almost too well from the side glances he got from women.

Women who I couldn't help but wonder if they did a comparison and judged me not good enough for him. Sort of like the chief.

"I'll give you one better," I said, refusing to be squeezed out of this impromptu brainstorming session. "Let's take up Mr. Shaw on his offer to put us at Indigo Plantation. Why not play the vacationing twosome to the max? He has no inkling of what we do for a living, and frankly, the only person who's heard what we do is you, Chief."

Wayne chewed the inside of his cheek, a habit I knew well. He liked the idea. Or at least he hadn't told me to hush. All he added was, "What about the rental we have?"

"It's paid for," I said. "Indigo's free. We haven't lost a thing; plus, this vacation has suddenly taken on new life for me." I elbowed him. "The chief can tell us what to do, and we do it. How hard can that be? Come on, Cowboy. You know you want to."

"But does she?" he said, turning toward our new friend in uniform.

A congressional debate practically took place in that woman's head. I could almost hear the arguments. I was naïve, not a real investigator, but Wayne was, or seemed to be. Easy enough to check out any badge. And who else would she get who wasn't known on the island? And damn, he was a fed, no less. I rode those coattails more times than I could count, so why couldn't she?

We weren't stealing her show, if that was her issue. We'd simply be tools at her disposal. It wasn't like Wayne and I hadn't solved a murder or taken down our share of miscreants. Our record might be bumpy and our methods . . . um . . . atypical, but we won in the end.

I took the ensuing silence as favorable. "I take it that's a yes?"

Rick wandered over. "It's getting on toward seven. I need to close. You reserving a kayak for tomorrow or not?"

"I'll go with *not*," I said, attempting to sound solid and professional. Inside, however, my belly did giddy dances. Back with Agriculture, management attempted to control my investigations with too tight a fist. Finally, a chance to snoop without all the accountability.

I feigned interest in a sand dollar display as we walked out the door to avoid them seeing the unavoidable grin on my face. Screw vacation. Wayne and I'd just landed a case.

Chapter 7

Callie

A LITTLE AFTER eight in the evening, Callie dragged herself up Chelsea Morning's two dozen steps to her front porch. Everyone who lived in the beach town referenced homes by their names. She often had to stop and look at a map to correctly type the mailing address on a report.

A breeze tried to make an appearance but without much effort, leaving the dusk air stifling and thick with humidity. She hadn't bothered to check in with Marie, her office manager. Not this late. In the air conditioning, she did call Raysor, though, already home in Walterboro, and updated him about the Charleston Sheriff's Office.

"And you took the case?" he asked in an almost bullhorn tone.

"Sort of had to, Don."

"You don't owe Charleston's people anything whatsoever, Doll. Hell, you don't even live in the county. Call him back and say no."

Peering in the fridge and finding little more than condiments and the take-home box of mostly eaten leftovers from McConkey's, she almost laughed at the comment. "Yeah, let's unring that bell. I think you know better."

From there on out, she was too tired to do more than listen to him, especially with the mood he was in. Piece by piece, she shed the uniform and almost fifteen pounds of belt as he ranted about her being dragged into something political. Letting him grump and moan until she was naked, she finished the call lying across her comforter under the ceiling fan, almost willing to forego dinner and a drink and go straight to bed. Dinner anyway. The drink was her evening ritual.

Touching thumb to fingers, Callie counted off the four months since she'd been pulled over at midnight by one of her own men because of that ritual. Not a pretty moment; one she still felt had been a bit overplayed.

Raysor hung up grumpy but obliged her by agreeing to help, as she knew he would. Sliding on her favorite khaki shorts unraveled in the cuffs, then a tank top, she padded barefoot to the refrigerator and poured herself a chilled gin and tonic, fighting to keep the measurements on the more respectable side of one to three. Cheese, crackers, an apple. Her yoga friend would be impressed, except for the contents of her glass, which Sophie continually attempted to find and dispose of during her impromptu visits. She hadn't been successful in months.

One drink per night now. Just one. The bigger the glass, the more tonic. She just refused to quit cold turkey, because she liked the taste too damn much. But she'd gotten a handle on the drinking.

She tired of being ever under someone's magnifying glass, but it came with the job. Heaven help that Charleston sheriff. He could have the more heavy-handed politics that came with that city: the being traded and bought while pretending you weren't. Her mother was the mayor of Middleton forty minutes away. Her father the previous mayor. Her grandfather before him. Yeah, she knew how the political game was played. She just didn't want to play.

Tonight she had plenty on her mind and needed to stay inside and research Callaway with a clear head. The silence since her son went to college deafened her some evenings, making her want to drive the Edisto streets or drink enough to preoccupy her mind with other topics, so she opened the turntable and put on three Neil Diamond vinyls.

Her favorite album dropped first. *Stones.* God, how did she get so exhausted? And hot. Temps had bumped a hundred before the day was out, and she couldn't stop sweating.

Rubbing the already moist glass against her cheek and temple, she grabbed her laptop, flipped on the ceiling fan, and planted herself in an Adirondack chair on the side porch, door open to hear the music and feel the AC draft. If there was one thing these Edisto houses did well, it was porches, fourteen feet off ground, propped on tall pillars that kept the homes above most hurricane storm surges. She had three porches: front, east side, and marsh view, but the screened east side suited her most, its mesh allowing soft winds to come from the beach on one side and travel through to the marsh on the back. The east side was the most obscure, too, facing the neighboring lot. Edisto Beach was too small for people not to know where she lived on Jungle Road.

A waft of air from her right barely stirred her hair as the tide came in.

From the periphery of her vision, she caught a bounced reflection of a blue light, and froze, listening. A whoop from the siren sounding not three doors down.

She phoned Thomas. "Is that you I hear?" she asked.

"Yeah, Chief. Traffic stop. I got it."

Good. She hung up. Thomas was her favorite of the crew. She'd promised her youngest officer that she'd refrain from drinking and cruising the streets late at night, a habit and a luxury she had pursued until he caught her in April. If she ever lifted a glass, she agreed to stay in. At least twice weekly he drove by, checking for her car. Probably had just then, too, before catching the speeder.

She took a sip, measured the level of the glass to ration the drink, and opened the laptop. The computer gave her all the light she needed in the waning day. She began a list which she'd transfer to her phone later. Calling the detective in the morning to get the coroner's cause of death ranked first. Next, digging more into Sweet's staff.

She added Sweet to the list to see what he thought once his mind had settled down after a night's sleep.

Sweet seemed innocent enough, but he wasn't the purest of sugar in her opinion. Not with that political play used to reel her in. And Roberts, damn. What the hell was she to do with him? She'd have an ulcer managing him if this thing dragged out too long, and she wasn't beyond calling the sheriff if Roberts got adversarial enough to tarnish the investigation.

But that's not how police treated issues regarding internal personnel clashes. Not and keep respect, anyway. Police tended to, well, self-police.

The coroner's prelim was crucial as to how this case developed. The missing wallet and cell maybe suggested involvement of a second party. But she'd leave the coroner to Roberts, giving him as much responsibility as she could. Surely Roberts was professional enough to keep her informed, because to sabotage her was to sabotage the entire case.

Finally, she plugged in a search for Addison Callaway, her main purpose for the night. His blog popped up front and center, and she dove into it. A counter stated a ridiculous eight-figure number of hits. His last post had been five days ago at a small restaurant in Charleston, a probable stopover on his way to Edisto. Most of his posts appeared weekly, leading her to believe he intended one over the next few days.

Listening to Rick at Craven's—assuming he wasn't exaggerating—Callaway had a rather belligerent method of gathering his blogging material. A business owner either allowed him to come into their place, gratis, or bear the wrath of a bad review to the world.

Or else he went incognito like at Indigo.

She flipped through posts about Charleston first. Then Asheville, Jacksonville, Roanoke, DC. Mouth-watering pictures, smiling chefs, wait staff in camaraderie poses as if what they did created world peace. Beautifully designed suites.

Then the copy. *Holy Bejesus.*

Sauce was colorless and gummy, as if they'd melted a jellyfish found washed up on Folly Beach.

A clueless staff, as if they'd been picked up from a parking lot group of unskilled laborers seeking hour landscape work. Salad, shrubs . . . what's the difference?

The terse and condescending verbiage made the happy people in the pics come off as saps, unaware the smiling shark behind the lens was about to take a chunk out of their livelihood. She'd checked. One restaurant in Tampa closed within months of their scathing review.

No, sir, no motive there. He ought to travel with a partner . . . aka body guard. She was surprised more fan pics hadn't appeared of the man, unless he was adept at slipping in, zinging a place, then slipping out. Who knew bad food and hotel reviews could be on-demand-entertainment?

New thought. The guy would practically sleep with a camera, unless he used his phone. Hard to tell anymore with photography technology. Where was either one and what had he taken pictures of lately?

Choosing Charleston again, since she had a decent knowledge of the city, she scrolled down to the comments from his fans, or rather, followers, because a good number of the remarks wanted Mr. Callaway as dead as the barbecue in one of his photos. Mostly anonymous remarks. The naysayers blasting the man with names like *phony, bastard, dickhead.* Callaway periodically responded, drinking in the attention, his wit jabbing in one-liner punches. *Your vocabulary matches your palate . . . limited and tasteless.*

Touché, said one fan.

Keeping it real, said another.

Then on the other hand, when he praised a venue, the comments exploded as did the hotel, B&B, or restaurant's business volume, if the thank-yous and capitulations were correct.

The banter and creative word usage hooked foodies like crack. The grovelers and the hecklers alike enjoyed the Caesarian thumbs-up or thumbs-down decisions. Before Callie knew it, she'd read an hour's worth of mindless tit-for-tat, almost wishing she hadn't contributed to the blog's number of visits. Callaway was not a nice man. Unless it was an act. Either way, one couldn't ignore his success, or his collection of haters.

If Addison Callaway didn't have enemies, nobody did.

She closed the laptop, threw back the last swallow of melted ice and gin, and stared out into the night, the empty glass balanced on the arm of the chair. The air had turned briny and dank this close to eleven.

A raccoon had come out of the marsh, its clicking noises evident in the bushes, testing trash can lids. Bugs and frogs sang in the trees with whirrs and mumbled ribbits. A stray gnat had squeezed through her screen, humming in dive-bombing swoops at her face, and she smacked him against her cheek then used moisture off the wet glass to wash him off.

She ought to go to bed but another concern worried her. The twosome she'd just accepted into the case. In hindsight, she'd accepted them too soon. Snatching the laptop open again, she fired it up and Googled *South Carolina + Agriculture + Wayne Largo*. Nothing. Not surprising since federal agencies attempted to keep their agents obscure.

Then she did the same with Carolina Slade. More success there. Headlines in places like Charleston, Beaufort, Columbia . . . the governor? Who was this woman? Apparently, she had assisted in a case or two with Agriculture, for whatever that meant. Short snippet articles, less than informative but long enough for the words *drugs* and *homicide* to be mentioned.

The United States Department of Agriculture. Huh, she pondered as she rose from her chair. Who'd have thought it?

That deserved another drink.

*

RUING THE THIRD gin, Callie awoke, moving a dry tongue around her mouth. Rapid, nervous knuckle raps banged on her front door that could only mean one person. Sophie Bianchi.

Everything the next-door neighbor was, Callie wasn't. Powerfully fit and lithe from decades of yoga, a health food freak who considered more than 800 calories a day to be binging. Naturally hyper, Sophie could be an insanely vexing morning person.

"Callie? Wanted to catch you before you left for work. Open the door."

After crawling out of bed, Callie opened her locked bedroom door, shut off the alarm, and fumbled toward the front door. While she slumped against the doorframe in one of Seabrook's old tee shirts, Sophie stood garbed in a baby blue tank, black leggings, and a sheer sarong affair. High-end sandals accented a fresh nail job on her toes. Her vividly colored eyes topped the ensemble; Sophie had as many colored contacts as shoes.

Sophie cocked a hip. "Well?"

"You aren't wearing your signature coral nail polish," Callie said.

Whooshing in uninvited, Sophie made for the kitchen. She opened the refrigerator and began pulling out items, smacking them on the kitchen table. "I went with blue this time, to match the clothes. In honor of Indigo Plantation. I'm headed out there today to see if they have a need for weekly yoga lessons."

Callie came to the entryway. "By all means make yourself at home, Soph. I'm going to take my shower."

The pixy shag shivered at Sophie's jerky movements at the sink. "I'm fixing you a smoothie to wake you up. To force that booze from your system."

Sighing, Callie lolled her head back, staring at the ceiling. "Only me and mornings. And I need to get to work."

The blender soon shouted its irritation at the vegetable overload. About the time Callie stuck her head under the hot water, Sophie's arm shot past the curtain. "Here, drink this."

"It's green," Callie shouted over the water.

"You didn't have enough carrots," Sophie shouted back. "I'll pick some up for you on my way home from Indigo."

Twisting the shower head away from diluting her drink, Callie downed half the glass and poured the rest down the drain. Booze couldn't even fix the taste of this. Hiding a belch, she thrust the glass outside the curtain. Sophie took it.

"Heard from Sprite?" Callie asked.

"Yeah, yeah, my baby girl's fine at college. Has practically forgotten me."

Callie managed a grin. "Jeb ignores me, too, but they'll take care of each other. Has Zeus changed his mind yet about returning to school now that his buddy and sister are there?"

"Nope. He likes his fishing charters. He's much more of free spirit, Callie. So like me."

More like lucky. Zeus's dad funded the lean months and had bought the fishing boat, keeping the ocean much more palatable than a classroom.

Callie dried off in the shower, reaching out for clothing articles, and began getting dressed. Sophie remained perched on the edge of the tub.

"What'd you come over for?" Callie asked, a quick brush of mascara to keep her face from looking naked.

"I wanted you to put in a good word for me at Indigo," she said. "Heard you went out there yesterday for lunch and didn't return until dark."

Callie stopped and turned. "Where'd you hear that?"

The yoga mistress hopped up and twirled. "Not saying. Anyway, does this blue match their blue? Do I fit in?"

Stepping back, Callie studied her friend. Outgoing and able to take flirty right to the line of impropriety, Sophie processed people on her own terms. Not sure how yoga classes would mesh with the historic flavor of Indigo, she threw her makeup in the drawer and left toward the bedroom. "Good enough to me."

"Come on," Sophie whined, on Callie's heels. "You're the famous lady chief on a tourist island."

Callie slid into her uniform slacks, leaving them open to tuck in her shirt over the vest. "Doesn't matter. You got this all by yourself."

A huge sigh from her friend almost ruffled Callie's hair.

"What're you really up to?" Callie asked, hustling once she glanced at her nightstand clock and saw she was already ten minutes late.

"You haven't heard?"

"No, apparently I haven't."

Sophie lowered her voice, as if they weren't by themselves. "Addison Callaway is staying there!" She shifted her weight, the cockiness she was so noted for radiating. "You don't even recognize who he is, do you?"

Callie cinched her belt, grateful Sophie spoke in the here and now about the man. Whoever told her about Callie's yesterday time at Indigo obviously hadn't understood the why. "The name sounds familiar. We get famous people out here all the time, Soph."

"And I heard the manager is hot. Was hoping since you're probably connected . . ." She hesitated. "Right?"

"Yes, I know Mr. Shaw."

"Good." Sophie scurried to block Callie's path to the bedroom door. "You can make introductions, then once I win over Mr. Shaw, he can introduce me to Mr. Callaway."

Amazing that Sweet hadn't heard of Callaway staying at Indigo, yet Sophie had. However, Soph made gossip her specialty, and Sweet had a grand opening to cope with. He might not have known, which he avowed yesterday, but it did make Callie wonder. Special guests needed special attention. If Indigo was so patron-friendly, and Callaway's name so commonplace in the hospitality industry, why risk assigning the case to her? Why wouldn't the sheriff retain it for safekeeping . . . and a feather in his cap?

And she couldn't ask Sophie how she heard . . . not yet. Not without giving away how Callie even knew about the existence of the illustrious, and very dead, Addison Callaway.

Chapter 8

Callie

SOPHIE LEFT CHELSEA Morning dancing on her tippy toes, eager for her meet-and-greet with Sweet. Reluctantly, Callie had promised to accompany her to Indigo if and when she landed an appointment. Which meant Callie would have to take care of routine tasks quickly, because Sophie would pull out all her coquettish social graces to finagle that appointment ASAP. When Soph smelled yoga opportunities, or more so, craved to learn the backstories of fresh residents, she wasted little time making connections. Nobody told the woman no.

Hmmm, like Callaway, if rumor proved correct.

The air-conditioning smacked her as she entered the station. Marie manned the station solo this a.m.

"Morning," Callie said, heading to the coffee pot. "Anything pressing?"

"A spousal squabble on Osceola Street, golf carts racing on the sound side of Myrtle, and someone tried to get out of a breakfast tab at the Seacow."

Turning, blowing on her black coffee, Callie leaned on the counter, so grateful for this lady. "A bit busy for this early. Taken care of?"

Marie, a frumpy blonde barely a year younger than Callie, continued to type as she spoke. "Spouses decided to pack and go home. Golf carts got tickets. Breakfast tab got paid with nobody pressing charges."

Having been born and raised on the island, Marie could recite names, addresses, birthdates, divorcees, prom dates, and the alma maters of the last four generations of families from the Atlantic to the McKinley Washington Bridge in one direction, from the South Edisto River to the North Edisto in the other. She remembered which skeletons used to be in which closets *and* all the versions misquoted since the original tale, and while she never bragged about said prowess, it came in handy when situations arose. Callie'd used Encyclopedia Marie as leverage in making several unsavory dilemmas disappear. They'd be lost without this almost invisible clerk who practically ran the station. And the woman who'd snubbed Callie upon her arrival to Edisto almost served as a sister some days when the men weren't around.

"Sounds like another day I barely needed to come in for," Callie said.

"Like yesterday?"

"Hmm, who hasn't had her second cup of coffee today?"

Marie's fingers paused on her keys, and she peered up, a motherly tenderness in her eyes in spite of their equal age. "I went home without you checking in last night. Are you doing okay?"

Callie nodded, genuinely appreciative of the clerk's concern. Marie had loved Seabrook, too, and his death eleven months ago still hung heavy over both ladies on some days. Marie would appreciate the weight thrust upon Callie to drive that road, past the place it all went down. "Yeah, thanks for asking. Just got caught up at Indigo." She shrugged. "I sent Don back when I saw how late I'd be."

Marie gave her a pregnant once-over, came to a silent conclusion, and returned to her work.

And guilt washed over Callie for misleading one of her best allies and got-your-back people she had on Edisto. "I've gotten sucked into a case out there," she ultimately added.

"Okay," her office manager said, not the least affected. No asking about the crime. No questioning how Callie came to work outside her jurisdiction.

"So if I need something," Callie continued, "keep it hushed. A man named Addison Callaway died out there, cause unknown."

Marie kept working. "Got it. Which means don't tell Brice, either, I take it. That all?"

"Believe so."

"You okay driving that road?" Marie asked, as if she'd raised Callie as her own.

Hesitating, Callie nodded, appreciative. "I think I'm good."

"No problem then." And Marie continued on being Marie, running the place.

Callie slid to her office, the only private room in the police station of seven officers and the one super-woman clerk whom Callie was coming to love more each day.

Door closed, she called Detective Roberts, now in her contacts list. Call went to voice mail. "Hey, this is, um, Callie Morgan." Concede to the familiar, she told herself. Meet him partway. "You heard from the coroner yet? I have his original driver's license, by the way. And while it's early, any chance you got a sense of his cause of death? Figured you'd have an inside track."

She stopped a second, wondering what else to say without squeezing it in and sounding breathless . . . and trying too hard. "Would like to update you on a thought I had, if you don't mind. No rush, but felt you'd want to collaborate."

As agreed to with the sheriff, Callie led the case but didn't own it. Roberts needed to be kept apprised, and whether or not she had anything, she'd call him twice a day until they concluded. He was unavailable this time, and she prayed it wasn't his norm. Even more so, hoped it wasn't because of animosity, jealousy, or spite.

But whether he liked her logic or not, he should be notified about Carolina Slade and Wayne Largo relocating to Indigo to keep an eye on things and speak to the pirate. These cooperating individuals held a few more qualifications than the standard CIs. At least when it came to Largo.

She placed a call. Raysor picked right up, his Southern Lowcountry lineage thick. "Been waiting to hear from you. You enjoying working for Charleston?"

"You enjoy working for me? No different," she said. Raysor was officially a Colleton County deputy with their sheriff's office, but he'd been on loan to Edisto Beach PD through five police chiefs now. "Hey, need you to stay close to the beach while I work this case. The guys listen to you."

He chuckled. "I'm your snitch."

"You're all my snitches," she answered. "You just don't see it."

"Keep thinking that," he said.

She relied on Don Raysor as much or more than she did Marie. Don and Marie . . . funny. She'd have to start calling them the Osmonds. Regardless, the two carried two lifetimes of Edisto secrets. "Listen, I don't want to pull you into the investigation quite yet. And don't share the case too readily with the others, okay? Turns out this floater might actually be somebody, which means—"

"Press, your favorite people." Most everyone was aware of the chief's scorn of paparazzi. She'd butted heads with a young blogger over a year ago and been hounded by reporters over the Jinx case. Then, of course, she shot a reporter on Pine Landing Road. The scum she should've seen coming way earlier than she had. The one who killed Seabrook.

That night had tarnished her image of the paparazzi species well beyond recovery.

"And politics are in play here," she added.

"Glad it's you and not me, Doll. Call when you need me," he said.

"Back at you."

She ended the call and was about to call Sweet when the phone rang in her hand. She answered, and Sophie's words spilled through the phone. "Can you collect me in your patrol car at eleven?"

"Absolutely not," Callie replied. "Civilians don't just ride in a police car unless you're misbehaving. Especially not to a job interview. He agreed to see you, I take it?"

"Yeah, and honey, I swear, I just dropped your name and *open sesame*, I was in."

That woman. "Doubt that, but I'll come home, and we can go in my personal car."

The sigh stretched long. "Not even a police escort?"

Probably not a bad idea. Sophie was like a sparrow distracted by the next bright shiny thing, and a thirty-minute chat with Sweet could stretch into her flitting around the plantation for hours.

"All right. Police escort. No siren or lights, though," Callie said in jest.

"Then what good's the escort?"

"Take it or leave it. The alternative is to ride in my Escape, meaning you'll leave when I say leave. Some of us have a job."

Sophie exhaled with an *oooh*. "Are you seriously telling me my yoga teaching is not a job?"

"It's a glorified hobby that pays you under the table, if I'm not wrong, and I don't want to know."

"Humph," Sophie said in a pout. "Bet I make more than you." She finished with a giggle, happy to win the spar. "Mr. Shaw sounds dreamy. Should I get my hopes up?"

"Gotta go," Callie said, recalling Sweet's shoulder and back rubbing at the crime scene. "I'll meet you at your place."

She hung up actually appreciating Sophie's timing. Callie wanted to see the scene again where they found the body. A night's sleep and fresh eyes might shed new light, then she'd interview an employee or two. With her visit being unscheduled, they'd have no prepared response.

And she'd corner Sweet, um, Mr. Shaw. Swinton? This had already gotten awkward since he'd pushed the informal on her first, and it had stuck. Truth was, he was not just the manager who'd had a body wash onto his place. The notes in the bedroom proved condemning of Indigo, and Swinton "Sweet" Shaw could easily become a person of interest.

SOPHIE PULLED INTO the parking lot in her baby blue vintage Mercedes convertible, like that car didn't make an entrance of its own without the police escort. Once Sophie committed to a parking place, Callie peeled over to the other side of the lot, leaving the patrol car a discreet distance away from tourists, beside a tall line of wax myrtles on the edge of the woods.

Meeting with Sophie at the front step, she started inside, only for the yoga maven to hang outside.

"It's hot, Soph," Callie said. "Marvel at everything in the cool."

"I remember how this place used to be, though." She did a 360. "I'm so impressed." Finally, she danced up the steps. "Can't wait to see the guy in charge."

Riley sat behind the concierge desk at a laptop, noting them when they approached. "May I help you . . . oh."

Callie approached the girl. "Hey, Riley. We have—"

A squeal arose behind Callie, and Sophie ran around the desk and hugged Riley. "Honey, I hadn't heard you worked here." She squeezed the girl again. "How's your momma? And your big sister. Didn't she get married and move to Atlanta? It's so good to see you!"

And there Sophie went—sucking the air out of the room.

Callie squeezed in the conversation. "We have an appointment with Mr. Shaw."

Riley appeared relieved for the interruption and extracted herself from the hug. "Let me go check and see if he's in his office." She disappeared.

"See?" Sophie said, all abuzz. "This is what we need on Edisto. Jobs like this. Not too detrimental to the island ways, yet good for the people who choose to live here." She leaned in when the room got quieter, as other employees took a moment to take in the energy of this new lady. "My yoga will fit right in."

Sweet appeared from the hallway to his office. "Callie. So nice to see you again." Once he shook her hand, he turned to Sophie who literally batted her eyes, the gaze from the blue contact lenses alive with adoration. "And this is the yoga mistress I hear so much about. Sophie Bianchi, how are you, my dear?" His handshake for Callie changed to a grasp of Sophie's hand in both of his.

Oh goodness, Sweet didn't know what he was in for.

The employees returned to work and noise recommenced, but Sophie tucked her chin, drew back her shoulders, and ever-so-gently let her posture remind the world she had the most incredible man-made boobs. Those abs, the taut glutes, yeah, she'd practiced in front of a mirror for moments like this.

Sweet cut a glance at Callie, who winked at him, offering a grin. "Well, when you two are done, I'd like to meet with Mr. Shaw myself, but no rush."

"You sure you don't want to join us?" he beckoned, and Callie shook her head.

"I want to see that spot we visited yesterday, if you don't mind," she said, not wanting to mention Callaway in front of Sophie. "But I'll be around."

"We won't be terribly long," Sophie said, inserting her arm around his.

Callie watched them walk down the hallway, then headed to the dining area. A mixed wave of aromas reached her as she rounded the corner. Grilled things, cheese maybe? Her stomach grumbled in approval.

In uniform, she couldn't ask anybody at the desk if her dynamic duo had checked in yet without blowing their cover. The grandfather clock in the corner of the lobby said five minutes to noon. She dared to peer in the dining room in hopes to catch Largo and Slade at lunch. Not expecting to find them, fingers already on her phone, she decided to text them to meet her at the marsh site.

The waitress recognized her first. "Hey, Chief. Craving some of that ice cream?"

"It's sure hot enough for it." Maybe she'd start with this woman. Jackie, she reminded herself with the nametag. "You got ten minutes you can give me? I thought of a question to ask you."

With only a flicker of concern, the waitress regrouped quickly. "Let me take the order from that table near the back, and I can probably work you in. Give me a second."

Callie squeezed into a niche between the kitchen and the hallway. Today, like yesterday, Jackie appeared in control of this part of the business. She might be able to direct Callie to other employees, even pave introductions.

Jackie soon returned. "There," she said, adjusting her apron. "I've got the kids covering. So what can I do for you?"

Callie scanned around with purpose to make her point. "Is there a place . . ."

"Oh, come to the break room." Jackie led them just eight feet away to a tiny room barely big enough for a table for four. "Not much, but then, this isn't the Hilton." She shut the door behind them.

There was a maturity about the woman. Personable and in control but without intimidation. She owned her job, not the least bit diminished by the fact she served food to guests. Callie could see why Sweet hired her.

"Now, what do you need?" Jackie asked. "Oh, can I get you a tea first?"

Callie smiled. "No, ma'am. Just wondered if you've ever heard of Addison Callaway."

Jackie sat back in her chair, pondering. "Is he a guest? I don't learn all their names. I mean, we try, but they don't exactly go around wearing name tags. Sometimes they're just room numbers, especially if they order room service." She gave a brief giggle. "I'm sorry. Guess I'm nervous talking to a policeman, um, police lady?"

"Think outside of Indigo. Not a guest. Have you heard the name?"

Puzzlement spread across Jackie's face. "Rings a teeny little bell, but I'm really sorry. I feel like I'm expected to recognize him for you."

"That's all right." Callie laid the driver's license picture on the table. "Forget the name. Do you recall seeing this gentleman here?"

Recognition grew in her eyes, and she pushed graying blond hair behind one ear. "Oh, yes. Yes, yes, I'm so sorry. He was here. Haven't seen him in a day or two, but he had breakfast last I did. He ordered a picnic lunch for two delivered to his room. Always liked the furthest table from the door, against the wall under that bay window. He was here at least two days, and I'm thinking maybe three. I oversee breakfasts and lunches, but someone else would've served him for dinner since I just work days. But he tried something different each time, and even asked me what I preferred to eat." She did a little dip with her head. "That was kind of special."

"Was he nice? Difficult?"

"Oh," she said, "Completely pleasant. No complaints, and he left a decent tip."

Callie tried not to sigh at the normalcy of the recounting. "I may need to speak to your staff, too."

"Yes, of course. Tito is on the floor now. Rose is here but on a break, I believe, and she's leaving early this afternoon. We have three others. May I ask which ones and why?"

"Just those on dining room duty like you during Callaway's time here."

"Oh, well. Want me to tell them to watch for you?"

"If you don't mind. I'll be asking if they had any conversations with him. How they perceived him."

Jackie blinked several times, silent.

Callie noticed. "Do you have a problem with that?"

The waitress snapped out of her reverie. "Oh, my, no. It's just they're young and highly opinionated as that age can be. Just hope they remember their place."

A term Callie hadn't heard in a while . . . except from her mayor mother's mouth. "Their place?"

Jackie shook herself. "Sorry. I meant I hope they act professional and cooperate completely with you."

"Okay, thanks. I won't keep you any longer."

Scrunching her nose, which Callie was beginning to see was her habit, the woman stood and pushed her chair under the table. "I sense I wasn't much help."

"Oh, but you were," Callie said. "And thanks for taking the time." She passed the woman her business card. "Call me if you think, or hear, of anything unusual about the man."

That made Jackie pause with a stunned expression. "Is he a criminal?"

"No, ma'am. Just missing. Probably a miscommunication with his family," she lied. "We're tracing his steps."

Concern gone. "Then I hope you find him." Jackie waved the card before tucking it in her apron. "I'll call if I learn anything."

Back at the entrance to the dining room, Callie hugged behind the hostess podium to make the uniform less obvious, and scanned the room, watching how people entered, both from inside the building through the lobby and out, the way she entered yesterday to meet with Raysor. Then peering around to her left, toward where Jackie said Callaway preferred to sit, she quickly pulled out of sight again.

Then slowly she eased out for another peek.

Slade and Largo sat at a table for four, at what could've been the so-called Callaway table, tucked out of the main traffic. And seated across from them was Roberts.

Son of a bitch.

Chapter 9

Slade

HAVING MISSED breakfast to hurriedly relocate to Indigo from our rental on Dolphin Road, my stomach hollered for sustenance. Quickly, we'd thrown our luggage into a room—the check-in slick and discreet thanks to an earlier call from Chief Morgan, and I dragged Wayne to the restaurant. In an attempt to not stand out, we settled at a table near the back window.

We'd just given our order to the waitress when a Detective Roberts made his way over, as if he knew us. Flashed his Charleston Sheriff's Office badge to Wayne, so others in the room wouldn't see. Said he asked for us at the desk. He didn't request permission to join us. He just did.

Being recognized by name in a place where we were expected to be covert sort of irritated me, raising my suspicion. And disappointed me. Thought the chief would've told us another LEO was involved. Didn't she understand the term undercover?

My trust-o-meter waned right now, and detective or no detective, this man owed me an explanation as much as he thought we owed him. I'd spent plenty of time around cop-types, and they'd quit intimidating me about ten investigations ago.

I noted an Edisto Beach police uniform depart from sight with our waitress. Hmm, so Chief Morgan was on duty as well. Roberts turned to see what I was looking at, and seeing nothing, returned his concentration to us. "I heard you found the body. Mind telling me about it?"

I told him in abbreviated sentences. Not sure how to act like a romantic couple on holiday with this intruder. Caught myself toying with the utensils and hid my hands in my lap.

He leaned heavy on the table. "Ms. Slade, let me get this right. You fell over the body, your boyfriend went and got the first policeman he could find, then once the authorities got there, you left."

"You listen well. Now, how'd you find us?" I asked.

From the extreme arch in his brow, he wasn't accustomed to witnesses asking questions right back. No poker face whatsoever.

Wayne's boot hit the side of my sneaker.

I nudged him back. I had the right to ask. "That's pretty much the facts," I continued. "I fell over the body, then we decided to spend the rest of our vacation out here. Trust me, a grand entry for my diary." A rippling wave of uncertainty made its way up my spine about this guy. So with my fingernail, I drew a question mark on his thigh. Wayne tapped me twice. Not sure when he thought I'd learned Morse code.

Roberts turned to Wayne. "And Mr. Largo, nobody touched the body?"

Wayne tried not to frown, his salt and pepper beard hiding the effort to anyone who didn't know him, but I saw it. "I flipped it and checked for a pulse," he said. "But I believe you knew that."

Ha, so Wayne wasn't too cozy with this guy either.

All we'd told the detective regarding our jobs was that we worked with the United States Department of Agriculture in Columbia. Nobody cares what you do with Agriculture, because everyone thinks you just help farmers grow crops or inspect meat and eggs. Mistake on his part. Yeah, and I was the only one without the real badge here.

"But," the detective said, with a pause, "you were a tourist on Edisto Beach yesterday, and a guest at Indigo Plantation today. Learned that only after I went to Dolphin Road hunting you."

"We found a body and won a prize," I said. "Lucky us." Hmm, so the chief had *not* brought him up to speed.

Wayne clarified. "We *won* our stay at Indigo because the manager felt he owed us something for our distress."

"Why not upgrade? It was free," I asked, feigning to be someone who thrived on BOGO offers and coupons. "We visited yesterday because of the, um, indigo. We don't see that much with Agriculture. And the basket weaving, of course."

Was that dumb enough for him?

"Of course," Roberts repeated.

Not exactly an inviting reply. You get people to talk by talking about *them*, showing interest in everything about them. You talk slow as if they were all you cared about. This guy must've been absent that day in cop class.

He should've said, "I know nothing about Agriculture." Or "Tell me about what you do." Yeah, then he might've learned we were investigators. Right now he just bordered on bully.

Still leaning on the table, fingers over his mouth, his stare settled on me.

"What?" I asked.

He didn't move.

So I leaned forward as well. "Are we mind melding?"

"Slade," Wayne warned. "The detective's just doing his job."

A young waiter arrived with my crab melt sandwich, the pimiento cheese oozing out the sides. Then he set Wayne's shrimp po' boy in front of him. "Are you joining us for lunch today, sir?" the kid asked Roberts.

Like statues, Wayne and I waited, clearly signaling with our Southern manners that we could not eat without Roberts deciding whether he stayed or left.

"Never mind," Roberts said, standing. "Now that I have where you are, I might be back with more questions."

We sat there mute. I mean, he hadn't exactly asked a question. Finally, he pulled out his business card, and Wayne snared it before the waiter would read it, tucking it in his shirt pocket.

Roberts walked away.

Satisfied he'd made us happy, the waiter left, too.

"After all that I'm starved," I said, wiping a finger across some cheese on the plate.

But Wayne concentrated on the detective's exit. "He's rogue," he said. "And he hates the chief."

"Duh, Cowboy." I took a monster bite and moaned. "This is so friggin' good," I mumbled. "I like the lettuce on it. Fresh."

"Eat fast," he said.

Shaking my head, I licked where a drip clung to the corner of my mouth. "Nope, I'm worshipping this meal for at least a half hour."

"Remember why we're here," he said. "I'd love to see who that detective went to talk to next."

"I say we stay where the chief can find us," I said. "She's here and has already seen us. I expect a text soon and suspect she trusts us to have the skills to poke around. At least she trusts you. I'm the village idiot."

That drew a chuckle out of the lawman.

"What?" I said. "I have my own methods of solving investigations."

He snorted right before taking a lawman-sized bite out of that sandwich. "That you do, Butterbean. That you do."

I kept eyeing the hostess podium, wondering if the chief would come to our table or keep her distance. "Hear from the pirate yet?"

Wayne wiped his beard and studied his phone. "Nope. Said he'd text us."

"Weird way to conduct pirate business, if you ask me." People walked outside heading to the water, to the indigo barn, in and out of the restaurant. Busy as heck. The restaurant had filled, and since people waited and my meal was comped, I did what Wayne asked and ate a little faster.

I wasn't sure what to snoop around and do yet. Wayne and I had wanted to touch base with the chief first before we were interrupted by Roberts, to inform we'd checked in. "You want to text the chief?"

"Already did," Wayne said, then added, "He's here."

"He who?"

"The pirate, Drummond." He scanned the windows. "Says he just arrived and would meet us outside."

I scanned the room. "Here? What happened to texting a meet?"

Wayne took a big swig of tea and stood. About that time, people began pointing outside, toward the parking area.

"Ho, ho, ho!" The voice boomed, such a contrast to the proper, old South charm of the place, the bellow reaching our ears even inside.

People laughed all around us.

"Sounds more like Santa than Blackbeard." I crammed in a last bite. "How do we meet him now?"

Wayne laughed. "Right out in the open, Slade. Right under everyone's noses. We're tourists, remember?"

Not having to pay for our meal, Wayne threw down a ten dollar tip, and we scooted out, keeping the pirate in view. There weren't many kids at Indigo, with it being more laid-back and less neon than a kid-type place. But that didn't stop a covey of folks from approaching him, assuming he was some part of Indigo's plan for entertainment. To me, he fit in like a frog in a chicken coop, but something about pirates seemed to bring out the children in adults.

Teach Drummond, a name I assumed the gent wasn't born with since it was a compilation of Blackbeard's presumed family heritage per the brochure, swung his arms wide, his white buccaneer shirt hanging loose. From a distance, the black knee pants and boots seemed out of a movie, his jet-black hair hanging in braids both from his temples and his beard, an old red bandana around his head. As we approached, however, I spotted white chest hairs, thirty years of beach sun, and an entire package sorely in need of a good scrub, but I bet Blackbeard wasn't very hygiene-oriented either.

"Avast ye mates," Drummond hollered as he doled out brochures I quickly recognized as his treasure maps. I took one. "There be treasure buried around these parts," he said. "And history sweeping back to the days when my ancestor owned all the Carolina waters." He bent at the waist, swinging his attention around in a half circle, bushy peaks over his eyes arched comically high into his hairline. "Now, I understand most of you be landlubbers, but no fret. There be chances for you to see the coves and hiding places where Blackbeard moored his ships." He gave out more papers. "And you'll find all the information on how to sign up for a trip my boat on the last page of the brochure."

I laughed, then couldn't stop laughing at the fake old seadog.

"I be seeking the likes of Wayne Largo," he bayed with a crescendo. "Now which one of you might be him?"

The crowd looked at each other, some choosing to leave, a few dropping their maps in a nearby trash bin. Drummond inched toward the can. "Mr. Wayne Largo?" he called again as he tried to nonchalantly fish the discarded maps out of the trash.

Wayne seemed to be waiting for the crowd to thin. One last lady asked the pirate a question, then left. Wayne approached the man. "I'm your guy," he said. "We texted?"

Drummond stacked the last of the retrieved maps then tapped their ends on the lip of the can. He tucked them into a knapsack strapped across his chest then offered a shake.

Ew, no hand sanitizer in sight, but Wayne accepted.

"My man," Drummond said. "I hear you're interested in a tour?"

I glanced at the brochure. No prices. "How much?" I asked.

Drummond smiled in a way that made me feel he was tasting me. "And who might the pretty lady be?"

"Carolina Slade," I said, holding the brochure tight to avoid the man's hand, and tilted my head toward Wayne. "I'm with him."

"And when would you like to book your reservation?" Drummond continued.

"Depends on your price," I said.

The pirate winked. "A hundred dollars for the two of ya."

"For how long?" I asked.

"An hour," he replied.

"Two hours," I countered.

"Heh, heh, heh." He turned to Wayne. "Bet this one keeps you hoppin', eh matey?"

Wayne smirked, letting me have my fun. "That she does."

Drummond retorted. "Ninety minutes."

Couldn't help myself. "Eighty dollars and you have a deal."

"Sold. I assume your time is limited, so what's your schedule like?" His accent had slipped into the contemporary with a hint of Charleston. A fortyish pair walked by, staring. Drummond waggled his forehead at them and offered a brochure they waved off.

"How about this afternoon?" Wayne said. "Around five?"

"Meet you at the marina," he said, then traipsed off without a congenial goodbye. We soon understood why.

"Drummond!" Coming around the back of the plantation house, Indigo's security Marion Tupper shouted. "You can't do business here!"

"So much for tact by the security guy," Wayne said, watching Drummond scurry in a cartoon zig-zag manner toward the parking lot, Marion trotting to catch up. Everyone chuckled, enjoying the show.

"Was hoping to pull him aside and ask him about Callaway," Wayne said.

"Hey." I patted his sleeve. "We can do that on the boat. Want to check out the crime scene again?"

"Wish we had some sort of game plan other than hang out here getting soppy in this heat, talking to pirates," Wayne said.

I snatched out my phone and group texted the chief and Wayne. *What the heck are we supposed to be doing? Want us to pretend we know Callaway? Interview staff?*

"There," I said.

The reply was immediate. *No and no. Meet me at the station in two hours.*

I motioned the phone toward Wayne. "Read that? It's like we work for her."

"We offered," he said.

"We'll be cutting things close meeting her in two hours."

"Maybe. Her office is down from the marina, so it's on our way," he said.

We'd asked and she'd accepted our help, but did she seriously need us, or were we being sent on a wild goose chase to stay out of her way? I pushed her pretty hard at the boat rental, fought to be involved, which had me wondering if this was her way of keeping us preoccupied and out of her hair instead of telling me no.

The opportunity of investigating a real murder separate and out from under my boss's nose had sucked me right in. Doubt niggled me now about whether we should be involved. Or if we were taken serious enough to make it worth our while. Wayne had already said as much, but the last thing I wanted to do was agree with him.

Besides, being run down by the Charleston Sheriff's Office without warning made this even more curious. It was almost as if this were two cases . . . or a race to see which investigator could solve the case first. That had me intrigued.

"Wayne," I started, an idea trying to take shape. "You think the chief and the detective are vying for what we find out . . . to use to their own best interest?"

Lawman studied me like I had purple horns growing out of my head. "No. Especially with a homicide."

Then why weren't these two LEOs communicating? Or did they not trust us, coming at us from two different directions to see if our stories changed.

"Don't overthink this, Slade."

"I don't think I am," I mumbled. Something wasn't gee-hawing here. And if these two uniforms were competing, why shouldn't Wayne and I play, too?

Chapter 10

Callie

CALLIE LEANED out of sight of the dining guests. What the hell was Roberts doing here without coordinating with her? She was there without his knowledge, but still, Callie had texted him, left a voice mail, and instead of replying, he'd driven an hour from Charleston to track down Slade and Largo. And he came in driving an unmarked vehicle or she'd have noticed.

Not cool. However, she had to work with the man. This was his ground.

A woman with a few years on her caught sight of the uniform behind the hostess podium and took a stunned step on her heel.

"Is the food good?" Callie asked.

Fear vanished from the guest's eyes, a smile emerging. "Their crab cakes are just about the best I've ever had." She giggled. "This place might be new, but it won't be much of a secret for long. You have a good lunch, sergeant."

Callie returned a discerning smile. "Thanks for the recommendation."

With a dip of her chin, the guest replied, "And thanks for your service." And left.

Peering around the corner, Callie noted Roberts still remained. Slade carried doubt in her expression. Wayne remained unreadable.

Callie'd withhold judgment for now. See if Roberts contacted her before she did him. See if his noticing *her* patrol car in the parking lot would prompt his call.

Once again she pondered whether she should've declined and probably would repeatedly before this was over. August was the wrong time of year to shirk her own duties. Not that she owed the town council an explanation since law enforcement networked and assisted each other often. She owed nobody anything and functioned purely out of courtesy. Different counties. Different jurisdictions. Different missions with hers not being political in spite of how Sweet had landed her the task.

But she'd accepted. And she'd never evaded responsibility before.

Returning to the break room, she pulled out the employee roster Sweet gave her yesterday. Riley, check. Jackie, check. Marion . . . still needed to speak to him. One waiter named Tito and a waitress named Rose worked during the time frame in question and would've served Callaway or at least been in the dining room. She couldn't tell which housekeeping staff might've cleaned his room.

She returned to the hostess podium and caught sign of a young waiter making his way into the dining room, delivering two plates. He set them at her duo's table, Roberts getting nothing. Good. Maybe he'd leave early . . . and call her with his results.

After a moment, the waiter returned, and quickly noting his name on his tag, Callie touched his arm. "Hey, Tito, got a moment?"

Her uniform made him jolt, and his ruddy complexion paled. "Um, why?"

She kept ahold of a pinch of sleeve, leading him away to the break room, leaving the door open to give him some ease. "Nobody's in trouble," she assured. She showed the driver's license picture. "Meet him before?"

He got even more rattled, eyes wide and leery. "Maybe."

One of the cooks walked by with a sideways peek. Callie pushed the door closed, giving the tiny eight-by-ten room the sense of vacuum.

"Come on, son," Callie said. "I assume Jackie told you I'd be asking questions. Either you've seen him or you haven't. He's missing with people worried."

He kept watching the door. "I remember him. He's a guest."

"Great." She smiled. "When did you last see him?"

Looking up, he queried his memory. "Day before yesterday, maybe? Breakfast? I didn't serve him. Jackie did. But . . ."

"Anyone seen Tito?" Jackie voiced rather loudly in the kitchen.

"But what?" Callie asked, attempting to hold onto the kid.

He couldn't stand still. "I was supposed to have taken his picnic lunch order to his room."

"But you didn't?"

He shook his head. "Jackie said I was too busy and was needed here. She'd take care of it."

Jackie had mentioned that lunch. "Lunch for one or two?"

"I didn't open the box, but it felt like two before she took it from me."

Callie waited.

His gaze went to the floor. Guilt. She waited.

Finally, the kid winced as he decided to spill. "Mr. Callaway paid me twenty bucks to sneak him into the kitchen to snoop around. And I gave him opinions on Mr. Shaw and Miss Jackie." His breath came out a little shaky.

Interesting. "Did you realize who he was?" she asked.

Shoulder slumping, he nodded. "Not then, but on break I Googled his name." A fear engulfed him, and he couldn't stand still. "I had no idea he was so big. Jesus, I'm gonna lose my job over this, aren't I? I volunteered to take him that lunch so he'd remember me, but like I said, Jackie stopped me." He shook his head, clearly miserable.

"Shhh, settle down," Callie said. "Nothing may come of it, so don't get all bothered." She hesitated to let that sink in. "But I take it you vented to him, and it wasn't all good?"

Hands rubbing across his tight-cut black hair, he shook his head. "I think I said too much, but it was little stuff. I need full-time hours but they give me just under thirty. It's all about getting out of paying the benefits." He'd flipped into defensive mode. "And Jackie thinks this is New York or Chicago or something the way she orders us around."

"She seems nice enough. Devoted to her job."

He snorted. "Understatement, for sure. Thinks she owns this place. Drill sergeant material."

Callie didn't goad him or push him one way or the other. The kid was vomiting his soul well enough on his own. "As to Callaway. Have any idea where he went? Hear him talk about any plans? See him with anyone since you said the lunch might've been for two?"

"Nope. But he showed me a page off the computer with a list of businesses out here. Asked me which I didn't like. This was before I knew who he was, you hear? So I went down and ranked everybody on a scale of one to ten. His idea, not mine," he added quickly. "I was laid off of half the places I ragged on. What if he quotes me or something?"

Again, not a problem, but she didn't tell him that. "When did you last see him?"

"The evening before, when I tried to get him to let me handle his lunch."

"Did he tell you how he hoped to spend the day?"

He shook his head again. Kind of pitiful. He wasn't much older than her son, and she couldn't help but pat his back. "I appreciate your help." She gave him her card. "Talk to the others. If they tell you anything, call me, okay? If any of this flares, I'll put in a good word for you with Mr. Shaw. How's that?"

He took the offer willingly, reading it like a get-out-of-jail-free card. "Yes, ma'am. Appreciate it, ma'am."

As he rushed out to work, Callie eased to the podium again and peered around for Roberts. Gone. So were her two undercover tourists. And everyone else's interest seemed drawn to a commotion outside. Moving to see better out the windows, she took a gander at what attracted the crowd. There was Largo, easy to spot with that height and that beard. Not a bad-looking guy either. And there . . . there was Slade. And in the middle of the mass of a dozen or more guests was Drummond. She sighed. The son of a gun just couldn't help himself. Indigo was the latest news, which meant a stage for Blackbeard's favorite doppelganger to make an appearance and skim whatever tourism he could off the backs of others.

A hand rested on her shoulder. "What's going on . . . well, damn," Sweet said. "Where's Marion?" he asked of the closest employee. "Go get him for me."

The young girl ran off as ordered.

"Not surprised," Callie said. "I'll let Marion take care of this business, if you don't mind." She didn't want to interfere with Wayne and Slade questioning the pirate. They'd planned to meet Drummond, but she wasn't sure this was what they had in mind. Best she remained out of sight. "Where's Sophie?"

"Scouting the place with one of my staff. Seeing if there's a location that suits her classes."

"Um, don't think so," she said, pointing. Sophie trotted over to Drummond, tiny compared to his stature. Poking him, she attempted to scold, drawing out only a guffaw from the buccaneer, which made her madder. After stomping her sandaled feet, she shook a finger at him and left.

"You're going to use yoga out here?" Callie asked, not seeing the Asian practice a part of eighteenth century Americana.

"We'll see," he replied, more honed on the continued disruption.

Callie checked her phone. Nothing from anyone except that last comment from Slade and Largo. "Have you seen Detective Roberts today?" she asked Sweet.

"No, why?" He scanned behind him, outside, head swiveling. "Where's Marion? This place isn't that damn big."

Second curse word. Interesting that the pirate drew curses sooner than the body had.

"I need to speak to you again when you get a moment," she said.

"Give me a half hour," he said. "My office."

"That works." She would need to speak to Marion, too. Mr. Security had the duty of watching the place, noting the unusual, keeping problems from disrupting tourists. Thus far she hadn't been overly impressed with him.

With both men unavailable, she slid to the break room which just might turn into her go-to hidey-hole while she worked this case. She approached the second-hand kitchen table, odd in contrast to the freshness of the rest of the place. Scanning the cases of non-food backup supplies, she went to the wall hooks holding assorted aprons and a windbreaker, feeling them over, then to a bulletin board flaunting the necessary labor law posters, and a tall, skinny stack of six twelve-inch lockers. Numbered, without names.

Suddenly, she'd kill for a glass of tea.

Someone tapped on the door. She waited to see who might've followed.

Jackie poked her head in the door. "Oh, I wondered who was in here."

Callie held up her phone. "Just me making calls."

"Making sure my staff hadn't slipped off. Care for something to drink?"

"Absolutely. Tea?"

"You got it." Jackie eased the door shut without the slightest whump, then seconds later reappeared. "Here you go," she said, setting the glass atop a branded white coaster on the table. "Leave the door open once you leave so we can see you're done, if you don't mind."

"Yes, ma'am."

Jackie seemed a woman always on her game. Might be prudent to ask her to question her staff since they seemed to have a healthy respect, or, um, fear, of her.

Alone again, Callie sat at the table and placed her call. She'd really hoped Roberts would've phoned her first. Number dialed, she halfway expected to hear his phone echo from someplace nearby.

"Chief," he answered.

"Detective," she replied.

Both waited until she felt childish at the standoff.

"I found Callaway's car," she said. "On the beach at Craven's. A boat rental place. That's where I retrieved his driver's license. He never came back to get it, yet somehow the boat he checked out was returned. And there's a possibility he went out in the boat with someone else."

"Who?"

"No idea yet. Just a description for now. Light skinned black girl half Callaway's age. In addition to her, Rick Craven, the manager, might just be one of the last people to see him alive, though."

Roberts grunted. "I see. When were you going to clue me in on all this?"

"I'm cluing you in now."

"Well," and his voice deepened, "we need a forensics team on that boat."

"Agreed. We don't have one on Edisto, so can you take care of that?"

"The oars, too, or whatever was loose in that boat," he said, as if piling on that he knew more.

This back and forth was old already. "I checked. The oars were placed in a pile. No sorting them out now."

She could almost hear his teeth biting his tongue. "I need better updates, Chief Morgan."

Now she was biting hers. "And I need you to answer your phone so you can get them."

More silence.

"Can we air some things?" she finally asked. His coarse attitude was raking her raw. "Since you're already out here, you could meet me inside." She let that sink in. "I saw you talking to Ms. Slade and Mr. Largo. Did you learn anything? I've met with them once already and would be happy to share."

"And when were you going to tell—"

She leaped from her chair, stabbing the air. "I briefed you yesterday after I interviewed them. Then last night they recommended they take Mr. Shaw's offer to stay at Indigo and be *our* eyes and ears."

Unfortunately, her telepathic connections were rusty these days, and he hadn't answered his phone this morning.

"Why would you let those two—"

"Because they have some experiences with investigations, Roberts, and they're a good opportunity for us. Just watching, I said. Jesus, would you get that damn chip off your shoulder?" Shoving the chair out of the way, she tried to pace the small room.

She took a cleansing breath, releasing it away from the phone.

"They'll just continue their vacation and inform if they hear something out of line, all right?" She rubbed her elbow, irritated. "When you're ready I have some questions." Then as if he could see her, she sat hard in a different chair, one leg thrown over the other, bobbing. Though the tea had watered down, she sucked down half of it.

A bear of a reluctant sigh sounded in her ear. "All right. What are your questions?" Then he added, "and I'm across the bridge, not at Indigo."

She let that settle. "Maybe next time."

"Yeah. So . . . your questions?"

"Did the sheriff give you an agenda unknown to me?"

He didn't miss a beat. "If he did, I wouldn't tell you. Next?"

Good answer. "Have you heard from the coroner?" she asked.

"No wounds. No bullet holes, no knives, no blunt force trauma. No water in the lungs."

She pulled out a memo pad. "Heart attack?"

"At first glance, no, he says. Toxicology will take a few days but thus far we're looking at natural causes since no evidence to the contrary. Sort of the reason I talked to that couple and left."

He was checking off boxes on *his* case.

"Missing his keys, wallet, and phone, right?" she asked.

"Right," he said.

"Hard to believe he abruptly died, then fell out of the boat dead since there was no water in his lungs, and in the jostle lost all his personal effects. And that the boat got out of the water and moored itself on its own."

She heard his radio shout with static, then someone call his name.

"Stranger things have happened," he said. The radio got quieter. "No offense, but I'm running more cases than this one, and I've got to go. Do you want me to accompany the forensics team or do you want to deal with them?"

"They're your people. And they need to do Callaway's suite at Indigo, too."

"Yeah, coulda guessed." He dropped the call.

Didn't matter how she presented things, Roberts was going to take them wrong. Time to just get used to the fact.

She needed to ask Slade and Largo what Roberts talked to them about. And what they might've told him about the pirate . . . if he'd stuck around long enough to *be* told.

She was almost investigating Roberts.

A text came in. *Still meeting Drummond at five this evening,* typed Largo. *Still meeting at your office in two hours?*

Changed plans, she typed. *Go ahead. Connect after.*

Then she left the breakroom and headed out to find Sweet. No one had talked to him specifically about the owners of this place. Or more precisely, why they didn't want the Charleston Sheriff's Office running this case instead of her. Her mind could easily run away with scenarios, but she didn't want to jump the gun too soon with the loose conspiracy theories eating into her head.

Chapter 11

Callie

CALLIE COULDN'T initially find Sweet, resorting to texts as she headed to his office, but she spotted Marion as she rounded the lobby corner, his attention on Riley at her concierge station. *Sure didn't take him long to get rid of Drummond.* The grandfather clock read five after three.

Straightening, he stepped away as if Callie couldn't see the flirtations, and when she beckoned with a finger, he followed her to Sweet's office down the hall.

Callie shut the door, and the lavish, vanilla-scented office immediately echoed the silence. "I need to ask when's the last time you saw Addison Callaway," she said low.

Though average height, he still had six or seven inches on her, his shoulders deceivingly broad in the tight, blue polo shirt. "The dead guy?"

Sweet apparently had informed Marion who the guy was. "Yes. When did you last see him alive?"

He cocked his head, thinking. "Maybe two days ago. Not sure the time. Not quite sure the day."

She took her seat and motioned for him to do the same, then she retrieved her notepad again from a pocket in her cargo pants. "Weren't you a Charleston deputy?"

He nodded, his effort to cooperate not hiding the analysis behind his eyes, as if pondering what she might be setting him up for.

"Then you understand perfectly well why I'm asking," she said. "We're establishing a timeline."

He sat rigid, his posture molded to the chair, both feet flat on the ground, arms on the chair arms. "Thought he died of natural causes."

Clearly, Roberts had briefed Marion, too. "That's not conclusive," she said.

Marion's forehead furrowed. Yeah, she understood the mixed signals he'd gotten today, but that was okay. "We're still running this like it was a questionable death, so I'd like to ask you to be aware. We're also keeping the death quiet. Heard any whispers amongst the staff?"

In the frozen seconds of his reaction, Callie read that Marion had already discussed Callaway. Possibly even bragged to his favorite girl. "When did you tell Riley?" she asked.

"Um, just now."

No wonder he was no longer a deputy. Yet the seasoned detective had also talked about the coroner's general thoughts before they were verified fact. "Did you use to work with Detective Roberts?" she asked.

"No, but saw him occasionally when I was still in uniform. Sat in a one-day class he gave once."

Hmm, a groupie? "Did you like the class?" she asked.

He pursed his mouth in recollection. "Yeah. He's damn smart."

And talked too damn much, she wanted to say, but she needed Marion's trust. "What are people saying about Callaway, if anything? I assume the news is leaking fast."

"Some liked him. Some weren't fond of him. Everyone sees him as a celebrity now, though I still don't get the attraction."

"Everyone?"

"Pretty much," he said, head bobbing in ignorance.

Stinkin' marvelous. She gave the press an hour tops to reach the island. Son of a frickin' bitch.

Sweet opened the door, stutter-stepping when he saw Marion with Callie. "Oh, am I interrupting?"

"No, Marion was about to leave," she said. "Thanks," she told the security guard. "Try to avoid the reporters. And spread the news for the others not to speak to them, please."

Marion appeared stymied and stood. "How do I deal with press, Mr. Shaw? What do I tell them? Where do I make them park? Who controls them once I go home?"

Callie bet Marion didn't even think he had a major hand in causing the bastards to show. "Call me when they're here," Sweet said. "Tell everyone not to talk to anyone who even appears to be a reporter." He glanced over at Callie who stared back, her mouth flat-lined. "And anyone who does risks their job."

"Copy that," Marion mumbled, then left.

Sweet took to the chair behind his desk and exhaled as he dropped into it, his gaze never leaving Callie. "What happened?"

She sank into her seat. "Roberts talked to Marion who talked to Riley and God knows who else." If everyone kept their mouths shut from this point forward, they could stem the flood a little. "Don't talk to them is about the best advice I can give you. And don't direct them anywhere else simply because they put pressure on you, and you want to send it elsewhere. I hope I'm making myself clear that means me, Roberts, anybody. That'll only fuel them, Sweet. Impede the investigation and tarnish Indigo's reputation." Her anger spiked at this change in events, and she worked to tamp it down. She could be mad at Sweet for not controlling his staff, but he didn't spill anything.

A seasoned detective such as Roberts, however, should've known better, unless he remained the sheriff's snitch . . . or saboteur.

"Before anyone shows," she said, "take me to Callaway's room if you don't mind." Then she hesitated. "You haven't let Roberts in there yet, have you?"

"No, ma'am," he said with emphasis, and rose to accommodate. "Not that he didn't ask."

Of course he did.

At the room, she noted the Do Not Disturb sign now on the handle. Sweet unlocked the door, letting her go first. "I had the key code changed," he said.

She walked around the room, slowly, studying while putting on gloves she'd stuffed into her pocket that morning. The computer. The suitcase. The toiletries. But she wanted to see the notes more closely before Roberts's forensics team addressed this room as well as the boat. With her phone, she snapped pictures as she made her way to the desk.

She lifted some of the spiral notebook pages with a pen. "Have you gone through these since I was here yesterday?"

"No, absolutely not," he said.

"I think there are pages missing." With the pen she noted the ripped edge of at least one missing page. Maybe two.

He rushed to her side and reached down to touch.

She shoved his hands away. "Don't touch anything, Sweet."

"Oh, yes. Sorry."

Snapping pictures, she lifted each page of the notes to read them later. The team would collect them, and they'd likely be pissed she was in here, but no doubt in her mind things had already been toyed with. "Someone's been in here. Any way you can determine who?"

"We're not New York, but I believe we can note which keycard let someone in. At least whether it was Callaway's card or housekeeping."

"Pull that record going back to the day before Callaway checked in, if you don't mind." She took all the pictures she could. She started to snag the laptop, then decided to leave that to the team. Best play nice and concede to one of the sheriff's office's technicians, not to mention her forte wasn't computer-dissection.

Motioning to the door, she put away her phone. "Let's leave the room as is. And let Roberts and/or his team in this evening."

With a pull on the door, Sweet made sure the lock caught, then they backtracked to the main house. "You think they'll actually come in tonight?"

"Cops don't work banker's hours," she said.

As they reached the lobby, Sweet stopped, as if to bid the chief goodbye. "I'm terribly sorry about the room, and I'll do my best to identify the persons entering. By tomorrow I ought to narrow it down."

He paused, and she sensed a change in topic.

"But when this is over with," he started . . . . "I mean when this whole Callaway deal is through, what do you say about dinner?" He gave a head motion toward the dining room. "I can get them to pull together quite the meal."

His timing was perfect from the scent of gravy and something sinfully savory drifting in from the kitchen. The clock read after five.

"No thanks, Sweet. Dating's not in my plans."

The freeze in his posture told her he wasn't sure how to read the remark. The no was transparent enough, but the other would leave him wondering why, maybe even lead him to think her gay. Uniforms could make a man think that about a girl. But whatever direction it took him, she didn't care.

"Okay, then. Well," he motioned toward the lobby registration desk. "I'll go do my thing with the room, and you'll go do what police people do. Thanks for your help." He left, maybe a hint scalded.

She felt badly. She didn't find him unattractive. Quite the contrary. The sun-kissed hair brushing his collar suited him in a type of Tarzan way. His slacks fit as if custom, and the college signet on his tanned ring finger added a nice touch she couldn't explain. He possessed a polished informality not easily ignored.

He turned from the counter. "Something else?"

"Yes, please," she said. "Your office?"

Kudos to him for almost hiding being caught off-guard. "Sure."

Once again, door closed, he started around his desk.

"Come sit here, next to me," she said, patting the guest chair. "No obstacles."

Meaning no symbols of hierarchy. No furniture to hide behind. He obliged her, resting an ankle on the other knee, back in the chair, continuing with the air of this being his domain.

She didn't hold that against him. On the contrary, it showed his attempt to control his insecurity, and while her aim wasn't to expose it, she definitely wanted to tap it.

She extracted her pad again. "Who are the owners of Indigo Plantation?"

Took him maybe three seconds to reply, but that long three seconds told her he wondered where this line of conversation was going. Good, he should if he were half as sharp as she thought.

"It's a partnership of five gentlemen," he said. "One from Charleston, the others from Atlanta, Mobile, Chicago, and Columbus, Ohio. Trent McKenzie, the owner from Charleston, went to school with two of the others. Georgia Tech, I believe. Each is a self-made entrepreneur with disposable monies. Indigo is one of their enterprises. No telling how many others they have, but this one is somewhat of a play-toy to them, I think. They fish, so they intend to use the dock they built up the river as a place to moor a boat or two on the occasional gentlemen's holiday. I've met Trent, but not the others." His shoulders seemed to ease some at the end of his presentation, and he smiled, grateful to be of assistance.

"I take it Trent McKenzie is the one with his grip on the sheriff?" she asked.

His eyes didn't darken, but they lost their twinkle. "He's active in politics, as would be anyone with his status."

For a second their gazes seemed to lock. Him trying to read her, and her daring him to try.

"But he's who you called when we found Callaway," she said.

"Of course. As a heads-up. For damage control. So that he would help me contain the spill. What else would you expect?"

"But why request me?" *And don't say because I understand Edisto.*

Hopefully she didn't sound paranoid, but she hadn't met Sweet but an hour before they found the body, so surely he hadn't decided in that short of time that he could manipulate her. Otherwise she had best change her image. He hadn't met Roberts before that afternoon, either, or so she assumed. And Sweet was already bending his boss's ear when Roberts showed, so a him-or-her comparison hadn't taken place.

"To keep the world around Indigo . . . around this death . . . as small as possible," Sweet said. "I'd already heard about you. How sharp you were. And yes, I saw you as devoted to this island. You would do what you could to both do right by Edisto and the dead man." He ran his hands across his thighs like a kid nervous about catechism.

"Nicely said," she replied.

His expression went blank.

Leaning forward, Callie brought home her point. "I don't think it was the right decision on your part, your boss's part, or the sheriff's part." She cleared her throat for effect. "Or on my part for accepting, for that matter. But what's done is done. My role is to solve this case which still falls in the ranks of suspicious. Yes, I care about this island, but Indigo's reputation falls far behind that of solving this man's cause of death. My duty is to him. Is that clear?"

"Perfectly."

She still felt the heavy bridle of politics at play, but she'd never get Sweet to admit it. Maybe he felt himself noble somehow in choosing her to protect them all.

But she bet he wasn't interested in a date now.

"That it?" he asked.

She stood. "For now."

She left the office, not surprised to not hear his footsteps behind her. Once she reached outside, she scanned the parking lot. Surprisingly, Sophie had left before she did, though once Callie realized it was close to five-thirty, she understood why. Afternoon yoga class. Good thing they took two cars after all.

About the time she buckled her seat belt, her phone rang. After a glance at the front porch of the B&B to see if Sweet watched her leave, she answered with a curt, "Hello."

"Hello, Chief Morgan? This is Sheriff Mosier."

Though the car was cranked, she held off pulling out. However, she did turn up the air conditioner. "Yes, Sheriff. What can I do for you?"

"How's it going?"

"We have an ID. We're establishing a timeline. Still questionable since the coroner hasn't yet determined exact cause of death." She didn't understand why he called her for this info. He could get those answers quicker from his own people. This was his county . . . and he had Roberts as his dog on point.

"Roberts is a good man," the sheriff said, as if reading her thoughts.

"Yes, sir."

"And I might've put you in a bind, but I've heard how incredibly qualified you were, plus you were requested by name."

"Yes, sir. I'm aware."

Seconds passed. "I'll owe you, Chief Morgan. This case is important."

"All deaths are important, sir."

More seconds passed. "So what can I do to make your job easier . . . and faster?"

"The job is what it is," she said. "Nothing's jumping at us as to what happened, though we're still working a few loose ends. But if the coroner could make us a higher priority, I'd be grateful. And make forensics jump a bit faster."

"Consider it done, Chief. Thanks again."

She'd wanted to ask him to snatch Roberts's leash a bit tighter, but that wasn't how to play this out. Besides, Roberts would resent her request that Mosier pressure his people.

Yet, she still felt an undercurrent of something else going on.

She received a text from Sweet. *Call from two TV stations.*

She typed back. *Don't talk to them.*

But that wouldn't stop them. Once they realized the body was Addison Callaway, they'd be relentless. If she were Sweet, she'd fire Marion.

Mentally she began her case "to do" list. Interview a few more employees. Do some research about Trenton McKenzie. And it wouldn't hurt to learn more about Swinton Shaw. What traits and experience crowned him the prince of Indigo Plantation?

Chapter 12

Slade

"SURELY YOU DIDN'T hire that old pirate."

A woman maybe five or six inches shorter than I am, dressed in flowing blue garb, yoga tights and sandals, judged us from behind Hollywood shades. With a body tight as a violin string, she had no qualms letting people see she stayed fit. I reached down as if to adjust my waistband, feeling if I had enough muffin-top for her to see through my shirt. Thank goodness the tee hung straight leaving my figure to the imagination.

Then I wondered how frumpy I looked.

"What if we did hire him?" Wayne asked.

She lifted her sunglasses, shifting her concentration from "us" to Wayne . . . and there it stayed. The Bohemian appearance gave her a youthful image, but the crow's feet belied her age maybe five or ten years older than I. However, that body. And those boobs. Boobs she thrust out as she stared up at the lawman's six-foot stance.

"Ooh, and who are you, handsome? I'm Sophie Bianchi."

Jesus, was she actually rubbing his arm?

"He's Wayne Largo. And I'm Carolina Slade." I held out my hand to give hers someplace else to be. "Call me Slade."

Her once-over of me told me I had competition . . . or fell below her expectations of who should be on this man's arm. After a limp-wristed dead fish of a shake, she gave me her shoulder. "Well, if you seek cheap comedy, you nailed it. Just don't fall for his historical bullshit about pirate ancestors. What'd he nick you for? A hundred? Hundred fifty?"

"Eighty," I said.

"Good for you," she said, and I wasn't sure if she'd delivered a compliment or sarcasm.

The corner of Wayne's mouth went up, enjoying the play between the two ladies in front of him. With a glower and intense mental telepathy steeped in cursing, I tried to remind him who he came with. And who he could leave without.

She held out a hand to him. "I'm the yoga mistress around here."

He shook the offering. "Nice to meet you."

She kept shaking, waiting. Then it hit me. She wanted us to ask about where she taught, how much, and when we wanted to attend her classes.

Not much different than Drummond.

When Wayne let go, she retreated with a hint of a pucker, causing her lashes to drop like her lip. "Boots? At the beach?" She climbed the elevator of his body up to his eyes. "Anybody ever call you Cowboy?"

"So what about Drummond?" I asked. "Are you telling us to steer clear of him? Is he dangerous?"

"Ha," she laughed. "Dangerous? Him and his make-believe ship. Planting his fake relics, even under the very noses of his so-called guests."

"But is he safe?"

A quick snap of her hip in the other direction, a dozen skinny bracelets dancing in the shift. "Oh, honey, of course he is, as long as you call taking your hard-earned money as being safe. If you don't mind losing your eighty dollars, he might entertain you a bit. Just don't take anything he says seriously."

"Oh," I said, almost adding *honey* on the end of it for her sake. "Eighty is worth a laugh, isn't it, baby?" And I sidled next to Wayne. Thank God he had sense enough to drape an arm across my shoulder or he might've gone home without it.

Sophie got the message. "Well, my signs are all over the beach and will be at Indigo soon. Yoga is a lifestyle, and . . ." she eyed us both again for emphasis, "I'd like to introduce you to it."

Like we were lacking in our calm.

"*Namaste*," I said.

Her cobalt blue eyes, courtesy of contacts I was sure, widened then softened. "*Namaste!*"

I held onto Wayne's shirt as she sashayed off, and she sashayed well. "Can you imagine that yoga class?"

"Sure can," he said, with a moan for effect.

Maybe I needed to start yoga.

"Wanna study the crime scene again since I assume we can't meet with the chief without revealing our *clandestine investigation*?" I positioned myself in front of him, reorienting his interest.

"It's miserable hot to be hiking, Slade. Plus, it's not a crime scene yet," he said.

"You get what I mean." And I struck out. Of course he followed. We'd sweat together.

Against orders and contrary to the Work Being Done sign on the path to where we found Callaway, we slipped down the trail fast until we were out of sight. When we reached the site, crime scene tape roped it off. "Thought forensics was done out here," I said. "And that the chief wanted this case kept low-key. Any tourist out here could do what we just did and traipse all over this place."

"He washed ashore, Slade, so I doubt there's much evidence other than what they found on the body." We analyzed the spot, where you could no longer tell the body had been. Then he scanned out across the river. "Surprised he made it to the bank," he said. "Bet there's things out there big as we are."

I shivered at the thought. The last place I wanted to die was dark water. "Think the chief will update us on what the coroner found when we see her?" In my tripping over, bumping, and leaning on the body the other day, I hadn't seen nor felt a wound. Not that I'd done a thorough examination. No blood in the water either. Just body parts with nibbles gone. I shivered again.

If this was not a crime, what was taking them so long to label the cause of death?

I stared out into the deeper water. "I bet his phone and wallet are somewhere out there," and I waved across the vista. "A scuba diver might find them."

"The two or three tides since then have hidden a lot of ills," he said.

"And the salt water would've completely wrecked the phone," I added.

In silence, we just studied the landscape, beautiful yet deadly, in my opinion. "How about we get Drummond to take us on the river? All the way here."

"I have no problem with that," Wayne said. "But expect the codger to charge you something for the effort because it's a few miles from the beach. Wouldn't be surprised he sets an alarm so he doesn't go a minute over the time you hired him for." He pulled out his phone. His fingers typed with me watching over his shoulder.

"Speaking of time," he said, doing a double-take at me reading his texts. "Apparently we can't see the chief until later, so let's get to Drummond."

"YOU SURE THIS thing's seaworthy?" I mumbled as Wayne helped me aboard the *Golden Pearl*. The air hung so thick with briny humidity my shirt already clung to my lower back. "And I thought Blackbeard's boat was the *Black Pearl*?"

"That was Jack Sparrow's ship," he whispered.

"Who?"

"Johnny Depp?"

"Oh, yeah."

Already wiping our temples, we assumed our obvious seats near the bow of the wooden ship, or rather an oversized dingy with sails, the craft barely thirty feet long and nine feet wide. Drummond—dressed in full regalia from his black, brocaded tricorn hat to his boots, from the cutlass hugging his left hip to a fake flintlock pistol on the other—told us right off the bat to don a life vest, to which I didn't argue. I searched every pocket first, halfway expecting to find something rotten, molded, or dead in one.

As I shrugged into a sour smelling vest that had entrapped God-knows-how-many sweaty, sticky, body-odor-reeking others before me, I scanned the boat. For what I had no clue. Holes maybe?

I'd never seen anything like the vessel, not that I was a seafaring woman, but I'd grown up coming to the beaches, especially this one, and had never experienced anything resembling the *Golden Pearl*. I wasn't the only one wary, judging by the vacationing onlookers gathering along the marina. They were probably gawking at the latest fools Drummond had weaseled into boarding the thing.

A breeze gushed by us, and I welcomed the evaporation of my sweat, enough to almost raise goose bumps.

"I hope we don't get a summer storm," Wayne said, leaning close to me.

"Storm?" I stood. "No way I'm riding this oversized bathtub in a storm."

"We be fine," Drummond said with his accent, running here and there, untying things and insuring others were fastened. He'd issued us each a card when we arrived, with his contact information on one side and how to talk pirate on the other. Didn't take long for him to approach us and say it was time to cast off, assuming we could pay in cash.

Wayne peeled off the twenties with Drummond eyeing the bills that went back in the cowboy's pocket. Then with flair, the pirate tucked away the money and swirled around for all the gawkers to hear. "Ahoy!" which meant *energetic hello* in pirate per my card. My chuckle bubbled at the overt effort toward the dramatic. "Avast ye mateys," he said, and again, waited for us to find it on the card. *Halt and listen.* Never knew that.

By now bystanders rolled with laughter with more bodies spilling out from the nearby restaurant. Drummond leaped with a hint of a limp atop the side of the boat, holding onto some boat part I couldn't name, with a leg and an arm swung out over the side in a sweeping motion. "I be your Cap'n," he shouted, though he played as much to the crowd as us. "Drummond's me name. Our adventure will take us to parts unknown, but before we return . . ." He waved wide again. "We'll see if you remain *landlubbers*, become just *Jack Tars*, or *go on account* as full blown pirates. Arg!" he shouted, as we made for the open bay, following our printed guide to catch the lingo. Funny how the jargon lined up in order as he spoke them, right down the card.

Applause exploded amongst the laughter from the dock as we drifted away, and I wondered if Drummond was crazy like a fox. And if I was crazy as a loon. However, I couldn't help but marvel at how spry our captain was for a man his age. He actually loved this stuff, or the acting . . . or both, and it seemed to keep him going strong.

We entered Saint Helena Sound at the mouth of South Edisto River, but that was all the geography I knew. I had no idea how close we were to the Atlantic or how far from Indigo. And as we skiffed across the water easier than expected, wind entangling my hair, my sinuses filled with sea air, I had to remind myself we were here to interview Drummond about Addison Callaway. As long as I didn't peek over the side, I'd be okay. The dark water was down there . . . me up here.

I caught Drummond going under his seat, catching sight of bags of maps, glittering souvenirs and seashells. His stash of treasures. I recalled Sophie's warning that he could be so bold as to plant treasure right under his passengers' noses, then aid them in finding them.

"Where are we going?" I asked, raising my voice over the water noises and gusts.

He dropped the lid, replacing the cushion. "Anywhere. Everywhere. Wherever you like!" A motor took us out, with only some of the sails open, but the force of ocean wind seemed to be taxing them. We cut expertly through the water, or so it felt like, and for a moment I may have understood the power and love of the open sea. Wayne stared at the horizon, his hair blown straight baring his forehead, giving his profile a hot, romance novel cover appearance with that beard.

I mentally snapped that image and filed it away for tonight, when we tested out the B&B's new mattress in our room.

Drummond started into a blatantly orchestrated tale of Blackbeard. His alliance of pirates, his stolen clutch of French ships, which somehow I figured looked nothing like ours. How the original Blackbeard rebuffed murder and violence, instead relying upon surprise and dramatics.

At a pause in his description of his ancestor, he flipped a switch or hit a button as sparklers crackled around the brim of his hat. With a boot propped on a bench, he withdrew his cutlass and aimed it at the sky, posing . . . holding it.

Oh, wait. I fumbled for my phone. We were expected to take his picture. Wayne got it before I did, so I clapped instead, rewarding the performance as the sparklers died.

This man was a riot! "Can we go up the Edisto River?" I shouted.

"Yes, ma'am," Drummond said, "But give me a hand with this sail, if you don't mind."

I stood and almost fell sideways into Wayne as a wave slapped the boat's side, gunnel, flank, whatever.

"I'll help," Wayne yelled, and quickly amazed me he knew what the hell he was doing.

Done, he sat back next to me. "Where'd you learn that?" I asked.

He reached over and tested my top life vest strap. "My sister and I took lessons in high school. Our grandfather had a boat. These vests are ancient. Don't let it get loose on you."

Drummond assumed his place at a center console and regained more control as we veered north.

"Will we see Indigo from the water?" I asked, turning around on my seat toward Drummond.

"That's quite a ways, lassie. Not sure we can get there and back in ninety minutes." He checked his watch. "More like sixty now." He glanced around behind him. "I'm not exactly liking those clouds to the southeast, either. Best we hang close, maybe venture no more than a mile, two tops. Let's head over to St. Pierre Creek where Blackbeard once hid out, running from Charlestown authorities after he took ships in their harbor."

I turned to Wayne who nodded at me. Proceed with the questioning.

"We heard from another guest about you," I yelled.

Drummond tipped his head to the side as if to hear, and I raised my voice and repeated. "We heard from another guest about you, but it wasn't until we heard from a second one that we read your brochure. The first person we talked to loved you. The other, well, he seemed sort of an ass, and frankly, it made us want to check you out for ourselves."

Drummond heard me that time and leered sideways. "An ass, eh?"

"Royal. Thought he was God's gift to, well, something."

His right brow cocked exceptionally high. I bet he practiced it for show or maybe to keep it from being singed from the sparklers, but once I realized he wondered who, I gave him the name. "Addison Callaway?"

Both brows dropped into a scowl. "You pegged him right, lassie. Tried to say I owed him a two-hour seafaring tour for no cost, all because he'd write about me on some website. Like the freebie would buy me favor. I never heard of the bum. Told him to take a hike. Pointed him to Craven's to get his own boat and follow the map, but he sure wasn't snaring me for free. If Rick gave him a free gratis boat rental, fine, but that trick don't work on ol' Drummond."

"That's where I last saw him," I said, pointing upward, as if a thought flashed to mind. "He was a frumpy old bastard. Was checking out the boats." I leaned in. "Frankly, Rick told us to give you a call. Said it would be a better experience."

Drummond grinned wide. "Yeah, he treats me right out here. Probably the best. That's why I returned his stray boat this morning."

"He loses boats? That happen much?" A fat drop hit my cheek, and I realized it was growing darker much too quickly.

"Sorry, lassie, but we're turning around and heading in," he said, his accent vanished.

The boat pitched left, aft, whatever.

And the bottom fell out of the clouds.

"Sorry, but ain't got no raincoats," Drummond shouted over the sudden roar, his arms intense into his steering.

Like it mattered now. Water poured between the vest and me, the floor getting slick.

The boat pitched right this time, and I didn't give a damn what you called that side because the jolt knocked me to the floor . . . into an inch of water. Six inches washed over when the boat rolled.

"Wayne?" I screamed, not trusting to ask Drummond a damn thing. "Are we sinking?"

While I tried to push wet hair from my eyes, Wayne drew me into my seat, the boat rocking one way, then another, no rhyme to the motion. "Hold on to me," he yelled, as I watched the deluge run into his eyes, running off the end of his nose. "I see the lights at the marina, but we've going against the wind."

"I don't think we're going anywhere," I yelled. "The boat isn't running."

Drummond had ceased talking, which told me even more about the seriousness of the situation. But when I turned to ask what we needed to do, I couldn't find him.

"Drummond! You stupid fraud!"

Standing, I gripped a handle here, a post there, the edge of the boat working toward where our guide had been. Drummond had fallen to his belly and laid still enough to warrant real concern.

"Slade!" Wayne yelled.

But as I turned to tell the lawman about Drummond, the bow went eerily skyward, and arms outstretched, Wayne slid into the console . . . and I flipped over the side.

I didn't think I'd ever stop sinking into the water, until it hit me I wore a life jacket. But in this storm Mother Nature wouldn't just bob me to the surface. She covered me with waves over my head, leaving me fretting over which end was up.

And what the hell size of a fish awaited below me!

As fear seized me, I screamed . . . and found myself without air . . . panicked . . . hysteria strangling me.

Pumping my arms, I clawed my way to the surface, more and more scared at drowning from the huge, undulating white caps in spite of the life preserver. Being still wasn't an option, because that's when I'd expect something to take a bite out of me.

If I breathed, I sucked in water, choking, so I held my breath. Oh my God, my lungs were on fire!

Breathing, drinking, choking.

Then the life jacket tried to slip off over my head. No bloody way I was losing this damn thing. So I tied whatever two straps I could find, then another two, my chin as high as I could thrust it, seeking oxygen. Knotting things around each other until I couldn't, continuing to kick with one-handed treading, the other fighting to maintain that life vest.

"Slade! Hold on!"

"Wayne," I attempted to say, only to choke again on a wave. My eyes burned with the rising, falling, bobbing, and sinking below the next mound of salt water.

When something hung the back of my vest, I screamed, and with bent fingers fought to reach out and grab something in the opposite direction to set me free.

"Slade! It's me."

But it took a moment for me to stop fleeing and clamoring. And in that ultimate second of awareness, when I realized the help was real, I'd realized it too late. My heart beat too hard to recover. I was done. And blackness came over me.

Chapter 13

Callie

THROWING THE patrol car's wipers into double-time, Callie headed to the beach, peering hard through the downpour to keep it between the lines, her shirt sticky from unsuccessfully dodging those initial hard raindrops of a storm. Reporters would be slowed by the weather, hopefully.

The storm had moved in eerily slick and fast, the clouds rupturing about the time they reached the island, as if targeted to saturate Edisto Beach.

Summer could do that, and tourists hated it. Not that they weren't already wet from the salty atmosphere, but the air practically dripped the humidity after an August rain, sweat riding in rivulets down backs, uncomfortably into cracks and crevices that underclothes could no longer contain. Lowcountry inhabitants took it in stride they might take two showers a day, or simply let the next air-conditioned building dry their underarms, but visitors panted, disappeared into their rentals, their chilly units cranked to the max.

Locals rolled with it. Tourists whined. Gave the Edisto PD a lull for an hour or two afterward.

Locals expected these storms, making Callie wonder if Slade and Largo had been inexperienced enough with the weather to take Drummond's offer to go out on the water. Or if Drummond had been dense enough to put out in his boat with the threat of storm in the sky.

Their appointment was five, wasn't it? She glanced at her dashboard. Almost six. Surely the idiot kept an eye on the weather.

"Marie?" she called on the radio. Informal, but that was how it worked on Edisto.

"Almost missed me," the office manager came back. "Was waiting for this shower to let up to run to the car."

"Anything for me?" Callie asked.

"Nothing. You expecting anything?"

"Sort of, but you go on home when you can. Be careful driving."
And she hung up.

Traffic was light, the ditches filling with water in places. The radio
beckoned. Expecting Marie, she keyed the mic. "Callie here."

Thomas sounded breathless, wind smacking the radio, an engine in
the background. "Chief, we got a boat in the sound dead in the water.
That crazy damn pirate, we think. In this storm that tub's at risk of going
down. Bobby Yeargin put in his boat to run out and grab 'em."

"Bobby's not by himself, is he?"

"Me and Terrance Matthews are with him. On our way. At least one
body in the water." She heard him echo to someone, "One right?" Then
he came back. "Son of a bitch, now it's two."

Her heart leaped in her chest. "Bodies?" Good God Almighty. And
she let them go out there. Damn it all!

Jesus, she couldn't stomach being responsible for the deaths of two
people. Having them die on her watch was horrible enough, but they
volunteered assistance. On a murder, no less. Bad move.

He yelled now, as though reading her mind. "Persons, Chief. Sorry."

Callie flipped on her lights and siren and almost mashed the
accelerator before realizing she was already doing seventy on the wet
roads. "Should be three counting Drummond," she yelled, as if the
storm's cacophony hindered her talking, too. She arrived at the
causeway, raced over it, and took Palmetto with its wider lanes, heading
toward the marina.

She hit her horn at a car still on the road. It froze and she veered
around it.

Catching water in the puddles enough to slide a few yards, she
pulled into Bay Creek Park and threw the car into park, donned her hat
and slammed the door. She bolted to the marina. And noted a WLSC
SUV in the lot.

The television station had sent Alex Hanson, the granddaughter to
a beach resident. Knew the people . . . knew the chief.

But Alex was a non-issue right now. A rumbling crawled across the
sky toward the mainland, threatening to turn this storm into something
nastier. Though the rain had lessened, the ceiling above Callie continued
to roil in dark, tangled clouds that couldn't decide whether to unite or
dissipate.

Clustered under rain slicks and umbrellas, two dozen people gawked,
some trying to photograph the rescue though the boats rocked a half
mile out. Alex held a camera wrapped in plastic, without a cameraman,

flying solo and questioning the crowd while hugging close enough to the cops to hear. Officer Ike Fenton spoke on his mic, keeping someone apprised.

By the time Callie reached him, she was half-drenched and breathless. "What you got?" Rubbing her sniffles, she fought to settle herself, trying to sound way less scared than the iron-fisted grip in her gut, while scouring the water for signs of life.

God Almighty, this was Francis, John, Lawton, even Seabrook, all over again. The loss of an officer, a husband, a father, and a lover who called themselves being there for her and paid the ultimate price for doing so. She hid the shake in her hands by shoving them into pockets.

Fenton waved out toward the water with a radio in his grip. "Half these people saw them go out. That idiot Drummond and two tourists. Someone said they saw someone fall in, though I wonder how they could see that far, but Thomas called and confirmed that two of them went in."

The two boats rose and fell, sometimes opposite and sometimes in tandem in the wind-fed waves. Though dying down on land, the open water still suffered the intensity.

Both knew to wait and let Thomas do his thing . . . to be the one to order the ambulance, if needed. But waiting dragged into long, breath-holding minutes. The rain weakened further, allowing the crowd to hear the first responders. Alex murmuring, recording the tension into her mic as she reported the scene.

"They're all right!" came Thomas's shout over the airwave. "Give us a sec to grab the boat and we'll be right there."

While the onlookers cheered, Callie released a breath she hadn't thought she'd been holding, willing her heart to stop beating her ribs.

Chatter circulated amongst the dock spectators, now that Thomas's news had opened the relief valve on their tension. Of course, they would all have time to kill until the boats moored. Nobody would leave until they'd seen the suckers who'd ventured out into a certain storm.

She never should've allowed them to be involved.

After ordering the crowd to remain out of the way, Callie and Fenton walked out to meet the arrival. Water dripped off roofs and seeped through dock planks with splashes and plops. Yeargin and Thomas finally pulled alongside.

A half dozen hands helped Slade off, with Largo refusing assistance. Though Slade seemed about the same age as she was, Callie's motherly instincts kicked in, and she reached to adjust the damp blanket tighter around the taller CI's shoulders and noted the shivers, though the air probably measured a solid eighty degrees. "I never should've listened to you," she uttered for only Slade to hear. "I'm so sorry."

"I got her," Largo said, taking Slade out of Callie's reach. He wore no blanket, nor shoes, and Callie theorized Slade fell in the water first, with Largo being the second one going in.

Callie glared at the boat, searching for Drummond. Thomas showed up with him by the arm, the old drenched pirate appearing shriveled, much more aged, but still forcing that crazy smile.

Callie let Largo escort Slade out of earshot then drew close to the pirate, teeth clenched. "You thoughtless son of a bitch. You almost killed these two in your half-assed crate of a vessel." She pointed at the listing ship, two marina workers attempting to tie it in a spare slip. "You're grounded, you hear? I'll do my damnedest to yank your registration until I say that boat's seaworthy."

Drummond leaned closer. "You can't do that, Chief."

She leaned in closer. "I bet I can find someone who can."

He tried to stand bolder, though his clothes fell wilted from his shoulders and hips.

"And you better give those people their money back," she added. Glancing around for Slade and Largo, she noticed them walking off alone, him hugging her close, talking. A shot of cold memory traveled through her veins. His concern for her reached inside Callie and tore her heart open.

Instinctively shedding his badge for his medical bag, Seabrook would've examined them for injuries. The man should've never become a cop. If he'd remained a doctor, he'd be alive today. Next month would be a year.

"Chief?" Thomas came around in her vision. "Want me to take those two back to their place? I suggested they see a doctor, but they said no. Just scared is all, he said." A collection of spectators escorted the pair to the restaurant. "She had a vest on, though it was half off. She tried to swim, but I think she got scared to death. Almost nonresponsive, you know?"

He waited for Callie to say something, then added, "Think I still ought to call EMS?"

"No, let me take it from here," she said, feeling worse than ever after her officer's report.

But Thomas bent down to her, inches from her ear. "This isn't like the others, Chief. None of this is on you, okay?"

All she could do was pat his arm in thanks and head to join the couple. But as Callie reached the main boardwalk, the young reporter caught up and matched her strides. "Care to elaborate on what happened out here this evening, Chief? Was the boat to standards? Was it licensed? Was anyone hurt?"

"Alex, stop it, damn it," Callie said. "I'll tell your grandmother how heartless you are."

She wouldn't want that on the evening news.

"I can cut that part out, Callie. And if you won't talk to me about the pirate, how about Indigo Plantation. Are you involved with the murder investigation over there?"

Alex was good, but baiting Callie with the word *murder* wouldn't get results. "No comment."

"You were seen at Indigo multiple times, but that's ten miles from Edisto Beach. How are you involved?"

Who the hell was she talking to? "No comment, Alex."

"Our van and others will be at Indigo in the morning, so you can tell me now or tell me later how Addison Callaway came to die there."

Pulse pounding in her neck, her head, Callie reached the seafood restaurant where they'd taken her undercover duo and locked the door behind her, leaving Thomas and Fenton to deal with the boats and the misguided pirate. She didn't trust herself to talk to Drummond anymore, much less the press.

Slade and Largo had coffees before them and towels around their necks, people peppering them with questions, the others just listening. *Damn.* Alex slid in from another entrance and hovered, one eye on Callie.

"Hey," Callie said to Largo, and the crew let her through. "Y'all want to come with me? Answer a few questions, then we'll get you back to your place?"

One woman frowned. "You're questioning them for something that wasn't their fault?"

"Routine, ma'am," Callie said.

Largo stood. "Sure. Frankly, we're happy to be able to."

Slade rose without speaking.

Outside and just past six-thirty, the evening sun shone sharp between thinning clouds, the storm no more than a gray horizon. An occasional, low-echoing thunder could be heard rolling inland. Largo motioned to the lot. "That's my Explorer. We'll follow you."

Callie led, only this time up Dock Site Road which entered Lybrand

Street, then she turned left onto Jungle Road, quickly reaching Chelsea Morning. She pulled beneath the house, then walked out to meet the Explorer.

Largo rolled down the window. "What's this?"

"My place," she said, "and hurry inside. That Charleston reporter is out here hunting two stories now, Callaway and Drummond. I can't follow you to Indigo without leading her and goodness knows who else, and I'm not sure I want you at my station."

Word would travel at light speed about Drummond's boat, and the unusual usually brought out Brice LeGrand, who would come knocking at the station seeking an explanation as if each case hung in the balance without the oversight of the self-imposed watchdog. "If you don't mind, of course," she added. "I might be able to find you some clothes."

Slade walked past, her shorts and tee half dry but wrinkled and stuck to her in places. "I doubt it," she said. "What are you, a size two?" She turned and clomped the two dozen stairs toward the door, Largo behind. He turned and gave Callie a wink and a motion to just give Slade space.

Before stepping inside, Callie scanned the Hanson house across the street and two doors down. She feared Alex spending the night at her grandmother's place to surveil Chelsea Morning and Callie's comings and goings.

She shut the door and motioned toward the kitchen. "Here, sit at the table," she said, hoping she hadn't just suggested she feared they'd get her sofa wet. "I'll be right back."

She returned with one of John's button-up shirts she hadn't been able to let go of since her husband's death four years earlier, and her largest cotton sweater for Slade. Both were old, and she prayed they didn't sport holes or unraveled seams. "And there's a hair blower in the bathroom if you want to rinse off."

They left and soon returned, their hair less disheveled.

"What can I get you?" Callie said, standing behind the chair opposite them, having shed her uniform and donned jeans and a tee. Largo studied the burn scar on her forearm but asked no questions.

Slade acted like it wasn't there. "I'll take a drink," she said. "A big one. Preferably bourbon."

"Whatever you've got," Largo replied. "But a bourbon would sure hit the spot."

"Um, Maker's Mark?" Callie hated breaking the seal on it, but she headed toward the shelf to the left of the refrigerator where her daddy used to keep his bottle. Callie had long finished that one off, but in honor of Lawton's memory, and as a challenge to herself, she kept a token bottle in the spot. Opening it would just create temptation, but so be it. She owed these two.

"Perfect," Largo said.

To which Slade added, "He'll take it neat with a splash. Coke in mine."

Attempting to smile, Callie poured as ordered, a third glass screaming her name . . . a glass she placed back on the shelf. Neither guest questioned her choice of ice water as she sat to talk, along with a notepad from her kitchen drawer.

"Call me Callie, and I profusely apologize for Drummond," she said. "This is my geography, and I feel responsible. You were vacationing, and I'm terribly sorry now you got sucked into this." She especially studied Slade. "What happened out there? You looked like warmed-over death when they brought you in. I'm having someone inspect that boat, hopefully pull his business license, and if you want to file charges against Drummond, I understand."

Instead of slurs and accusations, however, Slade's cheeks reddened, and she responded with a simple, "Not necessary." Then she filled her mouth with a large swallow, held it, and let it go down, as though buying time. Largo watched his glass and then took a gentle taste, as if already reading her mind.

Initially, Callie never saw this couple as much of a team, but somehow, they clicked. Slade was a looser cannon, but Largo seemed to enjoy the spice she contributed to his life and in return, seemed to have a certain hold on her. Slade gravitated to his level headedness. Opposites attracting. And dire straits only made them closer.

Seabrook used to retreat to his medical roots, nurturing instead of policing, often at the most inopportune times. Callie held citizens to the law, instilling criminals met justice. One more natural at enforcement than the other. The other more gifted with people.

But dire straits had instead split them forever.

"You had questions, Chief?" Largo asked, motioning with his glass, interrupting Callie's unexpected reverie.

Now warmth crept into her cheeks. "Just recap the boat trip for me, if you don't mind. And fill me in on anything about Drummond, assuming you got that far." She held her palms up. "Completely understandable if you didn't."

"We went out," Largo said. "He seemed innocent enough. The weather blew in rather fast, and the next thing we knew, he was sprawled on the deck, the boat had some malfunction. We were at the mercy of the wind, knocked all over the bay."

"And I fell overboard," Slade said, low and curt.

"And I went in after her," he said, watching her, his free hand disappearing under the table, presumed to hold hers.

Callie waited, observing.

"Anyway." Slade began again with a clearing of her throat, and a shift to reposition the chair, which scrubbed the linoleum. "I got him to mention Callaway. As suspected, Callaway asked Drummond to give him a free ride on the boat in exchange for a review on his blog. Drummond wasn't interested and basically told him to go to hell. All he saw was a freeloader and didn't understand the purpose of the blog, so they parted less than amicably, I guess you could say."

"How much less?" Callie asked.

Largo shook his head, his mouth mashed.

But Slade was the quicker to reply. "Nothing lethal, if that's what you're asking. Told Callaway to go rent his own damn boat, which it appears he did per the boat rental guy. I don't see a motive for murder. That pirate's dumb as a doorknob."

Slade swallowed a third of her drink and leaned a half-turn toward Largo. "Another one of these, and you'll be carrying me to the car."

Callie jumped up. "How rude of me. Let me boil you some shrimp or run some under the broiler." She glanced in the freezer for the staple every native on the beach kept in full stock. "Or pizza, if that's your preference. I'll call La Retta's and have them put a rush on it."

Largo met her at the refrigerator door, pushing it to. "We don't hold you responsible," he said. "Shit happens."

But Callie couldn't help but glance at Slade, and her periodic shivering. "But she—"

"Got scared," he finished. "We're still good, Chief. Just order the pizza and let's talk, if you don't mind."

"Yeah," Slade said. "From where we sit, it appears we're your only allies on this case." She twirled a finger. "Let's see if three heads together are better than however many other heads are out there getting in your way. 'Cause if Roberts is the typical example of your team, you're screwed."

Chapter 14

Callie

"I GOTTA PEE," Slade said after her second bourbon and Coke and three pieces of pizza at Callie's kitchen table.

Callie watched her disappear into the bathroom, weighing this woman and her worth. Largo didn't merit as much concern. The badge came with a degree of trust when it came to coping with crime. Especially a federal one. And he'd changed from bourbon to water some time ago, letting Slade drink as she wished.

But after conversation and half a pizza, Callie'd learned there was a certain renegade-yet-calculating caginess about Slade that Callie could not pin down. An uncertain style that could lead to mistakes. She understood the cost of that. Too many mishaps in her own life had happened because of mistakes.

"There's more to Slade than you can gather at first," Largo said, ice clinking. "And what she's not telling you is that she has a morbid fear of dark water. It's real. Right now she's embarrassed all those people at the marina saw it."

Nodding, Callie probably better understood that aspect of Slade than any other. On the most unexpected days her own chest tried to seize at dusk. The more intense the sunsets the greater the odds . . . the more the rays resembled fire, like that which took her husband in Boston. Took over two years to be able to go out after six p.m. without some sort of game plan to avoid the experience . . . and the same sort of embarrassment. "Oh, I get it," she mumbled. "Yet she was willing to go out on the water?"

"She's dogged that way. Did it once before, for me," he said, and Callie spotted a flash of serious adoration in those last two words.

No, he wasn't for sale. "And?"

"She saved my neck," he said. "And earned a scar across her ribs from a guy's knife. Coast Guard had to rescue us."

"Oh." *Shit.* She instinctively glanced over to the bathroom door. "Never would've guessed."

"Yeah, I know."

She'd avoided the intricacies of the Callaway details during the meal and ignored Slade's request to clue them in more, sliding the conversation more toward the pirate and his theoretical lineage, Edisto Island's history, how Indigo came to be. But more importantly, about *their* investigative past, which turned out to be quite novel, even dangerous. She had to respect them better to bring them into the fold. Fold. Hah. A fold of one right now, because she was about to cut these two loose.

The toilet flushed, and they hushed. Slade returned to the table. "Your turn," she told Largo, and he left the room.

Callie pointed to Slade then to Largo's empty seat. "Is this bathroom jockeying so I talk individually to you?"

"Maybe," Slade said, picking the mushrooms off a cold slice before taking a bite. "You dodged us about Roberts. And you changed subjects when we asked more about the case. You've heard about us now, so what's your verdict?"

Callie slid the last two pieces onto her guests' plates before rising to dispose of the pizza box.

"Lemme guess," Slade said. "You can't find info on Wayne without calling Ag, which you aren't sure you want to. You found info on me, which most likely surprised you since I don't wear the tin star that y'all do, and that info definitely surprised you." Slade held palms out like she was a balancing scale. "Do you or don't you?" And when Callie said nothing, she dropped her arms and returned elbows to the table.

Callie'd already decided that question, but even more so all Callie could think was why she accepted this case to start with.

Knocks sounded on the door, the fast, repetitive kind. The Sophie kind. She must have seen the different car in the drive, watched the pizza delivered, and heard about Drummond's boat. It's the kind of snooping she did.

"She's just a neighbor," Callie said, headed to the foyer, then opened the door.

Sophie craned her neck and scanned the area she could before stepping over the threshold. "Someone told me you're arresting Teach," she said, venturing in. "Are you really? He almost lost his boat. How did Alex hear about it so quick? I see her car across the street."

As expected, Sophie made her way to the kitchen, where she always went first, usually uninvited. "Oh," she said, seeing Slade.

The bathroom door opened and Largo exited. "My wallet and creds are going to take forever to dry."

"Oooh." Sophie let the expression drag out upon the sight, her turquoise contacts taking in every inch of him, to include his bare feet. "Haven't we met?"

The corner of his mouth tilted up. "You know we have." And he made his way to Slade.

"Well, not officially," Sophie said, letting herself slide into the end seat, at angle to Largo. "I'm Sophie."

"And I'm Carolina Slade . . . again," said the firm voice behind the hand that shot in front of Largo toward the yoga mistress. "And he's Wayne Largo, again. We're from Columbia, working with Chief Morgan."

Puzzlement crossed Sophie's face. "You're cops?"

"Agents," Slade said.

"Slade," Largo warned.

And somehow Callie could see these two behaving like this through each and every investigation. Slade overreaching, literally and figuratively, and Largo attempting to hold the reins, which Callie guessed he'd lost control of on more than one occasion with Slade having something to prove. And from the articles Callie read, Slade had indeed proven herself.

Intriguing.

Sophie gave them a theatrical ooh, eyes stretched wide. "Are y'all the ones they saved a little while ago?" She leaned forward and whispered. "Were y'all undercover?"

"They simply took Drummond's tourist offer and now regret it," Callie said. "So did you get the job, Soph?"

"Sweet said he'd call in a week." Her pixie nose scrunched, pushing into her eyes. "Don't you love that name? Bet I could eat him up in little bitty bites." A sensual growl crawled out and she winked at Largo. Then she turned to Callie. "But I got this, girl."

Callie laughed. "I'm sure."

"No, I'm serious," Sophie said. "I have connections."

"Um hum."

She rested her boobs on the table, arms crossed before her. "Honey, I'm friends with one of the owners. Trenton has a condo in Charleston and is a huge fan of my ex's football team. All I needed was an introduction, which you,"—she pointed a manicured nail at Callie—"promptly provided today. You got me in the door, but I nailed the deal." She acted as if she suddenly spotted the remnants of dinner. "How can you eat that junk?"

"A beer helps," Callie joked back, but Sophie scowled deeper.

"Oh, honey, you didn't," she said in pity.

Callie sighed and held up her water glass.

"Thank God," Sophie whispered.

"So," Slade said, diluting the awkwardness. "You're friends with the owner of Indigo?"

The turquoise eyes batted. "He's just one of them, but I don't understand all that corporate partner stuff."

"And he lives in Charleston?" Slade said, more attentive to Callie than the newest guest.

"Yep," Sophie said, oblivious. "Been in town the last two weeks. Had dinner with him not three days ago. I may have divorced my damn ex-linebacker, but his friends still remember me."

Slade pushed further. "I bet that guy has some ridiculous money and political influence."

Which drew a dramatic gasp from Sophie. "Of course. The names in his contacts list and what he owns would blow you off this island."

"I see," Slade continued but she'd ceased talking to Callie's hippie neighbor. "And Detective Chuck Roberts is a Charleston County Sheriff's Deputy."

"Who?" Sophie asked.

"Yes," Callie replied over the top of Sophie.

"And I bet someone asked for you by name to oversee a case, didn't they?" the Ag lady continued.

Callie didn't respond, but she caught Largo reading her.

"What case?" Sophie asked.

"One in Columbia," Slade said. "Thought while we were on vacation we'd ask the chief for advice."

"Oh." Sophie hopped up, bored. She danced a finger across Largo's forearm, and he didn't flinch. "Nice meeting you . . . Cowboy."

He lightly shook his head with a smile Callie couldn't help but admire. Slade rolled her eyes.

Callie's cell rang. Almost ten and she silently patted herself on the back for almost finishing a day without a drink. "Chief Morgan."

"Pulled all kinds of prints off that boat," Roberts said without salutation, "but guess who I have the honor of hauling into custody for having the cleanest, most recent set? With a criminal record, I might add."

Oh, good Lord. "You arrested him?" No point asking who. She didn't have to. And if Alex caught any whiff of this . . .

Callie *not* asking who he arrested gave Roberts a micro-pause. "Powers- that-be told me to give him to *you* to interview . . . since it's *your* case."

"Then shouldn't I have been the one to arrest him?" she asked.

"Teamwork," he said.

Teamwork her ass.

"So where do you want him?"

"At the station," she said, almost tacking on *you idiot bastard.* There wasn't another place on her beach to take someone arrested, and Brice kept eyes and ears open on that place.

"Too late," he said.

"What the hell, Roberts?"

He chuckled. "I'm already here, Chief. Waiting on you."

"Aren't you the boy scout." Ordinarily she'd call Raysor to accompany her to an interview, but it was late, and he was forty minutes away at home in bed. She glanced over at Largo. He quizzically waited.

While she'd decided to sever ties with Slade and Largo after the boat incident, she needed one of them at the moment. One last time. He would get it. Slade . . . well, she was no longer in play.

"Sit tight, Roberts," she said. "We'll be right there."

"We who?" he asked.

"Me and an . . . agent," she said, and disconnected.

The three stared at each other, Callie wondering how to use her new resource when she met Roberts. Resource, as in one.

The duo sat patient for whatever decision needed saying.

"You," and Callie pointed to Largo. "How would you like to come with me? Roberts arrested someone we need to interview."

Slade stiffened, but before Callie could explain, Largo did instead. "This is not Ag, Slade, and you have zero authority here. None. I'm helping a fellow officer, but you're pure civilian." He shook his head gently. "There is no rationalizing this one, Butterbean. It is what it is."

She took it, but not happily. "I'm not dumb. So what do I do in the interim?"

He reached into his damp pocket. "Here, take the keys. I'll get the chief to bring me back." He hesitated. "You can drive, right? Not too much to drink?"

Slade took the keys, staring at them more than him. "I'm fine."

The spark had left the Ag lady, and Callie wondered if being sidelined totally knocked her self-esteem askew. Largo touched the top of her head and ran fingers down to her shoulder. "Don't," he said.

"No, I'm good," she said with a grimace and a shrug.

Callie so understood the eagerness to chase. She gave Slade a mental moment of consolation then went to retrieve her wallet and keys.

This "interrogation" was a complete waste of time, in her opinion, but she'd use the night as a teaching moment for Roberts. The bastard ought to be leaning on the coroner. And she would've thought he had better forensics than simple fingerprinting.

"You coming?" she called to Largo.

"Wait," Largo said, standing puzzled in the middle of her living room. "What do I do about shoes?"

Chapter 15

Callie

CALLIE WALKED over to Roberts's patrol car, peering in the rear before she spoke to the detective. Drummond looked every bit the low-level con he could be, but she also caught a hint of shame, remorse . . . . That drew her pity. He might be a thorn under everyone's skin, but he was Edisto's thorn, and she should've been the one to bring him in. Assuming he even needed to be brought in.

"Bring him inside," she said, and turned to unlock the station door.

Largo, wearing deck shoes from one of Sophie's many past beaus, stayed to assist Roberts.

Hand on the door, Roberts hesitated. "Hold on a minute. You're the agent?"

"Yes, sir. Senior Special Agent Wayne Largo."

The detective stood tall, challenged. "And you didn't feel the need to tell me when we met today at lunch?"

"You asked the questions, Detective." Largo nodded toward Callie. "The chief knew, so I assumed you two communicated."

At that Roberts hushed and roughly extracted Drummond from the back seat, cuffed.

"Seriously, Roberts?" Callie said, seeing the pirate shackled.

"Standard protocol."

Drummond tried to shake loose from the detective's grip. "Ain't like I'm a murderer. And how was I to forecast the boat would give out when the wind blew in?"

"Shut up, Teach," Callie said. "Let's go inside and straighten this out."

As Callie flipped on the lights, Roberts scanned the facility and gave her a sarcastic "Impressive."

Which Callie ignored and unlocked the counter gate, leading them to her private office. She grabbed a chair en route since the room only allowed for two guests.

"Camera? Recorder?" Roberts asked, shoving Drummond into the chair immediately before Callie's desk.

Callie pulled out a portable recorder from her desk drawer, not mentioning she often just used her phone since she could count on one hand the number of recordings she'd had to make in the fourteen months she'd lived at Edisto. While Roberts set a chair beside Drummond, she quickly changed batteries in the device.

Largo, however, located his seat beside Callie, and she had to hide her grin at Roberts's note of the one-upmanship.

She read in date, time, place, and persons present onto the recording. "You brought him in, Detective Roberts, so you can kick us off."

"How'd you know Addison Callaway?" he asked.

"Didn't," the pirate replied.

"But you met him?"

"One evening at Craven's rental, when he asked for a free boat ride. I said no. He got mad. I left."

"Take any money from him?" Roberts asked.

Drummond shrugged awkwardly, the cuffs still on him. "I kept asking, but he thought I ought to give it away. If he'd have offered, I'd have gladly accepted."

"Did you part angry?"

The pirate worked his mouth around, thinking. "Not particularly. Insulted more than anything. How'm I supposed to earn a living giving away my services?" Then Drummond straightened his back, tucked his chin, and peered suspiciously at the detective. "What did that bastard say I did? What's he complaining about?"

Roberts ignored the questions. "How do you explain your fingerprints on his boat?"

With a bluster, he replied, "*His* boat? I didn't know he had a boat. Then why was he wanting to use mine?"

Roberts's frustration came untethered. "The boat he rented, you idiot."

Another shrug. "I don't know he rented a boat."

"Teach," Callie interrupted. "You took Callaway's rental to Craven's."

The pirate slumped and studied his thoughts a moment, trying to make sense of things. "I brought a boat back to Rick's rental place, yeah." Then he deliberated over what to say next. "But if that was his boat, and I found it loose . . . what happened to him?"

By now, holding Callaway's death secret was like holding water in her hands. "He was found washed up on the bank of the South Edisto River," Callie said.

His mouth dropped open, Drummond squinted. "You're shittin' me, right?"

The three watched him, each seeking tells in the old man, indications he was putting on a show versus being genuinely stunned. Callie saw the truth, and she glanced at Largo.

"I believe him," he said. "Same story he told us out on the boat this afternoon, and he had no idea who I was."

The room had warmed with the door shut, and Roberts's ire seemed to raise the temperature. "You already talked to this guy?"

Like a long-distance shot, the bullet finally hit the target with the pirate. "Oh, shit," he said, his voice higher pitched. "Surely you don't think I did it." It rose higher still. "All this over a stupid fare?"

"Just a second, Teach," Callie said. "Before we end this recording, Detective Roberts, do you have any additional questions to ask Mr. Drummond?"

"No," he said through his teeth.

Callie ended the recording, then rested crossed forearms on her desk, waiting.

Roberts spoke as if Drummond wasn't in the room. "Why'd you let me waste my time?"

"First," Largo said, "can we agree that we can't hold this man? I'm sure he'd love to go home. He's had a hard day."

"Damn if that ain't right," Drummond uttered and shook his cuffs. "I ought to file charges for false arrest."

"Or thank me," Callie said.

Roberts released him. "You're on your own getting home."

"Teach," Callie said. "I'll take you home if you want to wait in the lobby. Give us a few minutes."

Drummond gave a curt jerk of his head and left, grumbling. "I ain't forgettin' this." He shut the door behind him.

Roberts crammed himself against the edge of Callie's desk and leaned over, inches from her. "You've got some nerve. What else do you know that you aren't sharing? You've got me chasing my own damn tail, and I ain't got time for this."

Before she could answer, he began railing again, temper raised. "This two-bit police department has no business on this case, period. And you . . ." He raised a stiff finger in her face.

"Take it down a notch, Detective," Largo said, weight forward in his chair.

Which gave him Roberts's notice. "And you. Who the hell gave you any kind of authority here?"

Largo thumbed toward Callie. "She did."

"Roberts, we're working together at the request of your boss," she told the detective calmly. "But in all honesty, I never asked you to go find Drummond. You were to check the licenses of guests, backgrounds of all the employees, deal with the coroner to make sure we even *have* a suspicious death, and spearhead forensics. Enough to keep anyone busy. At the same time you bitched at me about having to juggle so many other cases. Yet you *clandestinely* interviewed Agent Largo and his friend, sought out Drummond, and wasted *all our* time, *Chuck*." She held up a hand. "Wait, I take that back. I think we can check Drummond off the list for now, though I hadn't been ready to talk to him yet. Sort of wanted to get forensics first."

The room thrummed with animosity, Roberts unable to take his narrowed eyes off her. Her holding back way more than she'd said. She was better than this, but this man went out of his way to push her buttons and prove her incompetent. She mentally scratched her brain on how to mend this rift, but they'd almost taken it beyond repair. And Largo had to witness it.

She scrambled to be the bigger person. "Can we move on to something more important? What did you get on the personnel at Indigo?"

But he didn't immediately answer.

"Twenty employees from Edisto or Charleston," he finally said. "Three imported from outside the state."

She gave him a soft nod, not too much. She didn't want to come off as superior.

"A few traffic incidents with one DUI," he continued. "Nothing NCIC except Tito Washington who has a simple larceny from three years ago."

Good. He'd checked the National Crime Info Center as he should.

So, this Tito was Edistonian, but Callie hadn't met the kid before today, much less heard of a record. "Think you could get all that to me?" she asked, wanting to run all the Edisto people by Marie.

He started to object, when she asked, "Could you also work your magic on the coroner, please? Cause of death would make our lives easier." She almost added, *so we don't arrest anyone else we don't have to.* And she darn sure wouldn't tell him that the sheriff promised her today to nudge the medical examiner himself. If Roberts got credit for that, all the better. Personally, she'd had her share of accolades in Boston, but this guy itched for recognition. She'd happily give him all she could.

Roberts typed on his phone, and she glanced at hers. It was just past eleven at night, and the small interruption seemed odd. Maybe he was taking notes? "Anything else, your highness?" he asked, still seduced by his phone.

Keep it together. "It's late. Let's reconnect tomorrow. Okay? I really need your help, Roberts. I can't do this alone."

"Then work with me."

"I'm trying." Could she try any harder?

He put away the device, rose, and made for the door. "Tomorrow I'll email you the employee data."

"I really appreciate it."

Probably the best two lines of conversation they'd had since Callaway was found.

His cell phone gave a ting . . . a text. Stopping in the doorway, he read it to himself. A half-grin slid up one side of his mouth, then he gave each of them a silent, cavalier expression.

"I take it you want us to ask what the text was?" Largo asked.

Roberts held one finger. "Time of death approximately ten a.m. to two p.m. on the day we found him."

Callie wrote it down.

He held up a second finger. "His last meal was a grilled pimiento cheese on a ciabatta bun, pickled okra, and a pecan tart."

Pretty chic picnic lunch. Something that nice was almost certainly shared.

Then with a finger rubbing his jaw, Roberts reread the text, teasing, dragging out the tension. "I was already all over the coroner," he said.

"Of course you were," Callie said. "I hadn't a doubt. Is that it?"

He held up three fingers. "No. One more item. He was poisoned."

"Poisoned?" Callie had about determined the death natural, believing the coroner had overlooked something the first go-around. No marks. No wounds. This she hadn't bargained for.

And she bet Sweet hadn't bargained for it, either. When word got out, the blame would go straight to Indigo. "Was it cyanide?" She remembered the employee in the barn talking to visitors about how the natural plant dye was not poisonous like the cheaper, artificial blue dyes that used cyanide.

"Why would you ask that?" he asked.

"Something to do with indigo dye," she said.

"No, it was hemlock," he said.

"What?"

Largo scowled. "Are you sure?"

Roberts scowled back.

"Ingested, I assume?" Callie asked.

"Like lettuce," he said. "On his sandwich."

There were two sandwiches packed for that outing per Tito. Meaning the companion could have been the one who doctored Callaway's sandwich or lay dead someplace like Callaway, unlucky enough to become fish food.

And if they had *another* body to hunt for, who the hell killed them?

With as many enemies as Callaway had in his profession, no telling what chef, waitress, restauranteur, or other hospitality employee had done the deed which raised suspicion on a slew of Indigo employees.

The girl mentioned at the boat rental shop fast flew to the top of her interest list. Someone needed to give Callie a firm description of the as-yet-unmet waitress, Rose Jenkins.

Chapter 16

Slade

I STOOD BESIDE Wayne's Explorer watching the taillights of the patrol car as he left for the station with Chief Morgan, or Callie, as she instructed us to call her. Admittedly, it was easier calling her that in jeans and a polo shirt, a shirt that showed a helluva scar on her arm. Despite how together an image she tried to project, I sensed her private self even more scarred than her arm.

And I wondered if she was in over her head.

Why did I have to find that damn body? Now, instead of a nice vacation with Wayne, we were in over *our* heads right along *with* Callie.

Damn, it was dark out here. I walked the half dozen steps back to the house and plopped down on the base of the beach house stairs. Chelsea Morning, she called it. My nose ran and I sniffled. Partly from bourbon and partly from the briny breeze meandering the four blocks from the rollers hitting the beach. I shivered and didn't want to ponder why. Dark water scared me shitless, and that's all there was to it. Only today there'd been an audience. And a reporter with a camera. *Sniffling.* Another wipe. No, I wasn't going to cry. And now was not a good time to call and speak to the kids. Wish I had a beer.

Damn press. Frankly, I was surprised they hadn't already made it out here, and kudos to Callie for keeping them at bay this long, but that honeymoon period after we found Callaway was about over, I suspected. The news whores would be out aplenty before we knew it.

"Psst."

Pretending I didn't hear, I kept watching the road, my eyes adjusting and trying to take in my surroundings.

"Slade, over here."

At my name, I turned to the yard next door.

"Up here."

On the porch, fifteen feet off the ground like all the other houses around here, that yoga lady motioned for me to come over. Hell, why not? Wasn't like I had an investigation to work.

"Inside before Alex sees you."

Already having been briefed on Alex, I fast-stepped the first dozen stairs, then slowed the second set. Who did these stairs every day?

"Quick. She lives right over there." Sophie pointed, then before I could follow her finger, she yanked me inside.

The door shut, and I entered the most beachy beach house I'd ever seen. Yellow paint, cast netting draped on the wall with crabs and little colored bobber things hanging on it. Driftwood. Cream colored sofa and chair each with pastel throws of seahorses and dolphins. White woodwork and a kitchen done in the same white, accented with sea glass colors.

Barefoot in tights and a tunic, she waved me to her living room. "I want to hear all about you. Sit over there, and I'll get you a water."

"Just water?" I asked.

"Sorry," she said, "but living this close to Callie, I try not to keep booze around." Swiftly, she covered her mouth. "Oh, not sure I should've said that."

I'd watched people flutter before, but not like this woman did. Like a hummingbird. It was after eleven at night. I would have thought this type of energy had to crash early.

And I hadn't realized the depth of the chief's alcohol problem.

"There," Sophie said, offering me my water then perching herself on the cushion's edge of the armchair opposite my couch. "So you're an agent? Not sure I've met an agent before. No, wait, I did meet that FBI guy a few months ago who came out here and worked with Callie. Is that what you are?"

"No, not FBI." I wondered how I could pump this lady for information. She'd been at Indigo and was about to be employed there. She was native. Would Callie consider using her as a CI?

She tucked both legs under her. My ankles would've popped doing that. "Okay, I see you're not going to release the particulars of who you are. That's fine." Sophie put a finger over her mouth and whispered, "I get that."

I smiled, legitimately amused.

"What's going on with Addison Callaway?" she asked.

Which immediately erased my smile. "What do you mean?"

She nodded. "Agents like you on the scene. Just the fact Callaway is even here is something. I've heard his name an incredible number of times lately." She crunched a shoulder toward her head. "Everyone's talking about him, but nobody's seen him in two days." She leaned forward. "Is he dead?"

Damn, the woman had a slick way of loosening people with her nonchalant innocence. Bet she could get whatever she wanted on this island—information, repairs, yard work—and make the other person grateful to give it away for free. People skills plus.

Already Sophie Bianchi was a better detective than Roberts.

"I can't talk about—"

"An active investigation," Sophie finished and then crossed two fingers. "Honey, I'm like this with Callie Jean Morgan, and she's cited that line to me more times than I can count."

Not surprising.

"But she gets this laser-like focus when there's something serious going on." Sophie allowed herself to sit up halfway. No wonder she didn't have a recliner; she hadn't the patience to use it.

"And she's doing it now," she continued. "Instead of holing up in her house after work drinking."

I lifted my glass. "I noted her drinking water while we had bourbon." In hindsight, that might've been difficult for her.

Sophie gasped. "You drank in front of her?"

"It's part of having to accept you're a recovering alcoholic, Sophie. Seeing other people drink while you don't. Plus, I didn't know."

But Sophie's immaculately plucked and penciled eyebrows took a slanted, skeptical stance. "So tell me this, Ms. Investigator. Why did she have it in the house in the first place?"

"She cracked the bottle open for us," I said, suddenly on the defensive.

"And now she can come home to that open bottle after she gets done tonight." And with that she rose and went to the kitchen again. "I need some carrot juice."

Callie had a friend who cared. She might be a nuisance, hovering, questioning, noseying in on everything Callie did, but she was there. "I take it you two are more than a little close?"

She fluttered into the room again. "Her son and my daughter are an item. My son and her son are good friends. And . . ." she raised a blue painted fingernail while she sipped a nasty-colored drink with a hue of rusty nails. "We solved a case together. I was kidnapped, and she saved me." Animated, she did an almost dance with her lithe arms waving and tiny hips sliding side to side. "Therefore, I'm rather well-versed in cop stuff."

"So you trust her as chief of police?" I asked, baiting.

"Honey . . ."

She loved that word, apparently.

"Callie's a blessing. It would take all night to tell you all she's done for this island . . . and sacrificed. Don't think she'll ever look at another man thanks to the crap she's endured."

Had to admit the chief did sport a wounded warrior air. I felt the urge to give her some sort of excuse, though. "Mr. Shaw at Indigo has eyes for her."

"That's because he's new. He'll learn."

Wow, that was sad. Surprisingly, my heart cracked a little for her.

Then Sophie cut loose. Telling me how Callie arrived, a widow, the tale surprising me that she'd discarded law enforcement before an officer named Seabrook coaxed her again into it. How she was almost killed, three times. A case called the Jinx that Sophie was especially fond of since she was an active participant. Then the loss of Seabrook after Callie'd fallen in love with him. Damn, movies weren't this complicated.

"Jesus," I said, then leery, asked, "why are you telling me all this?"

"So you'll help her."

"I am helping her," I said. "Wayne and I both are."

She smiled small. "I like your Wayne."

I frowned big. "I noticed."

"So we agree there's a case about Callaway?" she asked.

"No."

"Well, since we've confirmed there's probably a serious case that warrants foreign agents and Callie working twenty-four/seven, and that Callaway's name is the common denominator . . ."

My frown deepened. "I said none of that."

I recognized Sophie now. The queen of the beach's gossip.

"I can only assume that he's dead," she finished.

"Um, that's quite a leap, Sophie," I replied.

Lids closed, she frowned then eased it out. "I sense people. Living and dead." She opened her eyes. "You just gave me that vibe. Callie uses me all the time."

Shit, where did *that* come from?

"I just freaked you out, huh?"

"You think?" I said, hoping I didn't sound too unnerved.

She polished off her carrot juice. "Not that I'm trying to rush you, but it's bumping midnight. I teach yoga at eight and can't function without eight hours of zzzzzs."

"Wait, that's it?" I followed her to the door, still awed about this little tête-a-tête. A quick round of Callie, Wayne, Callaway, then me, and she was done. With a dash of otherworldly flavor.

So Sophie'd heard something was amiss about Callaway. Shocker. I did, however, gain insight into the chief. "Thanks for the chat," I said, reaching the porch, thinking what an adorable, yet deadly, relationship she offered. An asset I bet Callie took full advantage of. My sister could do me this way sometimes, but dang, Sophie led the parade.

And I liked her. With Wayne and Callie doing the "real stuff," I'd still managed to gain a little intel, plus Sophie'd lifted my spirits.

"Take care of yourself, and my friend," she said, the door half closed.

"Try not to spread rumors," I said. "It only complicates things for your friend."

In a cutesy *I know* eye batting, she sighed at me. "I realize my limitations. Oh, and Margaret asks if you've wrecked any more cars."

My brain fried a synapse or two. "What?"

Sophie winked. "Come to my yoga class."

I was still train-wrecked on the Margaret statement.

"Inner peace begins when you choose not to allow anything to control your emotions. Dark water won't kill you, Slade. But your fear of it could."

"Whoa, what?" Had I entered another dimension?

"Good night," Sophie said. "Take care of my friend. And she might just take care of you."

With that she shut her door.

She left me standing on a dark porch in the middle of the night, stunned. This guru, hippie, whatever-she-was person might've heard about my near-drowning and pulled a Sherlock on me, but Margaret was my old boss. My old *dead* boss. And she used to kid me about how many fender benders I had on my insurance.

Shivering down to my core, I studied the grounds, as if Margaret were literally watching. Then with quick footsteps I sort of ran to Wayne's SUV, got in, locked the doors, and cranked the engine. I couldn't scoot out of Callie's drive fast enough.

And noticed a car turn on its lights and follow.

So I gunned the gas. As I passed Matilda Street, a blue light flipped on and a patrol car turned onto Jungle Road behind me. The other car, a VW beetle, scooted on by.

Son of a bitch.

I pulled over, automatically reaching for registration . . . crap. This was Wayne's car. He'd have a fit.

"License and registration, please."

In the flicker of blue light, I gazed into the face of the cutest young, dark-haired officer with a perpetual twinkle in his eye. So familiar. The tag said Gage. "Sorry. I thought I was being followed. Guess I was speeding, huh?"

My insides still hadn't returned to normal after Sophie.

I showed him my license. "Um, this is my boyfriend's car." He kept a .38 in the glove box where I assumed the registration was. "Before I open the glovebox, I need to tell you—"

"You're that lady that Drummond almost drowned this evening," he said, peering up from the license. "I was there. You were pretty shook and probably don't remember me."

I studied him harder. "Yes, I am. Just came from the chief's house." I glanced behind me like the other car was still there. "When I left, this VW seemed to come after me." I shook my head. "Maybe I'm losing it. Just met some yoga lady who weirded me out. Oh, just write the ticket," I conceded.

He returned the license and laughed aloud. It sounded wonderful after my night, though I had no idea what the joke was.

"Drummond, Alex, and Sophie in one evening. You don't need a ticket. You need a drink."

Of course, I wasn't about to tell him I'd already partaken at Callie's. "Alex has the VW?"

"Yup. Go on and enjoy your evening," he said. "Just slow it down, get home, and chill."

I liked the Edisto police. "Yes, sir," I said to this kid who was almost young enough to be my son.

He watched as I rolled away in my most conservative manner. But as I reached Bi-Lo at the corner of Highway 174 that would take me toward Indigo, the VW pulled out of the parking lot and returned to my tail.

Creepy at this time of night. The lack of streetlights gave the jungle brush on either side of the narrow highway a horror feel. If the car had been a black SUV with tinted windows, I'd have waited at Bi-Lo and had Callie drop Wayne off there. The VW sort of diluted the fright to more of a frustration.

She stayed two car lengths behind me, regardless my speed. Studying her in my mirror, I saw only one head. I was armed, but no point in stopping and risking a confrontation, so I just headed to Indigo. Miss VW, however, had other plans.

At a white church hosting small streetlights, the car floored it around me and slowed. I veered right into the graveled parking lot, threw the car into park, and pulled the .38 from the glove box.

For a second we sat there. No point in me getting out first since she threw down the gauntlet.

As her car door opened, I tensed, gun now in my lap and seatbelt off. She exited with a camera. One of those you see on the shoulders of irritating cameramen on assignment.

My frustration grew to anger. I rolled down my window. "You come closer with that camera, and I'll shoot it off your shoulder."

She laughed. Laughed! And kept coming.

So I leaned against the door, gun in both hands. "Shine your light over here, Missy, and see if my .38 is still funny."

She screamed and ran in place, stomping with that damn camera bouncing on her shoulder, as if she wasn't sure where to go. Now things were funny.

I felt it safe to get out of the car now. Lowering the gun but keeping it in hand as I approached, I hollered, "What the ever-loving heck did you think you were doing?"

"You almost drowned," she answered, trying to sound strong but having killed that image with her fright dance. "I have some footage already of you getting off the pirate boat, but I wanted your comments."

She couldn't have been more than twenty-six or seven. Hair in a ponytail. Denim Bermudas and a lacy no-sleeve tunic. Cute . . . and lethal if she was indeed a reporter. I could see that package working her magic into the center of most any story. Except this one.

"Leave me alone," I said.

"What brought you to Edisto?" Some nervousness still sounded in her voice. "Were you afraid you almost died? Didn't you check the weather before you went out?"

Was that damn camera still going?

I walked to her, took the camera, having to yank it once when she tried to hold onto it. "Why were *you* on Edisto today?"

"My grandmother—"

I showed my Special Projects Representative badge, somewhat of an internal investigations ID that most people read as more than that. "So why were you here to begin with?"

"I have rights."

I twisted my mouth. "Hmm, I think I do, too. Let's go to the police station and compare notes to see whose rights carry more weight. Chief Morgan is still there, and we can let her be the judge."

Suddenly she took me seriously, with a pout that might seduce someone more like that young police officer. "Addison Callaway's dead," Alex said. "You were just a second coup of a story." Then when I didn't reply, she wised up. "Come to think of it, why is there a strange badge lurking around this late on the island? A badge who just came from Chief Morgan's home?"

She reached for the camera, but I slid it behind me.

"What's your part in the Callaway investigation?" she asked and went for her phone as a substitute.

"Who's Callaway?" I lied.

"Not swallowing that," she said.

"Who told you there was even a death out here?"

A waggle of her brow. "I have my sources."

I twisted all the knobs and adjustments on the camera and pulled out a plug of some sort. I knew nothing about the device, but hopefully this would disable it long enough to allow me to leave without becoming a starring role in her feature. Then I returned it to her, turned and walked to the SUV.

"I'm not the first one out here," she said loud. "When you get to Indigo, you'll find more of us."

I started the vehicle and drove around her, resisting the urge to squish her flat.

Chapter 17

Callie

"HEMLOCK," LARGO said from the passenger seat as Callie drove up Highway 174 toward Pine Landing. "That's some serious intent."

"Where do you even get that stuff?" she asked, her mind spinning as to what that meant for Indigo . . . and what her responsibilities were in possibly shutting it down. The crime had the B&B's name all over it.

"That's a question for Slade," he said. "She's the agriculture person. I just catch bad guys."

But Callie didn't want to ask Slade. After today, she'd reached the conclusion that these two shouldn't be involved at all. How insane to have invited them in in the first place. Yeah, they found the body, and if it had been natural causes or an accident, no harm, no foul. But murder . . . and poison at that.

Nope. She should fly solo on this one. Wouldn't even involve Don. The less of her world that mingled into this case the better. God, she'd lost Seabrook, her husband John, and Francis, her young deputy, to her zealous crime-solving tendencies, and while Slade and Wayne might be skilled enough to assist, today was at a minimum an omen, a reminder of what could happen.

So she changed the subject. "How the heck did Slade jump from planting corn to chasing murderers?"

Wayne gave a few chuckles. "Don't let her hear you ask like that."

"It's a valid question," she said. "How has she done what she's done with an agriculture degree?"

He reared in his seat. "Before she took this role, she was a loan officer who got backed into a corner by a client and had to fight her way out of it. About took down her job, her kids, hell, my job, and she almost died, twice. What would've given the average person PTSD only served to entice her, so they created a position. Special Projects Representative. She queries questionable situations, and often solves them herself unless they turn criminal. That's when she calls me . . . or someone like me. Currently I'm the only agent for both the Carolinas."

"And you two . . ." she trailed off, pointing at him in a side-to-side motion.

"Are an unofficial thing," he said as if well-practiced.

She slowed a bit when she spotted a white-tail doe off to the side of the road, unafraid this time of night, nibbling on honeysuckle trained up a mailbox. Where there was one, there were others. "You hunt?" she asked.

"Used to," he said. "I miss being in the woods."

"Biggest deer in the state are down here in these marshes. Call if you ever want to go out again. I'll set you up with somebody."

"Yeah, thanks."

There was an awkwardness to being in the car with a single guy with so much going for him . . . who understood law enforcement. But there was also an attraction. Her deceased husband and Seabrook, their professions had indeed added to their package. If asked, she'd say she never wanted to date another cop again, but for some reason they were the only breed she understood.

"What's next on your agenda?" he asked. "And ours."

There will be no ours, Lawman. Wasn't that the term Slade used for him?

"I'm headed out to Indigo in the morning for interviews," she said, mentally prioritizing the elusive Rose, then Sweet and Jackie. "I expect reporters to be all over the place. Hopefully, I can put the fear of God in the staff to avoid them, but not sure I can plug all those holes. As for you and Slade—"

Wayne's phone rang, and he answered. "Yo, Butterbean."

Such an endearment from a man unafraid of how it sounded to others. Reminded Callie of Seabrook yet again. A private pain she held onto because it was the only real feeling she had anymore. It was all she could afford, really.

He turned to Callie. "She's at a Presbyterian Church. One with the old cemetery?"

She acknowledged with the drop of her chin. Of course, she knew it. It's where Seabrook was buried.

"Chief?"

"Callie," she managed to say. "Call me Callie, but yeah, I know it. Why?"

"Slade's there. Said we didn't need to go all the way out to Indigo. She'd explain when she saw us."

Not a mile ahead. Callie had hoped she and that cemetery could pass in the darkness without much thought.

Wasn't five minutes before she recognized the Explorer and pulled in behind. Slade exited and came to them. Callie rolled down her window. Wayne got out and came around the car to meet his lady. "What's up?"

"Reporters," Slade said. "Had a run-in right here with your Alex friend a few moments ago. We parted with a better understanding about how I feel about her ilk, but she warned me that journalists were already at the plantation. I thought a patrol car showing this time of night might stir things and draw attention."

True that.

"So after we parted ways, she turned around and went home, I assume, and I went down the road, waited a minute, then returned. Wasn't too sure how many meeting places we'd have between here and the B&B. I assumed you'd want Wayne and me to remain rather clandestine out there?"

"Good move. Thanks." Callie sighed. She was surprised reporters hadn't been at the station, or on her doorstep as had happened in the past. Then it hit her. The media probably considered this a Charleston case. Truth was she had no idea how many phone calls had inundated the sheriff's office, but they hadn't exactly flooded hers. But then Marie went home by six.

Nobody knew she was in charge . . . and the SO wouldn't want the media to know they'd subbed out the case.

Apparently, Alex's Edisto roots had earned her some sort of leak.

Callie patted the open window ledge. "As I was telling Largo, I'm heading out there tomorrow. With this officially a murder, the pressure will be on the sheriff, and therefore me, to put these pieces together."

"It's officially a murder?" Slade asked. "You heard from the coroner?"

"Yes, and after you almost drowned today, I'm severing you two from this investigation."

Slade stared at her. "That's it? At the time you might need us most, you're ditching?" She patted her own body—her chest, her belly. "Honestly, I'm fine."

"Yep, and I could not have stood it if you weren't."

Callie hated and owed Drummond at the same time. His misjudgment today nailed her decision about these two.

"But we assume all responsibility," Slade said. "We understand how this game is played."

Wayne looked reluctant but empathetic. "The burden's on the

chief, and she's in charge, Slade."

One car went by and they hushed, as if the driver could overhear. Once the vehicle passed, the place turned dark again, with clicks and whistles echoing occasionally through the jungle that surrounded the church.

"But I still need information from you, Slade," she said. "And you have to keep it quiet."

Slade nodded.

"Largo says you're the agriculture person. Talk to me about hemlock."

Slade's eyes widened. "He was poisoned?"

Callie sighed. "Is it common? Is it really that lethal and how much does it take?"

Scratching her head, Slade leaned against Callie's car door. "Poison parsley, devil's flower, lady's lace. The novice thinks it resembles Queen Anne's Lace. It grows near water. Resembles other weeds, but it'll kill you deader-than-crap. Some people can simply touch a leaf and get a lesser reaction. The roots are the worst." She paused. "I've seen cattle die from it, but . . . not people."

This was a whole other world for Callie, and the uncertainty of it scared her nuts. What if this killer hated more people than Callaway? What if they hated Indigo as a whole, then what? "So is hemlock here?" she asked. "Would someone bring it with them or does it grow on Edisto? Have you seen it?"

Scrunching her face, Slade seemed to search her memory. "Can't say. Haven't been hunting for it, but I'll darn sure be tuned to it now. No doubt it grows in this region. I'll study the property tomorrow."

Fear rolled through Callie. Sounded like hemlock grew like crabgrass or goldenrod. Callie'd visited this island for decades, and now lived here. How the hell did nobody realize this? "How is it used? I mean, how would someone kill with it?"

Slade shrugged. "That's the thing. It's pretty potent."

"Meaning?"

She began counting off on fingers. "The root resembles parsley . . . tastes too nasty to cook it like a turnip. The seed looks like anise seed, so it can be substituted as an herb." Her words sped up the more she tapped into her knowledge bank. "The leaves are similar to wild carrots, fernlike, and it's actually related to both carrots and parsley, so you could put it in a salad. You can make a tea of the leaves. The hollow stems have killed children using them as whistles or straws. The fruit's poisonous, but not sure how you'd use it. It's not the season for the fruit now anyway, not that someone didn't bring something dried with them. Weed science 101 from school."

This couldn't be happening.

Slade leaned in to see the chief better. "Is the coroner sure?"

Callie didn't want to broadcast this. How many copycats would this generate across the Lowcountry? Why go to a hardware store for rat poison when you could pick it from the ditch out back? "So you have to ingest it, right? How quickly does it take effect?"

Slade raised both hands to the side. "Again, depends on how you ingest it and how much. A tea would take a day or so but ingesting the plant itself can kill damn quick. It's a nervous system thing. People suffocate in the end, but they act drunk before they do if it's anything like it does to cattle."

Which was probably why Callaway had no water in his lungs. Callie tried hiding the alarm in her voice. "Why don't people get rid of it? Why isn't it illegal?"

"It's a weed, Callie." Slade's voice attempted to soothe. "Nobody eats weeds. But what if someone brought it with them? It's most lethal in the spring, not in the heat of summer, not that it's ever not lethal. The flowers aren't growing this time of year, so it's harder to recognize. How much did the coroner find in his system?"

An urgency coursed through Callie at what Slade knew, and what Callie still didn't. "Can't say yet." With a firmness in her voice, she stared at Slade. "How would I identify it in a kitchen?"

Wayne, silent all this time with Slade the expert, stepped in. "Are you thinking someone is targeting more than Callaway? That's a bit of a leap, don't you think? We've seen no sign of that sort of motive."

"But can we ignore the possibility?" she asked. "Can we really take that chance?" She concentrated on Slade. "Can you spot it in a kitchen?"

"Sure, if it's sitting all by itself." Then Slade shook her head. "But not if it's mixed with greens, mingled with parsley, or hidden in a burger."

Callie rested her head on the steering wheel.

Slade touched her shoulder. "Let me scout the place tomorrow—"

She jerked her head back up. "No."

"But I can—"

"I said no." Callie's yell bounced off the front porch of the church and echoed back. "Pack your things. Leave tonight. Don't even think about eating there."

"Callie," Wayne said. "You're strapped for allies."

"If you need a rental on Edisto, call me. I'll arrange it. But otherwise, I expect to see you gone from the island tomorrow. Is that clear?"

The couple stood silent a moment.

"Yes," Slade finally said. "Perfectly."

Callie threw the transmission into drive and eased out of the gravel parking area, afraid to peer in her review mirror into the stunned faces of two people she'd decided she couldn't afford to care for.

CALLIE GOT HOME at almost one.

Her urgency was exacerbated by the fear of hemlock. She had to interview people tomorrow off the employee list . . . and the guest list . . . and somehow cross reference them with wherever trail of damage Addison Callaway had left. That could take weeks of one person doing nothing else but that, but odds were an employee or a guest did the deed. And that guest could be long gone.

So interviewing employees first mattered most. She needed to nail down who boated with Callaway. If Indigo prepared a meal for two, who says the staff wasn't aware who that companion was?

She'd put Roberts on this task . . . and Marie. The devil Callie knew, plus the angel she trusted. She already had the employee list from Sweet. On her way in tomorrow morning, she'd drop it off at the office and put her Edisto know-it-all to work cross-checking Callaway's blog, his travels over the last two years. Then came the more difficult part . . . checking each employee's work history for a year to see who had crossed his path before. And if that didn't kick up any dust, then go back two years. And then, the hardest part, she'd get Marie the guest list and start the exercise all over again.

Damn. Poisoned. School kids might not recall what Socrates did scientifically, but they knew he died from hemlock. Callie didn't see Callaway serving a nice cup of tea to kill himself, which told her she also needed to talk to the coroner to see what form and amount was traced in the blogger's digestive tract. The irony wasn't lost on her one damn bit that the man died of something he ate, making this awfully damn personal.

Somewhere, someone held a mighty serious motive. Lethal injection or electrocution was the death penalty in South Carolina. Too bad it couldn't be hemlock for this one.

Despite the hour, she called the sheriff, wanting to update him on a finding so critical, and after thirty minutes of arguing with various folks in the department, she'd finally been routed to Sheriff Mosier's personal number.

"I think we should close the Indigo restaurant," she said. "And I'm not saying this lightly."

"Have you linked this murder to someone specific there?" he asked, trying to shake off his sleep.

"Callaway ate something we're fairly sure was prepared in that kitchen."

"I'll send guys from the health department to inspect, but we're premature closing it down and doing that kind of damage to a new establishment," he grumbled. "This feels like a personal hit, not genocide, chief."

She'd hung up dumbfounded and gone to bed wide-eyed . . . unwilling to throw back a few shots of gin to make herself sleep. So she'd researched hemlock on her laptop until she was cross-eyed then dozed in her chair, rising as soon as the sun crept in around the blinds. Two hours sleep, max.

Calling Roberts at six, he didn't answer. Surprise. "How much hemlock did the coroner find in his system?" she asked. "And in what form. Was it specifically in the food? Any way to tell which item of food? I'm headed to Indigo this morning. You're welcome to come. I suspect the press will be present, and I might need your help interviewing people. And I need you to put someone on cross-referencing Callaway's professional travels over the last two years against the Indigo employee records. You already have those records, so I would appreciate it if you would have someone jump on it. Check in, please."

She dressed in khakis and a button-up shirt, rolled two cuffs but still hiding the burn scar. Nothing to draw notice. And she headed out while the dawn birds sang, first leaving notes for Marie on her desk, then on toward the B&B, unable to stop thinking of guests in that restaurant eating breakfast. She traveled down Pine Landing Road with the coroner's revelation first and foremost on her mind . . . along with who to interview when, and how hard. She'd decided to start with Sweet.

Two television vehicles already parked near the front of the lot, a van and a car, from two different stations. Could be worse . . . still meant treading carefully. Inside, she tried not to march too fast and too hard but monitored her stride through a clump of people and went quietly down the hall to Sweet's office.

The door was locked. She knocked. "You in there?"

No answer.

She fast-walked to the registration desk, but the collection of people blocked her way to the frantically working clerk. "I'll get to each of you as quickly as I can," she promised to no one person in particular.

Turning to the concierge desk, Callie hunted for Riley only to find her cornered by a cluster of fifty-ish tourists. The girl's young tender face fought her true feelings, but her mouth was pinched, and Callie noted worry in her eyes.

"Why weren't we told they found a body out here? There could be a serial killer running loose," exclaimed the woman.

"Ma'am, we've heard nothing about a serial killer. A man just drowned," Riley said.

"Wait, we heard he was killed," said the man.

Riley fought to maintain her cool. "I've heard none of that. Please. I'm here to help you with your entertainment and agenda."

"Well," said the woman. "Let me help you there. My plan is to get the hell out of here. I'm headed to my room to pack."

"Sandra," a man consoled as the woman spun on her heel and strutted off. The others drifted off with the mouthy one gone.

Relieved to be rid of the fracas, Riley sat at her station, letting go of a breath.

Callie slid over to the girl while she had a chance. "How long has it been this stirred?"

Riley jumped in her seat, startled. "Oh, Chief Morgan." The sign of a friendly face let her relax . . . and tear up. "Since I got here. Mr. Shaw sent us all email messages before work today, warning us the press might be here, but I don't think we expected anything like this. People are rattled. I'm scared. What's happening? Was Mr. Callaway really murdered?"

The girl deserved at least a half-truth. "We haven't totally nailed down how, but he was found on the edge of the water. Okay? Don't let the press push you into talking to them, either. They'll make you say something you don't want to."

Riley nodded. "Yes, that's sort of what Mr. Shaw told us."

"And a united front, steering clear of the gossip, will benefit you more than partaking in it. Understand?"

"Yes, ma'am."

An older gentleman in shorts and an Edisto tee came over, not talking, trying to listen.

"Oh, I'm done," Callie said, motioning for him to continue with Riley.

"Don't let me run you off," he said, smiling, so unlike everyone else in the room. "What's this gossip you speak of?"

"I know her mother," Callie said. "Nothing that would interest you."

"Shame," he said. "Was hoping to hear more about that dead man. Most interesting vacation I've had in ages. My kids in college will think it's a hoot if I can get interviewed by one of those television people outside."

Son of a biscuit. "What have you heard?" Callie asked. "I just got here."

"Oh, then let me fill you in," he said, easing closer, head down to Callie's short stature, keeping the conversation quasi-privileged. "Someone drowned this guy before he could write a bad review for Indigo."

Way too damn close to the truth. How was this getting out? "Was he famous?" she asked.

"Who cares?" he said.

And that was how the media worked its magic . . . or dug its claws into a story, depending on how you interpreted it.

Where the hell was Sweet? And why wasn't he out in front of this thing? He damn sure better not be behind that locked office door.

Or dead.

Chapter 18

Callie

REACHING THE restaurant area, Callie expected to find it vacant due to the tourist exodus. Instead it teemed with guests. Each and every table filled.

Jackie and Tito scurried between tables and the kitchen, Riley's same frustration clear in their expressions. Grabbing Tito's arm the third time he ran by, Callie asked, "What's going on?"

He glanced at Jackie, expecting to be scolded for the sidebar. "Mr. Shaw announced meals were free to keep guests from bailing. Rose called in sick, and we can't get the night people to come in after the news started spreading." He tried to turn and bolt.

Callie wouldn't release him. "Where's your boss? Mr. Shaw."

He shrugged and tore off when Jackie called from the kitchen.

Callie scouted the dining area, not finding Slade, Largo, or Roberts. Movement outside attracted her to a window, but instead of Drummond carrying on like before, a dolled-up reporter and her cameraman performed, him filming her while walking backwards—guests giving them almost a parade-route greeting and hoping to be seen in the background on the six o'clock news.

And still no sign of Sweet. So she called him. Took four calls for him to pick up.

"Callie?" he answered, winded.

"Meet me in your office," she said, a little frustrated at the man.

He spoke to someone else with him at the same time.

"Sweet! I said, 'Meet me in your office.'" Guests at the nearest two tables cut irritated glances at her.

"Busy," he said. "Doing my best to keep the guests from leaving."

He'd last seen her in uniform, and he wouldn't want a cop flaunting around the premises, so she used the hollow threat. "Yeah, but I need to talk to you. Now. And I don't think you want a uniform yanking you aside in public."

He answered someone's concern then put his mouth back to the phone. "Give me fifteen."

With those fifteen minutes to spare, Callie returned to the kitchen and walked in without invitation. Three cooks struggled to feed two dozen guests cramming the dining room, so they had no time to shoo her out. After five minutes of opening doors and analyzing prep areas, she tucked herself to the side of the kitchen and did a search on her phone. Not only did it all just seem like green stuff to her, but there were different kinds of hemlock. Damn. Her limited expertise wouldn't recognize squat.

Jackie whirled in and helped throw the last of two plates together, as adept as any of the cooks. Callie instinctively hunted for pimiento cheese on the plates before spotting scrambled eggs and parsley, remembering this was breakfast. Hell, didn't Slade say it resembled parsley?

"We really don't have time for you today," said the waitress as she whisked the two plates around Callie and out of the kitchen.

Callie exited and headed toward the lobby, making for Sweet's office around the corner, and bumped into a woman.

"Oh," Slade said. "Sorry. It's a madhouse around here." She gave the chief's civilian garb a once-over. "Didn't recognize you at all. Good cover."

Callie pulled her out of the busyness of the lobby to the side, where she could still see Sweet if he showed. "Have you seen hemlock around here?"

"Didn't think I was working for you anymore."

She had no time for this. "It's a question. A simple question. Yes or no."

"No, I haven't."

Damn it. Callie took a quick hard glare at the ceiling before planting it on Slade. "No, you haven't looked, or no, you haven't identified it."

Slade glowered. "I haven't seen it around the main facility, but otherwise I haven't gone out hunting for it. That good enough?"

Maybe she stepped too hard on this woman, but Callie had no time or patience to care. "I just saw parsley in the kitchen. Or what I thought was parsley."

The glare reduced to concern, even pity. "Good gracious alive, Callie, do you hear yourself overreacting?"

Callie gripped Slade's hand and hauled her inside the kitchen. She pushed Slade toward the prep area. "What do you see?"

Trying not to touch or contaminate the food, Slade wandered from station to station, even opening the refrigerator.

"What are you doing?" fussed a cook, only for Callie to throw up her badge to shut him down.

Returning to the chief, Slade touched her back gently and escorted *her* outside.

"I don't see anything," she said. "I'm not an herbalist or horticulturalist, but I'm not seeing a problem in there. But Callie, listen . . ."

Callie chewed her lip, fists on hips. "They could hide it in a pocket, or bring it in a lunch sack." She studied Slade harder. "You said it wouldn't take much, right?"

"Nope, it wouldn't, but you and I both think this was a one-on-one crime, don't we?"

Slade might be good at her work, but she wasn't trained or sworn law enforcement. "That changes when the criminal worries about being found, or takes issue with those seeking him out. His targets multiply depending on how paranoid he is." Callie hadn't time to train this woman. "That's why I told you and Agent Largo to get out of here. Why haven't you?"

With a short mocking laugh, Slade crossed her arms. "It's only ten till eight. If you wanted me gone before dawn, you could've said so. Damn. We haven't long finished breakfast, all right?"

Callie's eyes widened. "You ate here?"

"I picked off anything green, if that makes you feel better, but I don't eat that junk on my eggs anyway. Besides, don't you think more people would've dropped by now?" Slade laughed once again, but with the chief not finding the humor, the ag investigator gave a deep sound in her throat. "Wow. You're really losing it."

Callie wouldn't take water from this place unless it was bottled and even then she'd test whether the cap had been tampered with. This lulu of a woman wasn't appreciating the risk.

"Oh, get the hell out of here," Callie said. She hadn't seen Sweet and couldn't stand to miss him again. And whether she ticked off Slade and Largo or not, she'd sleep easier with them off-island.

She left for the lobby, but Slade followed.

Someone had cornered Riley again.

"Listen, I get that you're under a lot of stress," Slade said.

"Leave and I'll be under less."

"No," Slade replied, "I won't. Anyway, I talked to Sophie, and she mentioned you had a slight issue with drinking. Not sure if that's part of what's going on here, but we're here to help. Don't let all this—"

Callie stiffened, angry that she did. "Not. Your. Business."

"Hey, earlier you requested my help. Now you can listen to my feedback."

Eyes narrowing, Callie's jaw tightened. "Come again?" This half-baked investigator had her whole attention now. While this Slade person had five inches of height and twenty-five pounds of size on her, Callie had no qualms about showing her who could put who on the ground fastest. She almost itched to make her point, but that would appear like someone trying to prove herself.

"We're here to help," Slade repeated, enunciating each word. "That's all I'm saying. Don't get your panties in a wad."

Her elbow nudged from behind, Callie turned.

"My office," Sweet said without stopping, in an attempt to avoid complaining guests.

"Listen, we're done, and I don't have time to discuss it. I appreciate what you've done," Callie said for no other reason than to have the last word, then left, feeling Slade's gaze on her all the way down the hall.

Callie reached Sweet's office about the time he unlocked it, and they slid inside, him locking the door behind him.

"It already made the early morning news," he said, skirting his way to his safe haven behind the desk. "And I've lost a third of the guests and half the reservations for the next two months. Two housekeeping and one wait staff didn't show for work. Even Marion called in sick." He spoke with animated hands, ultimately embedding them in his long hair. "And of course, Trenton is livid."

"What did you learn about who slipped into Callaway's room, which is still off-limits, right?"

With an abrupt stare, he ceased his emotional gyrations. "With all that's going on, that's what you wanted to talk to me about?"

"That and a waitress named Rose I haven't been able to talk to yet. I assumed she's the one missing. Staff avoiding me raises concern."

"Who says she's avoiding you?"

Okay, okay. Slow down. The man was right.

"Just answer my questions, Sweet," she continued and motioned her chin toward the door. "We have a murder I'm pursuing full throttle. You hear me?"

He froze. "You just said murder."

"I did." Her words were clipped.

He slumped in his chair and whispered, "Holy Mother of God. How?"

If she told him those details first, she'd never keep his interest. "Tell me who got into the room after you told everyone to leave it closed?"

He blew out and coughed, as if he choked on words he worried about saying.

His nerves, her tension, they weren't working well together, and she knew better how to run an interview. Callie eased her shoulders, hoping that the appearance of her guard going down would lower his. She'd let all this get under her skin too deep. He would mirror her stress.

"The housekeeper said she misplaced her entry key sometime late in the day," he said.

"Which day?" she asked softly.

"The day Callaway died. She has no idea how it went missing, but the next morning someone had placed it in her locker, which had her thinking someone found and returned it. But the system shows her key was used after she lost it and left for the day."

Meaning anyone could've entered and taken those notes, to include the housekeeper herself. Callie wished she'd taken Callaway's notes the first time they'd entered the room, but they hadn't learned Callaway'd been murdered. Now reporters had everyone flustered, and anyone she interviewed would be worried about blowback on themselves.

What a screwed up case. A screwup that could inevitably be blamed on her instead of on the Charleston Sheriff's Office where the case should have remained.

"Is this housekeeper here?" she asked.

"Yes," he said. "But like I said—"

"I'll hear it from her." What Sweet said the woman told him, and what was fact, could be totally different things.

Someone knocked on the door.

"Be out in a minute." Sweet yelled a tad louder than seemed his nature, then to Callie said with a tired disgust, "Now, what about a murder?"

She was feeling fifty/fifty about telling him much. The culprit could be enjoying this melee, maybe having leaked the news him or *her*self, or in the complete opposite, have skedaddled five states distant, congratulating himself hourly that he got away. He. This was poison. This could just as easily be a woman. They tended to use poison more often than men, but poison was far from a popular weapon of murder in either sex.

"Callaway was poisoned," she said. "And we believe the food might've been fixed in your kitchen."

He didn't even ask what type of poison. Instead, he let his head drop, and sat there like that. "We're done. Not even thirty days open, and we're done."

Callie couldn't deny that Indigo was seriously damaged by all this, but as calloused as it seemed, she couldn't weigh the fallout. The case had advanced too far, the murder too premeditated, the risk too high to let Indigo's future be other than a passing thought. And that pained her. She'd seen the B&B as opportunity for the island and its people.

"I'm considering shutting down the restaurant," she said. "I don't have the details from the coroner yet about how much, what form, how it might have been prepared. Waiting on Roberts for that."

"Shit," he whispered, not raising his head, almost as if he hadn't heard.

"Where can I find the housekeeper?" she asked.

He finally made eye contact. "You'll find her cleaning all the empty rooms. Her name is Iris." Leaning on a fist, he asked, "What else?"

"I'll need to talk to your chef, then Jackie again, and whoever comes up in the conversation. As for Rose, care to try and coax her in?"

"Sure," he said, dejection pressing down on his posture like a wet blanket.

Just like Sweet, she had once pinned her hopes on a perfect career choice only to have it snatched away. From a glorified Boston detective to unemployed to embattled small beach police chief. Ultimate highs and pitiful lows, with nobody able to convince her one day it would be all right. When the sky is falling, you don't see the sun.

With a hand on his, she promised, "I'll keep you up to date best I can, okay?"

While she conducted face-to-face meets, Marie researched staff histories, the task's urgency intensified by the appearance of the press. Callie needed to speed her up.

Sweet slid his hand from under hers. Waved for her to go.

With that she left, heart heavy, to begin a round of questioning people who were probably a day or two from being unemployed. Because if she didn't start putting pieces together, with such hubbub, she didn't expect the killer to stay around for much longer, *if* they were still there. And once the killer left Charleston County, the sheriff would be almost as happy as if she'd caught the guy.

Coincidentally enough, she found Iris on Callaway's hall. Though she wore an Indigo blue housekeeping uniform, she flaunted a white iris wedged above her left ear. A white that shined big and bright against a puffy, glossy cheek of dark brown skin.

"Iris?" Callie asked.

The wide hips turned, a smile broad and pleasant, like she'd hug anyone within reach. "Yes'm? What can Iris do for you?"

The third person reference seemed to work, as if she were a benevolent deity, hidden on earth to be stumbled upon. Extracting her badge from her pants pocket, Callie flashed the shield.

Iris squinted. "Um hum?"

Motioning to the empty room beside them, Callie asked, "Can we talk?"

They entered, and Callie pushed the door shut.

When Iris faced Callie, the smile vanished. "Been wondering when the po-lice was gonna show up. What, you think someone took my keycard and robbed a guest? Well, all I can say, honey, is that it was gone at the end of the day and back the next morning."

Primed for questioning, and surprisingly not asking about Callaway's death. "Did you report the stolen card?" Callie asked.

The housekeeper leaned forward at the challenge. "Who said it was stolen? Coulda lost it and then it got found."

"But it was used that evening. What time did you leave that day?"

Iris didn't flinch. "Five-thirty. That's when I always leave. Gotta sit my grandbaby so my daughter can go to her night job. When was the card used?"

"A little after six."

"Hmph. I stopped by my ATM and got twenty dollars to give my daughter. If I can't find the receipt, I'll get the bank to give me something. Does that settle down your britches?"

Callie gave a reactive cringe as a memory flooded in. In grade school she was scared to death to cross Miss Peaches or break any of her house-cleaning rules, but she fondly recalled the fruity scent that smothered her when hugged against that ample bosom after a bad dream.

"If you could bring that receipt, I'd appreciate it," Callie said then thanked the woman. Check that one off. Too many people to see. Each one, like Iris, requiring a follow-up to completely rule them out.

In the lobby, the agitated crowd had died down with some people probably changing their minds due to the free food. Others already checked out and gone. The dining room in all its blues and whites had half cleared, looking every bit as prim, proper, cool, and vacation special as it had that first day Callie came in and met Raysor.

Still no Roberts. No call, no text, no appearance. She could hope he researched Callaway's past or met with the coroner. Anything other than ignoring her.

Jackie swooshed by. "Not now," she spat out in a hurry, leaving Callie behind.

The hell with this. Mid-morning and she had way too much to do. Waltzing through the kitchen entryway to snare Jackie for a chat, she drew up and measured two cooks at the grill, then one coming out of the freezer. She chose the pudgiest, the eldest, figuring he'd be the one who'd taste-tested his own recipes the longest.

"You're the head cook, right?"

"Chef," he corrected. "Roger McManus."

She showed her badge. "Were you working two days ago?"

He wiped his hands on a towel tucked in his apron tie, then after a quick shot of sanitizer, rubbed them and reached out to her. His grip was fleshy, firm, very warm. As pretentious as Roberts, he stared down his nose at Callie's petite frame, making her feel like he pondered ways of stomping her.

She got it. Nobody liked being questioned by the police, much less by one who they thought they could pick up and break in two. "Care to go someplace private?"

He shook his head. "Nothing to hide, little lady. Shoot me your questions so I can get back to work . . . while I have a job. I suspect you're here about Callaway?"

"Yes," she said, not shocked this guy had heard who the floater was. Both were culinary specialists with the dead one having once had the power to push the other into an unemployment line. "Did you prepare a picnic lunch that day for Mr. Callaway?" she asked.

His nose upturned, he gave his head a toss, his pinned back long hair swishing behind. "I have no idea for whom these meals are made. We use room and table numbers. We did prepare a take-out that day though. With it being this hot, most people choose to eat in the dining room, so I recall thinking someone crazy taking a meal in this heat."

"Who prepared it?" she asked.

"Why, I did," he said, a hint of nerves crawling into the creases around his eyes. "Jackie said it had to present especially nice, so I gave it my personal consideration. Why?"

"Just a piece of the puzzle," she said. "We're stymied as to his cause of death, so it's a slow process recreating the details of his last day, down to and including when and what he ate . . . and with whom." With a careful study, she let that settle into his brain. "So what was the meal?"

"Pimiento cheese on a ciabatta roll. Pickled okra on the side. Pecan tart for dessert. Simple. For two." He relaxed just a bit. "I suspected he had a guest he was trying to impress. With it being Addison Callaway—and honest to God, I had no idea before this morning's news—I could surmise that he was testing our take-out capabilities, which really was not fair considering it's August." He thought a second. "Or he simply entertained a lady. He had a reputation for snaring one at every venue, you know. A lusty bastard."

Good. Relaxed enough to gossip. No suspicion of poison. And thank goodness, Roberts didn't seem to have let that leak out.

"How was your special picnic delivered? Where? Or was it picked up?" she asked.

His wave motioned toward the dining room. "Ask Jackie. She oversaw that."

Her next move, regardless of how busy the head waitress was.

A short scream reached them from the same direction. Then a woman's yell. "Someone help, please!"

Chapter 19

Callie

CALLIE BOLTED OUT of the kitchen. A sinewy middle-aged man had stood from his table lurching forward, then rocking back. He fought for the best position to find air, his face already darkened. Across from him, his dining partner, a short, plump woman his age, half sat and half stood hollering in a panic. "Somebody do something!"

Jackie ran across from the other side of the room. "Sir? Can you breathe?"

He shook his head, grabbing at his throat.

"Can you cough?" she asked, in a firm but no-nonsense tone.

Clawing at his neck in desperation, he ignored her, eyes circles of panic, a blue discoloration around his mouth. The dining partner yelled, "He can't answer you. Do something!" Everyone in the room rose, craning.

Callie turned to the chef. "Call 911. Now!" But when she approached to assist, Jackie had already positioned herself behind the guy, arms around his midsection, one fist gripped in the other as she thrust pressure into his abdomen right under his ribs. Once, twice. Her height matching his, she squeezed with an uncanny strength.

Callie held her breath like everyone else. Poison or not? Premeditated or accident? Too many people sat in there having eaten food prepared on the same counter as Callaway's picnic lunch. What were the odds, or should she have not even played those odds at all and closed the place the instant Roberts delivered the coroner's findings?

A third thrust. Nothing. Whimpers came from a woman near the door. The chef stood in front of the hostess podium, phone to his ear, relaying events to an operator.

Tears pouring down her face, the dining partner gripped the table's edge, frozen as to what to do.

Then on the fourth jerk, a wadded piece of material flew out of the choker's gaping mouth, landing six feet away beside another diner who side-stepped as if it were a grenade.

Callie took a breath. The whole room took a collective breath.

Easing the man into his chair, Jackie pulled another in front of him, cooing how everything was all right. The partner ran around to join, with another diner donating his seat to her.

"An ambulance is on its way," Callie said, her heart beating almost as fast as the victim's. She held out a napkin to the crying woman.

Reluctantly, Callie turned to the room, holding her badge, slowly displaying it from her right to her left. "I'm sorry, folks, but we must close the kitchen. Don't take even one bite from your food. Just stand and leave in an orderly fashion. Police and an ambulance will be arriving shortly. We appreciate your cooperation."

Grumbles started. Some just uttered. Nobody seemed to put two and two together to suspect the food prep an issue. People patted the choking guy as they passed, wishing him the best. Several stared at Callie like she'd accused them of a misdeed, unhappy having been denied their free meals.

"Thanks, everyone," she added, though nobody cared for the gratitude.

At the open door, a voice was heard before Callie saw its owner, but she had no doubt as to the person. "What the hell, Chief," he said, announcing himself in his deepest crowd-controlling tone.

Callie met him halfway. "We had a man almost die at his table. Ambulance on its way. In light of recent events," she said, "I decided to close the kitchen. Better safe than sorry in light of Callaway since we aren't sure if this was simply a choking incident."

Roberts's glower tried to knock her back, and she fully expected another tirade of accusations, but instead he yanked out his phone. "This is Detective Roberts. Get me Sheriff Mosier. Now."

She didn't need to hear the conversation. The bellow had stopped people from exiting, guests eager to see who dared challenge the police, and when some saw two badges, the mystery became even more interesting. Outside, people scurried from one to another, relaying their version of events. Callie thought she saw the same reporter and her cameraman from earlier through the cluster of tourists. Tourists who mulled and chatted to each other like they'd arrived at a family reunion instead of never having seen each other before.

Aww, damn. There was Alex, talking at her camera, easing her way around people with smooth moves, fighting to keep the lens steady as she approached the restaurant. With the young reporter being a blogger at heart, Callie suspected a live broadcast on Facebook within the minute.

"Shut and lock that door," Callie shouted to Tito.

The waiter ran over and did as asked, but that didn't stop observers in the lobby from crowding the entrance from the other side.

Callie returned to Jackie. "Is he okay?"

Jackie nodded. "I believe so."

Running a palm over her face, Callie took a cleansing breath. "Impressive, Jackie. You thought quickly and saved his life."

"Just glad I had the training," she said. "It was mandatory at one place I worked before. They—"

"A word, Chief?" Roberts said in a less than mellow tone.

Stiffening, Callie turned to the man. "We cannot risk—"

"You're fired." The words came out loud, crisp, and full of effort to inform those in the room of the message as well.

"You can't fire me," she said, teeth clenched, holding her voice civil while fighting the craving to break his arm off and beat him with it.

He leaned in. "I damn sure can from this case. Sheriff says you stepped way over the line closing down Indigo. Out of your league. Arrogant. Impulsive. Just a few of his words, not mine."

"Of course not," she said, fighting the warmth crawling up her neck. Again her pulse. Throbbing. Double-time. "We need to talk in private. We have things to discuss. You've been running your own investigation, I believe, and we need to share notes."

He bent over, and with his mouth inches from her ear, growled, "Don't care. You're officially out of your jurisdiction, lady, and not welcomed in ours." Then straightening, he canvassed the room. "Ladies and gentleman, we apologize for the misunderstanding. The kitchen remains open." Then, "Hey, kid," he said to Tito. "Open the door. Tell those people outside there's been a mistake."

Tito froze, then looked out at the tourists. I figured he hated the thought of walking into a deluge of inevitable questions from diners.

Sweet, however, appeared, walked past him and opened the door. "Anyone wanting breakfast or early lunch is welcome to come in and dine. On the house." Then he told Tito, "Tell that to anyone who asks, sits, or even thinks they might be hungry, you got it?"

"Yes, sir," the kid said.

Seeing the manager made guests instantly overcome fears, and the room almost filled within minutes with eager expectation of compensation for inconvenience.

Sweet reached his two detectives in three long, purposeful steps. "What the hell?" he said under his breath. "Can we take this to my office?" Then with that buttery smile on a suntanned face, he went to the man who'd choked. "Would you care to wait in your room, sir? You still have a room, right? Don't think you want medics checking you out in front of all these people."

The man stated they still had a room, and Sweet asked if he could escort them to it, begging them to stay another two nights at no cost. But as Sweet headed toward the lobby, he turned to his two detectives. "Ten minutes."

Roberts bowed up, starting to retort, but Callie snatched his sleeve. "Don't. People are watching. Sweet's had enough catastrophes in one day, so let's move this out of the dining room."

Pretending to have no further concern, Callie exited. Not to be left alone in the aftermath, Roberts followed. Silently, they navigated the lobby down the hall to Sweet's office. Callie entered as if Roberts didn't exist, faced the window, and watched the Lowcountry jungle several dozen yards in the distance.

She wasn't sure what to say to the man, this adversarial partner she'd acquired. A man so not to her liking.

When she didn't open a dialogue, he said, "What the hell were you doing back there?"

"Not now," she said, and left it like that. For now she preferred to think . . . and to chill. She'd stirred a ruckus, for sure, but she still felt the threat of poison, delivered via food, warranted closing the dining area. But maybe she'd jumped too quick to announce it without discussion with Sweet.

As promised, Sweet soon blew into his office like he had a strong wind behind him. Callie remained standing to better address the expected emotional fallout. Then, as if to sit was a sense of submission, Roberts joined her and stood to her side.

Silence hung a moment. From the outside looking in, Callie suspected they appeared as three professionals with the same charge . . . solve a murder, avoid the press, right a wrong. But Callie couldn't swear she understood the privy, internal workings of the two men. Sweet worked for deep-pocket owners with a new venture at stake. Roberts seemed driven by forces she didn't comprehend, because if he solely acted out of spite and scorn, he was way more shallow than she had first given him credit for.

"Roberts," she started. "Callaway deserves our united intentions, using all our resources. There's a sick idiot out there who thinks they got away with killing. Someone who followed Callaway here is my guess, which is serious premeditation. Otherwise, someone recognized him and capitalized on the opportunity. Either way, their head isn't right." She paced the meager eight-foot span between the desk and cherry bookcase, reaching out to finger a tiny brass statue of a palmetto tree. "You think I can't investigate, and I don't exactly believe your way is covering all bases." She set down the tree. "Sweet, you called me in and now I'm gone? What would your all-knowing-and-powerful-Oz of a boss think about that?"

Sweet made little eye contact with her. A lot piled on his shoulders? Or pondering options?

"What he thinks no longer matters," Roberts said. "Fact is, the sheriff asked you on this case, and now he's saying you're no longer needed. Regardless of what Mr. Shaw here thinks. I'm investigating the employees and guests, seeing if any of them met Callaway before."

"Exactly," she said, but without telling him she had Marie doing the same at the beach. Something Roberts should've delegated to his own staff all along.

"You're done," Roberts spouted.

Callie peered over at Sweet.

"I have to agree," he said.

Heat drifted from her collar. "Feeling a bit used here, guys. Am I not doing enough, or is it more like I'm digging too hard?"

"In your dreams," Robert said, laughing on the end.

But Sweet only sat there, watching. She couldn't read his mind, but she recognized a mixture of confusion in those eyes. She let the silence grow.

"I'm just answering to the boss," he finally said. "He asked for you, it went sideways, and he no longer thinks he can afford you." He slowly blinked, as if his brain were tired. A man caught in the middle.

But two days since the death and Trenton was unsatisfied? It was inevitable the story would leak to the press, and she'd damn sure attempted to stopper it, but between Marion's talkative nature and Roberts's scorn, the news didn't spread . . . it exploded. Dumping her would make them lose ground, assuming their interest was solving the case.

And leaving the restaurant open meant politics reared its ugly head again.

"The kitchen needs inspection," she said after the long, drawn out pause between them. "And the property for hemlock."

Roberts stood braced, feet wide, silent. What the hell was wrong with him?

"Somebody needs to immediately interview Rose," she added. "That was my next step. She's a strong person of interest."

"Who's Rose?" he asked.

Who's Rose? He was supposed to be checking out staff, too. She turned to Sweet. "Did you try to contact her?"

"No" came the reply, the cavalier expression telling Callie he'd forgotten the request not long after it left Callie's mouth.

"Have either of you asked Jackie about her role in dealing with Callaway?"

Neither replied.

She could walk off, shout damn to the both of them, flip them the bird, but that accomplished nothing. She sensed with more than an inkling of concern that her dismissal was a first step in sweeping away the case. Making it disappear. Taking care of a rich man's investment, a manager's job, a detective's pride, and a sheriff's reputation.

She could read it in Sweet's eyes and Roberts's smirk . . . no one in here cared a scrap for justice.

Only one other time in her life had she had to walk away like this. Three years ago, when a Russian in Boston put a bullet in her husband's head, burned their house to the ground, and then died of a heart attack, denying her the satisfaction of taking him down. She about went mad from it all. The incompleteness tore her up and cost her a career, sending her back South.

But when a Russian relative pursued her, she didn't care about jurisdiction. She didn't even have a badge at the time, but she nailed him. Unsolved murder was one thing. But unsolved murder slipping through her fingers was another.

"Chief?" Sweet stood from his desk. "I have business to attend to."

Roberts grinned, not having to speak to make his point.

"Roberts, you can't afford to ruin this. In talking with these Indigo people, I've learned—"

"Our problem," he said.

On that she couldn't disagree.

"Nice working with you two," she finally said, leaving the door open wide behind her.

But where to now? Anyone else would give Roberts, Sweet, and the whole bloody crew their back, tell them to stuff it, and reap what they sow.

Pride wasn't the point here. She'd overcome that issue long ago. In the year she'd functioned as Chief for Edisto Beach, she'd almost lost her job more times than she could count, and she couldn't quite explain why she didn't give them her back either. Other than she knew she was more talent than they'd ever find and the best they could afford . . . by a long shot.

But even more, for personal sanity, she needed to live on Edisto, and just watching the tides change day in and day out wasn't her idea of life. She needed purpose. Seabrook dragged that out of her by relentlessly coaxing her to reclaim a badge, making her see she had to apply herself to regain her self-respect. Now that he was gone, she maintained the job as much in honor of him as for herself.

And Edisto Island was part of that vigil, because without the island there was no beach. It couldn't become a place where bodies disappeared and crimes went unsolved. How was she to walk away with so many loose threads—threads she had little hope of Roberts tying up?

She sat at the nearest empty table in the dining room, pondering.

Jackie brought her a water. "Someone seems in dire need of ice cream."

"Yes, bring me your favorite," she said. "Doesn't matter which kind it is."

She figured the ice cream came in its own container with least chance of contamination. That allayed her fears, that and Slade's daring-do to eat breakfast here.

In slow deliberate bites, Callie slid the banana praline dessert off its spoon, weighing options.

She could keep searching now, or possibly stumble upon the real answer somewhere downstream and kick herself for walking away.

Jackie and Tito continued to run table to table, never missing a beat with one staff down. Rose was scared to come in, they'd said. She might never come in. Callie took another bite and swallowed, thought harder about Rose, then turned the spoon over and licked it.

"What are you doing?" Slade said, sliding in across from her.

"Thought you were leaving."

Largo pulled out the chair beside Slade, curious. "What's happened?"

Callie took another bite. "I got fired from the case."

Slade reared back. "What?"

"Because of the press?" Largo asked.

Pointing her spoon at the tall man, Callie winked with sarcasm. "I see why you're Senior Special Agent."

With a heavy sigh, he leaned elbows on the table. "Politics is a bitch."

"That never stopped me," Slade said.

"Slade, not the place," Largo warned, and Callie let go a sad quiet chuckle at the now familiar dynamics between these two that really didn't matter anymore.

Waving off her lawman, Slade hunched forward. "Seriously. I just ignore whoever tells me no."

"She's not you," he said. "She's a legitimate—"

With a slap to his arm, Slade interrupted the remark. "If you tell me she's a real badge and I'm not, and that it makes a big difference whether you follow through on something you feel strongly about, then we're going home in two cars."

"We only have one car," he said, with half a grin creeping up the side of his face.

Slade frowned. "My daddy lives not too far, Cowboy. He might not take too kindly to you leaving his little girl stranded."

"He'll listen to me sooner than you, I bet," came his retort.

"Regardless," and Slade turned to Callie. "I once had a case in Beaufort—"

"Go home, Slade." Callie finished the last bite and set the spoon in the cup.

"What?"

"I said go home."

Slade and Largo couldn't help staring at each other. "You're not quitting, are you?" Largo asked.

"It's Roberts's problem." Callie pushed her chair from the table.

Largo continued to stare. She ignored it and left, her shoes squeaking on the polished wood.

They were baggage, she told herself. Nice, off-beat, generous to assist, but baggage.

She expected soon to be banned from the property. Did she keep going or not? If so, her time was now.

Her phone rang as she entered the lobby. The caller ID only angered her more.

Hustling to a corner, she turned away from the room. "What is it, Brice?"

"Since when are you working for Charleston County? We've got tourists running rampant at the beach that employs you, and you're carousing at that new resort? Hired by money? Double-dipping? The next council meeting isn't for two weeks, but nothing says I can't call an emergency summit about all this."

"Oh, shut the hell up." The shaking phone showed he'd gotten under her skin.

"What did you say?"

"Must be a bad connection on your end, because it was pretty damn clear on mine. Shut up, Brice. I've been asked to consult."

"Um, um. Got you now."

Brice had nothing, but he had a gift of turning shit into gold. At least on Edisto Beach.

Sweet walked through the room, and she turned aside. "I don't have time for your crap," she grumbled into the cell.

"Fine, don't take time for me. But you'll have to take time when I serve you a notice to be at the next meeting and discuss how you disregarded your duties and abandoned us. Again."

God, how many times was this man going to threaten her with that old trope? He'd followed through once and lost. But it wouldn't take long for the citizenry to tire of the small town battle between them, and assume where Brice found smoke there might eventually be fire. Then she'd be fired.

She'd been without a badge before. Developed a passion for gin. It wasn't pretty.

"Do what you gotta do, Brice."

"First thing I'm doing is calling the sheriff," he said. "Giving him a piece of my mind. Then you'll—"

She cut him off.

She threw her thoughts into overdrive. With Roberts on one side of her and Brice on the other, she had little time to follow through with any sort of plan. With a text, she ordered Marie to jump on the employee backgrounds ASAP. What a time to be without her patrol car and its computer. She texted again: *Shoot me the driver's licenses of the staff, starting with the wait staff, the cooks, and housekeeping.*

These were the ones with the best access to Callaway's food.

Time dwindled too quickly. Going out in search of Rose would kill all sorts of it, too, when Rose might not even be a concern. Callie might not find her, or get stonewalled. The day would be shot.

Her phone vibrated. Pictures coming through in texts. Driver's licenses. Damn, Marie was efficient.

Jackie, check. Lived in Charleston. Picture jived.

Tito, check. Lived on Edisto. Younger image but it was him.

Rose . . . lived on Edisto . . . but the picture took Callie by surprise.

Young, light-skinned black girl. Twenty-one. Pretty. Gold, short hair.

Callie scanned the room. To her left was Riley. To her right the male clerk at the desk. Jackie was just in the other room. With no time to spare, best to pick the brains here in the few moments she had left.

If she could trust the boat rental guy, Rose fit the description of Callaway's boating companion. *Son of a bitch.* She regretted urging Roberts to interview the waitress now. She bounced her cell on her chin, thinking, thinking. *Damn it!*

She could pray he'd ignore the suggestion on the merits that she suggested it. Hope against hope. But he could more easily pursue Rose *because* of the suggestion. Not bothering to connect the dots.

Maybe Rose did it. Maybe she didn't, but Indigo, and therefore the sheriff, needed someone to pin this murder on to save face, money, reputation, and the next election. Why not go with the easiest and quickest solution in the form of a low-income local who worked for minimum wage?

Callie's gut told her this murder was being quickly minimized by higher-ups with too much at stake.

Chapter 20

Callie

CALLIE APPROACHED check-in where a lone guy about thirty tended to whatever clerks tended behind the counter at hotel desks. He straightened when Callie approached. "Can I help you?"

"How do I find Rose?" Callie asked without badge or law enforcement air. "Didn't see her in the dining room where she waited on me before, and I promised to get something for her."

Reaching forward to lay forearms on the bar-level counter, he engaged. "I can take whatever it is and get it to her. She's not in today."

He sported a wedding ring. Callie didn't see much one-on-one time between these two, much less the exchange of confidences. "It was a website address, plus I said I'd locate some options . . . a little too much to write down on a post-it-note, if that makes sense." Feigning consternation, she waited for the desk clerk to offer assistance. Service staff were trained to solve problems. *Come on, dude.*

"Rose and I haven't talked much," he began, "but Riley might have. She has her finger on more goings-ons around here, plus she's closer to Rose's age. Maybe she can say when Rose reports in . . . or can relay the message." He gave a faux-expression of pity with a nice twinkle. "Sorry I couldn't help more."

Callie glanced at the concierge where Riley had returned and was putting away her purse.

The desk clerk straightened, craning his neck. "Hey, Riley."

The girl perked.

"Can you help this lady? She's hunting for Rose and has something for her."

Callie leaned over the counter. "Thanks so much." She hurried to the concierge who waited with a mildly puzzled smile.

"Chief Morgan?" she asked, unsure of the situation, her concern darting around the room until Callie stepped in front of her to capture her focus.

"How well do you know Rose?" she asked.

A shrug. "Enough to eat together, maybe talk dating sometimes. She only graduated high school, while I finished college. Sort of puts us on different levels?" she said, finishing on a question mark.

"Hear why she didn't come in to work?" Callie asked.

Another shrug. "Not a word. She's been rattled, though. Real rattled. Like if you spooked her from behind she'd wet her pants?"

The girl seemed likeable enough but that conversational style made her come across like a ditz. "How long?"

"Since, you know, the day that man died? But actually, a lot of us are rattled about that, so she's not the only one. After seeing how insane it got today, she seems like the smart one not coming in. Probably job hunting, something I might need to be doing."

The unspoken fear of unemployment had wormed its way through everyone at Indigo, for sure. "Had she served him? Talked to him? What did she think of Addison Callaway?"

That took Riley by surprise. "Have no idea about that, why?" Her voice took a conspiratorial tone. "Is she involved? Did he hit on her, too? God, that man was a sleaze."

Callie studied the young eyes for tells and saw nothing. "Not that I'm aware of, Riley. I was just asking questions I'd ask anyone. Don't mind speaking ill of the dead, huh?"

She gave a dramatic puff of a scoff. "Are you kidding? Not in the least. He'd, like, whisper these come-ons. Reminded me of something oily and dirty. Flat out harassed me every time he walked through."

"Thought he just asked you out once?"

That produced a laugh, and the desk clerk glanced over. Riley reined in her voice. "He kept trying. I mean, the perv had no concept of the word no."

"Maybe he came onto Rose, too?"

"Have no idea." Her shoulders eased. "Want her phone number?"

At the unexpected offer, Callie perked. "Sure. Thought you weren't close."

With a squint of her eyes and wrinkle of her nose, she scrolled through her phone as Callie pulled out hers. "Poor thing has unreliable transportation, and I've brought her to work a few times. Twice. She comes in way earlier than I do, so I'm sort of a last resort."

"Appreciate it." Callie typed in the number. "Speaking of missing staff, where's your boyfriend?" She tried to stay tuned to her phone to lessen Riley's curiosity, and waited to see what the girl had to say about

Marion. "He's cute. Not hard on the eyes at all." Then she smiled at the girl, as if to compliment her taste in men.

But instead, the question garnered a frown. "Jury's still out about him."

"Aww," Callie said. "Thought y'all made a cute couple."

A flip of her hair. "While I like chivalry and all that, he hovered. I kept telling him I wasn't his possession, but he kept saying cops have a sixth sense, and he understood people better than I did. He could protect me and all that. You realize how many psychology classes I took at school?" She blew out in indignation. "And him not even a real cop. I didn't even tell him about that morning Mr. Callaway *really* hit on me. Marion would've played the whole white knight thing and gone overboard with someone we had to respect as a guest, and the doofus would've lost his job." She touched her chest. "I might've lost *my* job."

Acting motherly, Callie widened her eyes. "Just how many times did this man hit on you? Did you report him?"

"Shoot," she said. "You can't do anything about that he-said-she-said stuff. He wasn't going to be here long, and from what I heard on the news this morning, that guy could've ripped this place to shreds with one of his posts." She stood and stepped around the desk and lifted a paper, pretending to show Callie details about the local attractions. "Between you and me . . ." and she paused. "You're not recording me, are you? I mean, this isn't an actual interrogation or anything?"

Callie gave the girl a serious quick shake of her head.

"Well," Riley said. "The night before, you know, he died, he came to me and told me I needed to show him the sights. I tried to nicely decline, but he wasn't having it, him bragging about his connections, that he would reward me with a better job offer in Charleston or even Atlanta. Wanted me to go boating with him the next morning. What made him think I'd spend five seconds with him here, much less half a day in a boat? I told him how to rent a boat, even suggested they'd find him someone to captain it for him since he said he'd never driven a boat before." Another little dramatic shake of her hair. "Just because I grew up out here doesn't mean I can maneuver a boat. I always let my daddy see to all that. Anyway, I said no, then said no again, but he left laughing. I forgot about him until I arrived at work the next day."

She eased closer to Callie's ear. "Then he shows up in the morning, struts his sorry ass self over to me and says he's talked to management, ordered a picnic lunch, and they approved me to be his guide for the day."

No question mark on the end of that sentence.

Callie showed the appropriate amazement and whispered. "What'd you do?"

"I ran to Jackie." The girl spoke in statements now, her words clearly truthful.

Itching to ask why Jackie, Callie let the story unwind. "Oh my, then what?"

Riley dipped her chin. "I hid in the ladies' room for an hour. That's what Jackie said to do and that she'd cover for me. When I came out, he'd left. Was horribly worried the whole rest of the day, waiting for him to come back and report me."

"Oh, my gosh," Callie said.

"Yeah. Can you believe it? If I'd gone out with him, I might've died, too." A shiver must've crawled over her shoulders, because she rotated them a little bit then settled herself down.

The desk clerk glanced over again, pausing just long enough for Callie to recognize the need to move on and make light of the moment. "Well, I'm glad you're all right," she said and rubbed the girl's arm, meaning it. She lifted her phone. "And thanks for Rose's number. That was sweet of you."

Riley acknowledged with a warm smile. "Thanks for letting me vent about that."

And Callie wondered why the girl didn't just spill all that the day before. "Honey, someone was watching over you that day. You take care."

"Yes, ma'am."

Callie left the lobby, disappearing in the same ladies' room that had harbored Riley in her hour of need. Locked in a stall, she rehashed the conversation in her head. Yes, she needed to speak to Rose, but the chat with Riley had shifted importance to someone right here on the plantation. Callie had spoken with Jackie yesterday, and she'd never mentioned this Riley-situation.

And Callie wanted to learn why. While she was still on Indigo property.

The dining room had settled, but instead of letting herself be seen there, she slid into the kitchen, hiding behind a large cabinet. She'd risked enough already standing in the open with Riley.

Jackie breezed in, moving as if in a hurry, dropped an order, grabbed a soft drink, then left. Callie tailed her to the breakroom and shut the door before Jackie could spot she'd been followed.

"What . . . oh," she said, recognizing Callie. "You unnerved me for a second. Feeling better? Told you ice cream was a cure-all."

"Can we talk again? I waited until the frenzy died down out there."

"Was going to take my break, but I guess this is good," she said, sat at the table and opened her bottle.

Callie took a seat. "You said Callaway requested a picnic lunch to go."

"Right," she said, eyes on Callie, putting the drink to her lips.

"And the chef said it was pimiento cheese and some other things."

Jackie took a second as if recalling. "I believe that's right, too."

"How was it wrapped?"

The bottle hung in mid-air. "How was it wrapped?"

"Yes. How does Indigo prepare such things and make them special?"

With a mash then release of her lips, Callie could see the waitress deemed the question reasonable. "Okay, we wrap sandwiches in wax paper with a trademark sticker then place them in a little cardboard box. Any side items go into something waterproof, but we do not use Styrofoam. At Indigo we try to be environmentally friendly, just like the indigo dye. Part of the brand is how they explained it to us during orientation. I love that."

"Rather cool," Callie said. "So then what. Such as how do they carry it? In a cardboard box like a tailgate dinner from KFC?"

With a humored bit of condescension, Jackie shook her head. "Think Edisto, my dear. Think the Lowcountry image."

Callie made an effort, but takeout meant bags and boxes to her.

Jackie rested elbows on the table and pleasantly smiled. "Baskets. Sweetgrass baskets."

"Oh . . . wow," Callie said, truly surprised. A genuine sweetgrass basket big enough to contain even a small lunch sold for two hundred dollars on the island. Three in Charleston. "Aren't you afraid those will disappear?" Then she paused. "Did you get that one back?"

"Well . . ." Jackie gave a drawn-out wince. "We haven't seen that one, not that I'm surprised. But we don't dole those out to just anybody, either. He was our first, and his reputation sort of earned him the right, I guess you could say." She took another sip. "Bet we won't be using them much in the future . . . assuming we have a future."

No, Callie wouldn't ask Jackie about Riley. Not quite yet. "How did he get the lunch?" she asked instead.

"I delivered it personally," she said, with aplomb. "While our staff is vetted and reliable, I wasn't putting that sort of financial temptation in front of Tito or Rose. Being locals, they'd recognize its value, and who would be the wiser?"

"Personally," Callie repeated. "You gave it to Callaway and his guest?"

Jackie shook her head. "No, I took it to his room."

"Left it in his room?"

"No, knocked and he answered. No need to use my key. He was there, alone, waiting for the delivery." She took another sip. Callie studied her, waiting to see if there was more to her comment. The quiet dragged.

"Jackie?" Callie finally asked. "What aren't you telling me?"

Pained lines appeared around her features as she made eye contact with the police chief. "I might've been one of the last people he spoke to. Wish I'd noticed more, maybe even asked more. What could I have done to alter the course of events?"

"And the killer could have been in the room with him," Callie said. "Let's worry more about finding the person rather than the what-ifs. Regretting the past doesn't do anyone any good."

A practice Callie understood intimately well.

"What about Rose?" the chief added.

Jackie sat stunned. "Pardon?"

Callie gave a mild frown. "Sorry, I didn't make myself clear. You told me she left early the other day and isn't here today. Has she quit?"

"Oh." The waitress's relief was palpable. "Yes, she did."

"Why?"

"Why? Why does it matter?"

Unusual question. "Tracing every employee, is all. I would've thought this job was a good one for her. A local with a local job, avoiding the Charleston commute."

"Well, I can't answer why." Another swig. The bottle was almost empty and she drank like she was parched. "You'd have to ask her."

"Thanks, hon." Callie rose and opened the door. "I just might do that."

Jackie had helped, whether she realized it or not. They weren't sure where Callaway had his lunch, or with whom, but that basket would not have been thrown in the trash along with sandwich wrappings and napkins. She wished she had time to revisit the person who found the boat. Might still do so, but her next course of action was to get to Rose. See what this girl had seen or heard. Jobs like this weren't common enough to let loose of lightly. Not on this island.

Chapter 21

Slade

WAYNE STOOD TO leave the dining room table, stretching his long self. "Guess the chief made that message clear. Bags are ready to go in the car. How about you?"

I hung back. "We could order a snack."

He gave me a scowl. "We not long ago had breakfast."

"But it's free." Then in a more serious light, I stood, no longer in the mood to joke. "This sucks, Wayne. I refuse to think Callie hates us."

"She doesn't hate us. She just doesn't need us in her way."

I threw my napkin on the table. "But we weren't in her way. She could still use our help."

"You almost drowned. She blames herself, Slade. Plus, we can't be sure of what's driving her, what's going on behind the scenes."

"But—"

He held a finger over my mouth. "And we aren't privileged to it."

We strolled out of the dining area. "I don't trust Roberts. And I don't believe that this famous dude came here, all clandestine to critique a new vacation spot, and accidentally got poisoned. And then they toss the lead investigator on her ear once she starts talking to people?"

"We're completely on the outside," he said. "And I smell lots of politics, just like she said. Let's head home. We can grab barbecue on the way for the kids."

"We could stick around and at least search for hemlock."

"*You* could search for hemlock. I don't have any idea what it looks like. Scared that once I see it, I'll start seeing it everywhere. Already wondering how many times I brushed it going out on so many farm cases."

"Red or purple stems," I said. "Just avoid plants with red or purple stems. I'll teach you. The walk will do us good."

We headed toward the exterior door leading from the dining room straight outside. "Well, you're coming with me anyway. Got your gun?" I asked.

A lady behind us caught my last words and froze. She stared at Wayne holding the door open for her, and reversed, hurrying back into the dining room.

"We're shooting hemlock?" he asked as we exited into the already ninety-degree temperature.

"No, but I'm not dealing with snakes."

He wasn't wearing a weapon, and his jeans fit too good for one to be hidden such that I couldn't see. I was about to ask him where it was, and that if he didn't bring his, I'd go grab my .38 from where I'd hidden it between the mattress and box springs, when a déjà vu walked across the graveled walkway twenty yards ahead.

"Yo ho ho, mateys!"

Capitalizing on the visiting press corps, Drummond had even washed and donned fresh ribbons in his braided beard. Boots polished. Same shirt, but it fluffed more, like it might have been exposed to soap and fabric softener. Amazed me it hadn't shredded in the wash.

While surprised to see him, I shouldn't have been. The press swell represented opportunity for the pirate. What he couldn't gain in reservations, he could acquire in free press. Sooner or later, a reporter would want his take on things, or at least learn who he was and what he was about.

Like now. A reporter headed his way. I started to wander closer to hear what sort of crazy spin he'd put on the Callaway deal, but Drummond bypassed the reporter and headed straight to me.

"Just the lady I wanted to see. Argh." With a swoop, he looped my arm into his and escorted me toward the barn. The reporter, however, continued to trail.

"Give me a second," he mumbled, and let me loose.

With one hand he slid out his cutlass, the other his flintlock, arms stretched wide, and leaped toward the dolled reporter screaming, "I'll have you walk my plank, wench! You hear me!" He jumped at her again. "Try me. See what happens to those who challenge Blackbeard's heir!"

On four-inch heels too high for a scare, the reporter dropped her microphone and did a fast tap dance backwards, a squeal escalating into a full-fledged shriek. Didn't take two steps on those stilettos to pitch her over a low rough-hewn fence between the asphalt and the grass. She sprawled with her skirt tossed around her hips, flashing pink undies.

And several guests caught smartphone footage of it.

Drummond tucked away his weapons, or props, depending on how you perceived them, reclaimed my arm, and escorted me toward the indigo barn. Even after such little time in the August sun, the air conditioning slid deliciously over my skin, sending goose prickles.

On second thought, he held the door open for Wayne. "You're welcome too, my matey."

He led me to the men's restroom, let Wayne follow, then closed the door with his back to it.

"We're in the men's bathroom," I said.

"That be true." He comically bowed. "Better than the ladies with men having different plumbing and all that, don't you think?"

He had me there.

Wayne wasn't charmed. "What's up, Drummond?" He'd been less forgiving of the pirate after the shipwreck in St. Helena Sound.

He peered down, braids falling over his face. "I felt I owed you an apology."

"You think?" I wanted to shove him as memories returned. "You about drowned me."

"Sorry," he said softly.

Images of dark water rushed into my head, my throat closing. Waves forcing water in my mouth. My nose.

Wayne rubbed my back. "Quit thinking about falling in the water, Butterbean."

Someone tried the door.

"Occupied!" Drummond shouted.

I shoved my nose six inches from his. "Your boat almost sank . . . after I got thrown overboard. Because you didn't respect the weather. I'd run you through with your own damn sword if I thought it was real, you damn fake."

"I can't return your money," he said. "At least not now."

Wayne had several inches of height on Drummond, and I swear he puffed himself bigger for effect. "So why'd you bother coming?"

Drummond's fingers played with a ribbon in his hair. "Just hoping you weren't planning to sue."

"I'm not believing this," Wayne said, rubbing his own cropped stubble. "We're holding you to the debt."

"What debt?" the pirate asked.

"Where's a reporter?" I replied.

"No, no," Drummond said. "Don't. It's hard enough as it is, and I'm not sure insurance is gonna cover my damaged ship."

"Ship?" I laughed. "That would almost make Callaway's boat a yacht."

"Callaway?"

I tapped my temple. "Cut the pretense, Blackbeard. Your prints were found on the boat Callaway rented, the reason Detective Roberts picked you up. Count your blessings Chief Morgan covered your butt."

"You found a dead man's boat," Wayne said.

"I found *a* boat," he quickly replied.

"Find anything in it?" the lawman asked. "A camera, for instance? A wallet?"

With a quizzical frown, Drummond hesitated. "Nobody was in it. I told the cops that already."

"No," I said. "What stuff was in it? Trash? Fishing tackle? A picnic basket? Snacks?"

His uncertainty was almost comical. "All this over a damn umbrella?"

Wayne intensely studied him. "No, Drummond," he said. "That boat might've been a murder scene, so keep talking. What else did you find?"

Fingering a knot in his beard, he seemed to take a mental accounting. "Empty water bottles? Well, one empty and the other half full."

How were we supposed to trust this idiot?

Sideways, he gave me the evil eye. "Was there something else of value in the boat?"

"You beat all I ever saw," I said. "Where'd you find it?"

"Past the Interpretive Center." He pointed downstream the river. "It almost got home on its own."

I reached over and tugged one of his chin braids.

He gave me a playacting *ouch,* gathering half his braids, stroking them, a shoulder moving between him and me to avoid another tug. "That's assault."

"So sue *me!*" I leaned toward him. "Argh."

His accent left him, his stance less pirate-ish. "What if I tell you there's something going on at Indigo?"

"Like what?" I asked, fully expecting another con.

Drummond shifted and leaned against the ceramic tiled walls. "In exchange for the fee?"

"In exchange for not suing," Wayne said, poking knuckles into the man's chest.

"Okay, okay. Listen," the pirate started. "I tried to do things legit with Indigo in the beginning. Talked to Shaw about him letting me collect people from their dock, but no, the dock is only for the owners, for

Shaw, and the occasional high-price party. You seen it? Outdoor air conditioning, televisions under a monstrous gazebo. Wonder whose palm they greased to get that thing built over the water? Ain't something they normally allow. Lots of money out there for just the owners. Bet they're writing it all off the business, though."

"You hear anything worthwhile?" I asked Wayne.

He shook his head, mouth pursed. "Nope."

Drummond bobbed his head. "Hold on, give me a chance." He grumbled something inaudible. "Anyway, wouldn't have hurt 'em a damn bit to let me provide their tourists easy access from there instead of going all the way down to the beach."

While I understood the logic, Drummond's private pirate tours weren't exactly the caliber of attraction Indigo represented. Also sort of my thought about them hiring Sophie to do yoga lessons at a place noted for its nineteenth century charm. But while Sophie had the owner in her pocket, I didn't see Drummond performing that trick.

Wayne scrutinized him, one eye narrowed. "I imagine your radar is keen on this island."

"It tis, it tis."

Some of the accent slipped in. Comical.

"You've watched Indigo come to life," Wayne said. "You've studied how to take advantage of that influx of economic opportunity. And excuse me for stating the obvious, but you sound bitter."

"Yeah, so?"

"Who says you didn't kill Callaway? To get back at Indigo. Get rid of the competition."

More pounding on the door, then a muffled cry. "Come on. How long are you gonna be in there?"

"Come with me." I forced the door open and left, the men behind me, the irritated party stunned at the exodus. I led us toward a corner of the barn.

Two guests walked by and did a double take at the pirate. He gave a pretend snarl of a smile at them, reached out, and offered a brochure. When they heard the indigo dye demonstration about to start, he acted like everyone was okayed to leave.

"No, you don't," I said and tugged his sleeve. "We're not done yet."

We'd fallen back into investigative mode, and I was glad. Callie was strapped for compadres. And I kinda liked being out here. Besides, like the meal, it was free.

But Wayne was better at this than I was. He knew it, and I knew it, and I couldn't often help but fuss at how his badge always trumped mine. However, I was learning when to remain quiet.

And Wayne's small smile said he appreciated the gesture. He addressed Drummond. "You're a natural born snoop. Why do you think Callaway died?"

"Fell out the damn boat and couldn't swim," Drummond replied.

Wayne looked deadpan. "You can do better than that. He tried to hire you because he needed a guide and couldn't drive a boat. He wouldn't have gone out alone. Did he say why he wanted to go out to begin with?"

With a toss of his hair, Drummond tried to be just as flippant with his reply. "Me. I'm colorful."

"Yet he couldn't have you and he still went out. Why?"

The pirate stared past us, to those intently listening to the indigo demonstrator. "He wanted to go all the way up the river to Indigo. That's a long way for a damn free ride. But I also turned him down on principle. The owner and his minion are assholes. About sank me. Not two months ago I was cruising the river, sort of scouting treasure sites. Came around the bend and there she was."

"Who?"

"Not who. What. The *Avarice*. Old man Trenton's yacht."

I studied Wayne to see if he made the same connection to the yacht name. He didn't. Trump one up for me.

Greed. Avarice meant greed. "What do you mean the owner about sank you?" I asked.

"They were just finishing that dock, so I took the *Golden Pearl* for a cruise on the river to check things out. Was gonna moor there and see what kind of agreement I could hammer out. Kind of a mutual sharing of skills and customer base." Thumbs slipped in his belt, he thrust out his belly. "Like the Edisto Island Welcome Wagon."

There was no end to this man's hubris. "And what happened?"

"Someone shot at me," he said, with a can-you-believe-that dip of his chin.

I was wary. Wayne waited for the rest of the story.

"I'm serious," Drummond added. "One of those morons put three holes in one of my sails."

"Just one sail?" Wayne asked.

The pirate nodded with vigor, eagerly telling his tale as he made a rough circle motion with his hands. "In a spot about a foot wide."

"Good thing they were bad shots," I said, trying not to sound rattled that people were shooting at each other on our proverbial laid-back island.

Wayne rubbed that wonderful square chin of his again. "Oh, quite the opposite, I'd say. If they grouped that close, that far, they were warning you, Drummond."

"What'd you do?" I asked.

Eyes wide, his answer gushed out almost in cartoon manner. "I got gone is what I did. Skedaddled. Nobody would take my word over all that money. But I figured they couldn't shoot me in front of *witnesses*, so I periodically wander onto the place and pitch customers. Straight through the front door and under their noses." He spit on the ground. "Asswipes."

"So that's why you didn't want to take Callaway on your boat? You were afraid of being shot at again?"

His mouth twisted as he tried to form his thoughts. "No, it was mostly about money, but I followed 'em partways. Wondered who was fool enough to get hired by him." He gave me a mild shrug. "Wanted to see who my competition was."

Holy bejesus. We'd interviewed this fool and endured a storm with him. Callie'd had him in cuffs in her office. I visually queried Wayne who stood there a little stunned, same as I was.

I fought so damn hard not to choke this guy. Fought harder not to yell. "You saw who was in the boat with Callaway?"

"It was a girl," he said.

"A girl? Which girl?" I asked.

He shrugged, and I clenched a fist to avoid slapping his face. "Why didn't you tell anyone about this before?"

With a snort through his nose, he straightened and gave a broad swipe through the air, his white blouson sleeve swinging. "Maybe you'll respect old Drummond now, huh?" He gave us one of those fake pirate chuckles. "Heh, heh, heh."

"I swear . . ." and I reached for his beard again.

Then reverting to his twenty-first century Lowcountry dialect, he added, "Frankly, nobody asked."

Glaring, I exhaled in disgust. "You fool. How old? Description?"

"A slight girl. Short gold hair from what I could see. Made me wonder why she didn't wear a hat. Tanned. Not particularly chummy with him either. Sat rigid as an Indian cigar statue."

"Would you recognize her again?" Wayne asked.

"Probably, and I'll tell you something else nobody asked me about, too," he said, and re-earned my interest. "Nobody's asked what happened to my boat."

And just as quickly, he lost half that interest. "Your boat tried to sink," I replied. "Should've known this was somehow about you and money. Not sure you even saw a girl."

His eyes narrowed, annoyed. "Oh, I saw her all right. Just shut up and listen to me."

Wayne moved in. "Dial it down, pirate."

Drummond gave a toss of his hair. "There was something seriously, mechanically wrong with the boat, I'm telling you."

Probably trying to get out of refunding our payment. "What? Poor maintenance? Cheap jerry-rigging with used parts? You're just trying to get out of being sued."

"Already got out of that by talking with you, remember?"

"You son of a—"

"Sabotage," the pirate said.

Wayne rolled his eyes this time. "Surprise."

"The bilge pumps didn't work."

"Sure."

This time he pushed a finger into Wayne's chest, and the lawman threw his shoulders back as if waiting for a chance to take a punch.

"Pumps. Two of them," the pirate said. "The hoses slit right next to the clamps . . . on both pumps."

Wayne and I sobered. "What exactly did you see that day they shot at you?" I asked.

"Nothing," Drummond replied. "But that doesn't mean I didn't see something a day later."

Chapter 22

Callie

CALLIE HEADED TO Highway 174 away from Indigo. Jackie had described the basket down to the love knots on the side and the Indigo stamp lightly burned into its base, so identifying it as the right basket wouldn't be hard. With that basket could come DNA.

But then someone could've just as easily burned it . . . or tossed it into the river with Callaway. Still, she had a tiny piece of fact to hold onto. All such tiny facts usually meant nothing when first learned . . . but one or two of them often came around in the end.

As much as she disliked the man, she'd connect with the Blackbeard wannabe herself. A year of shooing Drummond off other businesses left her with little trust in any answer he gave her. Assuming he even mattered once she ran down Rose. Assuming Roberts and the sheriff didn't stop her at any step in between.

Her intuition gnawed at her—this case was rapidly being swept under a rug, with her termination having being the first sweep.

While Slade proudly said she pursued cases whether invited or not, Callie didn't take over somebody else's business. However, they'd invited her in, put her in charge, then slammed the door on her. If that didn't scream trying to hide something, nothing did.

Their about-face might be nothing more than the press having caught wind, and the sheriff now felt obligated to do less outsourcing, but three days into the investigation, and they get nervous? In that case, they should've been nervous from the outset.

Trying to shut down the restaurant probably wasn't her best decision, and in hindsight, it gave them their excuse to cast her aside.

But just the idea of so many civilians being exposed to such a deceptive and lethal piece of greenery had her envisioning dropping bodies . . . in the restaurant, in the barn, all along the B&B's halls.

Shaking the images out of her head, she studied the road. More traffic than usual on the highway. Tourists cramming in the last days of summer. Raysor probably cursing her, leaving him and two others to cope with drunks, speeders, and squabbles egged on by almost a hundred degrees, but he'd understand once he heard the whole story.

Landmarks loomed into sight, and she watched on the left side for the county road marker. She hadn't driven down that road before.

Her phone rang. "Chief Morgan."

"Where the hell are you? I thought I made myself clear?"

Son of a bitch. Brice LeGrand. Again.

"In my car, why?" She pulled over. No telling where this discussion was going. And if he relayed some issue even halfway important on the beach, she'd have little choice but to return. "What's happened?"

"A three-car accident on Palmetto," he replied. "One person taken to the hospital."

Squinting at a grasshopper on her windshield, she let the words sink in. "Everything okay?"

"So you haven't heard?" he said.

There might've been an accident, but somehow the facts didn't seem right. Marie hadn't called her. "My people call when there's a situation, Brice."

Brice smelled opportunity to rekindle his campaign against her. Probably had thought of nothing else since the last call an hour ago.

He let the accident bluff die. "People are beginning to talk."

She scoffed at the second lie. People who were safe didn't hunt for the cops, especially the chief. "So what did the sheriff say?"

"Haven't reached Mosier yet." Brice dropped names like people changed underwear.

"When you get him," she said. "The detective's named Chuck Roberts. But since you need me, I'll be there in ten minutes. Just let me tell this detective that there's an emergency bigger than his."

She held her breath, watching traffic.

"So you'll be at the meeting tonight?" he asked.

Meeting? He'd cobbled that threat together this quickly? "If you need me. I don't remember being asked to be on the agenda."

"So I can tell the others you won't be there?"

Brice relished threats of emergency, last-minute council meetings to discuss her performance, and she always made plans to appear, just in case.

He raised his voice. "I said I can tell the others—"

"Brice? Are you moving? I can't hear you," she shouted, tired of the crap.

"Don't pull that shit with me, Chief. You know damn good and well—"

"You've hit a dead zone," she yelled. "Call Marie and tell her what I need to bring."

She dropped the phone in a cup holder. *Shit.* There was a ninety percent chance of no meeting. The man could be quite inventive with the truth, but when the town council met, she usually was mentioned, and it served her best to be there to hear it firsthand.

Thanks to some nasty, unexplained history between him and Callie's mother, Brice LeGrand wanted to fire Callie worse than he wanted to screw the waitress at McConkey's.

The clock read one-ish. But instead of texting Marie about a meeting or fictitious car accident, Callie reminded her admin miracle worker to expedite her research. The same research Roberts had his office doing, but Marie could ferret info like a seasoned PI.

Then Callie couldn't help herself. *Is there a town meeting tonight?*

Because if Brice connected with the sheriff and learned that Callie had stumbled into a murder, been given the reins, and then fired within two days, he'd attempt like the devil to hold that meeting.

She eased onto the road, then a quarter mile down she saw road on the left. She turned off the highway down a long, worn asphalt road with frequent potholes that wouldn't be filled any time soon based upon the economic level of the residents. The road wound through jungle, past pockets of marsh, until she reached a collection of small homes. Fairly neat with old, wide azaleas dotting the area, the plants thriving under the shade of oaks and pines, probably adding an uplifting personality in the spring when those plants bloomed loudest for Easter. Grass, however, hunted for sun and ran sparse.

Two basic brick houses, others concrete block, cloistered in a hard-worn cul-de-sac, the norm for heir property where families all laid claim to ground going way back into a family history with no wills.

A small blond-brick square box of a house had the right numbers on a porch post, if Rose's employment file was correct. The best quality house in the community of six though it had twenty years of age on it. Scuffed hand-me-down toys in the yard, but no kids in sight.

A curtain opened at the block house twenty yards to the left. A dark face.

Callie rapped knuckles on Rose's screen door, the loose wooden frame rattling as if coming loose from its hinges. No answer. She opened the outer door and knocked on the cheap wooden door. Still no one.

She peered through the small diamond-shaped window. A chihuahua poised itself on guard between a tiny living room and an even tinier kitchen. *Yap*. Testing. Then *yap*, *yap*, *yap*. Nonstop, the rat-sized canine bounced off its front feet with each protest, not looking aside or behind itself, as if nobody was there and the property was his to save. The television, however, was on along with two overhead lights. Matchbox cars strewn between Legos. Somebody hadn't been gone long.

She tried the door. Unlocked. Seeing Callie peer in, the dog backed up, fur raised. "Hello?" she called. "Rose?"

Nothing. Maybe these people left their doors unlocked out here like the beach residents, thinking crime couldn't penetrate their self-made bubbles. Callie never bought into the native mindset and kept her place locked, alarm set, cams at strategic parts of her house inside and out. Not everybody had seen the death she had.

Callie retreated and shut the door, to respect the owner's privacy . . . and avoid running into somebody's shotgun. After all, she wasn't dressed for work, and her firearm hid in the glovebox. She preferred fairer fights.

"What're you doing in our house?"

Despite her training, she jumped . . . the muzzle of a weapon caught her in the back.

"I'm Edisto Beach Police Chief Callie Morgan," she said, hands half-raised. "Not here to cause any harm. Just trying to find Rose Jenkins."

"Who says she lives here?"

The gun-toter delivered his question forceful and dominant. Island dialect. Callie guessed he held a multi-purpose hunting and protection weapon. If you couldn't afford but one, it was the one to have out here.

She hadn't the time nor the reason to fib. "Rose's employment papers at Indigo Plantation says she lives in this house. I came to ask questions about a missing guest. She waited on him a time or two."

He poked her harder. "She quit," he said, still not letting Callie turn. "Why?"

Another poke. "None of your damn business."

Sick of the prodding, she lowered her arms. "Do you have a name?"

"Again, none of your—"

"Do you live here?" she demanded, while her heart kicked her ribs. "I told you my name, my job, and my business. My officers are aware I'm out here." She wished. "You'd be better off taking whatever's stuck in the middle of my back and safely putting it away to save you from trouble you won't be able to crawl out of."

She turned to find a six-foot man, complexion dark as night, his big bones harboring at least three hundred pounds of muscle and over-zealous eating. Impressed he'd slipped up on her, she credited youth, maybe twenty-five. He still had another ten years of age on his side before cholesterol took charge. In other words, overweight or not he could still best her.

The gun didn't move, but her assertiveness took him by surprise. He was thinking.

She glanced left at the next house. Faces peered out of every opening in the place. Three of them kids, three of them adult women. Now empowered enough to be seen, two males stood on the porch in clear view, waiting for a signal from the guy holding her at bay.

Then she turned to the house to her right, the same person still peered out the curtain. A middle-aged man stood guard on that porch, a protective hand resting on the plump shoulder of a matriarchal figure. The glare in her eyes and firmness around her mouth relayed confidence, defiance, and a hint of regal authority. Age, maybe seventy-five. Callie guessed the alpha on this compound was a woman, not a man.

Then a girl about twenty slid out. The grandmother reached around, and by feel protectively positioned the girl behind her. Rose maybe?

"I ain't putting away the gun," her captor said.

"Have you heard of me?" Callie asked.

"Yeah."

"Then you're aware what I'm capable of."

The man gave no reply, but no doubt he heard the story of how she filled Seabrook's killer with six rounds last September. That story traveled the state, and for months afterwards those not close to her gave her size-four frame a wide berth.

The old grandma gave him a nod.

"Okay," he said.

"Okay what?" Callie replied.

"We'll all listen to you and then decide how this thing goes." He motioned with the shotgun toward the block house with the older woman. "Head on over there."

Together they walked, the weapon at ease, pointing down toward the thin, dry grass. The big man motioned her inside where the gawkers had retreated, and when Callie stepped through the threshold, fourteen people crammed into a room with one sofa, two chairs, and a cheap entertainment center. Two kids on their mothers' laps with the women elbow to elbow. Men leaned against the wall. Grandma, however, had retreated to an upholstered rocker in front of a fake fireplace maybe four-foot wide that cost no more than a hundred dollars and was worth no more than twenty. The thin metal mantle over it was adorned with a crocheted runner and an endless assortment of family photos with some going back generations from the black and white photography, bell bottoms, and hats.

Callie had no clue where to sit. Neither did the girl she thought was Rose.

Standing behind Grandma, the girl was way fairer than the others, and on the street would appear Caucasian. Here, however, the family resemblance appeared in one person, then another. The eyes, mainly, which right now flashed fear.

Someone brought in a kitchen chair and put it behind Callie. She sat without invitation and waited for Grandma, or whichever lieutenant she chose, to speak first. Being in their home, being grossly outnumbered, she could only garner respect by being respectful.

The room got quiet.

Her eyes a tad rheumy, Grandma stared without apology. "What you think my Rose done done, chief?"

"I'm not sure she's done anything, ma'am," Callie said firmly. "She didn't come to work today."

Shotgun man spouted out, "And that's worth the cops coming here?"

"Shush, Potluck," Grandma said.

Callie could see how he earned his name.

"No," she said. "She didn't show on the day the news broke about a man being killed on Indigo Plantation where she works. We're interviewing everyone employed there, but when she didn't come in, and left early a couple days ago, we especially wanted to talk to her." She eyed the girl. "I assume you're Rose?"

She was twenty-one per the employment file, but standing there lost and intimidated—the forced center of this family powwow—she'd pass for sixteen. Thin with gold hair cropped short and tight, she possessed a youthful beauty . . . and striking green eyes. Grandma tapped the girl's hand resting on the old lady's shoulder, giving the girl permission to finally concur that she indeed was Rose.

"You're scared to death," Callie said. "Not coming to work was a red flag. So what has you wanting to quit your job? There aren't many on the island like that available."

"I want a lawyer," she said, sending a ripple of murmurs around the room.

Callie gave it a second then replied, "But you're not under arrest."

"Don't you give me a free one if I ask for it?"

Shaking her head, Callie tried to appear sympathetic. Television distorted so many things when it came to cops and the law. "No, sorry. Like I said, you're not under arrest. I came to ask if you'd met Addison Callaway while working at Indigo. Did you ever see him meeting with anyone? Did you happen to overhear where he was going the day he disappeared? You were listed as working, so with a dining room that small, I figured you might've heard or seen something."

"She don't get no lawyer?" asked a woman on the sofa in her thirties.

Callie shook her head slowly. "The state doesn't assign her one just because she wants one. However, if Rose is involved in something, and I solve this without her cooperation, I don't need her."

"*Need* her?" Grandma's emphasis came with a heavy dose of sarcasm.

"Means if she don't spill to the cops before they figure it out, Rose is swinging out there on her own, Grandma," said a short, muscular family member maybe mid-twenties.

"Close," Callie said. "If she withholds information, she's totally on her own."

The room grumbled then, a few grousing about "that ain't right."

Palms out in peace, Callie calmly spoke. "But let's not get ahead of ourselves. From the looks of Rose, she's aware of something and it frightens her. Isn't that right, honey?"

Rose dropped her gaze. The others stared holes in me for making their sister uncomfortable.

This wasn't working. Something had the waitress tied in knots, and on trial in the middle of this packed living room wasn't the place to air it. Callie needed to take this one-on-one, which wasn't likely, but at least with no more than Grandma, and maybe one of her sergeant-at-arms.

"Someone in the yard, Grandma. Looks like a plain wrapper."

People started heading to windows, and Grandma stopped the surge. "Everyone stay where they are. Who is it, Potluck?"

He watched from beside the window, gingerly easing the curtain an inch. "White man. He's carrying on his belt and toting a badge."

"Dark hair?" Callie asked.

"Yeah."

"Wearing a polo shirt with a patch sewn on the chest? A little bit of a belly?" she added.

He turned to her. "Yeah."

Detective Roberts. Damn. He'd listened to Callie's comment about Rose needing to be questioned. She'd hoped he wouldn't react so soon. Having driven her personal car to avoid detection at Indigo, her plain gray Ford Escape would hopefully blend in with the other cars in the yard. She left stickers and identifying items off her vehicle just for situations like this.

"What you want me to do, Grandma?"

But Grandma laid a stare on Callie. "You familiar with this man?"

Callie nodded. "Yes, ma'am. He's from the Charleston Sheriff's Office. He's working the same case I'm asking about."

"So why's he here?" She turned her head a bit, analyzing. "And why did you come first and him come later? Either you came to butter up Rose for the taking . . . or this man doesn't know you're here." She lifted her chin, catching a thought. "You come here without a uniform, no patrol car."

Callie stood and dared to join Potluck at the window, unsure how to play this.

"Hello?" Roberts hollered, then like Callie, pushed the door open to the same empty house. He went in for all of five minutes, the living room crowd holding patiently still. Then he exited, studying his surroundings. "Someone has to be in one of these houses," he shouted. "I'm hunting for Rose Jenkins. It'd be easier if she comes out and talks to me."

Callie didn't trust the detective to manage the girl properly. Not with this sudden need for Indigo and the sheriff's office to put this case to bed to appease Trenton and curtail the press. Roberts was probably under double the pressure with Callie gone.

"What you think, Chief?" Grandma asked low, the request for advice catching Callie by surprise.

She stooped close to the old woman. "The dead man is famous," she said. "Authorities are pushing to solve this case fast. This man might not care who he arrests for the murder."

Grandma tensed, but her fingers worked the buttons on her house dress. Potluck kept watch on Roberts. "He's studying all the cars now. I think he's taking pictures of the tags."

He'd learn she was there soon enough, if that was the case.

Rose shook. A female family member eased her arms around the girl from behind. Tears welled in Rose's eyes.

"Why do you pretend to care?" Grandma asked.

To which Callie answered without hesitation. "I only want the one who's responsible, ma'am, and I don't think it's Rose."

Chapter 23

Slade

WHILE IT WAS cooler in the indigo processing barn, the oppressive heat fought to enter the open barn door. An overhead fan churned hard enough to ruffle hair, and a young teen motioned to his mother and then toward Drummond, making more people take note there was a pirate in the corner.

"We need to take this somewhere else," I said.

"We can't go inside the plantation house," Wayne said. "Not with Roberts mulling about. Besides, this guy's too . . . obvious."

Drummond stared through the nearest window. "It's hot as horny hell outside, but we can take it to shade. Follow me. You might as well see what I'm talking about." Then the damn idiot walked over to those noting him and passed out brochures with a bit of a tap dance and a signature *argh*.

Separating ourselves from the sideshow, Wayne and I drifted outside, figuring he would catch up. He did.

"Which way?" I asked. "And don't you have a tee shirt or something you can wear instead of . . ." and I swept a wave from his feet to his face, "instead of this getup?"

"It's called branding," he said, "and no. I rarely step outside my role. Besides," and he stroked his braided, ribboned beard. "This doesn't quite fit tee shirt and shorts garb." He leaned close enough that his hat shaded my face, his breath surprisingly hinting of spearmint. "Besides, these old frog legs of mine shine snow white, and I don't cater to sunburn."

And on we marched, which meant we caught gawks and sniggers as we fast-walked our way across the lot and toward one of the trails. Even if Roberts saw us, there wasn't a damn thing he could do since we were guests, but we preferred he not ask our business since he'd learned what we really did for Agriculture.

The guys watched the trail. I, however, scouted the weeds alongside the path, the undergrowth of the woods, judging the moisture levels and sunshine . . . hunting for hemlock.

It didn't take long for Drummond to detour at a fork marked, "Invitation only. Indigo Plantation" on one of Indigo's signature carved wooden signs. A black, rubber coated chain-link fence rose five feet tall and spread at least twenty feet into the jungle on either side, but the eight-foot locked gate indicated some sort of wheeled vehicle could come through as needed.

Drummond hopped over the fence spryer than I expected, but I scanned the area in front of us and behind, seeking witnesses. "Where're we going?"

"You'll see," he said. "Come on."

"Yeah, says the guy who almost drowned me." Digging my sneakered toes into the wire holes, I climbed over with Wayne's help. The cowboy easily followed, appearing less cowboy having lost his boots in the storm, and his deck shoes and khaki shorts gave his style a more Lowcountry appeal.

Water already trickled down my temples to my neck, clothes sticking. Every inch of Drummond's arms, neck and face slicked shiny with sweat. We walked into the dense vegetation, keeping to the path that became more obscure the farther we trekked. We were in the shade as he suggested but kept walking, and I chose not to ask why. Not conducive to hemlock, that's for sure. Too dark.

One could almost drink the humidity, feel it smack our skin like fly-paper, the no-see-um gnats digging into our ears, noses, and enjoying the salty taste of our necks, so I was game to come out on the other end of wherever this led as quickly as we could. Even into the intense August sun.

The pirate began to huff a bit, reminding me he was old enough to be my father, but before I could worry too hard about how to drag a sixty-plus gent out of the woods, sunlight beckoned ahead.

"How far was that?" Now I was huffing. "A mile? Two?"

"A half." His grin smeared up the side of one cheek.

To use his shirt as a handkerchief, Wayne lifted the tail exposing his decent abs, sopping the moisture dripping off his temples. "I take it that's what we came to see?"

I turned. We'd reached a part of the South Edisto River north of Indigo. Thirty yards across an open area of scrabble lay a complex dock, with two levels and an amazing craftsmanship compilation of spindles, steps, and cabling. The caps atop each post were lights. But at the end was quite the marina playground.

We took in the air-conditioners and big fans, the sound system, and the cabinets of what were probably televisions. This was party central for someone important, and probably not the likes of guests like Wayne and I were.

"Damn," I said, pulled like a magnet toward the thing. "I don't remember this being part of the B&B's accommodations."

Wayne reached for my wrist. "Is there an alarm?"

"Doubt it. Look how secluded this is." But then I thought about that. Secluded could be for any of a dozen reasons, some of which deserved guarding. "But if there is an alarm, we can say we thought being an overnight guest meant we had an invitation . . . and we'd come too far to go back for a key?"

Motioning to Drummond, Wayne said, "What about him?"

I shrugged. "He's on his own. He knows better. We're just ignorant saps from the city."

I wanted to see the gazebo, if you could call it that. I'd seen restaurants with outside eating over the water that dwarfed in comparison. "Is this where they shot at you from?"

"Yup," the pirate said, boots clomping on the decking. Twenty yards out, we reached a thirty-by-thirty covered patio with a stepdown to an uncovered second tier measuring about fifteen feet deep and running the full thirty-foot length of the upper level. Stained to give it a patina of age.

Drummond pointed south. "I was cruising in my ship coming around that bend. Didn't even get a chance to shout *ahoy* before they fired the shots."

"Okay, but you said you came back out after that. Why?"

The bushy black brows waggled twice. "To see whatever it was they didn't want me to see."

Wayne leaned on the railing. "So what did you learn?"

"And why didn't they shoot at you again?" I asked, setting my purse down next to Wayne and taking the steps to the lower level. "Hey, I think there are colored flood lights down here. How cool is that?"

"Came in the evening, to start with," Drummond said. "And came in my fishing boat, with a straw hat and jeans."

Wayne stared south at the vista, as if imagining the pirate's scenario. "What'd you do about all that hair?"

Another sneer. Drummond had pirate behavior down pat. "Wrapped a bandana around my neck, tucking it in. From a distance, just appeared like I'm fighting sunburn while fishing."

"So what'd you see?" I asked from below.

"Rich people," he said. "Lots of them. Being wined and dined and probably medicated. The only people under fifty were women, and they weren't acting especially wife-like, if you catch my drift."

"Sounds like a cliché," I said, still studying the dock, the water, seeing if I could spot fish . . . or a shark. Sea water gave me a quiver of dread and an abundance of imagination as to what I couldn't see down there that could peer up and see me.

"Trust me," Drummond said. "When the *Avarice* comes to town, they get it on out here. They don't let the average person like you or me use this dock."

I scoffed once, loud enough for him to hear. "Like you're average." What was that in the bottom of the water? I leaned over, but not too far. A rock, maybe? Something darted around it, and I left the edge.

"So you're thinking drugs and hookers?" Wayne asked.

"Tried and true drawing card for the rich and famous," Drummond said, sneering without the *arghs*.

A theory crossed my mind, and I stared at Wayne peering twelve feet down on me. "You thinking what I'm thinking, Cowboy?"

He was running a thumb over his bearded chin. I hoped he could think deeper than I could, though, because I couldn't make rhyme or reason out of how Callaway fit into all this. But I could see why Drummond was being *drummed* out of the area. He spied. He traveled by water. He'd probably seen too much. Frankly, with all the hoopla the pirate created, I was surprised he hadn't been conveniently disappeared. Then I remembered his accusations of boat sabotage.

Two pops rang out.

I ducked. "What the—"

"Slade, down!" Wayne shouted, bounding from the top gazebo to the bottom tier.

Then before I could put my thoughts together, he dove at me. He rammed into me about mid-section, my breath exploding from the hit, the momentum taking us into the water.

With no air in my lungs, I panicked. Underwater with no breath, my chest seizing . . . with Wayne's hold around me like he wasn't letting me come to the surface.

Writhing, I fought him, struggling to grapple loose, but he gripped me tighter. While I wanted to scream, I feared drinking in the water.

Bubbles, darkness, sunlight above us and oxygen out of my reach.

My feet bounced off the bottom once, twice, so if it wasn't that deep, why couldn't we get a damn breath!

Suddenly I could take a gasp, but a splash of the briny water came with it. As I started to sputter, lungs defiantly rejecting the liquid brine, Wayne clamped a hand over my mouth. Mouth to my ear, he whispered, "Don't cough."

But my throat wouldn't listen, so he crammed my head against his shirt.

Rebelling against nature, I tried swallowing the choke, willing every muscle in my chest, my throat, my mouth, to stop, to hold back. Tears welled at the effort, but just as I gained a semi-sense of control, I opened my eyes. It was dark. Underwater *and* dark!

Wait, there were slits of light.

Wayne had hidden us beneath the dock. The only fear worse than deep water was underneath a dock where everyone knew the ocean's creatures collected, the little fish feeding the bigger fish, and so on.

Eyes clenched shut, I crammed down the moan, mentally argued against the panic, because reality was someone had shot at us, neither of us was armed, and I bet they were trying to find us to finish the job.

And my purse was back on the gazebo. My eyes widened. They knew who I was. Where I lived.

"Shhh," Wayne said in my ear again.

I hadn't realized I made little noises until he told me yet again.

So I concentrated on baby inhales. In . . . out.

For forever we floated there, Wayne reaching out and bracing between joists. Me holding onto him, afraid to let go. Worried about some creature bumping into my legs.

"What happened to Drummond?" I whispered.

Wayne shook his head. "Didn't see."

"Did he shoot—"

"Shh," he said. "Wasn't him. Think I heard him go in the water."

Then all I could think of was his body floating out there, in the same water we bobbed in, little bitty fishes and crabs welcoming him for dinner.

God, don't let him play buoy near us.

"It's got to have been an hour," he said.

"What if they're still watching?" I asked.

He sighed and thought a moment. "We're swimming out of here."

"What?" The whisper came out more like a hiss. Shivers ran over me again.

"Assuming they're waiting for us, which I doubt, it's safer to swim downstream and come out on a bank." He gripped a joist with one hand, the other resting behind my neck. "You can do this, Slade. You can do anything you have to."

Holy Mother of God how I'd bragged about accomplishing anything I set my mind to do, but who thought that applied to swimming in salt water where things ate you? When there was a perfectly good dock right here.

Then before I could argue, he dragged me with a clipped "Come on."

Under we went, then out behind the dock. Wayne glanced around the corner of it, then upon seeing nothing, motioned toward the bend Drummond had spoken about earlier, and took off under water.

I kept scouting for Drummond all buoyant and dead, jerking like a fishing pole as something took a bite.

But Wayne was getting too far ahead, so under I went, shoving the pirate out of my head. I prayed Drummond wasn't shot . . . body waiting in the water for me to knock into.

I popped my head out only when I had to orient myself, each time not seeing Wayne, but I kept on. Once my foot knocked something fairly solid, and I practically climbed through that water to put distance between me and it. Plant stuff brushed me, and I wondered what wildlife hid in its leaves.

Never would I touch water again. Never, never, never. This trip had been enough to swear me off any vacation within ten miles of the stuff. And screw boats!

Finally, I came up gasping to see the bend not ten yards ahead, and Wayne squatted on the bank watching for me, reaching out.

And Drummond sat behind him.

"I see you made it," I growled, climbing out of the muck. Then I recognized the reeds, the location. "Isn't this where we found Callaway?"

Mud all over me, I tried to reach into cleaner part and splash undisturbed water on my legs, my arms. "What the hell happened back there?"

"Warning shots," Wayne said.

"Like at me," Drummond added.

Flying bullets were flying bullets. "And how can we be sure about that?"

"First, they missed us by a mile, Butterbean. Second, they never came hunting for us. We'd have heard them on the dock. Third . . . never mind."

"Oh no," I said, plopping on the damp ground beside him. "I just saw my life flash before my eyes about ten times. I'd almost rather take a bullet than do what we just did. I'll be having nightmares for six months about what probably chased me out there, tried to bite and missed. So what's the third?"

He stood, pulling down the legs and seat of his bunched khakis, stretching the soaked shirt riding his ribs. "They didn't shoot at us swimming away."

I just stared.

"I couldn't tell you that at the time, Slade."

A bout of temper threatened. "Yeah, well, thank God for small favors then, huh?"

He knew better than to reply.

By the time we walked back to the B&B, Drummond reminded me of how he appeared the first time I saw him, a bit on the grungy side, his clothes in need of wash, his beard ribbons in need of change. And thank goodness he drew more attention than we did, something he probably appreciated. Shame he had no dry brochures.

We parted without good-byes.

Back in the room, Wayne and I stripped clothes we'd never use again. Wayne had lost his second pair of shoes. Each unwilling to stand in the middle of the floor with pluff mud in our nooks and crannies, we both jumped into the shower. Any other time we'd have enjoyed checking each other over, making sure soap got everywhere it was intended. However, we'd been shot at, Wayne had lost his phone in the water, and mine still sat in my purse on the gazebo, proving I'd been there.

"Who the hell do we call about all this?" I asked, then spitting after soap bubbles sneaked into my mouth.

"Callie," he said.

"She fired us."

Kneading my scalp, washing my hair, trying hard to assure me the shots were no more than a warning to leave, Wayne didn't respond a while and instead did his best to soothe my nerves. But I was mad. Not at him, but at circumstances. Ultimately, I admitted the only person I trusted to call was Callie; however, I was leery about using the room's phone.

Something else was going on at Indigo Plantation, and I couldn't decide if Callaway had been involved, a coincidence, or simply got in the way. Like Wayne said, we swam from the dock to the crime scene without much trouble.

Why couldn't the crime have happened at the gazebo and Callaway drifted to the spot?

Wayne shut off the water, poised and listening.

I wiped water out of my face. "What?"

Then I heard the knock. "Hello? Ms. Slade? This is Gene Thurmond from the front desk."

"Just a minute," I shouted, scrambling for a towel. After a quick rub over my hair, I wrapped myself and hid behind the door when answering. "Yes?"

"Your purse, ma'am." He passed it through the opening.

Son of a gun. "You found it?"

"No, ma'am," he said. "Somebody turned it in. Said they found it on one of the trails. You must've set it down and forgotten where you left it. I hope everything's accounted for."

One of the trails?

Quickly I rummaged through it. Nothing missing, to include over a hundred dollars. Phone seemed fine. "Wow," I said. "I really appreciate it. Wish I could thank who turned it in."

He shrugged. "Not sure who it was, ma'am, but I'm glad it all turned out okay. We like to think we go above and beyond tending to our guests. You have a good rest of your afternoon and evening."

I pushed the door closed.

"They returned your purse?" Wayne entered, drying his hair. "Did not see that happening."

I kept going through it, expecting for something to be missing. Or expecting it to be contaminated somehow. "Yeah."

He gave a side tip of his head. "Like I said. A warning. We crossed a line, and we've been politely told not to go back. Wouldn't be surprised if the shooter was the one who turned in the purse."

I withdrew my phone, studied it for damage and use, finding neither. "And they know exactly who we are."

Chapter 24

Callie

POTLUCK BOUNCED the end of his shotgun on the toe of his shoe, clearly disgusted watching Roberts strut from car to car, snapping pictures of tags, watching periodically to see if anyone had the guts to come out and confront him. Grandma's boy then set his shotgun behind the door and exited, leaving the door wide open.

"Damn boy," the grandma uttered. "He's the one that's gonne get hisself killed one day."

"And some of us with him," said another member.

Then everyone hushed. The open door let them listen, and they listened hard.

"Got a warrant?" Potluck asked, meeting the detective halfway between the houses . . . his challenge clear in his swagger.

"No, sir," Roberts said, chin a tad too high to be respectful. "Easy enough to get one."

Potluck walked closer, keeping himself positioned between the house and Roberts. "Glad to hear it."

Then for a full minute the two men remained at a standoff. Inside the house, everyone held their breath.

"Well?" Potluck finally said.

Tight-jawed, Roberts studied his obstacle. "Tell Rose we'll find her."

At the mention of her name, Rose whimpered. A half dozen people shushed her.

Then attempting not to care about the inconvenience, Roberts moseyed to his vehicle, but before he got behind the wheel, he gave a defiant scan of the property, especially past Potluck at the house as if he sensed exactly where the girl was. "We found out you signed in to work the day that man died . . . but nobody can remember seeing you, Rose. Hope you can account for your whereabouts, young lady. You've got some explaining to do."

Callie's head snapped around toward the girl who wouldn't look back. Having checked the employee roster, she noted Rose reported in, too; however, nobody mentioned Rose hadn't worked. Just that she'd been on a break.

Rose had just become a person of interest.

The room full of folks remained frozen, awaiting Potluck's return. Silently, Callie eased into her chair, thinking Rose had some explaining to do. Only Callie wanted to hear all the details herself, before Roberts grabbed ahold of her.

The tires made little noise, but the engine did as it left by the road from whence it came, toward 174. Soon Potluck filled the open doorway. "I took care of him, Grandma."

"Boy," and the old woman hesitated, choosing words. "We could've just all sat here and let him come and go."

"Yeah, Grandma, but—"

"But nothing, boy! You better listen to me next time."

Then as Potluck hung his head, the matriarch turned to Callie. "Time you left, too."

"I'm nothing like him," Callie replied, working to undo the distrust Roberts's drop-in had exacerbated. "I care about the truth."

Potluck chimed in uninvited. "You're a cop." He jerked a fist in the direction Roberts left. "No different than him."

Grumbles ran around the room, which she could only assume agreed with their boy.

"Other than the badge, that detective and I are nothing alike," she said, her tone steady.

More griping, only a little louder. "Oh yeah?" Coming from behind her, she missed who spoke.

Who could blame them. Whatever experience they'd had with the police would encapsulate her. Who could afford to think the cop who pulled them over yesterday was any different than the one who questioned their sister today? Cops weren't people with varying personalities and work ethics to these folks. . . . Cops were homogenous and untrusted cardboard cutouts of each other, and they just showed when there was trouble.

"Go on," someone said. "You aren't wanted here."

Potluck approached Callie, his sneaker kicking the leg of her chair.

Grandma said nothing to make anyone behave this time.

Her phone rang. Slade. She clicked it to go to voicemail.

Callie remained in her seat, Potluck standing so close his body heat radiated off him. "Would you rather Roberts come back for Rose, or for me to try and figure this out?" she asked. "Sooner or later, Rose will have to talk to someone."

Nobody spoke, but the glares around the room could light a fire, so she made a final appeal to the girl. "Rose, your expression says you're hiding something. You saw something, heard something, and can't get it out of your head."

Rose kept her gaze on the back of her grandmother's pinned bun.

"But honey, the more you dodge this, whatever it is . . . the more you hide out and avoid the law, the guiltier you appear. Does that make sense?"

The girl gave no reply.

A text came through. Callie ignored it. Then another. Damn it, then another.

"Your people need you," Potluck said. "Time you got gone. Without some sort of court paper, you have to leave when we tell you to leave."

Yes and no, but Callie rose anyway and made slowly for the door, the family silence substantial and clear. She couldn't make the girl talk, couldn't bring the girl in, not the way things were with the sheriff's office and not without more evidence.

As if honoring the quiet, she let the screen door close easy and headed to her car, extracting her phone. All three texts from Slade's number.

Call me ASAP.

Then, *We have a witness.*

And finally, *We were shot at.*

Running, Callie leaped into her vehicle, turned on the engine for the air conditioning, and returned Slade's call.

"Hey," Slade answered.

"Told y'all to leave," Callie interrupted, surprised at her anger. "This is not your business. Anybody hurt?"

"Nope. Wayne says they didn't intend to hurt us."

"They? They who? Damn it, Slade, this is proof of why I ordered you to leave."

"First, nobody orders me. Second, I'll get to the shooting in a sec. Listen to me." Slade finished the fast string of words and sighed hard. "We met with Drummond."

Several of Rose's family members spilled onto the porch, watching.

"For God's sake why?" Callie's original opinion of this woman was returning to haunt her. She didn't have time for this.

"Well, he sort of ran us down," Slade said. "He was worried about us suing him after the boat almost sank."

Reaching in the door, Potluck pulled his shotgun out, again parking the butt on the toe of his shoe. Callie locked her car. "Fast forward, Slade. I've got seconds here."

"You okay? Need us—"

"Slade!"

"Bottom line is Drummond saw a girl in the boat with Callaway."

Callie's held her breath, then asked, "Did he recognize her?"

"Not by name, but he said he'd recognize her if she saw him again."

Another man joined Potluck, and Callie couldn't tell if he was armed or not with hands in his pockets. She put the car in reverse. "What'd she look like?"

Slade gave Drummond's description of the girl. Build, hair color . . . tanned complexion. Callie stopped backing and put the car in park. "I'll get back to you."

"Sure you don't still want us to leave?"

Callie ended the call. Rose peered out the door, matching the description to a T. Another law enforcement officer might've called in Roberts, but she wasn't so sure about his interest in all of this. After all, he'd been adversarial from the start.

And in some outer recess of her mind, where she tucked thoughts easily cast aside for not making sense, she had to wonder if Roberts was the shooter.

One problem at a time, though.

She exited her car. "We need to talk, Rose," she said loudly. "You can talk to me here, or meet Detective Roberts up close and personal at the sheriff's office."

"You ain't got no right," Potluck shouted.

Callie hollered so that Grandma inside caught the conversation, too. "I've got *every* right. Especially since someone saw Rose with the dead man before he died."

Mumbling and grumbling traveled from the porch to inside. Callie remained patient, standing in the dirt, gnats she refused to swat singing in her ears as she hoped what might happen did.

Potluck spoke. "Grandma says meet her around back at the shelling table."

Callie had no idea what a shelling table was, but assumed it'd jump out at her when she got there. Smoothly, not tentatively, and with clear effort to not appear dominant, threatening, or in charge, she strode across the front, past the audience, and around the corner of the small brick house.

Nobody was there yet. She waited, the sun bearing down and her pretending it didn't.

Finally, a screen door creaked open as Rose held it open and Grandma made her way out, balancing her hefty weight between wooden railings installed much more recent than the house.

Passing Callie, she gave a *humph*, then directed, "Time is ticking. Rose will speak to you, with me present, then you go keep her out of trouble. You hear me?"

"Yes, ma'am," Callie said, wishing the deal didn't come with such an unpredictable and unpromiseable promise. "I'll do what I can."

Rose at her elbow, Grandma shuffled toward a massive ancient live oak, its canopy at least sixty feet wide, the trunk six feet in diameter. Wandering, commanding roots pushed through sandy soil, claiming the moisture out of the ground for at least twenty feet out from around the base, leaving native silt, twigs, spits of grass, and the occasional cowpea hull.

Another rocker awaited Grandma with an assortment of straight-backs and lawn chairs randomly scattered around a paint-weary picnic table. Off and out from under the tree was a scorched fifty-five gallon metal drum that had held many a flame. A poor-man's fire pit . . . and trash compactor.

A scalded patch of land about thirty yards off held yellow and brown remnants of a summer garden. Now that August was half done, any beans had been long shelled and canned. Dehydrated hulls littered the ground, meaning they gleaned every pea they could as late in the season as they could go. Callie didn't doubt it. This family had a lot of mouths to feed.

Wiping one temple, then the other, Callie yearned to remind them of the heat and sweltering wet air but didn't dare. Rose, however, walked over to behind the tree to a cheap, square, eighteen-by-eighteen fan and turned it on high, positioning it toward the rocker. That's when Callie noted the hundred-foot extension cord leading to the house.

"Praise God," Grandma said, touching a carved crucifix on the tree truck before taking her seat in the rocker.

Air swirled softly around their legs. Thank God indeed. And the chattering racket of the fan would mask their conversation. This spot seemed the epitome of an outdoor praise house. Across the islands, praise houses were tiny, one-room mini churches where slaves used to extol Jesus . . . and self-govern each other, calling upon transgressors to appear and be chastised to avoid the discipline from those over in the plantation.

Keeping dirty laundry in the family.

Rose took a seat at the picnic table six feet from Grandma's rocker. Callie stepped across the bench and seated herself facing the young girl who, from the twisting and inability to relax, could break out in hives any moment.

"Now," Grandma said. "Speak your business to my girl, but there are some conditions."

"Yes'm. Thank you," Callie replied. "I wanted—"

"First condition," the old woman interrupted, "is that you don't lie, because this here girl ain't going to either."

Callie nodded, waiting for the next commandment.

"And no cursing or lip. Not in this place. Not on this dirt."

"Yes, ma'am," Callie replied again. "Is that it?"

An old, arthritic finger pointed skyward. "Hold up a bit. Rose?"

"Yes, Grandma."

"Like I told this lady here, be truthful. Don't mind me sitting here either, you hear me, girl?"

"Yes, Grandma."

Sure . . . like anyone could ignore the rules, the old woman's presence . . . or that cross on the tree.

Chapter 25

Callie

"I'LL NEED TO record this," Callie said, pulling out her phone.

Rose acted about to throw up, complexion pale, and Callie expected a second-thought reversal from the girl's hesitant offer to cooperate. Grandma, however, paused, thought, then gave the approving nod. Callie tried to hide her relief.

"Now, Rose," Callie began after recording the date, time, and persons present and positioning the phone between them. "Records show you were signed in to work at Indigo three days ago on the date when Addison Callaway disappeared, then later was found dead."

"Yes," she said.

"Yes, ma'am," Grandma corrected.

"Yes, ma'am," Rose replied.

No. Grandma wasn't there *at all.* "Did you work a full shift?"

"Um, no. I went home three hours early."

"Why?"

Her breathing quickened. "Miss Jackie told me to. I . . . wasn't feeling well."

One of Grandma's eyes widened. Just one. She was proving to be quite the lie detector.

Resting both elbows on the table, Callie signaled benign interest, attempting to relay to Rose that this was casual enough to relax. "Detective Roberts mentioned that nobody recalls seeing you at work." Callie gave a shrug, as if it could be a hoax. "What do you think he meant by that?"

"I wasn't always in the dining room?" The sentence ended with a question mark.

"Oh," Callie said. "So you were, what, making room deliveries? Taking orders to guests not in the dining room?"

"Y-yes. That's probably what he kinda meant."

"Tell me who you delivered to."

"I don't know their names."

"Okay," Callie said. "Tell me what you delivered, and to where."

"Um, the food was covered . . . and I'm not sure I remember which rooms."

Both of Grandma's white brows met in the middle. Rose was clearly lying.

Callie reached across the table to the girl's twiddling fingers. "Stop. Let's pretend you didn't just lie to me and start over, okay?"

Grandma gave a slight head dip. Callie wished she could use this woman on all her interviews.

Callie reworded the question. "Why weren't you in the dining room that day? Why didn't Jackie and Tito see you?"

"Miss Jackie did see me. She's the one who told me to . . . leave the dining room."

"And do what?" Callie asked.

Tears exploded from the girl. When she tried to leave the table, Grandma gave her an, "Oh, no, you don't, child. You sit your butt down there and answer this woman's questions."

"But I didn't want to do it, Grandma," she cried, blubbering and gasping between the words . . . scared to pieces.

"Do what?" Callie asked softly. "Just say it. I can't help you if you don't spit out what happened."

And the dam broke as terror escaped the shaking, tiny body. This was raw, in the open, with nobody around to give the girl as much as a tissue for solace. Callie's heart felt a pang of pity for her, but Grandma sat stoic as if the girl had to pay this penance.

"I don't think you're a killer," Callie said, filling in the awkwardness around the sobs. "If I'm wrong I'll be greatly shocked. But honey, right now I have a body in the morgue who you've not only met but spoken to at length, I'd guess. A conversation that you're afraid to share."

Callie gave the girl a moment. With the quiet wait hanging heavy, Rose's crying subsided. She wiped her nose on her sleeve, sniffled a few times, and heaved a deep breath.

Good. Callie pushed a little more. "If you want to stay out of jail, you just need to tell the truth. Because the truth's coming out. With or without you, the truth will spill."

The girl hung her head.

Grandma rapped knuckles on the arm of her rocker. "The first hog at the trough feeds, girl. If you ain't learned that from your boy cousins, you ain't up to learning." She leaned forward. "You hearin' me?"

"Yes, Grandma." Rose let loose a shaky exhale.

Sitting still, letting the girl build courage, Callie gave everyone a few seconds before saying, "You need to tell me everything that Miss Jackie told you to do, in painfully accurate detail."

Rose ran a short fingernail, painted soft blue, around a knot in the table top. "I reported to work like usual," she said. "But I wasn't there ten minutes, had just put on my apron, when Miss Jackie told me not to bother."

"Not bother what? Coming to work or putting on the apron?" Callie asked, giving her an easy question to answer.

"The apron."

"Okay. Why?"

Lips pinched, Rose continued. "She asked me if I knew how to drive a boat, and I said I've been fishing most my life. She said we had a guest who wanted a local to take him out on the river. I told her I didn't have a boat, thinking I could get out of whatever it was she wanted, but she said that had been taken care of. They'd already packed a lunch for us, and I was to ride with him in his car to where we'd get that boat. Then I was to have lunch with Mr. Callaway and—" She stopped.

Softly Callie took it a step further. "Were you told to do anything else with Mr. Callaway?"

"Not exactly," she said. "I really didn't understand what it was I was supposed to do other than drive the boat and eat with the man." Then she said in a hushed tone, "Not sure what I would've done if he'd tried something, though."

"So you didn't have sex with him?" Callie asked.

"No, ma'am. Didn't . . . have a chance. Not that I wanted to," she tacked on the end in a rush. "Or would have," she added with an eye on the old lady.

Grandma quit rocking.

Callie continued. "Where'd you go?"

"The South Edisto," she said. "All the way to Indigo. To the special dock. I hadn't never seen it before. Most of us aren't allowed to go there since it's for the owners and the special guests," she explained. "It's crazy fancy."

"Was this before or after lunch?"

Rose looked puzzled. "We went there *for* lunch," she said.

The logic escaped Callie. Why pack a picnic lunch, deliver it to the guest for an outing, travel several miles to lease a boat, then turn around and drive the boat back to where you started?

"So you drove Mr. Callaway to the dock, carried lunch onto the covered area, and the two of you ate there?"

Rose shook her head. "We didn't carry nothing, Ms. Morgan. We just boated. When we got there, Miss Jackie had it all set out nice for us. Linens on the table and everything." Her head now bobbed in the telling. "At first I thought it was oh so nice, but then it scared me."

"Humph," Grandma said.

"Go on," Callie prodded, immediately noting Jackie's lie about delivering the lunch basket to Callaway's room. "Why were you scared?"

Bending over the table, the girl mumbled, forgetting she spoke right into the recorder. "I just knew that eating lunch with a man like him, at a dressed-up setting like that, meant I'd have to put out as a thank-you. And I'd be afraid not to."

Jesus. Jackie had pimped the poor waitress out, and the girl felt she had no choice but to comply. And Jackie'd chosen Rose over Riley, who she told to hide in the ladies' room. What was the logic to that unless Jackie protected the wealthier white girl to the sacrifice of the poor half-black one. The whole sordid play of events turned her stomach. "Did you?"

"Like I said, had no chance," Rose answered.

Grandma did a *hunh, hunh, hunh* under her breath, her head shaking three times in rhythm. "Tell her why, baby."

Turning toward the old woman, Callie asked, "She tell you what happened?"

Grandma frowned and dipped her chin. "'Course she did, but she's gonna tell you. Go on, child."

Sweat trickled down the faces of them all, but Rose hugged herself in spite of the heat, tears welling again in red eyes. "Miss Jackie acted like she was our waitress. She brought over the picnic basket—"

"Wait. Jackie brought the basket?"

Rose nodded. "Like I said, she set it all out on china for us. A fancy picnic. Poured wine." She turned to the matriarch. "I don't even drink wine, Grandma, but they made me."

"Just go on, child."

"Anyway, we ate. Sandwiches, little pecan pies, and those okra appetizers the restaurant is so proud of. I tried not to drink, but Miss Jackie kept giving me the eye, motioning for me to keep sipping."

Callie stopped the girl. "Was the food on the plates when you sat down?"

Even Grandma had a quizzical expression at the question, but Rose slowly responded. "No. Just the clean plates, and napkins, and real silverware." She quickly added. "Oh, and the wine glasses. No paper cups or anything."

"Did you pull the food out of the basket yourselves?" Callie asked.

A fast shake of the girl's head. "Oh, no, ma'am. Miss Jackie served us. Set it right in front of me like I was royalty or something. Even served me first before him."

"What about the wine? Poured to each of you from the same bottle?"

To that, Rose pursed her lips, totally confused. "Um, yeah."

"There weren't two bottles?"

The girl turned toward her grandma, silently seeking advice. Grandma just tipped her head once. "Um, no, ma'am," Rose said. "Just one bottle."

Callie smiled, as if this were all routine. "Good. Go ahead. What did y'all do next?"

"Well, we finished eating, Mr. Callaway talking about what he does for a living, the places he's seen, naming people he said were famous that I never heard of. Miss Jackie talked some. She understood some of the stuff he was saying . . . better'n me anyway. I kept wondering if this was what rich folks did, ate and talked about nothing for a stupid long time, but I answered when they asked me stuff and laughed when they did."

The girl was slowly getting there, and while Callie hankered to speed things, she didn't want to break the momentum.

"But then he started acting drunk," Rose said.

"How much did y'all drink?" Callie asked, her adrenaline rising. She hoped this interview was taking her where she needed to be . . . to enough answers to tell her whether or not Rose would be leaving with her in cuffs.

"Not even the whole bottle. Split between two people, I didn't see how that would make him so sloppy and slurry. But then he stood, confused and totally unsteady on his feet."

"Then what?" Callie asked.

"He fell . . . and couldn't get back up," came the reply.

"What did you do?"

A new tear slid down the girl's face. "I ran, Ms. Morgan. After Miss Jackie saw I was scared out of my head, she told me to go home. Said that she'd take care of Mr. Callaway. Said he apparently couldn't hold his drink." She angrily wiped the moisture from her cheek. "And I ran faster than I ever run before. To my car. To home. I was thankful that Miss

Jackie took care of things for me."

The poor girl actually considered Jackie an ally, and Callie's anger spiked at the main waitress taking advantage of such a naïve soul. "So Mr. Callaway was alive when you left?"

"Oh, yes, ma'am. I don't know what happened to Mr. Callaway, but he was alive and . . . well, he wasn't well, but he was alive. A little drunk, I guess." She paused. "And that's all I want to know. Okay? That's all I want to know."

Callie rehashed the situation, then revisited points like what happened to the basket, which Rose knew nothing of . . . and the fact that Rose didn't get sick after the meal . . . and how Jackie never spoke of the incident again.

Rose was clueless, and Jackie had acted like nothing happened when questioned.

Callie concluded the recording. Then in a long silence, she reached across the table and squeezed the girl's hand.

Rose managed to force a smile, but it seemed way too hard an effort.

"So what you think?" Grandma asked, breaking the spell.

"I think Rose was smart leaving Indigo when she did," Callie said. "And she was smart not going back to her job."

Honestly, Callie was worried. Crap about this case was becoming not just front page news, but a story with potential national interest. Jackie was involved, yet she hung around like she hadn't a dog in this fight . . . or thought nobody could prove she did. Callie wasn't sure who planted the hemlock, but it was strategic. And the drunk behavior was most likely the hemlock taking effect. Rose escaped for some reason. Not poisoned. Maybe a fluke. Maybe not, but either way, she was a loose end.

And so was Jackie, unless she planned the down and dirty herself.

Chapter 26

Callie

ROSE RELOCATED to the top of the picnic table, feet on the bench, watching the distance yet awaiting Callie's verdict. Grandma rocked, likewise studying Callie, like she had all the time in the world and no frets to be bothered with.

Callie had walked away from the table, facing the garden. She believed Rose. No motive there, and if half of what she said was true, she'd been a pawn. But the girl would be snatched by Roberts. And whoever was really at fault could easily roll over on Rose in a second.

She fast-walked back to the tree. "Rose, I need you to stay out of sight. That detective might return at any time."

Grandma stopped her rocking. "How long does she need to hide?" Then she leaned forward. "At what point is she evading the law, Chief Morgan? And how long before you can fix the problem?"

Like there was a manual on all this.

"Until I call you," she replied. "Could be hours . . . could be days. And if they have no warrant, don't let them in, you hear?"

Both nodded. One scared, the other patient for now, willing to protect her own and trust Callie to help.

"Don't tell me where you are," Callie added, then gave Rose a card. Another to Grandma. "Don't flash those around, but call me if you don't hear from me first, okay?"

Callie took a second to pat the girl's shoulder then made a slow trot to her car. Plugging her phone in to charge, she cranked the engine and dialed what was her most familiar number.

"Edisto Police Department."

"Marie," she said, putting on sunglasses. Shifting from reverse to drive, she headed down the potholed road toward Indigo. Signs pointed to Jackie right now, and Callie might be able to back the waitress in a corner. Who was she working for, or what was her motive?

The trick was avoiding Roberts. And Sweet.

Without a doubt, someone had a secret to protect. Or a vendetta to fulfill. Maybe several somebodies.

"Marie? You there?"

"Yes, Chief."

And Roberts would be checking the tag numbers he snapped pics of.

"What've you got so far on the Indigo staff? Any of them connected to Callaway?"

Papers rustled. "I laid out a timeline for him, but there're still holes in it. Not sure where he goes or what he does when he isn't visiting places. Two weeks in between his posts tops, though most of the time it's no more than a week. Guess travel time can account for that."

"Marie! Come on. What did you learn?"

"Whup. Give me a sec. Got Thomas radioing in." Unrattled by her boss's frustration, Marie put her on hold.

Callie drove on. Houses sat several hundred yards apart, ranging from trailers to small boxes on stilts. The cars were older, taken past the point to be worth anything to trade. But as Callie passed one stained, wood-sided residence no bigger than a large shed, half-hidden behind an overgrown thicket of vines and myrtle, she thought she spotted movement. A car parked in the dirt drive. An SUV too clean for dirt roads. Not Roberts, but the visor was down, the sun glinting off the windshield.

She lightened the gas and avoided the brakes as she approached a curve. Peering into her rearview mirror, she noted the SUV pulling out and heading toward Rose's family commune.

Callie pulled a three-point turn and headed back way faster than she'd left.

Marie returned on the line. "Okay. Keep in mind I'm not through with all the employees, and that I started from the top down. Per what I've found so far, three people could've crossed Callaway's path. All three lived in Charleston during the time Callaway did reviews."

"Just tell me who, Marie."

"But you might want the context—"

"Names, Marie."

Callie caught up to the SUV as it turned into the drive.

"Wait! This first." Marie sounded urgent, so unlike her. "Brice's reserved the administrative meeting room for an emergency town council meeting about you. Tonight. He told me you better show."

Stupid ass. "Ain't happening, Marie. Tell him that or whatever you want to. Hell, tell him nothing for all I care. I won't be there."

"Should I get Raysor to go for you?"

"No. This is my business, not his. Just give me the names."

"Swinton Shaw, Jackie Ott, and Gene Thurmond."

"Thanks."

Brice's timing always stank, and sometime in the future he might win this game, but never at the sacrifice of a case or a civilian's life. Not the damn time for Edisto politics. Charleston politics had mucked up the island enough as it was. She didn't want to even think about Brice calling the sheriff. That just might end her career.

But she couldn't fret about that now.

Tucking the names aside, desperately wanting to mull over why Sweet hadn't revealed his affiliation with Callaway, nor Jackie, and who the hell Gene Thurmond was, Callie hung up and parked. She retrieved her Glock from the glove box, slipped its paddle holster into her waistband, and as the driver exited his vehicle she opened her door and left hers.

"Hold on, Marion," she shouted, hand on her weapon the second she noticed him wearing his. "What are you doing here?"

His stare clearly noted her stance. "I could ask the same thing, Chief."

"My rank outweighs yours. Answer me."

He slowly shut the car door. "I'm here protecting Indigo."

She stepped closer but left sufficient distance between them, so she could easily hear but avoid his reach. His being out here made zero sense, especially with paparazzi all over Indigo needing his oversight.

Which made him a wildcard.

And she'd love to get a hard look at his gun.

"Elaborate what *protecting Indigo* means," she said. "How does one little waitress matter in the grand scheme of a murder, Marion?"

Crossing his arms, fists pumping the biceps, he leaned a hip against his SUV. "Yet you're out here yourself . . . and no longer working this case."

His presence worried her. Marion hadn't been seen yet when she'd left Indigo earlier.

Faces peeked out of windows. One male member stood on the doorway two houses down. Innocents.

"Who sent you out here?" she asked.

Laughing, Marion relaxed his arms, using them to talk with. "Not your business, not your jurisdiction, and I'm not answering. Instead, I'm going to talk to Miss Rose in there." He looked toward the right address.

"No, you're not," she said.

He gave a half smirk. "You can't stop me from checking on an employee who didn't come to work."

"So Shaw sent you?" she said, fishing. "You wouldn't take orders from Jackie, though I imagine she's frantic being down a key staff member and others not willing to come in and deal with the chaos."

He began to approach. "Actually, I'm taking her to Roberts."

She scowled. "Why didn't he send a uniform?"

"I was handy, and the other guys were occupied."

Roberts hadn't given the kid a half second thought this whole time. "Try again," she said. "Just not believing you, Marion."

She read his face searching for signs of another lie, or an attempt to get away with a half-truth. Amazing how some people went with the latter in the hitch of a moment.

"The girl quit," she said. "And I'm beginning to wonder why."

He spat on the ground, totally unnatural in the effort.

There was a squirrelly sense about him. "Don't make a mistake you can't take back," she said cold and straight.

Another car approached. Last thing she needed was more people out here. Rose's family already outnumbered them, and if they had a serious desire to protect their little sister Rose, they could do what they wished with this man and lose him in the saltwater marsh.

But she also pictured herself in the middle of this, and Marion taking out a few of them in the process. Just depended on how rogue he was. She didn't suspect she'd find much level-headedness in his DNA. There had to be a reason he washed out of the sheriff's department.

"Get in your vehicle and leave," she said, praying Rose took the delay tactics as an opportunity to run.

"Afraid not, Chief."

The new driver pulled up. Had to be ten cars on the grounds now.

Marion flashed a hint of surprise then promptly hid it as Roberts got out.

"What the hell do we have here?" Roberts asked. "A rent-a-cop and the beach police, both trying to tamper with a witness." He waggled a finger at Callie, but there wasn't a smile behind it. "Imagine my surprise to find your tag amongst all these others."

"Imagine that."

Roberts's eyes narrowed. "I ought to run both of you in."

Marion pointed toward the house. "That girl Rose is a suspect. I was going to bring her to you."

Throwing a flashy impression of surprise, Roberts took a half step back, hand over his heart. "Oh no. Tell me it ain't so. A suspect? A real suspect?"

Then as Marion tried to shed his red-faced humiliation, Roberts gave a sarcastic chuckle and pointed to Callie. "What's your story, Chief? Somebody stealing seashells? A little far off the sand, isn't it?"

"Health and welfare check," she said, using a common law enforcement task. Checking on someone when their worried friends and family couldn't.

He sneered. "You're going with that?"

She shrugged. "Didn't realize Rose's grandmother lived here. Someone at the beach told me they were concerned about her, so I came out."

"And you didn't see me earlier? Hear me?"

She shrugged again. "Guess not. Was out back checking on the grandmother rocking under a tree."

Her phone dinged with a text. Extracting it from her pocket, she gave it a quick glance. Slade. *Did you know that Shaw knew Callaway?* And with the text appeared an attachment link Callie hadn't the time to download.

"Tell you what," Roberts said. "Let me go grab little miss Rose, and we'll all four head to Indigo where I have enough uniforms with cuffs for everybody." He strode to Rose's door and knocked.

Callie wasn't leaving now, not with Rose sandwiched in some scheme and at the risk of a quasi-posse. Taking the opportunity, she chose to call Marie in lieu of Slade. She didn't have time for both.

"Marie, talk fast," she said low. "And I mean lightning fast. Shaw, Jackie, and Thurmond. Go."

"Oh." Even stunned, Marie showed her efficiency. "Shaw worked at a place in Atlanta that Callaway blogged about, but he didn't work there when Callaway was there. Shaw arrived after the bad review, most likely hired to turn it around, but left six months later. Then four months later he appears at a place in Charleston where Callaway did a good review."

A black mark on his record, but an accolade later . . . a wash. "Next one."

"Gene Thurmond worked as a front desk clerk at the second place Shaw did in Charleston, again at the same time Callaway was there. Thurmond lived on Johns Island then and still lives there. He's worked at six hospitality venues in the last eight years."

Unable to hold employment or the nature of his profession? Did Callaway hurt him in any sort of comment? Still, it was a good review. But who the hell was he?

"And Jackie Ott worked in Charleston at the same place as Thurmond and Shaw, but she didn't get hired until three months after Callaway's review."

Callie glanced at the house. The family wasn't letting Roberts in, and the detective turned flustered, staring back at her with suspicion, wary.

"Nothing about a Rose Jenkins?" Callie asked quickly.

"No, ma'am."

"Thanks, Marie. I'll be in touch."

"Want me to—"

"You do whatever you feel the need to do. Gotta go."

Roberts waved with a snap to his wrist. Taking her time, Callie moseyed to the stoop of the porch. "Need me?"

"They don't know where the girl is. What the hell have you told them?"

"Not a thing," she said, giving Potluck a perceptive look. "Haven't told this man or anyone in this house a thing."

Not that she hadn't told Rose to skedaddle. She hoped the girl had listened.

Roberts pivoted, jumped down from the porch, skipping two steps, and marched toward the corner of the house. "Let's see if old Grandma's out back like you say."

Callie hurried to catch up about the time he reached the shade tree. Eyes closed, Grandma rocked under her oak, the fan blowing a breeze across her legs. Rose gone. As Roberts approached, Grandma opened her eyes. No words. Still rocking.

He strode to the woman. "Where's Rose?"

"Who're you to be asking?" Grandma asked.

Roberts pointed to the badge on his belt and spit out his name. "She's missing."

"She's at work," Grandma said.

Reaching out, he stopped the rocker with a grip on the arm. "Don't you lie to me."

But Grandma just smiled. A smile that seemed to express pity on an ignorant soul. "If she ain't at work, and ain't here, then no telling. Girl is grown and way past my influence. Tell her to call home when you find her." Then she closed her eyes, pushed the ground with her feet to dare him to stop her, and returned to her movements.

Roberts removed his hand, his jaw tight.

"She was my health and welfare check," Callie said, grateful Grandma owned such a stiff constitution, angry at Roberts's attitude toward an old woman. "Wouldn't appear so good listing you as the safety risk that warranted my trip. Don't touch that chair again."

His fluster shined clear. "Then the *three* of us will return to Indigo to answer questions."

"And I have a few of my own," she said.

"I'll take care of this case," he replied, his ire apparent.

And I'll let you think you are, she thought.

Time was of the essence now. A young girl might get railroaded by a detective too eager for another notch . . . too eager to show he should've been the one assigned lead in the first place.

Rose didn't kill anybody. And while she also might not know who did, someone could easily consider her too loose of an end. One potential reason Marion came out here to drag her back rather than simply trying to impress Roberts . . . an effort that died on the vine. Again, a guy vying for validation.

Questions needed answering. Roberts remained too much of an undefined entity. Raysor, Thomas, and anyone on her beach team would be too obvious arriving at Indigo, plus they hadn't been invited. Still the damn issue of jurisdiction.

Callie quickly texted the only other person she could semi-trust. The only other person with enough skin in the game to be of help. Slade.

Keep an eye on Jackie and Shaw. Identify Gene Thurmond? Ask if any met Callaway before Indigo. ASAP. Headed there. Stuck with Roberts on my tail.

If Slade and Largo wanted to help so badly, now was the time.

As Roberts and Marion entered their vehicles, Callie shut her door and cranked the engine. Amazing how fate happened. Before Roberts came out here, she was banned from the case, but with his surprise reappearance, he'd invited her right back in.

Time to see if the dynamic duo visiting Edisto were as good as they thought they were, because once Callie returned to Indigo, she needed to hit the ground running.

Chapter 27

Slade

FRESHLY SHOWERED, Wayne and I weren't eager to jump back into the heat so we assumed a place at what had become our standard dining room table. Over chilled crab dip and crackers, we watched the comings and goings of press and guests. Too hot to wander, plus we'd seen the indigo demonstration twice already. Jeans were dyed with carcinogens from China, and indigo jeans were too rich for my pocketbook. Guess I was stuck with khakis.

"The free food seems to have worked," I said, tired of crackers and daring to shove an entire spoonful of the dip in my mouth. A text came in. After one peek, I sat straight.

"You're a pig with that stuff," Wayne said, pulling the bowl from in front of me. "Who's the text from?"

Leaning forward, I tried not to hang too far over the table and be obvious. "Callie wants us to keep eyes on the head waitress and Shaw. And try to identify someone named Gene Thurmond. Just read it." I held the phone out. She needed us. I loved it.

Wayne rubbed a crumb off his beard after downing his fifth cracker and took the device. "No comment about the newspaper article you sent her, but she's apparently found some intel that connects folks to Callaway."

I nabbed one more bite and pushed my chair away. "Yep. I'm thinking ASAP means we jump on it."

"Loving this vacation," he said, rising. "Sun and surf to die for."

I pushed the chair under the table. "Beats the hell out of Disney World, Cowboy."

About that time, Jackie reappeared, skirting table to table. She'd delivered just about everything the kitchen had to offer in the hour we'd watched, Shaw's charitable open-menu offer making people try anything and everything.

She went to scoot past us when I tapped her arm. "Got a second?"

I asked, realizing how thoughtless that sounded in a dining room three-quarters filled and only two wait staff on duty.

"Who's Gene Thurmond?" I asked.

"Front desk. Need something else?" She barely constrained her itch to move on.

"No, ma'am. Thanks."

She hustled on, and we left, heading past the hostess podium toward the lobby.

"Well, as asked, we've laid eyes on Jackie," Wayne said. "But let's push her interview to last since there's no way we'll corral her now."

While the dining room remained abuzz, the rush had come and gone in the lobby. The disgruntled had gone, leaving only the opportunists on the grounds. They were at the water, in the indigo barn, and the dining room, and ready to take whatever else Indigo would offer for their so-called inconvenience. Gene Thurmond stood behind the desk's open laptop, no customers for a change.

"Hey," Wayne said.

His head snapped to attention. "Sir?"

Wayne took the first crack at most males. Harder for them to ignore him.

Elbows on the dark oak counter, the lawman relaxed. "Don't worry, we're not checking out."

A manikin smile. "Good to hear, sir."

"Bet your day's been crazy."

"Understatement for sure." Gene maintained the plastic image.

Wayne leaned a teeny bit further. "Had you met that guy?"

The facade vanished. "Which guy, sir?"

With cocked brow, Wayne said, "You know . . . the dead one. The Callaway fella on the news."

Nerves showed in Gene's micro-expressions, but then not many people spoke openly to strangers about dead bodies. The clerk didn't recognize Wayne from Adam, and with all the press, I presumed the clerk would distance himself from unexpected questions.

But surprisingly, Gene answered. "Met him once before in passing. Handled his check-in a few days ago."

"But not his checking out, huh?" I couldn't help myself. I pulled out the newspaper article I'd printed and laid it on the counter beside my internal investigator badge, halfway expecting Wayne to warn me with his routine, "Slade?" But he didn't. We both understood the urgent subtext of Callie's requests, and Gene was only the first of three we needed to talk to.

Gene's eyes widened and he wondered what to say. I rolled with it. "You ever meet Mr. Shaw before you worked here?"

He hadn't budged an inch since he saw my badge. Didn't even ask who I represented. Badges did that, and I'd gotten out of more situations thanks to such ignorance.

"Yes, ma'am, I worked for him. Mr. Shaw talked me into leaving where I was to come here when he did. I like him. Pays well. Respects a work ethic. There're three other staff here who came because of Mr. Shaw, too. Not just me."

"Sounds like a good manager," I said.

"The best," he said, without reserve.

I tapped the newspaper article. "I take it you're familiar with this story, then."

Barely a glance at it. "Um, yes?" He answered as if he wasn't sure of the right answer to give.

"Is that a good yes or a bad yes?"

His complexion reddened.

"We're just working with the investigation," I said with a wave. "Don't get upset. This story appeared in our search about Callaway. A picture of Mr. Shaw at Wisteria, in downtown Charleston, being interviewed as the manager, the story going on about him being distraught at the suicide of one of his waitresses." Of course he was familiar with it. "You ever meet the girl?"

"Worked with her," he said.

Wayne tried to act unaffected, but I saw a little tensing in his arms. "Wisteria was where you worked with Shaw?"

"Yes, sir. That's where we met."

"So this girl, what happened?"

Gene shrugged. "Nobody's really sure. Name was McKenzie. She wasn't a bad waitress and don't think she was worried about keeping her job. She seemed a bit depressed a lot of times, but it wasn't my place to infringe on her private stuff."

"What about Callaway?" I asked. "Says here he reviewed Wisteria and gave it a great rating. You meet him there?"

"He wouldn't have spoken to me, ma'am," the man said. "But Mr. Shaw would have, and he was over the moon for a month after that rating. Hung a framed sign of the review in the lobby. Gave us each a bonus."

"Anything else?" Wayne asked the standard final question in an interview, formal or informal. People loved to volunteer information.

Gene thought a second, then shrugged in the negative. "No sir. Sorry, sir."

I smiled warmly. "You've been a remarkable help, Gene. No wonder Mr. Shaw stole you from another venue. Professional through and through."

Gene's teeth could've shined in the dark. "Much obliged. If you don't mind . . ."

"Mention your cooperation to Mr. Shaw? Absolutely."

Wayne gave him a brisk shake. "Good man. Have a great day."

"Oh," I said, turning in afterthought. "Any idea where Mr. Shaw is at the moment? We owe him an update." I winked.

A grimace. "Wish I did. He's been helter-skelter all day long. Haven't seen him come through here for an hour, maybe more, but feel free to check his office." He pointed to his right, down the hallway. "That's where I'd go first."

Wayne gave him a two-fingered salute, and we hustled in that direction. One employee down and two to go with minimal time to spare.

I knocked on his door. "Mr. Shaw? It's Carolina Slade and Wayne Largo. We met over Callaway's body?"

Yep, the door opened at that remark.

"Not in the hall, please." Shaw invited us in, and with a robot gesture motioned us to two chairs. He stood beside his desk, not interested in a long-winded visit. "Your accommodations okay?" he asked. "Dining room taking care of you?" Rote phrasing meant to define the problem, fix it, and get us out of there.

Wayne showed his badge, the real one. "You knew Callaway before he came to Indigo."

A frozen moment of shock told us Shaw realized his magnanimous gesture for a free vacation had invited federal investigators onto his turf. A realization that shouldn't bother him. He had a crime on his grounds, and the more people searching for the killer the better. Or should be.

He protectively placed the desk between him and us. "Who wouldn't in this business? Callaway carries, um, carried, a lot of weight."

"You met him at Wisteria," and I laid out the article again, like with Gene.

With a quick scan, Shaw recognized the piece, not touching it nor taking time to read. "He gave Wisteria a good review. What of it?"

Defensive.

Wayne let me go with my questioning. After all, I'd stunned him finding the newspaper piece in the first place. "You led everyone to believe you had no affiliation with him," I said. "Said you didn't realize he was here."

"I didn't," he blurted. "Too busy with the grand opening to read the guest list. I've since groomed my staff about such things." He heaved a huge irritated sigh, probably aimed at us, scratching his scalp over one ear.

I believed him. "You really didn't realize he was here, did you? Did that piss you off?"

The hesitation said yes, and he didn't bother to answer.

"What haven't you said about his murder?" Wayne asked.

Shaw's fist slammed his Americana desk, rattling the cup of logo pens. "Not a damn thing. Wish I *had* something to say," he added, lowering his voice toward the end.

I remained level and calm. "Why do you think he was here?"

"To rape us," he said with the meagerest constraint.

That made not a damn bit of sense. His prior experience with Callaway had been positive, enthusiastic even. My puzzlement must've shown, because before I could question him further, Shaw kept talking. "We read his notes."

"We?"

"Um, me and housekeeping."

Wayne laid a hand on my knee, out of Shaw's sight. "Before or after Callaway died?"

Shaw's frustration disappeared, replaced with a guardedness and a steely brace of his shoulders. "Don't believe I want to answer that, Agent."

"Then answer this." I scooted to the edge of my chair and glared. "Why would anyone shoot at us out here?"

This time he turned the color of the ecru embossed stationary beside his blotter. "Where?"

Wayne joined me, edging forward in his chair. "That's your first concern?"

"Your private dock, about two hours ago," I said. "We're fine, thank you very much. And no, we have no idea who did it. Thought you might."

Shaw shook his head slowly. "Jesus, no."

I kept going. "You have no inkling as to who? I mean, that's a pretty harsh policy to take shots at visitors who wander off the main path, curiosity enticing them to take a peek at how the big money lives."

His eyes darting from us to the door to the bookshelves and window, Shaw couldn't seem to connect. So I went to the article while he hunted for surer footing, giving him a question he *could* answer. I tapped a finger on the newspaper piece. "Tell us about this Ott girl, then."

He jumped at the chance. "McKenzie Ott was just a waitress."

"You remember her, so tell me, why the suicide?"

"Nobody knew."

I highly doubted that. "Did you at least go to the funeral?"

His cheeks darkened. "Of course I did. A lot of us did."

"There wasn't a mother, a sister, a father or boyfriend who had the least idea why a twenty-three-year-old girl would take sleeping pills and drown herself at the beach?"

Head shaking. A lot of head shaking. "There was only a mother. The only relative at the service. She was bitter and wouldn't talk to us."

"Left you feeling rather guilty, I'm sure," Wayne added.

"Ungodly. While we basked in Callaway's review, that girl wasted away until she killed herself."

Shaw sounded hurt, the self-loathing clear. Maybe he did care for his employees like Gene indicated. "A mother losing her child," I said. "Bet you tried to do something to help. What was it?"

He swept his arm toward the door. I followed the gesture, couldn't read his meaning, and turned back to him. "What?"

"I gave the mother a job," he said. "Sent flowers and offered the woman a job." His sigh came from all the way down to his belt buckle. "She came to me later and accepted. Jackie Ott turned out to be one of the best staff members I've ever had."

Before Wayne and I could share astonishment and connect these new dots, Shaw rose. "We're done. I'm done. Hell, Indigo's done." His tone escalated with each word. "Which means you're done asking me questions until I have the company's attorney present."

"Mr. Shaw," Wayne started.

Two rapid knocks sounded. Roberts pushed his way in without waiting for an answer. "I need this room, Shaw."

Marion followed him. Callie trailed, our glances mutually communicating we needed to talk.

"Just a damn minute," Shaw bellowed, a two-handed grip on the edge of his desk. "I'm damn sick and tired of people telling me what to do at my own place." His wave addressed us all. "I don't trust a single one of the damn lot of you."

Callie moved near me.

"Shaw," Roberts started.

"My place, my office." The easy, Lowcountry demeanor Shaw had exuded since he so genteelly offered us a free Indigo stay, had vanished like mid-morning fog on the marsh.

"Need to talk," Callie whispered to me.

"You got that right," I whispered back.

I wasn't sure what to say to Callie or how to say it here, so I passed her the article.

Then I jumped when Roberts pointed at Wayne, then me, and gave us the thumb. "You two, out of here."

Empowered, Shaw took a side. "Was just trying to make them leave—"

"He's a federal agent, Roberts," Callie interrupted. "Respect the experience."

Roberts turned on her. "I don't care if he's J. Edgar Hoover. This is my investigation. If I want his help, I'll ask him for it."

"I'm needed elsewhere," Shaw said, coming around his desk.

"You," Roberts motioned to the Indigo manager. "Sit." Again he motioned to us. "You two, leave."

I slid the newspaper article out of Callie's grip and shoved it against Roberts's chest. "Here, dumbass, read this, assuming you can read. People knew Callaway before coming to Indigo."

Glowering, Roberts's inhale gathered strength like a Category Five hurricane. "Get the hell out—"

Taking my arm, Wayne tugged me toward the door, my backwards glare met by the pompous idiot whose anger slid into a grin.

In reaching for the door to slam it with all my worth, I grabbed air. Wayne had pulled me too far too quickly. I expected to vent in the lobby, but we didn't stop there. Instead, the cowboy—missing the clomp of boots that disappeared in St. Helena Sound—directed our momentum outside, away from the main building, to the shadowed side of the barn.

Only then did he let me loose and throw his opinion at me, no holds barred. "Dumbass? Have you learned nothing about running cases?" Leaning one hand against the wall, he studied the side of the barn, then the ground. The whiteness around his lips squished flat.

Yeah, I recognized all the moves . . . and totally disagreed.

Pointing toward the B&B, I tightened my own jaw. "That man has all but sabotaged this case with some sort of . . . of . . . haughty superiority, as if he were God Almighty and nobody else has half his skills."

Which earned me a sideways glance from Wayne. "When it comes to ego—"

"Nope." Now my finger found its way in front of his nose. "This is about solving a murder." Standing strong, I waved my arms wide in a dramatic arc. "Every person involved has an ego, you included. Me included. But do you see the only person in this mix who only wants the truth? Who doesn't need the accolades? Callie."

The cowboy had to think about that.

"She just does her job, Wayne. This isn't even her jurisdiction. They used her, and she let them. She only wants to live on this island, on her beach, and live out her life keeping beach people safe and happy." I couldn't believe how much frustration I'd harbored, or how much I wanted to protect her reputation.

"Roberts could still use us," he said. "We don't need to alienate him."

"Quit changing the topic."

His expression froze. "Didn't think I had."

"Well," I continued, "I don't want to talk about him right now. I'm talking about Callie."

To that, he had no reply.

"What I'm saying," and I paused. I wasn't sure what I was saying, and he sure as heck had no clue. "What I think I'm saying is that we ought to be loyal to Callie. She shooed us off for our own sake, not because we were in the way. She has no allies I've seen. At least other than that I-see-dead-people neighbor of hers."

His mouth flopped open, and he looked off to the side, shaking his head. I think he snorted once. "Who?"

"The yoga lady who thinks you're hot. Who came over to Callie's."

Out of the corner of my eye, I noted Marion come outside from the main building. Wayne noted as well and followed the security guard's movements to the parking lot. "Guess he got ousted, too."

We were straying. I reached across the space between us and sank fingers into his shirt. "Per this Sophie woman, Callie is a loner. Smart. But she has come through a past I cannot fathom. Seeing her fight this case without respect, with that, yes, dumbass walking all over her, infuriates me." I let go of him. "We will stay here until *she* needs us, not Roberts." There, guess I finally came around with a point.

It was hot, but we didn't want to be overheard. We could go to our room, our free room, at least until Shaw reneged on his offer, and weigh things there, but what exactly were we weighing? And the whole case could evolve while we hid behind a closed door. Raising my shoulder, I wiped sweat off the side of my face.

"This whole mess started with nobody claiming to know about Callaway's presence," I said. "Now we learn that Shaw, his desk clerk, and his dining room hostess had history with him. I'm not so concerned about Gene Thurmond. He simply saw Callaway via his duties at the front desk of both places. But Shaw lied to everyone. Said he didn't know Callaway'd checked in until after I found him dead."

Wayne tipped his head in agreement. "And why would Shaw request Callie take lead on the death—"

"Right. Unless they wanted smaller fish to keep everything subdued," I said.

"Thinking she wasn't good enough to catch details," he concluded.

Jackie exited the building. I wouldn't have noticed except she still had her apron on . . . and was running. She skirted around and through three lines of cars before reaching her Honda, jumped in, and left the premises.

Wayne and I studied each other.

"Thought they only had two servers," I said.

"And surely Shaw didn't fire her," he added.

"I would've thought Roberts needed to talk to her a lot longer than that."

About the time the cowboy lit out toward the restaurant, I started trotting. At the dining room entrance, the cook was trying to serve customers, Tito looking nothing like the calm, proficient waiter he'd appeared when we first met.

"Mr. Shaw! Can I see you a moment?" came a call from the direction of the lobby.

We turned in time to see Shaw exit behind us, out the exterior restaurant door. Gene Thurmond hurried into the dining room calling, "Mr. Shaw?" He stared at his boss, amazed Shaw had ignored him . . . run right by him.

Rushing to the windows, I followed Shaw's movements. Unlike Marion and Jackie, he broke into a run toward the pathways leading behind the agriculture area, toward where I found Callaway . . . toward the sweetgrass area . . . possibly toward the private dock. We couldn't be sure without tailing him.

First Marion drives off. Then Jackie vanishes in a hurry, shirking her job. Now Shaw, sprinting so unlike the decorous gent he purported himself to be.

I left the window and dashed around white and blue tables, past the podium, and through the lobby toward Shaw's office.

Seemed that rats were deserting a sinking ship, but my biggest concern was if they'd left damage behind them.

Chapter 28

Callie

CRAMMED WITH SO many bodies, Shaw's office warmed quickly, but nobody budged, allowing Roberts time to read the newspaper article Slade had so delightfully slammed into his chest. Fondly reliving Slade's spunk, Callie waited for the man to read. He didn't read very fast.

"Do you mind?" she asked, hand out.

He passed it over, and she scanned it, stopping more slowly at the names, date, and location.

"You recognize the names?" she finally asked, unsure if he'd finished before she took it.

"Shaw and Callaway, of course," he said, "but not this waitress."

"Read her last name."

"Ott. Ott." The detective studied Callie, then narrowed his eyes.

"Yeah," she said. "They're related. The dead waitress and the current head hostess."

Roberts stood and turned toward Marion hugging the doorknob. "Go get that head waitress in the dining room. Quick. And don't waste any more of my time than you and the beach police have already wasted today. You hear me?"

"Yes, sir," Marion said, bolting out, his relief clear to be out of the fluster.

The room fell quiet a moment, as if they needed Marion to recommence, but Callie saw no need to waste more time. "Explain to Roberts why you knew Callaway from before, but had no idea he was on your property at the time of his death."

"I swear." Shaw sounded spent, as if tired of repeating himself. "I'd have fawned all over him. Please, let me go. I have to salvage this place."

Maybe he hadn't fawned over the man but somebody else did. "Jackie fixed him the fancy meal, putting lunch in a three-hundred-dollar basket before delivering it to the private dock. You saying you didn't know about that either?"

Speechless, Shaw seemed unable to digest Callie's question. "I . . . I didn't. Maybe she took it upon herself to do Indigo proud. Trust me, that would be her way. Let me ask her. She'd be honest with me."

Callie started to add that Jackie had provided a female escort as well, but that would bring Rose back under Roberts's scrutiny. She was more curious in Shaw's angle first before throwing Rose to the wolves.

Roberts turned to Callie. "Go get that hostess."

"I'll get Jackie," Shaw said. "She's swamped out there, and she wouldn't leave her station for you like she would for me. Like I said, she's loyal."

"No, that's all right," I said, heading to the door. Shaw acted too odd, too nervous, too eager to get out of here.

Roberts thumbed toward the door. "Go on, Shaw. Don't care if the cook has to serve tables, get that woman's ass back here. The quicker you do, the quicker she returns to work."

Callie made for the door, as if to block it. Roberts held his arm in front of her. "Go on, Shaw!" he said. "Damn, Chief, do you feel you have to do everything yourself?"

Callie stared Shaw down as he exited, then tight-lipped and frustrated, positioned herself in Roberts's personal space. "What the hell do you think you're doing?"

"Investigating, princess. Like you should've done. Sheriff said to avoid embarrassing the management, so it appears more natural for Shaw to ask to speak to the waitress rather than one of us jerk her out of there. Finesse," he said. "And concern for the citizen."

Concern for the sheriff's campaign donors, he meant.

Restraining herself from smacking the man, and instead of putting space between them, Callie got in Roberts's space again. "Now. See if you can understand this, Neanderthal. I am not your enemy. The killer is, and that man you just let out of here has been too cloudy in his ways to be trusted."

The detective's nostrils flared. "That man represents a team of other men who hold lot of money, power, and something I thought you'd understand, economic opportunity for this area. No wonder you washed out of Boston. What were you doing up north anyway? Nobody down here willing to take you?"

A knock sounded.

"We're busy," Roberts shouted.

Largo opened the door.

"What the hell . . ." Roberts almost slung his arm out of the socket.

"I didn't call you. Get out of here."

"Guess you finished your meeting," Slade said, coming from behind Largo. Then overtly scanning the room, she asked, "Where's Shaw?"

"Gone to get the hostess," Roberts replied. "And you need to be gone before they get here."

Largo laughed once then started to speak, but Slade, smug and about to bust, said, "They scattered, dude."

Alarm crossed Callie's face. "Who?"

"Shaw, Jackie, and if it matters, Marion."

Callie wheeled on Roberts. "The only people in this room are the law," she said. "The people missing are persons of interest. Following the math now?" She motioned for Largo and Slade to go out first. "This isn't the way we conduct business in my shop . . . *on the beach.*"

The duo exited, Callie on their heels. Roberts behind her.

Callie quickly brought Largo and Slade up to speed. "I read the article. Didn't have much time to question Shaw about—"

"We did, though," Slade replied.

On the porch at the main entrance, they diverted several people to the restaurant side of the building, then Slade spoke of Shaw's discussion of McKenzie Ott, and how Jackie Ott came to work for Indigo. Callie relayed Shaw's earnest declaration of not being aware of Callaway and the lunch basket.

Roberts remained eerily silent, and Callie debated on whether to mention Rose. But time could be critical.

"Jackie set Callaway up for a picnic on the company dock," she finally said. "She lied to me about delivering the lunch to his room. Not only did she serve the meal, but she gave him a female escort to enjoy it with."

"No, never happened. The girl anyway." Slade crossed her arms. "We spoke to Riley, the concierge. She hid in the ladies' room to avoid going out with Callaway. The deal fell through."

Callie shook her head. "Not talking about Riley. It was Rose, a waitress. And since Riley was dating Marion, who's to say he didn't talk Jackie out of using Riley, protecting his girlfriend, meaning he also was aware of this clandestine outing."

"And now all three are in the wind," Wayne said. "What next?"

Roberts wasn't as stalwart and self-assured as he'd been. "I'll have more uniforms here in thirty, maybe fifteen."

Callie recalled one dark August night after she first moved to the island, when a kidnapper raced toward the mainland. The murderer, aka Jinx, who Sophie and friends had assumed was an island tradition affiliated with spirits. As on that night, with only one access, Edisto Island could be roadblocked.

"No, radio your people to block the bridge, Roberts. ASAP." Then she queried Slade. "Vehicle descriptions?"

"Jackie took off in a ten-year-old silver Honda. Marion in an old blue Camaro."

Roberts relayed the information to his counterparts, then paused. "Shaw's vehicle?"

"Shaw ran," she said.

"Ran?" Callie exclaimed.

"Yeah," Slade said, and pointed toward the paths that wandered into the jungle woods. "That way."

While Callie craved to chew out the pompous detective, they hadn't the time. Their suspects had rabbited in different directions, in different transportation.

Hands on her hips, Callie closed her eyes. "Stop and think."

"Oh, for God's sake," Roberts started.

But Slade interrupted. "Shut the hell up and pay attention, *dumbass*. Go ahead, Callie."

"Question," Callie said. "What did each of these three people have to lose?"

"Shaw loses Indigo and a reputation," Largo said. "Huge motive since he told us he read Callaway's notes which forecasted Callaway's opinion. And especially so if he had any idea Callaway was coming. He lied about other things, why not that?"

Slade chimed in. "Jackie lost a daughter, and Shaw gave her a job. Maybe she's not just loyal but crazy protective of the man? So if Shaw was at risk, she'd felt beholden?" Then she shrugged.

Largo added. "He still carries all that guilt so he'd take care of her in return."

"But what about Marion?" Callie asked, studying Roberts. "He idolized you. What's he about?"

"Damned if I can tell you. Taught him in a class, maybe two, then never saw him again. No telling why he left the department."

"More displaced loyalty, huh," Slade said, zinging Roberts whose cutting glance showed he didn't care what she thought.

Callie wasn't accepting the rationale that their suspects were simply being so devoted to each other. Much less all three involved in a murder that was dealt with so sloppily. Yes, he was poisoned, in a carefully orchestrated lunch. Premeditated, but not planned too far ahead because someone hadn't thought clearly about body disposal. These waters teamed with creatures that could make a quick meal of a carcass, if dumped right.

But what if there were bigger stakes in play? Or even multiple games. Even if Callaway was a crude, demented, misogynistic, boorish piece of shit, was he such a threat to warrant murder? As a semi-famous figure, his death on the premises could damage them as much or more than the review. Not everybody gave a damn about one person's opinion.

Unless Calloway stumbled on something bigger than a review?

Trenton and his buddies could incur an eight-figure loss if Indigo went under, but only if they rolled over and died. All that money meant they likewise had means and clout to damage Callaway, threaten him to behave or else. Somehow, she didn't see them letting one lone blogger do them in.

Callie opened her eyes. Millionaires had the means to most likely salvage Indigo. But what if this wasn't just about Indigo?

"What're you thinking, Callie?" Slade stood beside her, studying, as though afraid to touch her while she shuffled facts.

"Tell me about the shooting," Callie said.

Slade described the incident. "We were on Indigo's private dock with Drummond where he was showing us how and where he was shot at not long ago. New shots rang out, and we jumped in the water and swam downstream, coming out where Callaway did."

Slade looked at Largo. "Wayne thinks that if they meant to hit us, they would have. No signs we were chased."

"Head to the dock," Callie said.

With time short, the two women struck out in a run to the path leading past the barn and toward the crime scene. Slade climbed around the fence blocking the haves from the have-nots with Callie and Largo going over it, Roberts huffing a few yards behind.

Callie shouted at Slade. "Stop! Listen."

Fighting to hold back the heavy breathing, they heard a motor rumbling in the distance. Callie ran into the clearing leading to the dock and out to the water. No sign of the boat, but an eddy still slowly curled fifty yards up the river, surprisingly north rather than to the ocean, toward the intracoastal waterway. She turned to Slade.

"Yeah," Slade said, breathy. "The biggest boat is missing."

"Make, model?"

Slade, then Largo, and ultimately Roberts shook their heads. Nobody lived on water but Callie. Two other moored boats bobbed in the after wake of the leaving vessel.

"It had a sleep area," Slade said. "And a roll bar on the top. Measured about from here to here." She motioned between piers. "It was white with a tan bottom."

Tractors had roll bars. What Slade described was a thirty-foot, two-toned cabin cruiser with a tower.

Phone to her ear, Callie leaped into the biggest remaining craft, a twenty-four-foot Monterrey. Nothing to sneeze at, but it would be considered lower echelon for some of Indigo's more prestigious guests. But she couldn't find the key. Slade and Largo hunted through an eighteen-foot Carolina Skiff to her right.

"What the hell?" Robert said just as Callie heard it and straightened, scanning north.

Full throttle, his long Tarzan hair streaming, Shaw headed back toward the dock. His speed, however, indicated no sign of stopping.

Callie leaped into the skiff with the couple and keyed her radio. "Marie?"

Nothing.

"Marie?" she yelled.

Finally. "Yeah, Chief."

"Tell Don, Thomas, Bobby Yeargin and whoever else is available from the responder team to grab boats and head into the sound." She described Shaw's boat.

"Um, Don Raysor's not exactly the boating type."

"Don't care," she shouted, finding the key to the smallest vessel. "I need to flaunt uniforms and block the sound. Tell Thomas that means the Zodiac, too. STAT!"

Roberts pointed from where Shaw had come. Another boat.

A black and gray center console SLED patrol boat cut the water and came around, in chase. Then a second.

Slade shielded her eyes from the sun. "Is that . . ."

Marion hunkered down with five others in the first boat . . . the letters SLED across the back of his vest. State Law Enforcement Division. South Carolina's FBI.

Callie cranked on the first try. Largo untied the mooring.

"You coming, Roberts?" Callie shouted, giving the motor a jolt of gas. "This is your case, too."

Jumping in, Roberts's lack of sea legs cast him into the bottom of the boat at Slade's feet as Callie pulled away, cleared the dock, then thrust the throttle, shoving sunglasses on her face.

"Do you expect to catch them?" Slade yelled over the wind, her white-knuckled grip and squatted position a clear indication of her land-lubber nature.

"No."

"But you called your people," Slade replied, shoulders hunched at the hits and bumps forced by the wakes of the other boats.

"That's all right. They get to disrupt the getaway." Squinting, tight on the steering, Callie keyed her mic again. "Thomas? Move up the river. Suspect coming right at you, two boats in pursuit."

In the stretch toward Raccoon Island, Callie caught sight of the pursuit vessels, but their speed soon took them around a bend toward Fenwick Island.

"He might take Fenwick Cut, Thomas."

"Got it, Chief."

Roberts pulled himself to the center console. "What the hell are we doing?"

"Offering assistance," she shouted, swerving the boat enough to tip the guy off balance. "Something you don't seem to be very willing to do from what I've seen."

They reached Fenwick. Callie slowed a hint, analyzing the situation. No boats. They'd could've committed right, down the Ashepoo, or steered left toward the sound and the ocean. Bearing left and south, she scanned down the Edisto River. Pride swelled in her chest. All the more that her passengers saw it as well.

Stretched across the river like the rag-tag fleet of historic Dunkirk, the assorted captains, fishermen, and first-responder team members of tiny Edisto Beach stood fast in protection of whatever came their way. Whatever headed toward their beach. Doing whatever their police chief asked them to do.

And amidst them poised Drummond, his tricorn hat perched splendidly atop all those braids, standing on the gunwale of somebody else's boat. Even boatless, the pirate came to the defense of his home turf, regardless of what the natives thought of him.

How he talked someone into letting him on their boat was the mystery.

Thomas soon arrived in the department's Zodiac, the young officer stern and braced. A uniform ready to perform. "Want to come with us?"

"Damn right I do." Don sat low in the boat, his life vest barely connected around his girth. He just shook his head to which Callie grinned big. She turned to the team in her own boat. "Think y'all can take this in?"

Largo stood, an understanding smile in place. "We'll figure it out. Go take care of business, Chief."

Leaping into the Zodiac, she assumed her normal place in front of the console and let Thomas take them around. Without asking, she understood he headed south around Pine Island, then Otter Island, the exit of the Ashepoo River. If Shaw wasn't caught before they arrived, they'd at least be there to prevent his escape.

He could dodge around these waters all he wanted to, but he wasn't from here. She was, and all these other people were. Unless Shaw harbored some hidden marine prowess, he was done.

She watched the skiff get smaller behind her. Slade shouted, "Go get 'em."

Thomas raised his voice. "He saw us and turned tail," he shouted, the adrenaline keen in his cheeks and his inability to be still. "SLED went after him down the Ashepoo. Didn't think—"

"Kid did everything right," Don growled over the wind and water slapping the sides of the boat. "I, however, should've stayed on land."

They approached the southeast side of Otter Island. An afternoon summer storm began to take form. Waves took edgier shape, becoming wilder and more intense with each approaching cloud.

"Doubt we'll get there before he reaches the end. They should've caught him by now," Thomas hollered. Scattered drops pelted the sea around them.

"We can only hope," Callie hollered, wiping her mouth and chin where a few drops splashed.

The boat bumped, bumped and rode over the top of a few waves then came down bumping hard again. No longer a Grecian blue, the ocean had evolved into a gunmetal hue.

Thomas was right. Geography and distance would likely leave them as spectators, but Callie wasn't a case hog. She didn't care who caught him. She had little inkling of what Shaw had done to attract SLED. All she wanted was to understand, because whatever Shaw was involved in most likely impacted Callaway's death. The blogger might've stumbled on someone bigger and badder than he was.

The three of them scoured the distance ahead, hunting rooster spray from boats racing the hell out of their engines.

Callie pointed. "There!"

Shaw had rounded the tip of Otter, headed toward Edisto again. Aimed toward the Zodiac.

"Why isn't he going along the coast?" Thomas shouted, slowing.

"Because it isn't about him," Callie uttered to herself as the penny dropped. "It's about the boat. And maybe what's on it. It's about the dock and who goes there. Who sees what there," she added, thinking about Slade's talk of shootings. Still wanting to hear more about how Marion was SLED. How he had disappeared from Shaw's office not to run away, but to meet two boats waiting for him on the Intracoastal Waterway.

Fat rain fell, the outskirts of the storm roiling in ashen turmoil. Hair damp, Callie finger-raked wet tresses off her forehead.

She still didn't believe Shaw killed Callaway, because he was poisoned. There were better ways, more efficient ways to murder a person. Shaw and whoever he worked for, someone worthy of hitting the radar of state law enforcement's much-in-demand consideration, would've been cleaner with a murder, in her opinion, and made Callaway's body disappear without a trace. Especially with boats so readily at their disposal.

"Chief!" Thomas yelled.

Callie stood, tight-fisting a rail. "He's headed toward us."

"But we've got an entire ocean here. What's his deal?"

Callie stared at the oncoming vessel. "He recognizes me," she said.

"What the hell have you done this time?" Don bellowed over the motor and the weather.

"Pissed him off," she replied if only for her ears . . . words she could barely hear in ears filled with the heavy thumping of her heart.

Thomas tensed, biceps bulging, ready to turn from Shaw's path, fighting to read the direction of the much bigger vessel.

In the distance behind Shaw came SLED, but Shaw would reach the Zodiac before they could. Waves continued to chop with the gusts swept in by the hot summer afternoon storm.

Then a different sound interspersed itself amongst that of water, wind, and motors, and instead of peering far and wide for more boats, Callie and Raysor peered into the laden, gray clouds.

A chopper. Red and white. Doors open. Armed men primed in the opening on the chopper's side. SLED had called in the US Coast Guard.

Of the three scattered suspects, two were accounted for. Shaw and Marion, in an astonishing twist of facts that threw him on the law enforcement side of the house.

But as much as Callie wanted to watch the agents board Shaw's boat and cuff dear Sweet, she had Thomas turn toward the Edisto Marina. She wanted as much info as she could capture from Marion before he ran off to the interviews and paperwork of the capture, and she'd be waiting for him the second he docked. Per her orders the Marina was cleared to allow SLED to bring in the boat.

"Chief."

Roberts, over her mic. He'd run her down on the intrastate frequency.

"Morgan here," she said.

"Any chance of Jackie Ott being found out there?"

"Negative. Check in with your bridge guys?"

"Just did," he said. "She hasn't left the island. I even put someone at her residence, but nothing. She's still here."

A tremor rolled through her as much for the thought as the wet chill. Jackie lived in an apartment in West Ashley, on the outskirts of Charleston. And unless she'd flown like a bat out of hell, she remained on Edisto Island. And the only place that kept flashing in Callie's mind, the only place she could see Jackie attempting to hide at, was Rose's.

Chapter 29

Callie

AT THE MARINA, Callie anxiously awaited Marion's arrival, and when his boat docked, she strode with purpose through the black-garbed agents and took hold of Marion's vest, pulling his ear down to her height. "Give me five minutes. Not later and not once you get done here. Immediately, please. I deserve that much."

"Five minutes," he said in a voice so unlike the mild-mannered, cumbersome Indigo security guard.

Motioning for another guy to take over, he followed her to the end of the pier, facing the sound, backs to the busyness behind them.

She'd done undercover, so she wasn't irritated. On the contrary, she wished for a time the two of them could share their tales. But she couldn't proceed without at least a hint as to his knowledge of her case. Yes, she still felt committed. This was her geography. Roberts had taken over and immediately fumbled the ball. However, if he failed, she failed. Jackie was missing, on her island. Callaway was still dead, killed on her island. Those answers still needed addressing.

"First," she asked, "does Callaway play into any of this with Shaw?"

Marion shook his head. "I don't think Shaw had a thing to do with that murder. I was all over that man's business. The comings and goings on that dock in particular. This is about cocaine, Chief. Rich men getting stupid about getting richer. They used Indigo as cover to bring the stuff in, and sometimes deliver it elsewhere by water. I even guarded it some nights."

The cop in her itched to ask if the sheriff was involved, but that wasn't her business. "The pirate?" she asked.

"My shots," he replied. "Didn't want him getting hurt by learning too much. Same goes for that pair who came out with him the second time. Didn't need them there if and when things went down. Nobody hurt. I was careful."

Made sense. Per Largo, the grouping had been pretty tight in

Drummond's sail. "And his boat?"

Marion looked quizzically at her.

"His boat was supposedly sabotaged," she said. "I use *supposedly* in light of the fact it's Drummond, but I struggle with the idea that he'd go out in the sound without working bilge pumps."

Shrugging, he appeared genuinely stymied. "First, he wouldn't be the first captain to do that, but secondly, I have no idea. Since he'd nosed around, I wouldn't put it past Trenton to give such an order. I don't have the time to talk now, but even with your experience, you'd be surprised at this man's history of escaping detection. Without Callaway's death, things might not have gotten sloppy enough for detection *this* time."

Feeling a bit chagrined at not detecting Marion, she admitted to herself he'd pulled off his role quite well. "And Jackie Ott?"

He shook his head. "Never saw the needle move on the scale with her. Appeared straight up, but then, she wasn't my focus."

A new question flew in the face of facts. "If that was the case, then why come out to Rose's place?"

After a double check back to his team, he said, "I don't have a lot of time here, but in essence, I saw her run to her car scared the day Callaway died. When she never returned, I worried she'd seen something at the dock related to my case that might've put her at risk. I needed to talk to her, see she was safe, before she completely disappeared . . . in one fashion or another. Turns out you took care of her, and she had nothing to do with my deal."

"Which leaves Callaway," she said with a tilt of her head. With Marion being seasoned SLED, she'd have thought he could've spotted at least some sort of clue. "You really had no idea? Nobody got nervous? Nobody behaved differently after than before?"

With that question, he studied the water below their feet, and Callie easily recognized why before he could put the sentences together.

"Shocked me as much as you," he said. "And it's damn embarrassing to be undercover, on the job, eyes and ear open, and not see how a man got murdered."

Callie understood and let that feeling settle a second.

"As for Shaw, he was under Trenton's hold," he continued. "A buy was scheduled for today. You and Roberts and those other two sort of cramped Shaw's agenda. You saw his nerves in the office back there. Add to that the press. But powers higher than Shaw, one even higher than Trenton, couldn't change the meet. Shaw delegated me to make the appointment, and when I left the room to presumably retrieve Jackie, to head to the boat in Shaw's mind, I instead took off to meet and update my guys." He lowered his head down again. "You about messed up my operation."

"My apologies," she said.

He gave a half smirk of acceptance.

Thus explained Shaw's eagerness to collect Jackie when Marion didn't return. He wasn't sure Marion followed through, and if the product pick-up failed, Shaw would wind up like Callaway, only his body not found.

"So did you catch the other guys? The ones Shaw was to meet?"

A coy grin told her he couldn't say. "Gotta go, Chief."

"Later, Marion . . . or whoever you are. You can clue me in some other time."

Another half smirk on a guy who had morphed from a sheriff's deputy dropout to one of the state's esteemed SLED agents. Chances were Riley had been a source, and maybe an added perk, of the job.

Walking along the long dock, she halted briefly as she approached to pass Shaw. She never got close enough to him to be completely shocked at the turn of events. They hadn't known each other that long. But seeing him this way clashed intensely with how she'd met him that day with Raysor.

The agent holding onto the cuffs spoke in clipped words, not recognizing who she was in civvies. "Please back away, ma'am."

"Yes, please," Shaw said, resigned.

At hearing Shaw, Marion called over. "Give her a short word, Buster. She's all right."

Callie stepped in closer. No point in the world sharing in their conversation. "Got sucked in, huh?"

"That or drown." His arms were twisted behind him, pushing him to lean a little forward, but her diminutive height placed him closer to her level.

Shaw seemed out of place bound and detained. Not a thug, nor a slick money man. "I'm sad about all this, Sweet. I'm really sorry."

"Like I said, that dinner could've been sensational, in more ways than one."

In an agitated boredom, the agent shifted. "Ma'am?"

She waved him on. Saddened by Shaw, she wasn't crushed. It took a lot deeper relationship than that to touch her . . . touch that core she protected with her life. Had protected with her life.

Letting them go ahead, she followed to the end of the Marina where

Slade and Largo waited under the awning of a seafood place, chatting with Thomas.

Roberts stood to the side, out of place. None of these LEOs were his, but if he partnered better, that would not have mattered. The case he'd flagrantly demanded had turned upside down, and she doubted he'd updated his department about it yet.

From behind the small gathering, Alex, the young reporter, popped out, about to raise her camera. Slade's expression turned sour, and instead of backing off, she inserted herself in front of the girl. The movement gave Alex obvious pause, making her sidestep. Slade sidestepped, too.

Callie wished she'd heard the late night conversation between those two on the road. Nobody chased off Alex easily.

Her phone vibrated on her belt, and she let it go to voicemail.

"I got this, Slade." Callie reached over and firmly pushed the camera down, making Alex stop trying to land the shot. "Leave me alone and I'll give you an exclusive on Callaway," Callie said.

Lowering the camera, Alex acted hopeful. "When?"

"When it breaks," she said. "Otherwise I call another station. Move on."

Alex craned to peer at the activity around Shaw. "That isn't about your case?"

"Nope, it's not," Callie replied. "That's a whole different animal there, and I'm not involved with SLED. They're just using our real estate. You've on your own with them."

"Will you—"

"Introduce you?" Callie scoffed once. "Like I said, you're on your own."

Which gave Alex enough permission to leave Callie and seek out the hotter story.

Largo let the reporter leave earshot. "What now, Chief?"

Callie twisted toward Roberts. "Your case, but . . ."

Her phone vibrated with another call. Instinctively her hand went to the device, but this wasn't the time. "Like I said, your case."

The detective shrugged. "You call it."

The closest to an apology Callie'd ever get. "Largo, come with me in my patrol car." Or rather Thomas's car. Her officer could find another way to the station. "Roberts . . ." They'd all arrived by boat. "Guess you're coming with me, too."

She had several places in mind to hunt for Jackie, the first being

Rose's. But if Rose took off and hid as Callie told her to do, Jackie would've taken off as well. She could use Largo, and she owed Roberts out of courtesy.

But that left Slade, the wannabe, pretend investigator from agriculture who could see what was coming and couldn't hide her disappointment.

Sliding shades on, Callie attempted an explanation. "I have no idea who or what we'll be confronting, Slade. LEOs only. Nothing personal, but if you were there we'd be distracted, protective, and—"

With a slight bow, Slade accepted the decision. "Sort of used to that. Just bring him back," she said, lightly punching Largo.

And there it was again. That sting. The not-so-old wound of losing Seabrook during the peak of a case. When the crap hit the fan. When they thought they were headed one way with an investigation only to be caught in a cross that cost them dearly.

Of course she'd protect Largo . . . like he was her own.

As the crew of three fast-walked to the parking lot, Callie hung next to Roberts. "We good?"

"Good," he said.

No shake or oaths in blood, but Callie could live with that. Everybody at one time or another did something wrong. She'd made her living as a detective, noting those wrongs, seeing things through different eyes than most, but on the other side she'd erred enough times for an assortment of dreams to send her to the gin bottle in the dark early hours of morning. They really didn't need to say much more about who did wrong.

Besides, she'd learned long ago that when you wanted something from somebody, you didn't make him feel like crap when he gave it.

Lightning forked the sky. A few fat drops hit already damp heads.

"Hustle," she yelled and struck out for Thomas's patrol car. They leaped in. Each of them took a second to check phones. Only the two voicemails on hers, both from a cell she didn't recognize. She put the device to her ear for the first.

"This here's Rose's Grandma. Rose's boss is here. What you want us to do about that?"

"Roberts," she ordered, cranking the car. "See if your guys can head to Sugar Hill Road. Give them Rose's address but tell them to just block the road until we get there. Work for you?"

Roberts jumped on his radio.

One-handed, she peeled out of the parking lot, headed off the beach, the few drops turned into many, and by the time they reached the end of Palmetto Boulevard, they watched the water reflected in their headlights hit and bounce knee-high. The other hand keyed in the second voice mail.

"This here's Rose's Grandma again. We're not needing you now."

What the hell did that mean?

"Here," she said, passing her phone to Largo. "Listen to those voice mails. Put them on speaker."

The car hit a puddle, and Callie quickly righted the skid. Wipers ran high, and she put on the air conditioner in attempt to reduce the moisture building inside the windows. A shiver coursed through her thanks to dank clothes.

"Ott's in the wind," Roberts said.

Largo returned the cell. "Not if you shut off the island quick enough. And who is the *we* they reference?"

"Family," Roberts said. "A passel of them to include a guy in his twenties who could stand to lose a hundred pounds. Doubt they'd let that Ott woman in the front door."

Two-fisted on the wheel, Callie stared hard at the slick, shiny road, speeding more than she'd like under these conditions, but her gut told her not to take those two calls lightly. While she'd given a card to both Rose and Grandma, she'd hoped to hear from Rose.

The bottom dropped out of the sky, and she eased the gas, trying to recall exactly where the road turned. Coming from this direction, it would be on her right. "That family," she said, "is rabid about protecting their own."

Roberts disagreed. "The guy was big, but I read him as harmless."

"You didn't sit in their living room surrounded by sixteen scrutinizing sets of stares," she said. "And that was just one house of them."

"You counted them?"

"Wouldn't you?"

She used to be more trusting. Used to think that a person gave a straight deal if they got one themselves. As much as her work let her see humanity as it really was, people were squirrelly, not nearly as trusting these days. While Grandma was old school, more to Callie's liking, she managed a team of younger folk eager to protect their own, not eager to trust the likes of Roberts to do right by them.

Callie sped up. She had no idea what was going down at Rose's place and hated the scenarios playing in her head. If Rose was correct in her story, Jackie set her up, endangered her. Opened her to rape. What brother, sister, cousin, or parent wouldn't want justice for that?

In a quick back and forth, the trio exchanged intel. The history of Gene, Shaw and Jackie at Wisteria in Charleston. Callaway's timeline of hotel visits and blog posts. The shots at the party dock.

"So Marion shot at us," Largo said. "Hunh. Still makes me want to punch him."

"I'd have shot back," Roberts grumbled from the rear.

They reached the turn. A county cruiser guarded the entrance, assigned the task of checking the comings and goings of traffic. Two hundred yards down the potholed asphalt, another car waited to the side. A bit further, once the aged road deteriorated to silt, a third sat in the middle of the road, the heavy rain having compromised the edges into automobile quagmires.

As Callie eased around the third officer, Roberts stated the obvious. "The houses are just around the bend."

Callie registered the unspoken question of *what next* and pulled to the side, leaving the car running. "Let me exit first. You guys hang. Let me try this alone."

The detective had a habit of growling before speaking, and this time was no different. "Either of those women from Indigo could be a killer. Or be hiding one. Do I need to elaborate the scenarios that could happen if they see some tiny wisp of a woman standing on the porch?"

Callie turned in her seat to see him. "I have a good relationship with both those women as well as the grandmother. You, however, pissed the whole bloody lot of them off with your car tag performance. Who do you think will threaten them the most?"

"Maybe I ought to go with you," Largo said.

"What, and appear like I brought backup to return and nab Rose?"

She lifted her phone and dialed. Nobody answered. "Rose?" she said to voice mail. "This is Chief Morgan. I'm coming your way. I have good news for you." She clicked off.

"That's how you're going in?" Roberts asked over the rain beating the roof harder in a surge of storm.

"It's a matriarchal household I've identified with. It's all I've got right now, but I'm thinking it might be all I need."

She put the car back in gear, and with soft bumps over the wet silt, she slowly pulled the car toward the houses.

"Anyone see Jackie's car?" she asked.

Largo pointed. "There. Dated silver Honda behind that oak and old pick-up."

Callie tried to call Rose again. No answer. Either the girl was in hiding or not there . . . or preoccupied . . . hopefully not dead.

Jackie's car indicated she was there, or recently had been. Dead or alive, she wasn't far.

Chapter 30

Callie

THE RAIN LESSENED. Potluck lumbered out on the porch, his shot-gun again resting as usual on the toe of his shoe.

Largo's eyes widened. "You don't want backup with that?"

Callie keyed her mic open for the two men to hear her and whomever she approached. "Nope. Not yet. He's Grandma's boy. Like Roberts said, not too much of a threat. How about throwing me that windbreaker, Roberts."

With clothes sticking to her, she exited the vehicle into the light rain, weapon in its paddle holster on her hip covered by the light jacket. By the time she reached Grandma's boy, the rain stopped, but she was tacky warm under the cover.

"Hey, Potluck," she said. "Miss me?"

He raised his foot, also raising the weapon so it slid more appropriately in his hand. "Who're those two guys?"

"Mine. They'll stay there as long as everyone behaves. Consider them my bodyguards," she said. He'd understand that. After all, wasn't that his job for Rose?

He nodded, but continued to stare at the car.

"Is your Grandma here?" she asked.

"Grandma's always here."

Callie subtly thumbed to her right. "Who's that silver Honda belong to?"

He didn't bite, continuing to stare hard at her. "Grandma says we got this."

Shaking her head, she tried to keep it nonthreatening. "That won't cut it, Potluck. This is beyond Rose. Beyond all of y'all. Take me to Grandma."

The house seemed dead inside. No movement she could see or hear. No faces peering out of windows, here or in the other houses.

"I'm told to stop you or anyone else," he said.

"Funny, that's sort of my job, too."

A girl cried, followed by a distant, tearful, "No!"

Rose.

Callie retreated to the steps. "They're around at the tree, aren't they? The one with the cross."

Potluck's bottom lip pooched out over his top, his scowl digging deep between his brows. "Ain't saying."

She eased down a step. "Then I'll mosey back there and see."

"Not your business."

She took another step. One more to go. "Afraid it is this time. Don't try to get in my way. It wouldn't turn out well for you. You hear? That would break my heart. Just so we're clear, I'm not here for Rose."

At least she hoped she wasn't. Callie didn't hold all the cards, but she'd lay her bet on someone else for Callaway's murder, and that someone arrived in that Honda and was with Rose. She motioned toward the corner of the house. "So I'm heading around back. You coming? Or you can stay and watch those bored guys in the car. Your choice."

Without waiting for Potluck's decision, she left.

Blotched with patches of grass, the sandy yard oozed water under her feet as she rounded the house. She slowed seeing backs of several people sharing or holding umbrellas, their pants and legs wet from enduring the recent downpour, their attention toward the tree farther out in the yard she'd seen earlier.

The closer she came, the more people she saw. Glancing behind, she spotted Grandma's boy who'd meandered over, watching her while peeking once at the car. By the time she reached the rear, she roughly counted thirty people hovering in a loose arc around that oak. Even without the ability to see through them, she presumed Grandma held court from her rocker. The sobs sounded like Rose.

Potluck had stepped closer and stopped, preferring to maintain vigil from a middle position, but he seemed to have more interest in what ruckus might evolve from Callie's presence.

Callie inched closer.

"It's okay, Rose," said another recognizable voice from the center of the group.

Jackie.

"Rose, you hush. Ms. Ott, you be talking to me now," Grandma was saying.

A cousin, or whatever she was, tugged on the sleeve of the woman next to her. Heads slowly began to redirect from the trial to Callie.

But she rerouted, choosing to work around the crowd, to a side wrapping the tree. To a spot less visible to Jackie who sat in what resembled the chair Callie'd used inside. Not restrained in any way . . . just held hostage by the sheer numbers of bodies strewn around the yard under so many umbrellas.

Jackie was soaked to the skin, her hair in disarray, stuck to her cheeks and neck. And she'd been crying.

Drops continued to drip through the huge oak tree, plopping on umbrellas, the picnic table, but falling silently into the sand leaving perfectly formed circles. Air thick enough with heat and moisture to raise a sweat standing still.

Pushing past several people, Callie peered through. Grandma saw her.

Callie shook her head and held a finger over her mouth, hoping Grandma read the signs. She couldn't stay tucked out of sight for long with so many of these souls seeing her, but at least they recognized her . . . and respected Grandma enough not to react until the matriarch did. Besides, Callie only wanted to remain hidden from one. Jackie Ott.

"I just want to apologize to Rose. What about that don't you understand?" cried Indigo's head waitress.

"Say it again," Grandma said.

"Say what?" Jackie whined.

"What you did."

"But I explained it already. What I want is for you to understand is why." Jackie fell forward, head in her hands.

"Unh uh," Grandma replied. "Don't care why. We're not here for why. We're here for Rose. You dragged yourself out here stating *you* were here for Rose. Needed to apologize, so tell it again. Why did you send our child out with that man?" In slow motion, Grandma extended her arms. "Not all these people, Rose's people, heard what you first told me." The wrinkles in her neck stretched in her reaching. "Let Rose's people maybe decide your fate."

A zing of concern ripped through Callie as the attendees all but surged forward. She'd not envisioned Grandma as anything but righteous, and wanting her offspring to be equally righteous. But that last line didn't sound too terribly moral.

Suddenly the throng took on the potential for a mob.

Rose stood beside the matron. "Grandma, I told you she was helping me. She's not a bad woman. Let her apologize and go."

But Grandma only ordered, "Talk, Ms. Ott."

"But Grandma—"

"Shush!" Grandma yelled. "That goes for all of you. This spot is sacred. It's where each and every one of you has at one time or another been called to account for your misgivings and sins. This woman came on her own. So here she sits. Let Ms. Ott speak." The rocker slowly rolled forward with the old lady's size. The understanding eyes from my earlier visit had turned hard as stone. "What did you do? What do you seek penance for?"

Jackie sniffled, rubbed her eyes, and tried to stiffen with resolve. A weighted warmth in the air promised more rain. Light waned as evening approached under sagging, gray clouds.

"The man was named Addison Callaway," she said. "He was an ugly man. A blogger who made a living criticizing restaurants, hotels, and spas."

At the word spas, a few laughs of sarcasm spilt from the family. At least until Grandma stared them silent.

Jackie continued. "He came to Indigo and asked us to fix him a picnic lunch for two. Then I learned he asked one of our young girls to go out in a boat with him. She was petrified. I had her hide, thinking he'd change his plans." Her chin fell, touching her neck. "But he didn't."

"He didn't change his mind about what?" Grandma demanded.

"He didn't change his mind about wanting a girl." She lowered her voice. "So I asked Rose to go with him."

"He might've cost us our jobs," Rose shouted. "I wanted my job. I liked my job. Ms. Ott was protecting us all. So I went."

"What about the other girl?" a middle-aged female shouted across the way from Callie. "What was her problem?"

"You don't understand," Jackie shouted, fingers bent and crooked in an effort to enforce her point. "Riley knew nothing about all this. When she hid, she thought Callaway left. I *told* her it would all go away."

"Whiter than Rose, too, I bet," screamed the same woman. "She's half white but never will be white enough."

"Hush, Daffney," Grandma said, cutting a warning stare at the out-crier. "Go on," she told Jackie.

"Rose went with him. So instead of giving them the picnic basket, I told them to bring the boat to Indigo's dock and I'd serve them." Tears rolled down cheeks now chapped from emotion. "Thought I could somewhat protect Rose."

"Yes," Rose said, emboldened. "She served me like I was special.

She was apologizing in her own way, and I was trying to go along best I could. That's what I've been trying to tell you. She was taking care of me."

Callie caught herself covering her mouth, dumbfounded at Rose's naïvete, and Jackie's belief she'd made good choices. Too crazy. There was more to this story, at least when it came to Jackie.

The teenage girl on one side of her and a fifty-something man on the other remained silent, hanging on the words. Callie doubted any of them had attended an atonement ceremony of an outsider, and like her, wondered how it would end.

"I was lost," Jackie whispered.

"Can't hear you," came a shout.

"I was lost and confused," she repeated louder. "On the way to the dock with the meal, I vowed to confront this man . . . but couldn't decide how. Then I truly believe God showed me a sign."

Several people gasped at the hint of blasphemy. Grandma frowned, shook her head twice, and they quieted.

Jackie reached into a pocket of the Indigo apron she still wore. When she extracted a large wadded bouquet of wilted greenery, Callie busted into the open. "Put it down, Jackie."

"This is what God showed me," she said as if Callie wasn't there. "It was growing right there, off the path, calling to me from my childhood summers on my uncle's farm. So I picked it."

Undertones floated through the crowd again. This time Grandma waited and in the way she stared at the cop in her midst, Callie guessed she recognized the weed.

Uncertain whether touching the plant mattered, Callie hesitated, replaying all she remembered Slade teaching her about hemlock, stymied whether to take it from the Indigo waitress or smack it out of her grip. "Lay it on the ground," she finally said.

But Jackie held the floor . . . and the hemlock. "And I put about this much on his sandwich." She gave a lackadaisical *whatever* look.

Rose cried. "Oh, Miss Jackie. I told you you shouldn't of come here. Shoulda just run."

"You coulda poisoned Rose." This time Potluck marched up. "You coulda made a mistake and killed her."

"But I didn't!" Jackie shouted, mighty and ugly. The crowd quieted. "I thought Rose was more street smart, more savvy to handle herself. When Callaway dropped I saw Rose's fear and told her to leave. None of this was her fault. She'd done what she was told." She smiled at Rose. "Such a sweet girl."

"We get it," Callie said. "Put the plant down, okay?"

But Jackie only scrunched it tighter. "I panicked not knowing what to do with him once he died. So after I cleaned up, I tossed the leftovers into the water. I untied their boat, letting the tide take it. Then I pushed Callaway into the deepest water, off the end of the dock, in hope the tide would take him, too."

Various family members, patient too long, raised their voices. Barks and accusations, each one thinking, as Callie did with them, how easily Rose could've lost her life.

Three of the younger women crossed the invisible line that had kept them at bay. While one stopped a few feet from the waitress, the other reached the chair and slapped Jackie. The third scampered back after spotting the evil-eye from Grandma, but the taste of violence only served to stir the others into action.

With Callie in the midst of them.

A shove almost tripped her to the ground at Jackie's feet.

Jackie leaped to her feet, arms fisted to her sides. "But she didn't get *raped!*"

Her complexion red from the effort. A scream that had to rake her throat raw.

People checked themselves, some just frozen in place.

"He raped my daughter," Jackie cried, her fingernails digging in her palms, back arched . . . her scream shouting to the sky. "The son of a bitch raped my daughter in Charleston. She couldn't tell without the restaurant paying the price. So she kept it to herself until she couldn't take it anymore."

She launched another wail into the trees thick, moss- and rain-laden limbs. It seemed to stick there and hang until she turned limp and let it trail to a whimper. "Until she drowned herself," she moaned.

Callie gently slid two ladies aside to reach Jackie. "Come on," she said, reaching to take hold of her arms. "Let's get you out of here."

But the waitress reared her left arm to the right and hurled a backhanded slam that knocked Callie to the ground. Before Callie could scramble, Jackie jammed the wilted wad of hemlock in her mouth.

"No, Jackie!" Callie fought past the woman's flailing arms in effort to grip her jaw. "Don't eat it!"

But Jackie windmilled, blocking, chewing for all she was worth, then swallowed. And swallowed again, repeatedly swallowing as she stared at Callie in defiance.

The melee spread, with half the shouting mass demanding Jackie's life. "Let her die" turned into a chant.

Largo appeared, ordering the mob on one side to back off. Roberts split off another set. And the three deputies from the road block showed with shotguns at the ready, one engaging Potluck to drop his weapon.

Orders pummeled the group. "Hands. We want to see hands."

Callie shoved Jackie into her chair and took a protective stance before her. Grabbing her mic, she called dispatch, shouting over the din for a medivac chopper, hollering to give the address. Rose came over, becoming a second shield.

Grandma rose and lifted her cane. The women calmed first. Then with grumbles, so did the men.

Shotguns still drawn, deputies took quick glimpses at the rocker, trying to analyze the power that quieted the mob. And while Grandma didn't tell them to lower their weapons, one by one they did, their chests rising and falling faster than any of the family members.

Roberts appeared at Callie's side. "We've got to get her to the highway for that chopper," he said. "Too many trees out here."

They lifted Jackie from her seat. She could still stand, but seconds mattered. Callie hunted for Largo, but he waved for them to go on without him, remaining behind to aid the deputies. She and Roberts gripped the waitress from either side and ran to their vehicle.

They pushed Jackie into the rear seat with Roberts getting in behind her. She already held her stomach, a dribble of saliva escaping the corner of her mouth. Callie hurled herself into the front and drove, ignoring the speedometer to reach Highway 174 before seizures set in.

"How involved was Shaw?" Roberts asked after strapping her in.

Jackie shook her head, distress having replaced the craziness in her eyes as though she'd just realized what she'd done. "I told him nothing. He's a good man, and I didn't want him burdened." She moaned. "Help me."

"Doing our damnedest, Jackie," Callie yelled. "So Rose wasn't aware of your plan?"

"No," she said with another painful groan, clutching her stomach.

Callie righted a skid. One more question needed an answer before Jackie lost touch, addressing the concern Callie'd had all along. "Where's the hemlock at Indigo?"

Jackie stared at the rearview mirror, not understanding.

"Where exactly did you pick the hemlock?" Callie shouted.

But Jackie doubled over, shaking.

"Think we're out of luck on that one," Roberts said, then answered his radio. He hung up. "The chopper will meet us at the highway in ten."

Almost a mile ahead.

Callie peered in the mirror again. Jackie's complexion had paled, a tremor taking over.

Damn it.

At least Rose was in the clear. After all, Jackie had just spoken to a sea of people in what would likely be considered a dying woman's confession.

Chapter 31

Slade

THE TAILLIGHTS LEFT the marina shining a wet, bleary-eyed red as I stood alone under a borrowed umbrella. Left behind again, the forgotten spectator as Wayne took off with Callie. If I didn't know him better, I'd be jealous, but life had used that woman up too much anyway. She was married to her work, by choice.

I was still left to my own devices to get back to Indigo, so how was that going down? I started to ask that nice young deputy who pulled me out last night, but he seemed steeped in cop work with SLED.

I reached into my damp back pocket and drew out the sundry business cards doled out to me in my short week on Edisto. The boat rental place, Indigo, Edisto PD, the Sea Cow, and this one . . . Sophie Bianchi, yogi extraordinaire.

She answered on the second ring. When I identified myself, she asked, "Are they gone yet?"

"Pardon?"

"The SLED boys, silly. Heard they arrested somebody right there in the sound. Were you there?" The enthusiasm sounded like a thirteen-year-old girl reincarnated in a forty-five-year-old body.

I saw nothing super-secretive about the arrest. After all, a reporter showed. Plus, I really needed a ride. "I was there."

"Really there?"

"Smack dab in the middle of it," I said. "But listen, what I called about was—"

"Wanna come over?" she asked.

She sure bit fast. "Well, I called because Callie and Wayne left me at the marina while they pursued more important business. Not being law enforcement, I can't go play with them. Hopefully you won't find me too forward, but I was hoping—"

"On my way," she said.

Didn't get a chance to finish saying *take me to Indigo*.

I moved inside the local seafood restaurant, ordered an iced tea, and waited. They'd barely delivered the Styrofoam cup before a powder blue vintage Mercedes convertible, covered, pulled as close as it could to the marina entrance. The driver flashed lights and tooted the horn. A waitress stopped mid-stride with plates balanced and glanced out the window. "Wonder who Sophie's honking at?"

"Oh," I said. "That'd be me. Wasn't sure that was her."

The waitress snickered. "Honey, that lady ain't getting in the rain with that pedicure. Better hightail it out there before she finds some other shiny object to chase."

The rain plummeted, but I wasn't passing on the ride. Running, shoes soaked as I jumped a puddle and misjudged the distance, I reached the little car and crawled in. "Whew," I said. "Sorry you had to come out in this."

She tossed a towel at me smelling like mint. Before I wiped down my arms and legs, I had to bury my nose in the scent.

"Eucalyptus and spearmint," she said, pulling out, her little body perched almost on the edge of her seat. "Good for stress."

I finished dabbing. "You have towels for different emotions? And who says I'm stressed?"

Bangles jingled as she gave me a swoop of her hand, sending some other scent my way. "Cops, an arrest, on top of this storm? Please."

The beach being so tiny, we were already almost to her house . . . and Callie's.

"Would you mind taking me back to Indigo? That's where I'm staying, and where my car is. You're welcome to come in." I said that last part with as little reservation as I could muster.

She sped past her house. "Sure . . . as long as you fill me in on today. I'll drive slow to give you time."

I wasn't sure what slow meant, but her version exceeded the posted limit. We hit the turn onto Highway 174. The light slide gave me pause, but Ubers didn't exist on Edisto Island, and her Mercedes beat me thumbing in the rain.

By the time we reached Pine Landing Road, she'd heard that Callaway was dead, I found him, Callie had been helping the sheriff, and that Swinton Shaw had been arrested for something I wasn't quite sure of yet. I must've said too much, though, because she wanted to stick to me like glue once we arrived at Indigo.

"It's late afternoon and cloudy," I said. "Don't you want to hurry home before it starts raining again?"

Sophie parked, landing a convenient spot not far from the B&B's front door. "Heavens, no," she said. "I'm sensing you're a lightning rod of activity."

"You are, are you?" I tried little to hide the sarcasm at the ESP stuff.

She eased out of the low-riding vehicle much easier than I did. "Yes, ma'am. So want to show me where you found the body? I want to see if I can sense him."

The laugh fell out before I thought to contain it.

She thrust a hand on her hip. "That's the thanks I get?"

"No, no." I inhaled and made my smile disappear. "That's the least I can do." I glanced at the sky. "Got another umbrella?"

Sure enough she did . . . covered with yoga ohm symbols. Sophie the Yogi repeated itself around the lower edge when she popped it open. She saw me studying it and grinned wide. "A gift from my son, Zeus, when I opened shop."

O-kay. She named her son after the Greek god of sky and thunder. There was no end to this lady's profile.

The place wasn't too active, the parking lot still. The walkway area between the restaurant and the barn lightly steamed from the moist heat, our umbrellas capturing some of it in our faces as we walked toward the paths. A thin gathering of tourists stood along the water, a few with raincoats, most with assorted borrowed parasols in Indigo blue. The air smelled thick with organic matter, salt, and ozone.

"This way," I said, ignoring puddles with already soaked shoes while Sophie hovered; whatever it was, she didn't bob up and down. She glided, pointing, never hushing about anything and everything. How did she stay quiet on the yoga mat?

Brushing the occasional plant, we arrived at the scene with my pants and her tights damp to our knees. My heart did a little flip, my mind's eye recalling the body tipping, floating . . . the feel of him when I bumped, then tripped over him, hitting his dead leg. The nibbles on his face.

Then the gasping, terrifying memory of swimming here from the dock while envisioning a school of man-eaters sniffing at my toes.

I turned to Sophie who'd become quiet. Both hands on her umbrella, her eyes were shut, chin toward the sky as if the umbrella weren't on her shoulder to block the view.

I waited before asking, "He feel like talking yet?"

She made a slow, open-palmed arc in front of her. "He's confused."

"Yeah, I could see that."

Trees dripped collected rain, the occasional minor breeze making the foliage let loose of it quicker in miniature showers, enough for us to keep ourselves covered. With each waft came a more intense odor of dying greenery in the woods.

"He didn't die here," she said, eyes still shut.

"No, he didn't," but I didn't tell her where, curious enough to wait and see her next move.

"Take me to where he did."

"I'm not sure—"

She went to the edge of the water and stretched to look north. "Tide would've brought him down . . . bet he fell in at Trenton's party dock."

"You're aware of the dock?"

With a wink and a click of her tongue, her mouth grinned to the right. "Of course I am. Told you I was friends. I rode his boat here once. He stopped at the Marina, picked me up, and escorted me out here for an evening of fun."

I couldn't believe this. Callie's neighbor with intel on a case she had no idea was taking place. "What kind of party?"

She ignored the question. "Let's go see it. I haven't been there from the land, just the water."

I glanced around, seeing no one. "It stays locked."

"Can we get around it?"

How could I tell her no since I'd scaled it already. And it wasn't like Shaw or Marion would stop us. "Come on."

But when we reached it, I studied her feet. "Can you climb with those?"

"Oh, honey, I'm not ruining these sandals."

Whew, good. We could turn around.

But instead, she kicked them off, slung them over the fence, and climbed with her size ten toes like a frickin' monkey. I had no choice but to follow.

Sophie continued on the path shoeless like she'd been reared barefoot on a farm. Like before, we soon reached the dock just as the wooded path curved and came out in the hardscrabble opening. She ran once the dock came into view. "Yes! Look at this place! Appears so different in the sun." She bolted onto the gazebo area, then scurried down to the floating dock where Wayne had knocked me into the water.

I finally caught up to her. "How was the party? I've never hob-knobbed with deep pockets. what's that like?"

She inhaled, paused and searched for the words. "I guess the best way to describe it is exhilarating . . . and highly pretentious. Exciting and daring, because you never predict how these people can help you . . . or hurt you." Her eyes sparkled, and I could read she enjoyed dancing on those edges.

"Not too appealing in my book," I said. "So who was there? Was Callaway?"

She shook her head. "No. These were bigger people than he was, but you have to be careful with those sorts of get-togethers," she said with a worried, yet all-knowing pout. "Part of the reason I left my husband, the ball player."

"Ball?"

"NFL," she said. "The reason Trenton got familiar with me."

"Oh," I replied, easily seeing this flamboyant woman thriving amongst VIPs.

"Anyway, they party hard, and I leave before it gets wild, because wild can scar you forever." She'd turned serious there to the end. "That's for another time, girl."

She walked around the dock, peering into the water. "Tide's out."

I joined her, hoping she'd talk more. "Drugs?" I asked.

"Loads," she said. "I called my son to come get me that evening. Things got rowdy fast." She peered harder, bending over. "What's that?"

I leaned forward but not as deeply as she, Wayne toppling me over too recent in my head. "Can't tell. Saw it earlier today. What do you think it is?"

She ran around to the lone moored boat and hauled out a pole with a hook on the end. She scurried back. "Let's see."

"What is that?" I asked.

"A gaff, for hauling your fish in."

"Big fish," I added, studying the size of the thing.

"The ocean grows them like that," she said, only accenting my mantra not to set foot in water where fish could grow bigger than me.

Without her asking, I held her ankles as she got on her knees, groping in the water. Finally, after stirred mud made spotting difficult, she lucked out, and retrieved the icky, mud-coated item. Dripping, a piece of paper peering out of the inside of it, greased with the muck that only saltwater estuaries can create, Sophie set a basket on the deck.

Then she took it by the handle, laid herself on the dock, and dipped it in and out of the water.

"A sweetgrass basket," I said.

Sophie picked out the paper. "Indigo sticker. Somebody ate lunch here." She tucked the paper back inside. "I'll toss that at home, but I'm keeping this jewel. You recognize what this is? How much it's worth?"

I sure did. And Callie would be most interested, too.

"Might belong to Indigo," I said.

"Belongs to me now, honey. Nobody throws these babies away like that."

We then returned, Sophie eager to clean her treasure, and me scared of the dark skies. With assistance for each other, we scaled the fence again, but as I hit the ground on the other side, I slipped and fell.

"You okay?" Sophie reached down to help me.

But as I rose off my knees, I caught sight of the vegetation off the small beaten path.

It was too late in the season for it to flower, but there it was, roots anchored in a small ditch. Hemlock. About a ten-foot long and five-foot wide patch.

"Hey, give me that paper in the basket," I said. Then with the paper between my fingers and the plant, I tore off a long section of the greenery.

"What're you doing?"

I folded the plant in the paper. "I, um, have a degree in agriculture, remember? It's a hobby of mine. Don't recall what this is. Hoping that guy in the barn can tell me since my guess is he's an agronomist."

Quizzically she raised her brow. "Oh, do you sage?"

"Why yes," I lied.

She popped me in the arm. "There was a reason I took to you."

Rain began again, and we fast-walked, sometimes trotted, to the main grounds, stopping in the barn first. Not a soul in the place, and the demonstration guy sat off to the side texting, checking email.

"Hey, you wouldn't happen to be as educated about plants as you put on in your demonstrations, would you?"

He tucked away his phone, smiled, and met us across the open floor. "Why, you thinking about testing me?"

I opened the paper, holding the specimen out. "Is this what I think it is?"

He had this comical buggy-eyed expression. "Depends. What do you think you've got?"

But he wasn't touching it.

"Wild carrot?" I said, using the most commonly mistaken plant.

"No, ma'am," he said with a long red-neck sounding drawl. "That's hemlock, and you best be disposing of it."

Sophie gasped and hopped back. "Oh my gosh."

Oh my gosh, indeed.

Chapter 32

Callie

THE NEXT MORNING shone bright on the sand. Callie and her two guests, in shorts, walked the beach for half an hour. Tourists packed the water line with August being the last hurrah for inland people before they packed it in and returned to normalcy, car pools, and commutes. Some regulars hollered "Hello, Chief."

Sweated a bit, the three then veered onto Palmetto Boulevard, down Portia Street toward Callie's street. To their right, a fresh white For Sale sign stood out on a vacant lot near the corner of Dolphin and Portia. "There you go," Callie said. "Your future home. One block over from me."

They diverted to the front of it. Six live oaks shadowed the place, giving it an ominous yet romantic feel. The rear fronted a creek. Two huge modern homes with loads of porches bordered either side. Silt instead of asphalt on the road, lending itself to a more private feel.

"Close enough to the beach, too," Largo said, holding back in a cheeky way.

"Label me a perpetual visitor," Slade said. "Love my lake, less things that eat you there." She pointed to one spot, then another, then another. "Besides, get a load of all that poison ivy. There, and there. God, get a load of that six-inch diameter vine of it crawling up that tree."

Callie laughed, and it felt good. "Ever the agriculture lady, huh?"

They resumed their walk toward Jungle Road, Callie smiling at the casual banter between the couple. She enjoyed their company, more so than she'd enjoyed the company of anyone in a long time. She'd been serious singling out the empty lot to them, but she understood their work took them across the state, Largo's across two states. To live on Edisto would mean they'd exist at the end of the world, far removed from civilization. While it made no sense for them to relocate, she could wish.

Her closest friends were Stan, her old Boston boss who retired on

Edisto, Sophie, and Raysor. Nobody really like her. Some nights got lonely.

They resumed walking, Largo with an arm across Slade's shoulders, and in an unexpected bittersweet realization, Callie took pleasure in seeing their natural, easy-going rapport. It did her heart good, like a healed broken bone with only the occasional twinge of a reminder of the accident.

They reached Chelsea Morning. Callie started up the stairs, pausing after three steps. "It's only ten thirty. Come sit on the porch and cool down."

"I guess we've got time," Slade said and followed.

Positioned on the side porch, the one that caught breezes both from the ocean and the marsh, they relaxed in Adirondack chairs with waters. In Sophie style, Callie'd sliced lemons in them, and thrown some cheese, crackers, and apple on a seashell plate. Staring off through the screen into the branches of a live oak, they sat silent for a while, watching two squirrels in a spiral chase around the massive trunk.

Each of them understanding that the other remembered the week in their own unique way.

"Sophie told me you were in trouble with the town council," Slade said. "What's going on with that?"

Callie scrunched her face and shook her head. "More like Brice LeGrand instead of the whole council. He happens to be the chair. Has some axe to grind with my mother from years ago before I was born, something I have no desire of knowing. He stays in my shadow a lot. Always looking for buttons to push."

Largo studied Callie. "Anything serious?"

"Not this time." She messed with the condensation on her glass. "But he'll stay on my butt. When the town is through with me, they'll tell me. Otherwise, this back and forth rivalry is part of our fabric here." She took a drink, not stating how much better Edisto would be without the man. The emergency town meeting he'd called last night fell flat with only two council members showing along with Marie, Sophie, and two firemen who'd strolled over from their station when they saw the lights on. Second time Callie'd dodged the Brice bullet.

"Makes being a fed so much more appealing," Largo said.

Slade's foot tapped Largo's. "Reminds me of my own nemesis. Had a guy vowing to do me in for a year or two for something from our past."

The situation did seem to parallel her own. "What happened with him or is he still in your business?"

"Put his ass in jail," she said.

Leaning forward a little, Callie gave the agriculture lady another look. "Seriously?" She chuckled and settled in her chair. "That's an option I hadn't considered."

An option that never would be considered, though. Brice had deep roots in Edisto. Not to say that if the man broke the law she wouldn't deal with him, but she recognized Brice as much a part of this environment as September hurricanes, and she protected all the people of Edisto Beach, those for and against Brice LeGrand. Not easy straddling that fence sometimes.

"Guess it's sort of good that Roberts took over the case, huh?" Slade said, cutting the reverie. "No paperwork for you."

"No credit, either," Largo said.

Callie swirled her glass. "I can do without the credit."

Unable to stand much more quiet, Slade leaned forward in her chair. "I hate to say it, but I'm going to. I liked Jackie. She seemed like a decent person."

Largo nodded. "She did, but you understand as well as anyone that family changes how we think . . . how we react and behave."

She sat back. "Ain't that the damn truth."

Callie had to ask. "You lost someone?" Did they really have that much in common?

"Almost," she said, mouth a bit tight. "A guy we were after stole my children."

"They're . . ."

Slade gave a light smile and waved her off. "They're fine. I found them."

"Against all advice, including mine," Largo said. "Almost lost her in the process as well."

And so the conversation went. Slade revealing how the same culprit had partnered with Slade's ex . . . then killed the ex in front of her. Callie expressed in general terms the loss of her husband to the Russian mob because of one of her own cases.

They spoke of children. They spoke of investigations, coming around to the one they'd fought together, finally cycling Largo into a conversation the ladies had run away with.

"Riley looked a lot like McKenzie Ott from that article, which probably made Jackie possessive and fearful for her," he said. "Also reminded her how miserable she was at how Callaway got off with raping her daughter. And here he was threatening Riley *and* Indigo. The plantation had become her new home, and she'd turned loyal to Shaw. She wasn't going to let Callaway ruin her employer, a man who'd helped her get her life back, after Callaway'd destroyed hers."

Slade tapped fingers on the chair arm. "I sincerely think the whole ordeal spun out in a rather spontaneous way, though."

Callie gave a light shrug. "Yeah, but a jury would consider half a day premeditated, Slade." She took another sip from a glass almost empty. "Not that anyone has to worry about that."

She stopped short of describing Jackie's miserable state by the time the helicopter arrived. Partial paralysis, tremors, the wide-eyed, inescapable fear of seeing death slowly seep into her nerves until it shut her down en route to the hospital.

"I hate we lost such a good venue for tourists and employment for the natives," she said.

"In theory," Largo said. "From a bigger picture view, you got rid of a drug port."

Callie's phone rang, and she hesitated answering. "Roberts," she told her company.

"Take it." Slade lifted out of her seat. "I need to visit your bathroom anyway." Peering at Largo, he got the message and left as well.

"Morgan," Callie answered.

"It's a sticky situation with the politics and all, but the sheriff's grateful he learned about Trenton and his ilk before he got in too deep with them."

"Glad to hear it." She and Roberts hadn't held many talkative chats before, so she didn't expect this one to last much longer than Slade's potty break.

"When the dust settles, I'm getting a commendation. Probably in some back room somewhere, but still, it's something."

"Again," she said. "Glad to hear it."

He cleared his throat. Then he cleared it again. "This was yours."

"I don't keep tallies, Roberts. Got over that in Boston. Take it. Enjoy it. Just be there for me someday. With our territories butting each other, I'm sure one of us will get thrown in the other's path."

Silence hung heavy on the line.

"Deal?" she asked.

"Absolutely. And Chief."

"Yes?"

"I did wrong by you. Just wanted you to hear that I see that."

"And I'm glad to hear that, too. Have a good day, Roberts."

"You, too . . . Callie."

Setting the phone on the side table, she repeated the conversation in her head. She might not have a buddy in the sheriff . . . he'd be too embarrassed to confront her . . . but Roberts might be another story. A good feeling to end the case on. Excellent, actually. Cases didn't always close that tidy.

Slade stepped onto the porch. "Guess who I found—"

Sophie pushed past, swinging the sweetgrass basket. "And see what I found!"

"Pretty," Callie said. "How much did that set you back?"

"Not a dime." Sophie slipped onto a rattan settee across from the chairs.

Slade made eye rolls and returned inside.

Noted for pilfering through belongings put on the curb, sometimes a lucrative hobby considering the economic scale of most of the rental owners, Sophie had furnished her porches and half her kitchen from such treasure-seeking quests. "Guess where I found it," she said.

"On somebody's trash heap several blocks over."

"No, not in Edisto Beach," Sophie teased, waiting for another guess.

"Have no idea, Soph. Where?"

"Indigo," she replied with the enthusiasm of a second grader getting the answer right. "Off the dock where they hold parties. Didn't I clean it up nice? It needs to dry a bit. Still a tad swollen from being in the water."

Callie sat rigid. "Let me see that."

The yoga teacher passed the basket. Callie flipped it over. Branded into the base was the Indigo logo.

Slade and Largo reappeared with bottles of soft drinks. Slade stopped short watching Callie examine the basket. "I think that's the one," she said.

Sophie looked from Callie to Slade. "What does that mean? Which one? Slade saw me fish this out of the river, so it's finders keepers."

Handing it back, Callie shrugged. "It's yours to keep, I'd think. I won't take it. Wouldn't want it, and am frankly surprised you'd put it in your house."

"Why?" she asked low and long, curiosity piqued.

"Because a woman who died last night used it to carry poisoned food to kill Callaway."

Sophie leaped, squealing, shoving the sweetgrass container off her lap and onto the floor. "Why didn't Slade tell me? On my gosh. Oh my gosh. I've got to sage my house." She pointed to Callie. "You need to sage *your* house! Do you understand the energy that comes with that thing? Holy Mother of God . . ." She wheeled on Slade. "Why didn't you tell me?"

"Wasn't sure. Didn't have all the facts. But I know one thing." She swooped up the basket. "I have a boss who could use this. He told me to quit scouting for investigations that didn't exist and take a vacation. Get out of his hair for a week. Learn basket weaving, he said." She swung it on the end of a finger. "Karma or not, this is going on his desk bright and early Monday morning."

Jumping to her feet, Sophie stepped around Slade. "On that note I'm out of here." But when she came to Largo, she dragged her exit, giving him another visual once over and a stroke across the chest. "Honey, if you ever dump her, you know where to find me."

She went inside then poked her head back in. "I'm returning ASAP to smudge this house, Callie. Just give me time to do mine."

"Appreciate it," Callie said, smirking.

They waited until the door closed.

"She's fun," Largo finally said. "Nuts, but fun."

"Yeah." Callie relaxed into her chair. "She's been there for me. All but lived here when . . ." She trailed off as if needing something to drink.

Slade held out a bottle of Bleinhem's ginger ale. "When you lost Seabrook," finished Slade. "I can't imagine. From what she said, he was a really good guy."

Callie took the bottle, grateful for the distraction. "What's this?"

"A special South Carolina ginger ale I like every now and then. Saw it in the Bi-Lo just by accident. For those special nights when you're craving something with more kick."

Callie's jaw tightened. "In lieu of gin, you mean."

"Just my way of giving you options. You told me it was none of my business, but according to him," she did a head toss toward Largo, "I tend to blur those lines."

Largo had already opened his, and Slade returned to her chair and opened hers. "Besides, you'll think of us every time you open one."

The liquid went down cold with a bite, one that could broach the level of alcoholic . . . almost. Callie licked her lips. "Thanks." She waved the bottle, pointing it at Slade, then Largo. "So y'all met on a case."

Slade rested fingers on her chest. "I was the one who called in a bribe. We sort of clicked. Got in a little trouble for it, but came out good in the end." She smiled at the lawman. "He liked me. Thought I was wonderful. I still don't see why."

"You're quirky, Butterbean," he said.

"Oh, I'm more than that, and you know it."

They laughed.

Tears crept into Callie's eyes before she realized, and it was too late not to wipe them away.

A touch of emotion softened Slade's expression. "Honey, you've got this hard finish, but I don't believe you're nearly as hard underneath the surface. You've seen too much of the wrong in people, and it's calloused you."

Turning toward the marsh, Callie fought the sniffle but had to. Where was all this coming from?

"Slade," Largo warned gently.

"No, it's okay," Slade said in reply. "She'll stop me when she needs to." She left her chair, kneeled, and laid a hand on Callie's knee. "You come across as tough and crisp, but I think you're just playing a part for the world. Only at home can you afford to be real."

Callie was glad she didn't have to describe what being real meant.

She reached out and drew Slade to her. "But you have him," she whispered in her new friend's ear.

"You'll have someone like him, too. Give it a chance," she whispered back.

They parted, Largo acting like the squirrels' new activity intrigued him. "We've got to go," he said.

Rising, they silently headed toward the door, Callie walking them down the stairs to the car. She hugged them both at the bottom.

"We don't ever find all the answers, do we?" Slade said, slipping into the passenger seat. "Guess that's why we do this line of work."

Callie laughed. "Slade, most of the time we don't understand the questions."

"Makes us crazy that way, I guess. Take care. We'll be back, assuming we're invited."

With a warm touch of poignancy, Callie grinned. "Always," she said. "And that lot is still available on Dolphin Road."

They pulled out slowly, waving out their windows. As the vehicle disappeared into traffic down the road, she started to turn only to see a familiar sedan.

With a quick pivot she made eye contact with Brice LeGrand. She waved big and smiled. He accelerated, snapping his attention around to the road.

Like she told Slade, he was just as much a part of Edisto as she was now, and if the pompous silliness of that man was Callie's worst of living on the beach, then she counted herself mighty damn lucky.

Now to see if she could get used to that spicy ginger ale.

The End

Acknowledgements

In the past I've had help with each novel. Writer's groups, reviewers, people interviewed for their ideas, a myriad of people who infused thoughts into a manuscript. This time, not by choice, I pretty much winged this book on my own while in hospitals, in a nursing home, in a car, in other words, alone. Not by plan but by necessity to meet a deadline while also tending to Alzheimer's parents. I came close to giving up, but there has been support, and they need to be recognized.

First, thanks to my husband to stepping up in all facets of my world so that I could write. A lot of female writers would kill for this level of encouragement in a spouse.

Second, thanks to my publisher and editor, Debra Dixon. The initial concept of this book was hers, and her support for me through these trying times has been nothing but exceptional. She believes in me, and who wouldn't kill for a taste of that?

Third, thanks always to my Edisto fans, particularly those on the island. They help create bookstore events to die for and keep putting Edisto books in all those lovely rental houses down there on the Atlantic for more and more tourists to read.

Finally, thanks to my regular readers. The ones who cannot wait for the next book, who have been patiently awaiting this release, reminding me on Facebook that they are there for me. This is the book where the Slade readers get to meet the Edisto readers and learn about each other's worlds . . . and hopefully realize that both heroines need to be on their TBR list.

About the Author

C. HOPE CLARK holds a fascination with the mystery genre and is author of the Carolina Slade Mystery Series as well as the Edisto Island Series, both set in her home state of South Carolina. In her previous federal life, she performed administrative investigations and married the agent she met on a bribery investigation. She enjoys nothing more than editing her books on the back porch with him, overlooking the lake with bourbons in hand. She can be found either on the banks of Lake Murray or Edisto Beach with one or two dachshunds in her lap. Hope is also editor of the award-winning FundsforWriters.com.

C. Hope Clark

Website: chopeclark.com

Twitter: twitter.com/hopeclark

Facebook: facebook.com/chopeclark

Goodreads: goodreads.com/hopeclark

Editor, FundsforWriters: fundsforwriters.com

CPSIA information can be obtained
at www.ICGtesting.com
Printed in the USA
FSHW012206051019
62638FS